golden state

best new
writing from
california

2017

edited by
lisa locascio

Outpost19
San Francisco

Copyright 2017 by Outpost19.
Published 2017 by Outpost19.

Locascio, Lisa (ed.)
    Golden State 2017: The Best New Writing from California /
    Lisa Locascio, editor.
    ISBN 9781944853235 (pbk)

Library of Congress Control Number: 2016918548

Cover art by Axel Wilhite

OUTPOST19

ORIGINAL
PROVOCATIVE
READING

Golden State is the latest in a series
originally conceived as the California
Prose Directory by Charles McLeod
in 2013. J. Ryan Stradal edited the
2014 edition, and Sarah LaBrie edited
the 2016 edition.

golden
state

CONTENTS

EDITOR'S NOTE

Lisa Locascio

In California we dream coming and going. Where we've been and where we'll be. In honeyed Beach Boys past and neon *Blade Runner* future, our dream state promises that newness will be the only constant. Maybe it's the scale of the landscape, or the indomitability of the sunshine that increasingly seems the last vestige of American optimism: for all its subdivisions and startup money, Cali has never lost its frontier bona fides. Here each of us must decide at which destiny to manifest. The twentieth-century mirage that calls German tourists West on the Hertz package deal that includes a Mustang convertible and a slate of stops up and down Highway One? Hale Thorp's log house? Or the still-halcyon days to come, in which our Golden State is promised to lead the resistance?

Lush diversity is the defining feature of California's people, literature, and fantasias. So maybe it makes sense, given the vagaries of time in Pacific standard, that in this book you will find an idiosyncratic set of wayward fathers, lodestars of a kaleidoscopic and evolving notion of the Western Family immortalized as one of our grocery store chains. Parents and children at war and in love, unflinching flashes of mysterious self and other, and a singing joy of place expressed through rich humor and powerhouse language.

Before I moved to Los Angeles, I dreamed a long time about California. In the first photograph of me here I'm about six months old, in my dad's arms, Big Sur a green smear behind us.

I wear a poofy pink parka onesie, he aviators; it's indubitably the Eighties, and we are breathing big tree air in the decade's capitol region. Sixteen years later, my family spent a spring break in L.A. and San Francisco, checking out colleges I wouldn't attend. In Hollywood I met up with a much-older penpal, my favorite band's videographer, who took me to see *Before Night Falls* at the Laemmle Sunset 5. We scandalously held hands throughout, but that was it: my dad was our ride to and from the movie and waited out our pseudodate in the bar at the Chateau Marmont. That was 2001, a year after *Mulholland Dr.* made it clear to me exactly what the city had to offer. I wanted all of it.

I went to school in New York City, where I liked to pick fights with people about California. They all seemed to hate it, especially Los Angeles, where I wanted so badly to live. "The thing about L.A.," I insisted with the hauteur of someone who had never lived there, "is that if New York is a luxurious black Town Car, L.A. is a flaming orange Lamborghini. Stupid, and loud, and fun, and unashamed."

So of course I fell in love with a classmate of Angeleno vintage. When I visited him in the summers he took me to Westside Chinese restaurants with long white tablecloths and pearl carpeting and backyards set with gemlike oblong lap pools. He grew up in Hancock Park, attended Palisades High, and later lived with his mother on Abbot Kinney; I wouldn't understand the absurdity of the commutes that shaped his childhood until long after we broke up. Only then did I, too, finally get to live in the amalgam I had so long wanted, a chimera of the orange-scented whirligig at California Adventure, sexy-sweet violet dusks, and inky, electric dark movie star nights. Every morning featured the return of that inimitable, purely penetrating light. My hero David Lynch had written about L.A. sunlight what I came to feel about the whole state: "It fills me with the feeling that all possibilities are available."

My seven years in California took me from Niland's Salvation Mountain to Humboldt Bay, which I cruised on *Madaket*, the oldest operating ferry in the United States. I drank banana rum cocktails on Malibu Pier and celebrated Thanksgiving in Stinson Beach, wowed by the preponderance of independent bookstores in Marin County. Weekdays I drove or rode the L.A. Metro to the universities where I taught, climbing the hill up to my apartment in the purple gloaming that never lost its magic. I won a scholarship to attend a writing conference in Mendocino and returned three years later as faculty, convinced now that the Golden State was my destiny. When my insomnia acted up, the only thing that could soothe me back to sleep was a California guidebook, oneiric journeys that came true as I visited General Sherman in Sequoia National Park, the ruins of the Llano del Rio commune, and the kelp forests off Monterey. As Mae Van Norman Long put it in her 1926 novel *The Canyon of the Stars,* "California has driven me quite mad with its beauty."

In California it's always a little messy, that line between reality and invention. Last year I was bidden back Eastward, and on my last drive out of L.A. my whole dream of the city crystallized in one moment and vanished the next. As I pulled onto the 405 North out of Santa Monica, an actual orange Lamborghini merged in front of me and escorted me up the 101 to Santa Barbara, until the freeway curved away from the ocean and it, too, left me.

I write these words from Connecticut. It's a nice place, rich with trees and cool, humid nights. Thunderstorms. Snow. It's hard to get used to the abundance of water, the fact that the desert doesn't open up around the car when I get outside of town. I can't quite square the landscape with what I see. Inside me is a California space, tall and slick like trees in rain, spiky as a cactus, wet as the ocean, a place that will never leave me.

THE VIEW LIKE AN ASHTRAY

Andrea Lambert

The woman under the spotlight at Beyond Baroque read lines about licking the view like an ashtray. The smoldering palm trees. I imagined her hair catching on fire under the light. I thought about how her eyes kept flickering up at the audience to make sure we were watching her. I was watching her. So were they.

It's a good technique, they say, to make eye contact.

I was thinking about the ashtray. The view like an ashtray. The fact that no one was smoking at this party. Well, I guess it's California. The picture I did not take was the view in front of me. Stephen was in the hot tub with a woman named Zelda. The neon blue angles of the light on the water hung between her body. Black. His gangly arms along the side of the tub. The two men embracing at the far end. I loved when people came together under the awkward shimmy of an afternoon party to take off their clothes and soak in the darkness. The release of the awkward it's too bright I don't know anyone here to: Well, I'm a little stoned and my feet are in the hot tub, so I guess the palms will sparkle a little brighter tonight.

I pulled my boots on too fast. My feet were wet. Release is a difficult thing. It's best not to let oneself go too far into the moment, especially among strangers.

When I awoke it was eleven thirty. I took two pills because I must. The cat is awake. This was usual. The cat was awake. She leapt on the counter. Rubbed her head all over my hand as I tried to make coffee. I told her, "This is about to get very hot, Nevada. You will not want to touch this."

I filled the paper filter with grounds. Set it in the coffeemaker while her grey head bobbed and whirled around my hands.

I thought about how I wanted to like Sandra Cisneros' poetry, but found that I did not.

I thought about how I missed a rival's book party last night. Felt guilty about it

I thought about how my best friend, Stephen, thought he had herpes. He drove us around all yesterday trying to find a clinic that was open.

I was a little stoned. I am often these days, since my girlfriend Katie has a medical marijuana prescription. I was a little high so it seemed like more fun then the death march towards diagnosis really should be. Riding around Echo Park in his old Buick with the windows down and the summer outside. Watching the orange stucco. Ferns. Palms. Warm air streaming in with music of ice cream trucks and far-away sirens. I remember I had my arm slung on the window. I was watching the tattoo I had always wanted to get color put onto. The white hairs above the black nurse shape. My tan skin.

Stephen was talking. Talking about the size of the pustules. How he was afraid his new boyfriend Billy would leave him. We had been talking about all of this on Gchat for an hour before he picked us up.

"There is an electronic record of almost everything we talk about these days." I said.

Katie said, "You're so paranoid, so what if there's a record."

"I'm not saying it's bad. It just is what it is. It's kind of nice. It's like, we can look it up later."

"Oh my god! So, like, someone could look later and see that I was offering to show you my pustulant herpes-covered penis? To see if you could tell me what it was?"

"Okay," Katie said, "Lena, pie chart. How much of your life

do you spend talking about herpes?"

"Okay," I said, "Pie chart. How much time do you spend making fun of me?"

"But it's so easy."

"Guys... is Billy going to want to keep going out with me? Is anyone ever going to want to date me again?"

He swerved into the parking lot of Los Angeles Presbyterian Medical Center.

The coffee was too hot. I put the carafe into the refrigerator as soon as it was done brewing. The Men's Health clinic had been closed. We had returned to Stephen's house.

Plans made in the summer were never quite followed through on. A party with free entry and drinks that we all were going to meet at, then Stephen and Billy showed up at our door to let us know that we had missed the whole thing.

We ended up sitting in 4100 Bar, which was fine with me. I drank the gin that Billy had bought me. Watched the texture of sequins and velvet against the wall. The gilt mirror hanging there that reminded me of the Cat Club where I spent so many nights long ago. I couldn't hear what anyone was saying so we communicated by gestures. When they laughed, I laughed. I bought Katie a Newcastle. We kissed. Cold lips in the warm room. When "It's Getting Hot in Here" came on everyone laughed and I went inside myself to a summer in 2002, where that was the song that swelled the dance floor in a bar in San Francisco. We would dance. Everything would seem simple. Right. Beautiful. We were young and slutty. Full of cocaine, beer and cheap synthetic fibers. That was all there was. At the end of the night we would whisper out in pairs and go home in new combinations and that was all there was.

But the song ended. I was still sitting in the bar with Stephen, Billy and Katie. And she was my fiancée. And she was beautiful. And now she made things seem right and real. Not endless strands of half-seen faces.

She was asleep now. She slept in her lavender panties wrapped in a white comforter with a tattoo that said *amnesiac* visible on her left shoulder. She was young. She did not have these memories. She did not have these past flowerings and faces in the night. She spoke of forgetting because she wanted me to forget. Forget and remember only her. I wanted this, I wanted this more than I could say.

SAVAGE BREAST

Elizabeth McKenzie

It had been an ordinary day, to a point. I had a headache that wouldn't let up, and there was a party I'd promised I'd go to—I'd said see you soon to the people at work. But after I unlocked my door and kicked off my shoes all I could think about was jumping into bed. Once I allowed myself to think that this was a reasonable idea, I felt released from the grip of the party; I realized that if I slept right through nobody would really care.

I threw down my bag in the hall. A stale smell engulfed me, as if from a storage room that had not been opened for a long time, but I was too dead to investigate. I groped for the light switch, but instead felt a warm furry thing on my hand.

Next thing I knew, I was lying on my back in a bed.

The bed was hard, and there was a thin blue blanket over me. Looking up, I saw light coming through an old-fashioned shade that had been pulled down over a window. There was nothing like this in my apartment. Slightly yellowed, it had a cord hanging from it which had been crocheted around a plastic pull ring. There was a familiar water stain on the shade, a lion's head coming out of a rose, and I sat up in bed with a gasp.

Across the room, on the opposite wall, two pink-framed pictures were precisely where I remembered them. In one was a fluffy, cartoonish-looking kitten wearing a tuxedo with a white carnation on the lapel, and a tall top hat that reflected light in the pattern of a hazard symbol. The other showed a kitten wearing blue earmuffs sitting at the bottom of a snowy slope in skis. As a child, I used to stare at these pink-framed kittens from my bed and think of them as significant features of my universe. There were other familiar items—on the bureau was a red enamel poodle pin I'd baked in a kiln for my mother, even though she hated poodles. Beside it was a keychain lanyard I'd made for my father, with yellow and brown braided plastic twine.

"Mama?" I called, for it seemed perfectly natural to say that, even though of course she was no longer living, and I had recently forced myself to stop talking to her when I was alone.

Instead, a large beast swept in. This explained the furry touch on my hand. The beast stood on two legs and was about the same size as my mother, but it was covered in a mat of brindled fur that obscured the contours of its body, as thick as the coat on a sheep dog.

The beast sneezed. Dust flew in the small sliver of light that came in at the edge of the blind.

I said, "O.K. if I open the window?"

The beast crossed the room and pulled the little hoop—once, twice, until the blind caught and rolled up. I realized that it had been a long while since I'd seen blinds like this. They had fallen out of favor for some reason, though they were really very functional.

With a shock, I saw the trees that had been outside my bedroom when I was a kid—the mulberry, the elm, and the peach tree, all in scale to my youth, stopped in time.

"How did we get here?" I said, noticing how thin my voice sounded.

But the beast was gone.

I jumped up and started looking around. A few of my games and toys sat in the closet, right where they belonged. I had often thought of our old house, and thought I could remember it perfectly, but there were all sorts of things I had forgotten. The map of the United States in the hallway, for instance. My parents had mounted it on cardboard, and made a frame for it out of binding tape. Beside it was the hall closet. Yes, there was the old

6

hospital-green vacuum cleaner that rolled, nestled between my mother's wool coats, which smelled of mothballs.

The bathroom was as it was before we fixed it up. I liked it better this way. Original wallpaper, which I remembered later helping my mother strip with a steamer and a scraper, a good example of false progress. I peeked around the corner into the living room, wondering if the illusion was complete.

It was, in every detail. The brown sofa, the basket full of magazines, the bookshelves, the ceramic owls. I crossed the braided rug, followed the hall on the other side, and went into my parents' bedroom; there was the beast, lying on its side, as my mother used to in the afternoons.

I knew exactly what to do, and I wasn't afraid.

I came around the bed and sat next to the beast, situating myself near its upended hip. The beast stirred, and peered up at me.

It reached out one of its furry arms and put its large paw on my arm. Exactly how my mother used to. I lay down beside it, and the beast hugged me to its breast.

We snoozed like this a long while, in great contentment; when I woke, the beast was gone. My back was cold, and a cool draft blew in from the window, making the curtain billow lazily. Somewhere in the distance I could hear a chain saw, and the low hum of rush-hour traffic.

In the kitchen, the beast was pushing onions around in a pan. It glanced up, not minding me at all. I could hear a rustling sound just around the corner, where our kitchen table used to be, like the sound of my sister doing her homework or cutting pictures out of magazines. There was a small beast doing exactly that, holding a small red plastic pair of scissors, snipping out pictures of animals. She was arranging the cutouts on the table: a cow, a giraffe, two dogs, and a bear.

I sat in my good old chair. The small beast was kicking the center pole of the round table, pinging it with her bullet-like toes, just as my sister used to, but I didn't feel comfortable kicking the little beast or complaining. Instead, I picked up a magazine from the pile and began to leaf through it. It was *Life*, April 13, 1953. Before I was born, but my parents had been alive. I flipped through it—there was an ad for the GE Range that thinks, a letter to the editor about Igor Stravinsky: "Stravinsky's statement that music is incapable of expressing emotion is a reflection of the sorry state modern composers have entered…" There was a strongly worded editorial about Korea and ending the bloodshed; I barely knew anything about that war. A photo of demonstrators being clubbed in Brazil, a photo of massacred and "Disarmed Kikuyus" in Kenya, ads for a Spinet piano and a full page for Hunt's catsup and another for Hertz—for "the woman who needs a car." Strangely, I knew much more about the piano and the catsup than the events in Brazil and Kenya. I wasn't sure if I'd ever really thought about 1953 in any specific way—a whole year of people's lives, a whole year of history, a whole year that all years since had built on. I didn't want the little beast to cut this magazine up, so I hid it under the table on my lap.

By the old clock on the stove, I could see that it was precisely six when a large, father-shaped beast came through the backdoor as my father used to do. He greeted us all with hugs—me as well, as if I were no different to him than the others—and took a large tumbler etched with Greeks in togas and filled it with ice and gin and just a dash of vermouth. I knew exactly what was next. He removed a jar of dry-roasted peanuts from the cupboard and poured some into a bowl and shook it until the peanuts leveled out. And then he sat with us at the table, tossing a few into his mouth while enjoying his martini. Shortly, dinner was served: peas, small steaks covered with onions, and baked potatoes, all on the green melmac plates we used to have. It was all too remarkable for me to feel hungry, but I tried to eat, wanting to fit in.

I had wished many times to reinhabit my childhood home. For years, I dreamed about the house and its every corner. Many of the dreams involved getting the house back, either magically or simply by having it come on the market. In some dreams, the house was different and yet I recognized it as my house. In others, the house was backed by vast tracts of land that descended into canyons and valleys, even though it was nothing like that where we had lived. We had not been especially happy there, nor was it an especially beautiful house or neighborhood. I could never really understand why it had haunted me.

Now I saw that over our old back fence were acres and acres of grass and alfalfa, with solid granite outcroppings here and there. There were footholds in the rocks where local tribes used to climb them. There were also mortar holes they had used for grinding pemmican, and narrow pits where they sharpened arrows. No one had graffitied the rocks or left them covered with bottles and cans, which surprised me. It would have meant so much to me to wander back there when we lived there. How could we not have known? My mother would have loved it, and it might have saved her mental health. She could have roamed during the day while we were at school, looking for arrowheads, taking notes in her field journal, making sketches, completely in her element.

We once found a trading bead in our small backyard. It was cornflower blue, caked with mud. My mother rinsed it in the sink, just about the most excited I'd ever seen her. I started digging holes in the backyard after that, hoping to find more relics and antiquities to please her. I wondered what it would be like to live along the trail on which Napoleon marched to Moscow. Or along the path that Hannibal and the elephants took across the Alps. The soil where we lived was very hard and difficult to dig in. I kept digging, though. I liked having an ongoing project. Every week I made progress, and got a little deeper, hoping to find something.

This interlude, or whatever it was, carried on. Days went by in what felt like the usual fashion. I could barely remember my recent life—there had been a lot of rushing around in uncomfortable shoes and meeting with people and always having to play some game from which I was supposed to receive some gain. I didn't miss it at all. My surroundings in the past several years had become unimportant to me, and whenever I transferred jobs I moved from one serviceable apartment to the next, not the least attached to any of them. Now here I was, walking my old route to school and revisiting the houses of childhood friends, who had been supplanted by beasts of appropriate shapes and sizes, relishing every iconic detail. Each reunion thrilled me in a way that is almost impossible to describe, and sometimes I found myself smiling so hard that tears came to my eyes.

And so I settled in, enjoying the chance to investigate all the old drawers and cabinets in my house, to examine the simple artifacts of that life with wonder, and to accept the genuine warmth of the beasts and their embrace of me, which was what I'd always felt was fragile in my own family. The motherly beast who cuddled me that first day remained gentle and warm. The childish beast played happily, without much complication. I did not have to struggle to express myself, and felt included and appreciated and somehow that was more than enough. I started to feel as if words had somehow been my undoing, that in trying to explain anything I'd ever thought or felt, I'd only driven a wedge between me and other people. Sometimes, after I'd spent a long afternoon pulling books off the shelves, looking at the inscriptions, or actually reading the books to gain greater insight into my parents' interests, I'd find myself feeling slightly unmoored, and before I knew it, the beasts would come to me and surround me in a circle, hugging me. There was such pleasure in their warm soft bodies and in how they responded to my unspoken moods.

They fed me old favorites and new things, too, such as flavorful bowls of mush, rich and delicious, as if filled with butter and nut meats. An old beast visited regularly who enjoyed brushing my hair, something that I knew other girls' mothers did. Another prepared baths, and scrubbed my back and washed my hair patiently when I sat in the warm fragrant water, as if it were some kind of honor to take care of me. The beasts didn't wear clothing, yet someone

10

always washed and ironed the clothes that were in the closet—yes, clothes I'd had as a child that somehow still fit me. The weather cooperated with all this kindness, every day sunny and bright and warm. I'd sit in the yard and pick a peach or an orange or a fig off trees that I knew had long ago died of disease and been chopped down.

Looking around my old room one day, I saw a book on my shelf that reminded me of a long forgotten incident. There was a phrase in this book that had caused me some trouble, and sure enough, thumbing through the soft, worn pages I found it quickly enough. The book was about a big lucky family of English children and their wonderful summer adventures of complete freedom with their sailboat. Here it was, Nancy speaking: "And then we've got to be all proper in party dresses ready to soothe the savage breast when the Great Aunt comes gorgoning in." I laughed out loud. This phrase had made me shriek during free-reading at school. Surely it was a typo, surely it was supposed to say "savage beast." My fifth-grade teacher was an old woman with legs so swollen she could barely stand up long enough to write things on the chalkboard, and, when I showed her why I was so worked up, she sent me to the principal.

It was not the first time that she'd sent me, and Mr. Leonard knew me by now.

"What is it this time?" he asked. He was a giant, probably 6 foot 6, with close cropped curly hair and teeth like piano keys.

"I just wanted to know if it's valid to say 'soothe the savage breast' instead of 'soothe the savage beast.'"

"Is this in dispute?" the principal asked. I showed him the passage.

"I believe Mrs. Hayman is embarrassed by the word 'breast.' Not to mention 'bosom,'" he said, and then it was me who blushed.

A few weeks before, I'd been sent to Mr. Leonard for saying that word, a word which struck me as nasty. "Breast" was a firm and lean term, but "bosom" sounded dangling and clammy.

"It's true I said that to cause trouble, but I didn't say this to cause trouble."

"I also understand that you've continued to pronounce 'ed' at the end of all verbs?" It was an annoying compulsion, that I felt I had to say "walk-ed" instead of "walkt." "Why does it matter to her so much?"

"She thinks you're trying to annoy her on purpose. Would you be opposed to doing it a little less, just to keep the peace?"

"It's just that . . ." Should I tell him that if I didn't do it, the core of the world would collapse? That it was an outlet, that I needed to be absorbed with small, manageable projects like that? But he was cutting me some slack, and I agreed to stifle myself.

I had seldom thought about Mrs. Hayman's hatred for me in the years since, nor of the strange pleasure I got from provoking her. She was a lonely old woman with fat legs who was probably miserable. She had to be dead by now, buried and forgotten. And she wasn't the only person I'd been mean to back then. I used to enjoy frightening my sister, chasing her around with the roaring open hose of the vacuum cleaner, letting it clamp onto her skin like a viper, leaving round marks on her while she screamed. But we're close now, aren't we? I believe we are; I am sure we are. We talk all the time on the phone.

And then one day, when my guard was down and I simply believed I deserved all this warmth and comfort, the beasts began to hurry around with great agitation and it was plain that something had changed and we would have to clear out.

To tell the truth, I'd stopped questioning the nature of this reality. I didn't know what the world was like outside of the neighborhood—if the whole world was as it had been, or if this was a bubble within the world as it was now. Would we stay in the bubble, or have to go back?

We left all at once, at night.

I ran to keep up, guided by the jagged breath of the beasts around me. We rushed down a long alley to the wash, pushed through the wire and ambled down to the concrete platform by the waterway. A small boat waited for us there, a beast at the helm. We climbed in as if we were being chased, though looking over my shoulder I couldn't see or hear anything. The beasts formed a circle and allowed me to sink in between them, cushioned by their luxurious fur. The captain started the motor, and we set off down the culvert under a sky of silvery stars.

I wondered what the danger was. I trusted them completely.

We passed down the channel a good distance before the boat slowed. Ahead, a lantern was swinging in the dark, signaling to us. As we pulled closer, I saw that the lantern was held by a large bear wearing a ranger's outfit.

"Smokey Bear's a py-ro-ma-ni-ac," I sang out without thinking, and all the beasts turned on me. They grabbed me by the shoulders and pushed me down, burying me between them, out of sight. I was smothered by fur and ashamed. The boat rocked as if we were taking on a passenger or some freight, and then the engine kicked in again, and the boat picked up speed, and, after a few more minutes, breathing shallowly, I was released.

"I didn't mean anything bad," I said.

The beasts were waving their arms and I could tell by their eyes that it had been very important not to offend the Bear. They seemed angry with me, as if I were more of a loose cannon than they realized. They surrounded me as if demanding an answer.

"I used to sing it when I was a kid," I tried to explain. "To bother my sister. She was obsessed with him."

It was the first time that the beasts had been angry with me, and I felt discouraged and insecure.

I lacked, it had been said, pragmatic language skills. They had tested me at school. It meant that, even though I seemed smart, I didn't know how to talk to people in day-to-day life. I wondered if that was true. Didn't I talk to people a lot? Maybe I wasn't really talking, maybe I was only listening. It was true that whenever I wanted to say something I had all these thoughts and feelings but it was sometimes hard to find words for them.

The beasts parked the boat. I had no idea what time it was,

but I was tired. They climbed out and I followed. We ran single file up a staircase covered with litter, and when we reached the top we had to climb over a chain-link fence. Though it was dark, I could see that we were near a freeway overpass. There were a number of trucks parked in the darkness. Some of them had their refrigerator units on, humming steadily.

The backs of the trucks opened up. Other beasts appeared, and piled in. The heavy smell of diesel panicked them, and I grabbed onto one of my beasts for fear I'd get separated. All at once I was being boosted into a truck by someone with skin and hands. The back of the truck rolled down with a crash, and I settled down on the floor.

The truck rumbled on through the night. I found a comfortable place for my head, on the thigh of a beast, and felt relieved that I had been forgiven for my earlier mistake.

When I woke up the beasts were stirring and the truck was slowing, and then it stopped. Before long the back rolled up. Daylight streamed in, and what I saw was nowhere I'd seen before.

It was a desert landscape, flat, dusty, yellow, dry. The air was hot, and fine particles of sand blew in, and a man was helping the beasts climb down. When it was my turn, he nodded but didn't appear to care that I wasn't a beast.

He was maybe in his mid-twenties, with golden hair pulled into a pony tail, and he wore a Levi jacket and a worn leather belt and had big sideburns and a scar above one of his eyes, and he was barefoot, and looked a lot like a boy that had mattered to me in high school.

He took out a box cutter and opened a container full of water bottles that had been in the truck. He passed them out to everyone standing there. The others had fanned out to relieve themselves in the dust. Furry backs faced us in all directions. I counted—I'd been sharing the back of the truck with thirty-three beasts of all ages.

"Where are we?" I asked, but the man just opened another box. He pulled out lunch sacks and distributed them to all present, until there were no more boxes in the truck. In mine was a sandwich wrapped in cellophane, a big oatmeal cookie in a wax paper sleeve, a bag of corn chips, and a perfect looking peach.

Beasts bit at their food and tore it apart, and little pieces flew. Ants attacked the crumbs on the ground around us. I stepped away from the truck to look at the condition of the road, but there was no road. I couldn't see one anywhere around the truck, and so I walked in larger and larger circles. The sand was blowing, but not so hard that it could hide a highway. Could we have driven all this way without a road?

The sand was blowing hard. I saw tufts of hair coming off the beasts, flying away in the wind. The beasts were shivering and scratching themselves as if the sand really irritated them. Some of us huddled in circles. "Why did he bring us out here?" I asked, but that didn't seem to be the main question on everybody's mind. It was more like, What now? Some of the beasts began digging. Others wandered away, towards the distant, uninterrupted horizon. My beasts dug, but it seemed futile. The sand kept blowing back into the holes, filling them up again. I wanted to help, but I had no idea how to help or even what I should hope for. The beasts had been scratching themselves so violently that in places they had lost almost all their fur, and the skin underneath was bleeding. As they lost fur from their faces, they began to look more human. Their facial structure was almost the same as mine, or maybe just like mine. They had cheekbones and chins and lips and noses. With the fur they all looked mostly the same, but without fur they looked very different from one another.

I realized that without his fur one of the beasts looked almost exactly like our next-door neighbor, Bill McGee, an insurance salesman, a nice man with a nice wife named Marion. They had seven cats, and whenever they went on vacation we'd offer to feed and play with the cats. They were the only neighbors my mother ever made friends with. One day, they announced that they were moving far away, and from that day forward my mother felt her world was crumbling. Some essential component of her well being never recovered.

"Mr. McGee?" I found myself saying to the scraggly beast. But the beast merely glanced at me and continued to dig in the sand.

More fur flew away in the wind, and the beasts began to shiver.

I was growing despondent, as the beasts lost their fur and continued to dig. Everything felt futile, like madness. I was hungry and thirsty again and I came around to find the driver, who was sitting in the cab of the truck smoking a cigarette, staring out at the vast nothingness. I waved up at him.

"Can you understand me?"

"Sometimes," he said.

"Is there some reason we had to stop here?"

He climbed out of the cab, his shirt blowing open. He handed me a plastic cup filled with hot black coffee from a thermos, the last of it. Then we walked around and sat on the truck's lift gate. I didn't ask any questions; I just drank my coffee. I had a hunch that we'd run out of fuel, and it was embarrassing him. He lifted one of his bare feet to pull a thorn out of his heel.

I reached over and touched his stomach, and my hand slipped down under his belt. He lay back on the wooden floor of the truck, which was scarred by many years of yielding to the rough wood of palettes and the scrape of palette jacks and forklifts. I didn't want to kiss him, but his lips parted; the remains of his breakfast were at the corners of his mouth and a smear of peach flesh was in the stubble on his chin. I simply moved my hand in the way that was necessary, rubbing my knuckles on the inside of his zipper. His ponytail lay off to the side, and I found myself repelled by the smell of his flesh, so used to the soft fur of the beasts had I become. An exhausted groan erupted from his throat, and I managed to withdraw my hand dry.

He was not the boy who had mattered to me, that much was for sure.

16

Some of the beasts were losing their claws and ripping their skin as they dug into the ground. Their toes were getting bloody but it didn't stop them. The little fur they had left was clotted with blood, and the sand was sticking to it, and they were wiping their paws on their sides in bold, bloody, sandy streaks and continuing on. The reddish-brown streaks on their fur and foreheads began to resemble war paint. Frantically they scratched on, finding occasionally a beetle in the cooler parts of the soil, or a ground rat's tunnel, or a snake hole with bones in it.

All around, the beasts were slowing down. One was up to its neck in a pit, still flinging out clumps of roots and sand in sporadic bursts. Retreating figures weaved uncertainly, weak and purposeless, broken. Several of the beasts were dead. Flies attacked them, lighting on the blood on their bodies and remaining patches of fur. I wandered across the field where all this purposeless digging and clinging to life was happening, until I came upon the beast I'd known in the way I'd known my mother. She was lying on her side, panting with great effort, and like the other beasts, much of her lovely fur had been stripped. There was a pattern of freckles on the beast's arm much as there had been on my mother's arm, a constellation of freckles that I had known better than the night sky. I touched the beast's skin there, and it flinched, but then relaxed. I held its hand. I'd missed my mother's death—I'd been at work, I hadn't come fast enough. Now, for the first time, I could clearly see the beast's teeth. When my mother died and was sent to be cremated I had cried, ridiculously, about her teeth, which I had always loved, unable to conceive of a world where I could no longer see them.

I sat with the beast until sometime in the middle of the night, when the sky was very black and the stars were bright. I held its hand all through the panting, rumbling breaths that would lead to the last one, like an old engine going still.

I was hungry. It was cold. I had a conscience. I had a sister I never spoke to. Dear history, dear life. Hadn't I been glad enough?

WONDER VALLEY

William Hillyard

You might have passed through here, maybe. Out for a drive with time on your hands, you might have taken the long-cut to the casinos of Vegas from the soulless sprawl of L.A. You'd have driven way beyond the outer reaches of suburbia, beyond its neglected fringe of citrus groves, past the outlet malls and the desert resorts, past that remote high desert national park and the Marine base, past the Next Services 100 Miles sign and any reason anybody really drives out this way anyway. You'd have blown through here at 60 miles an hour, probably, along a potholed and corrugated tarmac, the only asphalt for miles. If you were messing with your radio or fiddling with your phone, you might not have even noticed the grid of washboard tracks scraped from the sparse hardscrabble of greasewood scrub in this nowhere corner of the Mojave.

You can turn off of the pavement, of course, turn onto any one of the bumpy dirt roads. These are public rights-of-way, county maintained easements between dry homesteads. You probably didn't, though. Few people do. And that's the way the people who live out here like it.

If you turned off onto dusty Steeg Road, however, driven north through the miles of stinted scrub, past the empty shells of abandoned shacks, the sparsely spaced shanties of cobbled together junk, you'd come to the dilapidated cabin where Ricka McGuire once lay nude in the old cream-colored school bus that was her home.

You won't find the old Wayne school bus parked there now, though. Ricka's son towed it to his place, then Ned Bray bought it. It's now another mile up the road, past Willie Mitchell's place, and the old circus elephant trailer and the rusty Volvo once owned by one of the Beach Boys. It's parked on Ned's five-acre parcel next to what's left of his homestead cabin way up there at the northern edge of Wonder Valley.

Wonder Valley. This patch of desert gets its incongruous name from a joke, really, a sign out on the paved road that once marked an old cabin. Wonder Valley just as easily could have been called "Calloused Palms" or "Withering Heights," the names of other homestead parcels in the area. Back in those days anyone could get a parcel out here, get a homestead spread for the cost of the filing fee, make a claim under the Small Tract Homestead Act of 1938.

Congress passed the Small Tract Act to give land to veterans of the Great War, land in this dry desert climate, a climate thought recuperative to mustard gas-scorched lungs. It opened lands to homesteading from Nevada to the Mexican border, throwaway land the government deemed otherwise useless. The Act opened the land to anyone, too, not just veterans, made land available for health, convalescent and recreational use. Mostly, though, the government just wanted rid of it.

This land had been open to homesteading before 1938, too. There are a few remnants of original homesteads in Wonder Valley, the quarter section, 160-acre type filed under the Homestead Acts that privatized much of the west with the goal of turning America's vast God-given wastes into bountiful, man-made gardens of Eden. Under previous homestead acts, however, you were required to build a home, live there, not an easy venture in place like Wonder Valley, a place not at all conducive to human habitation. A few homesteaders made a go here, and a few of those homesteads survived, only to be divided and subdivided into remnants, parted out piecemeal over the generations so that most have been whittled down to fewer than twenty acres each.

The small tract act, however, waved the residency requirements. All you had to do was choose a five-acre rectangle from the General Land Office map and pay your five-dollar filing fee. They had divided the valley on paper, 336-by-660-foot parcels— roughly two city blocks each—and overlaid that on the land without regard to topography. There were no roads back then, few markers; it was up to you to find the property you chose. Parcel locater services popped up: for a fee, they'd help you locate your land.

There were one hundred and forty-two small tract homestead applications filed in 1941, the first year land became available. But by year's end, World War II preoccupied America. Gasoline and tires for travel grew scarce; the strong legs and backs needed to improve this land were off fighting tyranny abroad. After the war, however, things changed. The fifties saw the advent of California car culture, the Atomic Age, the Cold War, nuclear families, bomb shelters. Hollywood westerns fed nostalgia for simpler times. Out in the desert, the old west lived—the purple mountains majesty, the changing colors of the desert sunset, the wide-open skies, the limitless stars. In Wonder Valley, people discovered, you could get your very own home on the range, claim your own personal piece of the Wild Wild West. Magazines published pieces: it's easy to make a small tract claim, anybody can get land, inciting what the *Los Angeles Times* called "one of the strangest land rushes in Southern California history." By 1952 the Federal General Land Office had processed more than 12,000 homestead applications in the area, and by the mid-fifties they had a backlog of some 60,000. They could no longer keep up. Lines trailed out of the government land office. Even movie cowboy Ronald Reagan staked a Wonder Valley claim.

Once you chose your plot and located it, you had three years to "prove-up" your parcel, clear the land, build a cabin. Ronald Reagan didn't "prove up" his parcel. In fact, few people did. Few could stand the scorching months of triple-digit heat or the icy winter chill, the snow and the flash floods, or the constant wind that blasts like a furnace in the summer and bites to the bone in the winter. Most drove the three hours out here from L.A., took one look at the dry, scruffy land blistering in the summer heat—no roads, no water—and they got right back into their cars and drove right back home. Those folks lost their homesteads, gave up their claim. Their parcel went back on the block, became available for some other soul to select.

Many did tough it out, though. They spent their weekends banging nails into lumber and mortaring desert rocks together into walls. Others bought prefab units or hired the construction companies that sprang up across the desert offering units designed specifically to satisfy Land Office requirements. Over the years, the flat valley filled up with cookie-cutter cabins, each a couple hundred square feet, an outhouse out back. Some cabins grew into houses: rooms were added, water wells drilled, flush toilets and indoor plumbing installed. Most, however, sagged into disrepair.

After the homestead blip of the fifties, this corner of the Mojave became a blank space on the map once again. The interstate freeways had bypassed the area; any tinge of a town died on the desert's withered vine. Homesteaders passed properties to heirs with no interest in grandpa's wasteland clapboard shack. Congress repealed the Small Tract Homestead Act in 1976 and by then thirty-six percent of the land the act had opened to homesteading was privately owned. The rest, the government reckoned, merited federal protection. Now Wonder Valley is a pixelated patchwork of public and private land.

Through the eighties and nineties, Wonder Valley crumbled into a sort of post-modern ghost town, an eerie ghost suburbia in the dry desert wastes. Squatters squatted in the old, forgotten cabins. L.A.'s downtrodden, drifting east from town to town chasing cheaper and cheaper rent, occupied others. Mental institutions resettled patients out here, prisons dumped inmates out on early release. Vacant cabins had their windows scrapped, their metal scavenged, the shacks stripped to bare shells, doors and chairs and siding and walls hauled away and burned to heat the newcomers' homes in the freezing high-desert winter. Open squatters' fires built on bare concrete floors sometimes spread to the walls, the roof. "Improvement fires" the fire department calls them. They let them burn, let them "prove up" Wonder Valley by removing another run-down shanty. Remaining residents burned down eyesores, too, tore down drug dens, dismantled desert blight. A federally funded program, "Shack Attack," actually paid contractors to demolish the development it once encouraged. Today, few of the original 4,000 cabins remain.

When the nearby national park was established in the Nineties, however, others began to venture out this way. Snowbirds' motor homes retraced the corrugated pavement of this forgotten byway. Retirees discovered the quaint little cabins—the rustic charm! Writers found solitude in the lonely desert; artists, inspiration. The artists and writers and snowbirds and retirees look at the mountains, this is the real purple mountains majesty, they say, the changing colors of the desert sunset, the wide-open skies, the limitless stars—it's like living in a painting!

These days, maybe a couple thousand artists and writers and snowbirds and retirees, drifters and squatters, mental patients and ex-cons people the three hundred square miles of Wonder Valley, each on the vestige of a homestead. You can tell the artists and retirees by their satellite TV dishes, their raked-sand, Zen-garden yards, their manicured desert landscaping carefully sculpted and formed—nature "proved-up." You know them by their cars: how few of them there are, none of them on blocks, all of them running. They live in houses, proper houses, with windows and walls and rooms, kitchens with running water, garages. Pride of ownership. They look out over the desert, look out at the sagging shacks and single family slums of scavenged cast-offs, old lumber, scrap metal, weathered furniture, the cars on blocks or left for dead where they died. Can you believe the way some people live? they say. The empty shells of homestead cabins are historic, they tell themselves, quaint reminders of a bygone era—little ghost towns now being trashed by indolent little ghosts.

Ned Bray lives on a five-acre homestead plot up at the northern edge of the valley. His parents bought him the place twenty-five years ago, sight unseen, then they packed him up and shipped him out here. Figured he couldn't harm anyone way out here in the middle of nowhere. Recently, some anonymous artist or retiree called the county, reported Ned: His place is an eyesore, they said, it needs to be cleaned up, junk everywhere, the mounds of wood and stucco, the piles of parts, the wind-blown trash that flaps from the greasewood scrub like withered fruit. Ned's parcel had been "proved-up": at one time it had a cabin on it, indoor plumbing even, and a big mesquite tree out front near the road. Ned used to live in the cabin on his property, and for a while Cindy McCollum and her son Danny lived there, too. Cindy had lost her home in town and Ned invited her to share his Wonder Valley cabin with him. Back then it had a bedroom and bathroom. Lace curtains. But that damn tree out front, that big mesquite tree had spread its roots like tentacles under the house, into the walls, and would give Ned no rest with its constant talking, five different voices from the walls, the swamp cooler, the toilet. It was like five radios you could never turn off, man. Ned had to keep the toilet sealed tightly to keep that demon thing from getting out into the house. He spent nights on end crouched there waiting for it. He caught the demon thing once, caught it running back to the bathroom. He beat and beat the little bastard with a baseball bat, tried to kill it. He tore the walls out looking for the voices, destroyed the cabin, chopped down the tree and dug out the stump. He dug down into the septic tank and flung the muck out, disgusting work, man, until he got that thing out and the voices were gone.

It was Ricka McGuire who finally got Cindy out of Ned's place, took her and her son Danny to a friend's to stay. Ned had been ranting about the voices, that damn tree, its roots! He had been sitting in the corner rocking back and forth waiting for the demon when four-year-old Danny stumbled sleepy-eyed to the bathroom. Ned beat him with that bat until the child passed out. Danny woke up vomiting blood. The police were called; they wouldn't come. It was too far, it was a domestic dispute. Ricka came and got Cindy and Danny out of Ned's house. There was no ambulance, no hospital. Children heal.

Ricka didn't live in her old cream-colored school bus back then. She had ten acres in a sandy pass on Valley Mountain, the rocky crag that scars deeply into Wonder Valley. She had her bus parked there, though, next to the cabin. She'd had the bus for years, had bought it when she lived in Oregon, kept it outside the Portland Victorian where she raised her family. There, a single mother on welfare, she picked beans and berries to get by. Her kids never realized they were poor. But after those kids had grown and gone, a heavy weight lifted and Ricka McGuire floated free. In that Wayne school bus, she set out south, an old hippy bumping down the coast. She spent some years in Humboldt trimming marijuana bud for cash and living in the school bus she had outfitted like a motorhome. From there she pressed further south, drifted to the edge of town after town until the towns ran out at Wonder Valley. She parked her bus behind the cluttered cabin where her son had settled his family. It was tough on her at first, but she came to love the desert, the wide-open skies, the limitless stars. When the wind wasn't blowing and the heat wasn't so bad, the ear-ringing quiet was more calming than lonely. After a while, she found a place, that old homestead cabin on ten acres nestled in the rocks of Valley Mountain. An old woman agreed to sell it to her—$15,000—she'd make payments, a couple of hundred a month. She had no well, no water, but that didn't matter. You can't drink the well water out here anyway, it's too full of salt and minerals, and comes out of the ground at 140 degrees. No, Ricka would haul water like most everyone else. Her cabin had a two-thousand-gallon tank—that would last her about a month.

Ricka had contracted polio as a child and wore a leg brace, but that disability meant she got $750 Supplemental Security Income each month from the government. She could live pretty good out here on that. And she was smart, she learned the system, the way things worked. Once she got a real address, became settled, she could take advantage of county services. She hired Cindy McCollum as a county-paid in-home service worker. Cindy would clean Ricka's cabin periodically and help her get around. Ricka also convinced Meals-On-Wheels to drive all the way out to her place; she was the last stop on the route, got the last of the food—enough for her and her dogs and her cats. For a while, things were pretty good for her.

But only a few years later, Ricka McGuire was back in her old Wayne school bus, parked in front of that dilapidated cabin down by her son's ramshackle shack. She'd moved back into it, had it towed off the Valley Mountain property, the property that was no longer hers. You see, Congress had voted to purge fugitive felons off the SSI roles; they matched old arrest warrants with Social Security records, tracked down the aged and infirm, revoked their benefits. That's how Ricka lost hers. She got a letter in the mail: "We are writing to let you know that we have paid you $17,323.00 too much Supplemental Security Income (SSI) money. You were overpaid because our records show that you have an outstanding arrest warrant." Her SSI payments abruptly ended. And the government wanted its seventeen thousand dollars back.

Back in 1965, Ricka had done something dumb. She was raising three children on welfare when she found some woman's checkbook. As another mother drove her around town, Ricka wrote bad checks. Busted and booked, she did time—five months. But she never completed her probation.

Now, forty years later, she was back in the bus. It no longer ran; she towed it place to place behind an old yellow van she had. She bootlegged power at vacant shacks using her daughter's info or made-up names until the power company caught on. She was smart, she knew the system, but without a fixed address, she lost other benefits, too, the Meals-On-Wheels, the county-paid in-home service worker. The artists and writers and snowbirds and retirees watched her through their tinted windows, Can you believe the way she lives? Her son had gotten into meth; his wife had left him. He had moved to an apartment in town and left his place to a crew of low-lifes. And in her struggle to survive Ricka had burned some bridges. Now she was all but alone in the desert.

The heat peaked at 118 degrees the day Ned Bray stopped by to check on Ricka and found her lying nude on the bed in her cream-colored bus. Ned had been worried about her—she'd run out of water, she wasn't tolerating the heat so well. He had convinced her to go to town the day before, to get out of the record heat, to go to the library where there was air conditioning. Wonder Valley has a community center—it's on the paved road next door to the fire station. The county runs it, residents pay for it with their taxes. The community center is supposed to be a sanctuary from the heat. It's supposed to be air-conditioned; it's supposed to be opened to the public on days when it's really hot. But it wasn't open. Wasn't open because the plumbing was bad, or the floors needed work, or because the last time someone used it they didn't keep it clean. So Ricka and Ned drove her old yellow van through the miles of stinted scrub to town. She had no air conditioning in that van of hers, the heat was unbearable.

They never made it. On the way, Ricka had a seizure or something, right in the middle of the road. She just stopped. Ned got the van over to the side. Sheriff deputies came by: move that damn thing or you'll be ticketed or towed. But they just sat there, four hours. As the sun set and the day cooled, Ricka recovered; she drove herself home. Ned brought her a couple of jugs of water. When he returned the next afternoon, walked the mile from his place to hers, past Willie Mitchell's place and the circus elephant trailer and the sunbaked Volvo once owned by one of the Beach Boys, he found the water untouched.

In the stifling heat, Ned ran to Willie Mitchell's. Willie had a phone; he called 911. It took the paramedics thirty-seven minutes to drive out over the forgotten remnant of corrugated asphalt, up the washboard dirt road, past the remains of old homestead cabins, cross over the wash, past Ricka's son's ramshackle shack to the dilapidated cabin where Ricka had parked her bus. It didn't matter. Ricka McGuire, lying in the bed of her bus, had long been dead.

I drove out there, beyond the outer reaches of suburbia, beyond its neglected fringe of citrus groves, the remote high desert national park. Out past the Next Services 100 Miles sign, I turned off the corrugated pavement and rattled north through the miles of stinted scrub, billows of dust roiling behind my car. It was hot. Ahead of me, a dust devil stumbled like a drunk across the sandy road ripping wind-blown trash from the greasewood scrub and flinging it into the air, up and over the dilapidated shack where Ned Bray had found Ricka McGuire dead.

I had gotten the county coroner's report. It concluded "Probable Heat Stroke" was a "significant condition" contributing to Ricka's death. But not the cause. Ned had tried to explain to the officials that Ricka hadn't been well. She had run out of water; the week of record high temperatures had taken its toll. But they had found some pot in the bus, a pipe, determined she had a "history of smoking cigarettes and marijuana," and listed the cause of her death as "Chronic Drug Abuse." There was no toxicology report. When I asked about it, the coroner's people just shrugged, agreed it made no sense, there was nothing in the report to justify those conclusions. They'd have to look into it. Pull the file. Call down to archives and have it brought up. They'd have to talk to so-and-so when she got back from wherever.

Out in Wonder Valley I parked my car in front of the dilapidated cabin where Ricka had parked her bus, the spot where Ned had found her. The lonely silence made my ears buzz. Ricka McGuire isn't the only one who has died out here, died from the heat. A man lived in the cabin right next door to the parcel where Ricka died. His truck broke down between here and town; he tried to walk home. He didn't make it. And there's Shawn Pritchard. Shawn grew up in Wonder Valley, lived for a time in the cabin just next door to the east. He was out with his girlfriend scrapping on the Marine base, out collecting bombs and bullets to recycle when his car got stuck. She stayed with it, he walked for help. The Marines found their raven-picked and coyote-eaten corpses weeks later. There have been others too, others who no one bothered to look for, who no one knew were missing. Like the guy whose femur Jill Davis shows to visitors. Jill has the place still further to the east. She found the leg bone in the wash at the end of the valley. Poor chump. The cops couldn't even be troubled to drive out from town to retrieve the guy's sun-bleached remains.

You can see Ricka's son's ramshackle shack from the place where Ricka died. From there, it looked like a pile, a swept together pile that no one ever bothered to pick up. An old Fotomat booth stood like a gatehouse in front of the shack, walled-in from the world by parapets of scavenged lumber, campers, and cars. Jill Davis wanted to buy it, buy it just to clean it up. Can you believe people the way some people live?

Up close, the son's house looked like it had exploded. The doors were flung open, the windows smashed out, the insides thrown outside, scattered everywhere—household items, children's clothes, books and papers. Cars left where they died. A Bible standing on end blocked the dirt drive, its pages swollen thick in the heat. A couple of pitbulls bounded at me from under a ten-foot travel trailer parked behind the cabin.

"You looking for Nutty Ned?" a woman answered me through the window of the trailer; her short, blond hair and bare shoulders visible through the ragged curtains. She didn't seem too used to visitors. Plopping out of the trailer, she pulled an oversized shirt over her body; her heavy pale breasts squished out through the cut-off armholes as she pointed the direction to Ned's. She's been living out here for a couple of years, she said, waiting for her SSI to come through, then she's moving, going to get an apartment somewhere out of the dirt and the heat.

I drove the mile up the road, past Willie Mitchell's place, the circus elephant trailer, the Volvo once owned by one of the Beach Boys. Ned lives in Ricka's old Wayne school bus now; he towed it up there and parked it next to the ruins of his homestead shack.

28

He tore the cabinets out of the bus and the bed and the floors, stripping it down to a shell. People are too attached to things, he said. You've got to simplify your life, man. As I walked up, Ned was organizing: moving carburetors to the carburetor pile, the rearview mirrors to the rearview mirror pile, the bicycle wheels, toilet seats. He stacked and restacked his stuff with swift jerky movements, winding his way through an elaborate maze of things. He handed me a paper, a notice of violation from the county. "What does it say," he asked me. Ned couldn't read. I told him a neighbor had complained, the county insists he clean the place up. "It's not right what they're doing, man," he said. "I use everything here once a year!" I didn't understand what he meant.

Behind me, a water truck lumbered up the road, turned and backed onto Ned's property, sinking into the soft sand. Ned threaded his way through the maze of stuff to a group of blue plastic barrels. He rolled them close to the belly of the truck as the driver, Moose, a burly guy with a grizzly beard, unwound a section of canvas hose, sticking the end into one of the drums. He opened the valve and water began to flow, droning into the hollow of the barrel, drumming its sides. Ned moved the hose from barrel to barrel, filling half a dozen, 55 gallons each, splashing water over his dirty feet and tattered flip-flops as he stepped around white flags of toilet paper waving surrender from desiccated clumps of human shit. As the last barrel filled he dug his hands into the water. Reaching up with arms full, the water cascaded over his tanned face, through his stubble of hair, his shadow of whiskers, and over his thin, leathery body, darkening the waistband of his frayed shorts.

"I'm going put the rest of this water in that hole there," he shouted to Moose, gesturing to an open pit in the dirt. "I dug a well down there, I'm going to fill it up."

Ned dragged the hose to the hole. Moose shot me a hesitant look, then opened the valve on the truck. We stood with our hands in our pockets and watched the water gush forth from the open end of the canvas hose.

"You got to have water, man," Ned said as the remaining thousand gallons of water sank into the thirsty desert sand. "You can't live out here without water."

WINTER OF DEPARTURES

Susanna Kwan

Recently, at a neighbor's memorial, I saw a young man in uniform press a button inside the barrel of his bugle, his white gloves bright against the polished yellow metal, before bringing the instrument to his lips and filling the cemetery with the sound of "Taps." During the minute the song played, the muscles in his cheeks and neck did not move. No one else seemed to notice it was a recording. Another man in uniform presented the family with a flag folded into a soft-cornered triangle like a chain letter or the notes girls used to pass in Language Arts.

When I was very young, I lived downstairs from a retired band director who volunteered as a bugler for military funerals. I could tell from Mr. O'Rourke's footsteps when he was preparing to leave his apartment. Sometimes when I heard his door shut I would open mine to catch him on his way down.

"The twenty-four hardest notes to play," he'd say, lifting his trumpet case and pointing the bell end at me.

Once, he had seen me use a watering pot to write the alphabet on the cement in our shared backyard, and soon after small boxes of colored sidewalk chalk began to appear at my front door. From the street or the yard, where I drew hopscotches with my new chalk, I could see the blackened walls of the building beside ours.

The building had been boarded up since the year before, when a fire had killed a family of squatters who had moved into the top

31

floor after word got out that the bank, which owned the property, had given up on collecting rent. They had run an extension cord to the downstairs unit to siphon power, and the plug had sparked and ignited the apartment, trapping them inside.

I woke up outside in my mother's arms as smoke pumped out of the windows next door. All down the block, which was riddled with half-patched potholes, residents huddled outside their buildings as firemen pointed water hoses at the flames. Beside me and my mother were the rest of the neighbors from our building: Avis, along with her hulking boyfriend, Cedric, both of them in their fluffy bathrobes; Mr. O'Rourke in flannel pajamas, his silver hair smashed and tangled and his trumpet case in hand; and Wilson, gaunt and shivering in his underwear and faux-fur slippers. All five of us—and Cedric—together in one place.

On Sunday mornings I woke to the warbled sound of Mr. O'Rourke playing the trumpet and the slip and swish of scissor blades as my mother clipped coupons from the newspaper. After listening awhile to the brass notes twisting through Mr. O'Rourke's floorboards and into my room, I would kick off my covers, pad into the narrow kitchen, climb onto the other stool at the rolling island we used as our dining table, and watch my mother stack perfect rectangles of thin, smooth paper. I wanted to help, but my hands were too small and the scissors squeaked at the pivot and resisted straight lines.

"Don't mess up my piles," she would say when I ran my thumb along the soft corners. "I have those organized like that for a reason." After checking every page, she would secure each pile with a paper clip and place them all in a brown plastic sleeve that fit inside her wallet. She never went anywhere without that sleeve.

Afternoons, my aunt, who lived a six-hour drive south in Los Angeles, would call to complain to my mother about their mother.

"What do you expect," my mother would say. "They fried her brains, remember?"

When she talked on the phone, she would huddle over her

32

crossed legs and twist the cord with a finger. If I laid my chin on the island counter, I could see into her ear—dark corners and crevices, shadowed shapes. When she noticed me staring and listening, she'd wave me out of the room, and I would lie on my belly in the hall and peer into the kitchen from the floor. With my cheek against the coarse, lumpy carpet that smelled of previous tenants' cigarette smoke, I could see her toes curled on the bottom stool rung and feel the entire building vibrating with trumpet noise.

"No, thanks," she said into the receiver some days. "We have enough right now, but thanks for offering."

"Someone broke into my car," she said on other days. "With the tires and now this window I have to replace, we're already down to almost nothing this month."

I loved how the whole building was home on Sundays. Avis, who lived upstairs across from Mr. O'Rourke, would knock on the door with a Pyrex measuring cup my mother would fill to the top red line with sugar. Two hours later, Avis would return with half a dozen warm peanut butter cookies, and, on occasion, some plastic jewelry for me—dangling chili pepper earrings, pearls with seams that scratched my skin. She was a round woman whose hairstyle changed weekly—from tiny braids that hung straight to her shoulders to bouncing ringlets to a shiny red bob. Sometimes she even had long blond waves. She pinched my nose with her knuckles when she passed by, and when she laughed—when Cedric, who worked nights as a bouncer and security guard, came around and made her laugh—the sound was loud and full, like dinner with my extended family. Her perfume made my head throb, but I held my breath happily because I liked when she visited. From my window, I'd see her waiting, in a brown blazer and matching pants, all of her brown, for the bus that went downtown. My mother said she worked retail at one of the department stores.

Wilson, the forty-something-year-old Chinese man who lived opposite us, would step out for a smoke every hour or so. I'd follow him down the stairs, admiring his neat ballerina bun and perfect posture, to watch him from inside as he blew smoke rings on the stoop. He wore jeans torn at both knees, one of the holes patched with pink sequined thread, its seam puckered, the scales forming a sparkling wad, which I imagined would do damage to his skin if he fell. The other hole hung open like a lazy mouth with frayed threads for lips. I thought he looked lonely and told my mother so.

"I think you're right," she said. "You were too young to remember, but a very nice man named Leo used to live with him. He got sick and died a few years ago."

"Cigarettes are no good for little girls," Wilson would shout through the glass-paned front door, and I'd stare at the dramatic slope of his cheekbones as he inhaled, his cheeks rosy, as if a sheet of coal was glowing under the rugged skin. He seemed thinner and paler every time I saw him. I wondered, as I wondered of all men his age, if he might be my father.

"No, he isn't." My mother took my chin between her thumb and pointer finger. "I would tell you if it were him."

In the cement yard, weeds shot up through the cracks and wilted, too tall to stand. Poppies sprouted from the fence corners like static bonfires. Cats covered in cuts and sores, their ribs visible beneath the fur, slunk through the lawn, which was ravaged from winter and littered with mascara tubes and beer bottles and bullet casings. At night we heard the cats yowl as they scavenged in the dumpster. When they came to the back door, my mother would put out a shallow bowl of milk. She said their bones were stretching like mine, that their cries were from growing pains.

The winter I was seven was the coldest in Northern California in decades, and I hoped to see my first snow. Icicles formed on our windows. The radiator hissed and clicked, but failed to generate heat. My nose was raw and peeling from weeks of emptying my sinuses into toilet paper. My mother filled a baking pan with half an inch of water and set it on the back step so we could marvel at the ice an hour later.

One afternoon I left a Coke can, the one soft drink I was allowed for the week, in the back seat of her car, and the can froze and exploded overnight. Early the next morning on our way to school, we found the can blown cleanly in two, its contents on the seat, not yet slush—a cylinder of brown snow. I reached for the aluminum pieces, and my mother pushed me back on the sidewalk and placed them in a plastic bag in the glove compartment, saying, "It's sharper than it looks." Then she tossed the cold brown lump to the curb and brushed away the ice shards that had formed on the seat.

Several shelters had shut down that year. Homeless men slept on the front stoop of our building, huddled beneath the thick glass windows on either side of the door, one beneath the four mailboxes and another beneath the four doorbells, their shopping carts pulled up on the step, partially blocking the entryway. My mother never said a word to them, not *good morning* or *hello* or *get out*. I asked why we couldn't let them bring their sleeping bags and coats inside, just to the ground level where nobody lived, where it was warmer, and my mother said, "Don't ever open your door for someone you don't know and trust." But I saw empty yogurt containers—the same kind she bought for me—and plastic baggies flecked with white rice or Cheerios left in the corner. One morning I even glimpsed, beneath the layers of military green, a corner of the pink polyester blanket my aunt had given me, patterned with rainbows and ponies, which my mother had refused to let me use because it was flammable.

A few days after Christmas, I was bundled in wool and playing in the yard when I saw Avis hurrying down her back steps, running so fast I was sure she would miss a step and fall. She squeezed herself behind the dumpster. Disheveled and trembling, she was almost unrecognizable. I had never seen an adult hide or look so terrified. I don't think I'd have known it was her if I hadn't seen the whole thing.

She put her fingers to her lips when she saw me. "Shhh."

I ran inside and told my mother, who dropped the knife she'd been using to chop ginger and went straight to the yard. She came right back with Avis and latched the door behind them. After checking the locks on the front door, she sat Avis down on the living room couch, pulling a blanket around her. I positioned myself on the floor between the two of them.

"The 9 is gone from my phone." Avis was panting, and her voice was raspy.

"What?" my mother said.

"I look out the window and see him get out of his truck and he has a baseball bat. I pick up the phone to call the police because this morning he said he was going to kill me. But there's no 9 on my phone anymore. He took the 9 off my phone."

"You're safe here," my mother said.

The main door to the building opened and slammed below. Heavy, slow footsteps came up the stairs, past our apartment door, and up the next flight, followed by a boom.

"He just kicked my door open," Avis said.

"I'll call the police."

"Please, please don't."

My mother went to the kitchen and came back with an envelope. She kept a thin stack of cash hidden under slabs of frozen chicken in the icebox for emergencies, the bills so old they looked counterfeit.

"Here," she said. "You can stay with us for a few days, but you have to get out of here. It's not going to get better."

Avis shook her head. "I can't take your money."

She spent the next few nights on our couch, and my mother monitored the window for Cedric. At one point, Wilson and Mr. O'Rourke came over. They had heard the commotion. Wilson's arms were covered in rashes, and he was so thin I couldn't look at his face, so I stared at his sparkling pink knee. Mr. O'Rourke didn't have much to say, but he pulled a harmonica from his shirt pocket and blew a ragged tune into the hollow metal, making Avis smile.

"You must have been a great dad," she said, and he nodded, just barely, and gripped the harmonica in his hand.

"You deserve better," Wilson said to her. We could barely understand him over his cough.

"You take care of *you*," Avis said.

The year was coming to a close. I don't think we had ever all been in the same room together. My mother filled an old takeout container with leftovers from Christmas and handed it to Wilson, who requested another song from Mr. O'Rourke.

In the mornings of her brief stay, Avis would ask to use the phone. I overheard her calling in sick and then telling my mother she was afraid of losing her job. "This is the busy season," she said. "I can't miss any more shifts, I can't."

I kept returning to the scene in the backyard. I could not understand who Cedric was, or had become, to her. I wanted to know what he had done. "It's not our business," my mother said. She didn't ask questions, but she always opened her door at the right time.

The landlord had the door fixed and the locks changed a few days later, on New Year's Eve, and Avis went back upstairs.

That was the first time I stayed up for the New Year, and I remember feeling older, the way I expected to on birthdays but never did. Earlier that day, my mother had let me try arugula, which she had grown in a plastic milk jug on the back step. I remember that first pinch on my tongue, the flood of bitter and sweet, the surprise that there could be spice in a leaf. I resisted spitting it out, and this, too, made me feel grown-up. For the last half hour of the year, my mother and I sat next to the radio with cups of sparkling cider she'd saved from last January's clearances, waiting for the recorded moment when somewhere, three hours earlier and thousands of miles away, in a city I could not yet imagine, a glowing ball dropped. We heard cheers from the neighbors watching a broadcast down the street, and we clinked our cups and sipped the cider. Upstairs Mr. O'Rourke played "Auld Lang Syne," and when I woke I felt, for the first time, the loneliness of morning on New Year's Day.

It must have been a Sunday in mid-March the last time we heard from Avis because I remember we were on our fourth or fifth or sixth day of eating corned beef. My mother would buy it once a year, on sale, and we would eat it all week, stuffed into sandwiches when the cabbage ran out, or sprinkled into omelets, the clipped red threads of meat flaking like eraser shavings. Sick of the taste, I pretended I was eating pieces of barbequed pork or duck with glistening chocolate-red skin. When that didn't work, I tried to conjure the taste of ham.

Earlier that day I watched my mother cut coupons and place them into neat stacks, and we ate brunch to the dampened trumpet soundtrack. My aunt called, as usual, and my mother sat hunched on the kitchen stool for hours, talking in a low voice.

"We have to move out of this place," I heard her say. "It's just not safe."

Wilson had been moved into hospice care, and the afternoon felt empty without his ritual smoking breaks. Outside, the cherry trees had blossomed and clouds of pink and white floated over the sidewalk, dropping petals that browned under foot traffic.

My mother had decided it was time for me to start learning how to cook. For dinner, she started with a simple lesson. After checking to see how much corned beef was left, she instructed me to rinse and soak the rice while she took a quick shower. In a series of washes, I sifted out the bugs that had invaded the stock. The tap water smelled like chlorine that day. The rice water was just starting to run clear.

That's when I heard the knocking—insistent, loud, so powerful I thought the front door would break open. I listened for a reaction from my mother, but she must not have been able to hear over the water. The pounding didn't stop, so I set down the pot and crept into the hall and saw the front door shaking, and then I heard Avis yelling right into the wood, *open the door, please, please, open the door*, and I wanted to but didn't know if I should, and instead I dropped to the carpet and clamped my hands over my ears and tried to stop my whole body from shaking. My shoulders wouldn't stop shuddering, and the rough carpet burned against my cheek, and the clamor did not subside. I brought my hands from my ears, and just kept grabbing handfuls of carpet and pulling and pulling, willing the moment to stop, feeling my fingertips go raw. It sounded like a giant was sprinting down the stairs. I heard a man's voice, full of rage. The thumping was different now. She might have been throwing her shoulder against the door. *Please.* After a minute it stopped. I heard a tiny muffled yelp, then nothing.

I crawled onto my knees and into the kitchen where I stood up and stared at the coupons stacked on the island. I picked them up and tore them in half and in half again, not knowing why I was doing it, and when I was done the counter and the floor were covered in shreds of colorful paper. I stood there breathing only through my nose until alongside the fear I felt sorry, the most sorry and scared I had ever felt about anything, and my breathing got even faster.

The bathtub faucet squeaked shut. I wanted to make those pieces of paper whole again, I wished I had opened the door, I wanted to take it all back. I ran to my room and hid under the covers, trying to make myself undetectable.

I listened as my mother dried her hair. I heard her feet on the kitchen linoleum and waited.

"What is this?" she shouted. "Get in here. Now."

All I wanted was her arms around me, but I shrank and shut my eyes and pressed myself closer to the wall. I don't think I could've made a sound if I had tried.

She came into my room but didn't see me because I heard the hall closet creak and I heard her yanking the shower curtain to the side and even opening the refrigerator door moments later. Never had I felt my heart going so fast, so fast I thought I would go blind.

I tried to breathe but I couldn't control the air, just kept hearing the footsteps and Avis pounding and yelling at the door, and I don't know how much time had passed but when I opened my eyes my mother was beside me in my bed, under my blanket, holding my head in her hands.

"I'm not mad. It's okay," she kept saying. "Whatever it is, it's okay."

I let her hold me, but even her hands and arms and voice could not make the terror that had bloomed inside me leave.

We can't predict the ways we will fall short, those vital, ordinary slips. Some days my girlhood closes in around me, and it's like I'm living in that building again, in that time when people had run out of just about everything and still had something to give. When I think of that apartment now, I see my mother closing her checkbook and leaning over the table with her palms pressed against her temples, saying, "It's like the ocean is inside my head." From a stool by the window, I see cherry blossoms and an older couple with stooped backs carrying boxes from Avis's apartment, one by one, as Mr. O'Rourke's mournful trumpet music reverberates against the walls.

He had been the one to call the police. They found Avis's body in her apartment. From under my blanket my mother and I heard the sirens and saw the lights flashing rapid-fire like a bright drumbeat. She pulled back and tried to see my face in the shadow. "Oh no, oh no," she said. "What happened?"

"The schedules they handed him at the cemetery got longer and longer," my mother told me years later, when I had just graduated from college. We were on the eve of a new, undeclared war, and for the first time I wondered what had become of Mr. O'Rourke. "He stopped volunteering. I don't know what happened to him after that."

My mother was Wilson's only visitor at the nursing facility. When I asked after him, she told me that his parents had disowned him when he was sixteen and that they hadn't spoken since. She tried to get in touch with them—at that point he was in and out of a drugged sleep, half-lucid and unable to protest. She was certain they would forgive their child anything on his deathbed. And she was right. They bought plane tickets and made hotel reservations, but by the time they got there it was too late. He never regained consciousness.

SPEAKEASY TACOS

Michael Jaime-Becerra

Your family makes it all by hand. The meat. Beans and rice, nopales and potato salad. A large platter of freshly cut fruit. Garnishes of finely minced white onions and cilantro and two kinds of salsa, red and green. One spiced enough to thrill the palate. One for those that prefer to be set aflame, because it is better to make your clients sweat and suffer than to overhear veiled insults about the salsa being tasty, but not hot.

Including your mother, Concha, there are four of you. You may be Miriam, the oldest child, now in your twenties. Your high school years would have been spent either making tacos or keeping an eye on your brothers, but now you have a chair in an upscale hair salon and you plan on owning your own shop one day. Or you are Samuel, just old enough to buy beer, but already showing the talent and sensibility of a chef on the way to greatness. You were hired at Pollo Loco to wipe down tables and your years of making tacos vaulted you to unofficial Grill Master in a week. Now the goal is to be a nurse. To have solid, stable, official work. Or you are Eli, the youngest. The one who gets to go to college, to study United States history and try out accounting because it seems like it would be interesting and useful.

For three hours of catered taco service at a Saturday party, the preparation begins the Wednesday before. While you're cutting hair or tending to convalescents or studying, your mother is beating other taqueros to the best produce when local markets post their weekly specials. With the meat, she insists that the beef for her carne asada be shredded by the wholesale butchers' knives because it is damaged when they do it with the machine. Purchased in El Monte, it's the best any of you have ever found, the contents of the ten-pound bags tender and raw, blood pooling at the corners. Her pork adobada and her chicken come from a second wholesaler in Azusa. He's from Jalisco as well. Not the same pueblo as your family, but close enough that his seasoning is correct and trustworthy, the chicken tinged the yellow of saffron, the chunks of pork a deep orange that will become the color of charred brick as you tend to it in the pan. When beef tongue is requested, your mother will poach it in a broth of onion and garlic. In the morning, one of you will peel the rough outer layer, then dice the rich inner meat into tiny, succulent cubes to later be simmered in their own fat.

The prep work continues on Friday. In South El Monte, your mother picks lemons from her cousin's tree, and that night, instead of going out, you watch *Qué bonito amor* together, peeling and chopping into the early hours of Saturday. After a few hours' rest, you start again. Your hands become pruned because they're constantly wet--from bloody meat, from rinsing radishes, and dozens of white onions releasing musky milk. You wash and rewash the same knife and cutting board. You work the knife until it seems the top of the blade is slicing your index finger. A quick double-check to make sure you're holding the blade with the sharp side down.

Sweating constantly and eating as you go. No stopping for breakfast or lunch because time is passing and you're expected to serve a hundred hungry people in a few hours. Sampling along the way, carne asada scooped from the pan, salsa spooned out of the blender jar, pineapple plucked from the cutting board. Eat something now, your mother reminds you. There won't be time to eat later.

The stove is on the entire time, the same four gas burners as any household stove, but on this one, only two still work. Three of

42

the four knobs are gone, a remaining white plastic stem melted like a used birthday candle. The large pans atop it are blackened and a little misshapen from countless hours of simmering meat. The pots' plastic handles are cracked or missing.

Stirring, keeping things in motion because whatever isn't moving is absorbing heat immediately and might soon burn. In the minute it takes to transfer rice from the pot to the chafing dish, the chafing dish will get hot enough to scorch your hand, pain then pulsing under cool water. A rookie mistake. For the next two weeks, your fingerprints will have the smooth, warped texture of Silly Putty.

Concha has made airplane parts in one El Monte factory and has assembled trophies in another. To clean offices in downtown Los Angeles high rises, she had to learn how to drive, doing so in a car so questionable that the steering wheel popped off during the test drive. Thereafter, she'd stick to the first lane of the 10 freeway until she reached the Alameda exit. Before that, she sold popsicles at the Edward's Drive-In swap meet in Arcadia, her first job in the U.S., one that made her cry at night from the shame of being recognized by others from home. Remembering her as a proud, willful young woman, they asked, "¿Que haces aquí? ¿Por qué haces esto?"

What are you doing here?

Why are you doing this?

Thirty-some years later and she is still willful, still proud, though these aspects of her personality are now applied to the things that matter most: her three children and her taco business.

The business became "The Business" nearly a decade ago in the emergency room at Queen of the Valley Hospital, on the evening when her husband died. Prior to this, Concha and her husband would sometimes make tacos on the weekends in the backyards of relatives and family friends. It had been extra money, supplementary to his work as a gardener and her time in the factories. Miriam was seventeen then. Samuel was thirteen. Eli, twelve. In the plain white room, where the doctor said he had done everything he could, that the heart attack was just too much, the moment was a whirlwind of shock, grief, and panic about what to do next.

There was also the understanding that God had to take him. Miriam remembers a sense of peace accompanying this thought. Responsibility settling in. Certainty that they would eventually be fine.

Tacos then become the means to survive. How the mortgage gets paid. How the utilities stay on. Literally putting food on their table. Without any licenses, permits, or written contracts. No Yelp reviews and no requests to friend them on Facebook. Just business cards with two phone numbers, one for Spanish-speaking clients and one for those that only know English. Those who have this card have probably been at a party Concha's family catered, because this is the main way they're distributed. But word of mouth is fluid, and with Concha's food, the word is good. Her tacos are the sort that is remembered. *She* is remembered.

When she is not working the business, she is searching out cardboard and scrap metal, and on trash nights, she goes through a regular route of recyling bins. She keeps busy not just for the extra income, but because when she stops moving, her body is wracked with mysterious pain. Her hands now shake so uncontrollably that she has trouble serving tacos. Some regular clients have promised her a cure from Mexico, medicine purportedly blessed by the Pope, and when she falls asleep, her children witness her exhaustion and wonder about Parkinson's. Despite all this, Concha will still say that the taco business is greatest job she's ever had. It allows her to meet people from all walks of life, to be at a different party every week. But the very best part about the business is that has kept her children with her. It has ensured that they remain together.

For one event, it's relentless heat all the way to Lancaster. In their father's truck, named "Guapa" by its original owners, now dented and scratched, flaking blue paint, something always needing to be fixed. Now the temperature gauge is creeping up. The event is at a retirement home, and when they arrive, radiator steam gushes

44

from the hood.

The business grows to the point that they are often booked for two parties on the same day, with half the calls coming from clients in increasingly higher tax brackets. While Guapa isn't out of place on the eastern side of Los Angeles, she might not seem presentable to an NBC producer or a trust-fund kid or a family that spent thirty-thousand dollars to celebrate their daughter turning sixteen.

Miriam stretches her credit to its limit on a new truck, a V-8 engine to haul all the equipment and an extra cab fit the family. Still at the Toyota dealership, the negotiations over, the loan papers signed in the sales manager's office. Since she's given him some business, why not return the favor? Two weeks later, she's back, the grill set up beside the service bays. Tacos for fifty: car techs, salesmen, the girls who answer the phones.

The business is torn between two different philosophies:

Concha accommodates her clients as fully as possible. If she's told that there are still people coming at the end of her three contracted hours, she'll wait for the latecomers at no extra charge. Fifteen minutes. Thirty minutes. An hour. The extra time doesn't matter because it lets her become part of the party. She'll gather everyone around the cake to sing "Las mañanitas" or "Happy Birthday." If there's dancing to be done, she'll get it started. Pour her a shot of Patrón and she'll cheer loudest during the toast. Her spirit is infectious, and it is genuine, for these are not just clients to her. Concha considers those who book her for recurring annual or semi-annual parties as family. These clients often call her "Tía Concha" and their children are encouraged to say hello and hug her as if she were a blood relative. Sometimes these hugs seem awkward, the child's embrace tentative and reluctant. Sometimes the hugs are real because Concha is kindly remembered from the last time as "la señora de los tacos."

Besides the extra time, these are the people who also get a tray of potato salad and an overloaded fruit platter they didn't specify in their order. They might also get an added portion of lengua or fifteen pounds of carne asada instead of ten, the extra meat packed in one of the family's clear Tupperware containers that Samuel and Eli are reminded and reminded and reminded not to forget.

Concha sees these extras both as gifts to her regular clients for their loyalty and as investments in the business's future. She believes a potential new client will recall being poolside or before an inflatable jumper, in their hand an empty Styrofoam plate smeared with the last swirls of orange grease and salsa, their mouth pleasantly smoldering. Their appetite called for more and their body didn't have room for another bite. This person won't know that their satisfaction is the same satisfaction Concha and her children get from having seen their food enjoyed.

Concha's children know that each of those extras cuts into the profit margin. At $4.99 per pound, the two beef tongues for an extra chafing dish of lengua cost nearly fifty dollars, and that's without the additional garlic, onions, and seasonings to prepare them, the cooking time, and the time needed for peeling and cubing them the following morning. It all might be used for something else. Like a new stove or a professional-grade onion cutter. At the end of the night, Concha's boys can wait another ten or twenty minutes if the party hosts were generally respectful and paid what they owe. But, unlike their mother, Samuel and Eli believe that when the three hours are up, the three hours are up. Part of this is the fact that it is Saturday night. They both have girlfriends waiting for them and their phones buzz with text messages.

But their thinking is also rooted in confidence. Samuel and Eli have been doing this work, weekend after weekend, since they were in junior high. Eli knows that if you're calling him, you've probably had their tacos and you know they are very, very good. If you try to talk down the price he quotes you, he will feel mildly insulted because he knows eight dollars per person is more or less what other people charge. He'll work with you, removing extras until he hits a number you like. But if you live outside a ten-mile radius, he'll also charge you a fifty-dollar transportation fee to cover the cost of extra gas.

You are up in Silverlake, up a narrow street, both sides lined with cars. Just enough room for the truck to approach the two-story glass-wall experiment attached to the hillside. Up concrete steps, a geometric hike past ripening grapefruit and cumquats, to the patio, the lighter of the two grill pans, a seventy-pound slab of stainless steel, hoisted by your brother. The grill stand is next, a two-person task guided by someone on the other end, you backing up and being careful to not scratch the silver Jaguar parked at the base of the steps, lifting, angling your way. Next is a second, smaller and circular grill for today's requested vegetarian preparation of grilled mushrooms, multi-colored bell peppers, and onions. Up with the propane tanks and a cooler the size of a coffin for anything perishable.

Most times the event is a birthday party, and today is no different. Today a father turns eighty, the milestone used to reunite three generations. T-shirts for the occasion sported by family from all over California. Nashville also represented. Munich, too. Talk of how cousins are related. Grandmothers the children never got to meet. The mandatory trip to Disneyland.

A quick connection to the propane tank under the grill stand, followed by three flicks from a long-stemmed lighter, and then the grill begins radiating unceasing heat at four-hundred degrees. There are four different kinds of tacos this afternoon. Rice and beans in the chafing trays beside the grill pan, a separate table with the potato salad, nopales, and fruit. The two kinds of salsa and a tray of freshly roasted jalapeños. The line moves quickly, forty-some curious and hungry people. Orders for one of each taco, absolutely to beans and rice because this is better than anything they've had in Tennessee, because there's absolutely no Mexican food in Germany. The men ask if the jalapeños are hot, then goad one another to try them. You suggest that two be taken in case they're not lucky with the first one.

Your family has worked parties at this home for nearly a decade. These clients, a husband and wife, know your family. They ask how your mother's doing. They knew your father. When they found out that he'd died, they took up a tip collection that amounted to over five hundred dollars. As the years went by, their friends began to hire you. Their friends' friends too. Each of them in parts of L.A. you'd never been to before. And so this husband and wife have become two of the business's most important clients, meaning that with them you adhere to your mother's philosophy of giving out extras for free. After a full shift at the hair salon the day before, your sister worked until three, peeling, blanching, and chopping the nopales, nopales that go untouched--partly because the tacos rule the evening and partly because this clientele doesn't really have the appetite or appreciation for a salad of minced cactus paddles.

The grill is cleared to make way for a slide show, and you remove the other equipment and supplies with the same sort of hurry you had when carrying them up. There is plenty of remaining food--food for days, as the host notes with resignation. People did come back for seconds, a few for thirds, and still the meat is piled high in the chafing dishes. Emptied, packaged up and set next to the other side dishes with the inescapable sense that much of it will eventually be in trash. Even as you prepared it, you knew this would happen. When you were younger, the squandered expense, the wasted labor and time bothered you. Maybe it still does. Your mother's way of doing things makes you want to leave the business to focus on your hairdressing clients. Or move out of the house. Or dream of teaching high school students about the Louisiana Purchase. When there was nothing else, tacos allowed your family to live on. Now they hold you back. Each job comes with the deepening sense that either you or the business must change. And until something gives, you must tell yourself that wasted side dishes don't matter because your tacos were loved by those that ate them. You must tell yourself that's what matters most.

A few words on tortillas: The ones that Concha uses are slightly smaller than a compact disc, ordered by the box from a tortilleria in Baldwin Park and picked up the morning of the event. There are at least three other tortillerias minutes from her home, but they've never been considered because as far as Concha's concerned, the Baldwin Park tortillas are perfect. A supple texture that gives slightly to the touch. That doesn't harden easily when heated. The subtle, sweet taste of the corn coming through each bite.

One Christmas Eve is spent doing the usual prep work, all four of them. Christmas morning in an industrial park. A bakery assembly line. Tacos intended as a thank-you for employees packing trays of fancy Danishes and madeleines. Afterwards, a fifty-dollar tip to be split four ways. That night it's decided they'll no longer work holidays.

Next it's nightfall at a horse property at the easternmost edge of the county. A full banda going. White Stetsons and white ostrich-skin belts and white boots that curl upward at the toe. Synchronized trumpets and trombones. A tuba. Dancing makes dancers hungry, and soon the chafing dishes are empty. The host sends someone out and he returns with another twenty-five pounds of carne asada. The tacos keep coming and the banda keeps playing, horses trained to prance in time with the music. Tamborazo a toda madre. Tipped $150 at the end of the night.

After three hours over the grill, your face is always sunburned, no matter if you've been outside or indoors. You've sweated enough to have felt embarrassed as you served food to your clients and to also feel thoroughly wrung out. Dehydrated. Now that the gear has cooled off and has been loaded onto the truck, everything about you also seems coated with the unique oily sheen that comes from adobada and asada smoke.

The ride home is quiet. Relief that cash is in your pocket and that looming bills will be paid, that this job is over. Curving along dark freeway lanes, all roads leading back to El Monte, the occasional rattles of shifting equipment in the truck bed reminding you that there is still more to be done once you get home.

You swing the cooler through the front door and collapse

onto the couch. The answering machine blinks, the house quiet because your mother is still out at the other event booked for today. Everything in the back of your truck must be washed and cleaned, but if this evening is the first of a weekend with back-to-back events, the washing and cleaning must happen tonight instead of tomorrow. This maintenance will be the last thing you want to do. If you wait until tomorrow, your mother will be up before you, with degreaser and a pumice stone, scouring blackened oil off the spots where the grill pan gets hottest. You can already hear her complaining that you always use too much oil when you cook.

The chaffing dishes and the utensils are waiting for you too, as are the pans and pots from the morning's prep work. And because they'll be the first things you'll need tomorrow morning, you begin by washing them. You can hear your mother saying, "Cada quien tiene que traer su tortilla a la casa." And you can sense the answering machine's light pulsing behind you. The empty weekend spaces on the calendar will taunt you until you play the message.

It will be a woman looking for tacos. She will be someone you don't already know and she will start in English, her voice unsure of itself because there is purposely no identifying greeting on the answering machine. She will switch to Spanish, and it will be clear from how poorly she speaks it, her pronunciation wooden and stilted, that this was the language of her parents or her grandparents, that it is no longer her own. She will sound out her phone number in the protracted manner of someone recollecting numerals for an exam.

She may be from someplace that you've never heard of before except for traffic updates and weather reports. She will say that she is a friend of Vijay. Or that she knows Adriana. Or that she was at the party for someone named Douglas. She will be expecting fifty people, but from the way she will describe the event, you can tell that it will more likely be twenty. Or a hundred. She will hope that you can work with her budget and you can already sense that she's the kind that probably won't tip.

In a few years, there may not be a business to receive this call.

The business depends on your mother's health. And it depends on what you decide to do with your life. These ideas press intense guilt upon you, and yet the business no longer existing may also be its best possible outcome. If that day comes, it will be because you've each achieved something with your individual lives, something greater than what tacos can currently offer it. And you will have used skills passed down from your mother and honed in front of the grill: resourcefulness, tenacity, and the ability to be fearless in front of strangers.

But on this evening you will write down the woman's phone number and her name. You will do this with the same pen that you use to book appointments for your hairdressing clients, or that you used to fill out the paperwork for a position as a certified nursing assistant, or that you have in History class when you're taking notes on the Great Depression.

It will be too late to call the woman back tonight, but tomorrow morning, early, she will definitely hear from you.

RAINY DAY SCHEDULE

Anthony J. Mohr

It was February 1963. Beverly Hills High School's morning bulletin read "RAINY DAY SCHEDULE TODAY," and I was not thinking about my father, who was missing. I was thinking about Mr. Occhipinti's class, where I felt calm and safe. Along with twenty-three other sophomores at the door to Room 121, I was waiting for him to arrive.

He taught modern history, my favorite subject that year, and he was my favorite teacher, even if he was the only one I knew who locked his room between periods. To this day I don't know why he did so. Mr. Occhipinti was a small man who wore black suits and black-rimmed glasses and something slick in his thick black hair. His head was a little too narrow. His tenor voice was ideal for formal lectures, which he tape-recorded in order to make sure that each of his classes heard the same material, delivered in prose that verged on the lyrical. ("And they drank the intoxicating wine of Renaissance culture that suffused their continent.") He drove an Edsel. Every summer he haunted Europe's museums and brought home postcards with which he festooned the classroom walls. Wherever we looked, we saw little pictures of battles, landscapes, saints, and monarchs.

He also served as the faculty sponsor of the Squires, Beverly High's honors service club for freshmen and sophomore boys, who had voted me in a week earlier.

I was in Mr. Occhipinti's honors section (the school adored the word honors), with the type of kids who remained in their car outside a party until the symphony on KFAC finished, in order to learn if they had correctly guessed its composer and number. My closest friends—Bobby and Larry—were among them. So were some of the brightest girls, a couple of whom had invited me to their parties, even though I was a newcomer who had only lived in Beverly Hills since the sixth grade. They had known each other since kindergarten. Their families defined the ethos of Beverly Hills, then a small town despite its wealth, a Mayberry in the middle of Los Angeles.

We dressed in accordance with the school manual: the boys, clean slacks or tan Levi's; the girls, tailored dresses, skirts that reached below the knees, oxfords or flats, socks, hose or peds. At least half the class wore Honor Club sweaters: blue pullovers for the boys, red cardigans for the girls. Hardly anyone had acne, but I kept Clearasil in business. Our hair was combed just so, except for mine, forever a dark thicket of messy curls. I glowed when we were together. They made me happy and Room 121 felt like the stable center of my world.

As I settled into my seat and waited for class to start, I thought about Evelyn, a blonde, brown-eyed actress my father had introduced to me and whom I lacked the nerve to call. Then the bell rang, and Mr. Occhipinti began his lesson.

Mr. Occhipinti's reel-to-reel tape recorder was out of sight that morning, along with his solemn demeanor. Our lesson about Louis XVI and the French Revolution called for ironic humor. I leaned forward. It was clear from the mischievous expression on Mr. Occhipinti's face that we were about to hear another one of his good stories.

The Tuileries had been Louis XVI's palace in the heart of Paris. During the French Revolution he had decamped from there and fled to Versailles, a secure place far from the mob. Yet he came back. He didn't have to, Mr. Occhipinti said, but he did, and that triggered the events leading to Louis XVI's imprisonment and execution.

A titter escaped from a boy one row over. Behind him a girl with black hair and a sweet face perked up.

Mr. Occhipinti ignored the lectern and moved about like a windup doll. He circled back to Marie Antoinette and her "Let them eat cake" comment. He lingered over the wealth on display in the Louis XVI court. I knew he was building to something.

Rainwater poured into the bushes outside. I wished that on rainy days, the school didn't send us home ten minutes early. I wanted modern history to go on forever.

"And why," Mr. Occhipinti asked, "did Louis XVI return to the Tuileries?"

Either the answer itself or the tone in Mr. Occhipinti's voice turned us into a collection of hysterical teens. Bobby laughed so hard he nearly fell out of his seat. He had the face of a lovable genius and a voice that, the following year, would make him California's speech champion. I hooted and howled.

Mr. Occhipinti didn't resume his lesson until we calmed down and one of us—me, I think—let out the final whoop. At least precipitation did not shorten modern history, but it made me wonder whether it had rained when Louis XVI had traveled to Versailles or when he'd returned. Our history textbook ignored the weather.

By the time school let out, the rain was pounding down, and someone who had just obtained his driver's license offered me a ride home. I chose to walk, which meant jumping over puddles because the runoff overloaded the drains and water flowed over the curbs, a frequent problem in the Los Angeles basin despite the flood control channels that had been built a decade earlier. During the four blocks between Beverly High and my house, I stopped thinking about Louis XVI.

That's because my father had been missing for three days.

He was an actor, and although he wasn't a star, he was known. In 1956 he had left my mother for Mai, the Swedish script girl on his television series, which, within a year, had left the air. He married her in July 1958, five months before my mother remarried. Now, five years on, his marriage was failing.

Mai must have been frantic. She had called my mother to ask if she or I had heard from my father. We hadn't. I guess Dad had not warned his bride that whenever his life faltered, he disappeared for a while. Dad had vanished a few months before he left my mother, but just for the day. He had come home before I awoke the following morning. I had no idea where he had gone or why. After all, I was eight, too young to understand, but now I'm sure he had driven to Mai's apartment.

So, unlike Mai, I wasn't panicked. I was more concerned about what my honors class would say if the newspapers learned of my father's latest absence. My group came from two-parent families who, at least on the surface, seemed happy.

I pulled a bowl of red Jell-O from the fridge, leaned against the door, and started to devour it. My mother walked into the kitchen and put a bag of groceries on the counter.

"You shouldn't eat so fast," she said gently and then she hugged me. Her blue eyes were full of love. Her short brown hair was perfectly arranged. Her white blouse was spotless, like her kitchen. I picked up the spoon, continued eating, and listened to the rain.

"I know Daddy will come back," she said in a soft tone. As usual she was trying to be sympathetic, but she probably felt relieved that my father was no longer her problem and that Stan, her new husband, loved her without letup. I'm sure Mom would have hugged me again if I had moved even slightly in her direction, as I should have. She would have said more soothing things to me, had I given her the opening.

But I didn't. All I said was, "I guess so," and suppressed my lack of feelings by swallowing quivering dollops of Jell-O until no more of the goo remained.

We walked into the den. On the small off-white sofa sandwiched between two built-in counters, Stan was talking on "CRestview

188," the telephone line we reserved for his work calls. He looked nothing like my dashing father. All they had in common was their six-foot-two-inch height. Dad was wiry with thick black hair. Stan had lost most of his, but not, unfortunately, his extra weight. My father could seduce anyone with his mellifluous baritone. Stan tended to mumble, which I heard him do now, into the receiver: "If Mr. Hughes is listening, tell him to go to hell." Hughes, as in Howard Hughes. One of his enterprises was negotiating to buy Stan's business machine company. Stan waved as he continued to talk, and I went upstairs to study.

Shortly after 8 p.m., my father telephoned. I answered on the first ring. His voice sounded tinny against background noise that resembled rushing water, typical for long-distance calls in 1963. I sat on the edge of my bed, and as we talked, one of my fingers drifted from hole to hole along the rotary dial, moving it slightly but not enough to make it click.

"I want you to know I'm all right," he said.

I said, "Good." I didn't feel relieved. I didn't feel anything.

"Everything is OK," he said.

I asked, "Where are you?"

"Up the coast." That probably meant San Luis Obispo, the town where he and my mother had honeymooned. I pictured him there, alone, calling from a phone booth at the entrance to a motor court near the beach. Was he looking at the ground as he pressed the receiver to his ear, or was he peering through the glass door—closed against the rain—at his 1952 Jaguar, parked in the gravel next to a faded bungalow where he was staying? Ensconced at Versailles, pondering his future, did Louis XVI stare—in the rain?—at one of his chariots? Didn't my father have a phone in his room? While tracing calls was difficult then, it could be arranged, especially when a person went missing. Maybe that's why he was calling from outside.

I asked when he was coming back.

"I can't say." The interference on the line, probably due to the rain, rose until it almost drowned him out.

I asked what he planned to do the next day. He didn't know. I think I asked again how he was, and I think he said "Fine." With exchanges like this we consumed almost three minutes, the time after which the cost of a long-distance call mounted furiously.

He said, "We're still pals, right?"

"Yeah."

"Great," he said before he hung up.

I didn't ask why he had vanished. Mai had to be the reason. The first fight I witnessed between them had occurred at least three years earlier; over what, I don't remember. The quarrels had become so frequent that any peccadillo could trigger an outburst. Alcohol was never involved. During one of my every-other-weekend stays, a month or so earlier, Mai had ordered me to put their parakeet back in his cage. We were in a little room that served as the den of my father's rented house in Hollywood.

"Why?" I asked. Trixie appeared happy perched on my shoulder.

"Those are the rules," she snapped in her singsong accent. Her eyebrows furrowed and her lips tightened. "You only get ten minutes with the bird." She and my father had initiated that protocol when, once, her two young sons and I had wanted to play with Trixie at the same time. But today they were away.

My father looked up from his script. "What are we doing? Timing this with a stopwatch?"

Mai stormed from the den and left the house.

"Oh, shit," my father said. He tried to follow her, but she slammed the front door before he could catch up. I had no idea what to say when my father came back into the room. So I said nothing. Neither did he, but Trixie remained on my shoulder.

I thought Dad was right. The rule seemed pointless if Mai's children were not home. But then I recalled my summer-school driver's education class. Some kid had said there was no need to obey a stop sign late at night in Beverly Hills. After all, our residential streets were wide, with few blind intersections, and no other cars were about. The teacher, a man with a severe face and remnants of red hair, glared at him. "Stop means stop. I don't care what time it is. That's the law and you better follow it." If Dad and Mai had made a rule about the bird, did it matter if, at the moment, there was no reason to enforce it? After all, what if her children were about to come through the door?

Shortly before 8:30 p.m., Stan eased into my bedroom. "How's school?" This was not his normal opening. Usually Stan would ask, "What did you learn today?" He sounded tired, due, I'm sure, to his sessions with Hughes.

"Okay," I said. Rain played across the roof and plinked through the downspouts.

For a few seconds Stan said nothing, which made me uncomfortable. I was grateful that he had rescued my mother and me from the scary backwash of a divorce, but I was not entirely used to him yet. Put another way, despite having lived with him over four years, I was not perceptive enough to read many of his signals. I looked down at my history book and wished one of his business associates would telephone.

He said, "Want to come sailing this weekend?" He had recently built a 58-foot catamaran. Sailing was the only way he could relax. In 1949, with his first wife and two children, Stan had boarded a schooner and cruised from Michigan through the Great Lakes, down the Atlantic Coast, and into the West Indies. A year and a half later, the family arrived in Los Angeles and settled there.

"Can I see how homework goes?" I had a test the following week and had to write a paper for Mr. Occhipinti. I also had a tendency to get seasick.

He lingered. "We're going Sunday too." He'd take his boat out even if it rained.

The salon was meeting Sunday. I knew he'd approve of that excuse. The salon was Bobby's brainchild, typical of his brilliance. Every few weeks he gathered our friends and invited an expert in some field to meet with us for a discussion, followed by dinner. Finding speakers was easy; most of our fathers were authorities on something. I hoped Stan didn't expect an invitation, because I'd have to introduce him and didn't want to use the word "stepfather" in front of twenty kids from solid homes. If he asked (he never did), I'd say that Bobby and I had passed on our own fathers. Like mine, Bobby's dad worked in the film industry, not a unique topic at Beverly High. For this coming Sunday Bobby's uncle, the editor of an essay collection titled *The Meaning of Death*, would ask us to answer a "death questionnaire" he had written to gauge people's attitudes on his favorite subject.

Stan nodded. After a pause he said, "Looks like we're going to sell the company."

I said, "Good," and I meant it. But all I wanted to do at that moment was study.

"I think we'll make a deal."

Months earlier my father's agent—a man I'd never met—had said that a "deal" to cast him as the lead in a new series was "99 percent done." The final 1 percent had never materialized. I didn't say that to Stan.

Stan must have been concerned about me, his chubby stepson who preferred lectures on death to sailing, but he seemed unsure how to pull us closer, and I was too withdrawn to help. I wonder how I would have acted if Stan had sat on my bed and asked, "Tell me how you're feeling. You're worried about your father, aren't you?" What if he had said, "I love your mother so much; I promise I'll never run away"? Would I have felt less hollow? Would I have shared whatever hurt may have surfaced—or simply cried?

I glanced at my history text, open to the Napoleonic Wars, tonight's soothing balm.

Stan said softly, "When we close the deal, I think I should get your mother a mink coat."

"She'll like that," I said, and kept listening to the rain.

"Get a hundred, make a million," my mother said the next morning before Stan and I left the house. Normally I walked to school, but the rain had not stopped, and Stan wanted to drive me.

I asked him if there was a chance he'd meet Howard Hughes. *How many eighteenth century French kids asked their fathers, "Will you ever meet the King?"*

"He's an odd man," Stan said. *How many said that about Louis XVI?* Stan and Hughes never would meet. He'd been dealing with Hughes' underlings.

Stan got in line with the Falcons, Mercurys, Tempests, and Thunderbirds that were entering the student parking lot, and then he pulled as close to the main entrance as possible. After a quick embrace, he told me to have a good day. I neglected to thank him for the ride.

I burst through the double doors like an animal returned to its habitat. A girl with freckles yelled to a boy that his Sting Ray "looked sharp." Under their raincoats a couple held hands. From a record player in a room near the auditorium came the rollicking final fugue of Benjamin Britten's *Young Person's Guide to the Orchestra,* loud enough to compete with the slamming of locker doors. A girl with dimples and a pageboy haircut poked a member of the football team, just enough to make him turn, and then, without stopping, she waved. Somebody dropped a copy of *Ivanhoe.* A fellow Squire said something about our upcoming picnic with the Adelphians, the lower division girls' honor club. The student body coursed up the stairs to the math department, out to the language wing or, like me, over to the social studies department. A boy lobbed a tennis ball in the air as he walked. Someone bellowed, "Party at 980 Roxbury Friday." I wondered if I should invite Evelyn. I felt a lift each time someone said "Hi" and a locker door banged. I was surrounded by the smiles of companions free from worry—or so it seemed.

I want to say that I remember what I was doing when my father called to say, "Hi, pal. I'm home now." I don't, other than it was still raining. I want to say that despite having a mere learner's permit, I hijacked one of the family cars and drove into Hollywood to see him and that, after a long hug, he said his agent had called with a script. But that's not what happened. All I know is that he showed up at the end of the week at the house he shared with Mai, and another week passed before I saw him. I spent Sunday as planned, in Bobby's living room with my friends, bantering until his uncle handed out his death questionnaire. The booklet had the heft of an aptitude test. One question required a choice among similes: "To me, death is like (a) a beach at sunset, (b) the end of a song, (c) a curtain coming down in a theater." With my No. 2 pencil, I filled in the oval next to the curtain. The room turned quiet as we worked, save for the rustle of pages and some nervous giggles.

My father picked me up the following Saturday morning. We drove east out of Beverly Hills and along the Sunset Strip. The sun hovered between two massive cumulus clouds. The smog was gone, washed away by the rain. In the car, we talked about nothing. He didn't tell me how he and Mai had greeted each other after his absence—whether with yells, tears, or silence—and I didn't ask.

We passed a modern building of mostly glass that housed Scandia, an elegant Scandinavian restaurant to which Dad could not afford to take Mai. We drove by Ciro's, an iconic nightclub, and kept going until the buildings became more ordinary and we reached Carolina Pines Jr., one of my father's favorite coffee shops, a Googie structure with a wavy roof at the intersection of Sunset Boulevard and La Brea Avenue.

As usual we sat in a booth next to one of the bay windows. After ordering scrambled eggs and onions with burnt bacon on the side, Dad said to the waitress—a plump woman with frosted hair and puffy cheeks who looked as though she had worked there for years—"Darling, can I have coffee while I wait?" And then, as always, he lit a cigarette. His black hair was turning gray. His face looked ready to sag.

He didn't say where he had been. I didn't wonder whether he had been wise to leave. Or return. But I was glad we were together. I still felt more at ease with him than with Stan, and part of me felt guilty about that.

"Is school okay?" he asked.

I described our lesson about the French Revolution, beginning with Mr. Occhipinti pacing in front of us with his crescent-moon grin. My dad nodded and sipped his coffee.

I took my time. There was a lot to say before I reached Mr. Occhipinti's question: "'And why did Louis XVI return to the Tuileries?'" I wanted to put it in context, build to it, and then imitate Mr. Occhipinti's tone of voice, which I think I did reasonably well.

My father nodded at me.

I told him the reasons my classmates had offered for the king's decision to return there. Then I shook my head, the way Mr. Occhipinti had shaken his when he said that was wrong.

"So what's the answer?" my father asked with a tinge of impatience.

Easing from word to word in slow but cheery singsong, I tried to mimic Mr. Occhipinti. "The king was—stupid."

Then I laughed, exactly as I—as the entire class—had: so loudly that a couple across the aisle turned and watched me almost spill my glass of skim milk. I was laughing too hard to tell my father what had occurred next: that Larry had stretched out his arms as he repeated the answer, and since Larry was tall and sat in the front row, his arms had framed the scene of our classroom roaring into bedlam, hooting the word "stupid" while Mr. Occhipinti beamed at us. Nor did I tell my father that each day since then, when Larry and I had seen each other, we'd said, in synchrony, "The king was stupid." Dad smiled. A courteous grin to humor his son. He lit another cigarette and sipped his coffee before he asked if I liked any girls.

I looked down at my napkin. I took a breath. I said, "Evelyn."

Dad had introduced us at a party for celebrities whom the Hollywood Chamber of Commerce had invited to ride in its annual Santa Claus Lane Parade. I had not forgotten her smile and the way she'd said, so clearly and confidently, "How do you do?" Nor had I forgotten what Evelyn said with such poise to the emcee who had interviewed her: "I hope that this Christmas everybody gets what they want." I was smitten.

My excuse for not calling was that she lived too far away for a boy without a driver's license.

"Call her. I'll arrange something," Dad said. He added that she was a good actress. She and Mamie Eisenhower had posed together once to promote United States savings bonds.

I nodded and didn't say anything.

"You still have her phone number?" my father asked.

"Yes." I should have asked my father to feed me some opening lines—he knew them all—but I didn't.

He leaned back and puffed on his cigarette. When Evelyn was nine, he said, she had wanted to see Mamie Eisenhower again, and to do so, she had sneaked out of her house and flown alone across the country. The event had made the newspapers.

I asked, "How could a nine-year-old manage such a thing?"

The check arrived and my father put down three or four one-dollar bills plus a silver half dollar. Then he said, "She emptied her piggy bank, called a cab to the airport, and bought a ticket."

The way my father told the story made it clear that he admired her confidence and derring-do, qualities we both knew I lacked.

"Wow," was all I could say. I wondered if she would tolerate a timid boy like me.

My father got up from the table and I followed him outside. The clouds had departed, leaving behind a sky about as blue as it could become in Los Angeles.

As soon as we left the parking lot, Dad said, "Look. Before we see Mai, I want you to know that Trixie flew away." The parakeet had escaped through a door she had left open. "Please don't get upset with her over that," he said.

He turned onto Santa Monica Boulevard. The afternoon traffic was wretched and made worse by the abandoned trolley tracks that ran down the middle of the two-lane street.

I promised not to say anything.

In April 1963, Stan sold his business to the Hughes Tool Company. By then he'd developed a thorough dislike of Howard Hughes' minions. Once over breakfast, he called them stupid, punctuating the word hard. I broke out laughing and didn't say why.

The night after the closing, several of Stan's friends came for dinner, close friends who knew how badly he had needed to make the sale. Stan said his company had been bleeding money, a fact he wanted to keep secret, "but the Hughes people probably knew. I wouldn't be surprised if our phones were bugged." I'd sensed Stan's tension over the past weeks, but tapping telephones? Suddenly the son in me worried about him. Then the teenager in me took over and wished that I had called Evelyn. What would we have talked about—schoolwork? Whether she had enjoyed playing Eloise?—while an eavesdropping Howard Hughes licked his lips? I would see Evelyn again at the 1963 Christmas parade party, where I would join her and her parents for dinner at one of the long tables the Chamber of Commerce set up for us, but I'd still balk at asking for a date. I'd even been hesitant to name her in response to one of the questions Bobby's uncle had included in his survey: "When you die, whom would you like to be buried with?" I'd thought of her; then I had looked about the room, searching for the right honors-class girl and, too embarrassed to pick any of them, wrote down "my mother."

After dessert, I excused myself to finish a paper for Mr. Occhipinti. He was guiding us through the nineteenth century, a calmer time thanks in part to kings who were less stupid than Louis XVI. While Mr. Occhipinti focused on the treaties and diplomacy that kept Europe peaceful, one of his quick asides—another factoid not in our textbook—grabbed at me. In 1816, a year after the Congress of Vienna, the summer turned wintry, perpetually cold, overcast and rainy to the point that crops failed in several countries, including France. The season became so miserable that, confined to a house in Switzerland, several writers challenged themselves to create dark stories. One member of the group, Mary Shelley, ended up with *Frankenstein*. Predictably, that made the class laugh, almost as much as we had over Louis XVI, and while we did, I looked out the window at a day of brilliant sunshine and wondered if it had been the rain that had driven my father to flee from Mai—or return to her.

Before he said good night, Stan asked if I needed a ride on Saturday to the Squire-Adelphian picnic. The annual event took place in Coldwater Park, an isolated sward on the northern edge of Beverly Hills, at the foot of the mountains that bisected the L.A. area. No buses ran near it, and many of us, myself included, had yet to turn sixteen and get our driver's licenses. Coldwater Park was no Versailles, but with clipped hedges along the perimeter, walkways across the lawn, and an ornamental stone fountain in the middle, it offered hints of a French baroque garden: not too shady, not too exposed, a place to feel as though we'd escaped the world without actually quitting Beverly Hills. Sitting on blankets, eating sandwiches the Adelphians would prepare, I'd feel like a character from one of the paintings by Fragonard and Watteau that Mr. Occhipinti had shown us in class, royals at play in their woods. I envisioned all of us imitating them, albeit dressed in shorts. I hoped it wouldn't rain.

CRYING WITH THE COSMIC COWBOY

Elizabeth Hall

I am in Mendocino, driving through a light rain, towards a grove of redwoods. The road ahead drops off into the mist, into the ocean. I drive slowly. I am in Mendocino to do research for an essay about the musician Doug Sahm. But I could be anywhere. I am telling myself that I am here to learn about the town that inspired Sahm's 1969 record *Mendocino*, a record that defined a particular time in my life. I say I am here to eat fresh sole, sleep in a tent shaded by a live oak, drink strong coffee on a crumbling bluff, ask locals about Sahm, nose through the library. I am telling myself I am here for all these reasons. But I know better. I am in Mendocino because I do not know how not to be driving down the fogged-out road. I could be anywhere, but since I am in Mendocino, I decide to try to find out why Sahm moved to Northern California and why he left.

When Doug Sahm moved to California in the spring of 1966, he was fleeing a drug bust in Texas. The story goes like this: he moved to Salinas from San Antonio with his family and without his band, The Sir Douglas Quintet, which had reached national fame the previous year with their pop song "She's About a Mover." After their drug bust in the Corpus Christi airport, several band members, including keyboard player Augie Meyers, were put on probation, forbidden from crossing state lines. The band languished. Sahm, however, was lucky. The terms of his probation differed: he was allowed to rove.

Sahm bought a tract house in Prunedale, a city of dying plum trees on the outer edge of Salinas. His true home, however, was not in the valley with his family, but in San Francisco, specifically the Haight-Ashbury, where he dropped acid, lolled around Golden Gate Park, jammed with the Dead, smoked bricks of potent Mexican weed, cut tight records in brightly lit studios as the fog rolled in. He had different girlfriends stashed all over town, cute chicks holed up in cold apartments with cats and crates of records beside their beds. In San Francisco — and only in San Francisco — Sahm was finally able to indulge, full-time, in the one activity he loved most: grooving. He was free.

Or so the story goes.

The first year I lived in Los Angeles I wrote an email to an old friend, a former roommate, who still lived in Georgia: *everything you've heard about L.A. is a lie.* My apartment, a dingbat on the east side, was far from Hollywood and Beverly Hills and their stereotypes of Botox and Bentleys with blacked out windows. Instead, I wrote about skinny, sickly palms and pink stucco condos, greasy potato tacos, sitting on the roof of my building at dawn smoking, watching the pigeons peck the chickweed clean. I wrote many such letters: *succulents in bloom, jacarandas shedding, rotting all over the sidewalk.* I told everyone the same story. *The city is magic.*

I did not mention that I was incapable of starting the day without smoking a tidy joint, without sobbing on the roof of my building, pink sky and all. During this time I listened to the same record, every day, over and over — Sir Douglas Quintet's *Mendocino.* It was the band's third album. An autobiographical trip through Texas and Northern California as narrated by Sahm. The record told intertwined stories. One concerned a man who simply wanted to cruise through life, to groove. The other, a man in the midst of losing it all: his family, his youth, his sense of self. This was the story I heard.

Mendocino was recorded in Los Angeles and San Francisco in a few quick sessions in September 1968. Although released under the Sir Douglas Quintet name, the lineup was new: Augie Meyers on keys and organ, Harvey Kagan on bass, John Perez on drums, and Frank Morin and Martin Fierro on horns. When the band entered the studio, Sahm was keening for a distraction. He had recently started and ended an affair with a 16-year-old girl up the coast in Mendocino. He was heartsick, or so people said.

The first song on the record, the title track, charts Sahm's affair with the girl. At first listen, "Mendocino" is a sunny pop song featuring a choppy, driving organ, an infectious loose rhythm. I danced to it often, in the living room of my apartment in L.A., lights off, mouthing the words *teenybopper, my teenage lover.* I listened to it on repeat. It was not long before I began to hear a different story. One of longing. A longing obscured by a pulsing bass, Meyer's staccato Vox throbbing on and on.

The plot was simple enough: a man and his teenage lover, a shack in a beach town, by a river, a grove of redwoods; two lovers, walking through a sun-drenched park, kissing beneath a eucalyptus tree, a perfect afternoon, save the man's insistent pleading *please don't go.* Sahm repeats: *please don't go. Please stay here with me in Mendocino.* I imagined the scene: they make love in the dirt, the soft dirt along the river, he holds her naked in his arms, already aware he's losing her to another, a "fast-talkin' guy with strange red eyes," a man who makes her "mind wonder." The song's lyrics swerve between tenses, between the past — that is, the night he falls in love with her, the early days of their affair, making love on a bluff — and the present, his aching *don't go.* He has not lost her yet. He grieves nonetheless. The song ends in this suspended present-tense moment. No resolution in sight.

I first heard *Mendocino* on my weeklong drive from Georgia to California. It was late summer. I was 23. A friend had given me the record as a going-away gift. Doug Sahm and his band were strangers to me. I stared at Sahm's picture on the cover of the CD:

limp brown hair, big black shades, pert cowboy hat perched on his head. I slid the record into the player where it stayed.

Oh, baby, it just don't matter were the words I mouthed as I kissed Georgia goodbye, crossed into Alabama, the highway lined with pines. It was the last track on the record. A raunchy garage jam with distorted vocals and a driving guitar. A song just heavy and loud enough to snuff the stray thoughts.

Oh, baby, it just don't matter, I sang as I sped through Mississippi's swamp lands, floated belly up in a chalky pool outside Shreveport, pissed on the side of the road in Beaumont, the noon sun sapping the spit from my mouth. Somewhere outside Houston, my car's air conditioner failed. *It just don't matter,* I sang out loud. Windows rolled down, hair sticking to the sides of my lips. *Oh baby, oh baby. It just don't matter.* Up through the cattle country, the cut-up crust of Arizona. A brief detour: I sat in the back of a black SUV sweating through my shorts while two plain-clothes cops illegally searched my car for marijuana, wrote me a $1,000 ticket for possession, then slapped my back and said *have a safe trip.* I drove off into the red cliffs. *It just don't matter,* I sang. As if casting a spell. *It just don't matter.*

I sang all the way to LA.

Like every track on *Mendocino*, "Oh, Baby It Just Don't Matter," obscures more than it reveals. The more I listened to the song the more I began to question the singer's confidence, began to wonder if the refrain — *it just don't matter* — was less a declaration and more a necessary repetition.

Behind the veneer of good-timin' was a deep-seated sense of longing, a longing for a world in which one can waltz through any and all experiences no matter how unpleasant, with the insouciance of John Wayne riding away on a dappled paint waving his hand: *baby, I don't care.* A fantasy.

Another fantasy: a woman moves to L.A. to write. She tells everyone she is moving West with her boyfriend to write a novel. A murder mystery set at a yoga retreat. She says she has waited her entire life to see the Pacific, to sniff the wet seaweed, crush jacarandas in her palm.

None of this is true.

She fled.

When I moved to California, less than a month had passed since my mother announced that she was divorcing her husband, my stepfather of 20 years, after discovering that he had lived a secret life for almost the entire extent of the marriage, including sexually abusing my older sister throughout her childhood. This was not the first time my stepfather had been accused of sexual indiscretion. It was, however, the only time the accusations were accepted by the family as fact. Within weeks of my departure, my mother listed our family farm for sale, and my ex-stepfather began dating another woman, an ex-nurse he met at a bar. By the time I had unpacked and settled in L.A., they had married. I called him only once that first year. The ex-nurse answered. I asked to speak with "my father." She said, he does not have any children by your name. Then, she hung up.

The first year in L.A. I wrote little and read even less. Which was unfortunate: reading was my only hobby. I struggled to sleep. I took to walking the city late at night, fingers trailing the clipped hedges, the metal fences enclosing nearly every yard. I watched punks in the industrial park pass glass bottles hand to mouth. I paced the flood tunnels, my shadow large on the smooth, concrete walls. I walked to exhaust myself. I tried to focus on the alder leaves above my head, the scratching of the rats. My mind roved. I wondered what I could not bear to know: how was it possible that I lived alongside a man for two decades without ever once glimpsing his nature? I had missed all the signs. I had lost the through line of my life.

It sounded as if the man who had written *Mendocino* was even less sure than I of where he was going or why. I listened to "At the

Crossroads," the tender ballad that had replaced "Oh, Baby" as my favorite song on the record. I loved Meyer's churchy organ. The overall religious tone of the song. Sahm sings every single word. The song begins with the line: *leaving you now for the very last time.* Again Sahm plays the confident narrator, a man who knows what he wants. It is easy to picture the "crossroads" Sahm found himself straddling — whether to move home to Texas with his wife and his band or to stay in San Francisco, the "great big freaky city." Sahm sings: *crossroads of my life passed her by.* It appears he has made his decision: he will stay in the city. He has accepted his choice. Yet a residue of sadness lingers. The decision has brought him little solace. No closure. No sooner has Sahm announced — *I'm leaving her* — does he sing, just as surely, *someday a change will come and you'll be beside me one more time.* He repeats *one more time, one more time, one more time you'll be beside me.* As if he, too, is trying to convince himself.

The picture of a man who is sure of nothing. A man bewildered by his appetites. A man playing a fool in the city of his dreams.

In "Lawd I'm Just a County Boy" Sahm willingly plays the fool, the wide-eyed dreamer adrift in a city of dive bars, bad vibes, and cable cars. *Really did mess up my mind,* Sahm sings mid-song, referencing all that he's seen in the Haight-Ashbury. *Lawd I'm just a country boy in this great big freaky city.*

In truth, Sahm was no longer simply a country boy. Could never be one again. This, too, he mourns.

Sahm openly grieves the loss of this particular identity in "Texas Me," a sublime slice of autobiography. He sings, *I wonder what happened to that man inside, that real old Texas me?* The question hangs. Sahm's fiddle plays on. The fiddle itself is played with heavy reverb, an especially trippy touch that seemed to answer the question Sahm posed earlier: no, he can never return, will never be that good old Texas boy again. The steel guitar whines. He can never return.

In "I Don't Want," a song written around the same period as

those on *Mendocino*, Sahm yet again refers to himself as a fool. A man who has changed so irrevocably as to become unrecognizable even to himself. *The changes in the city made a fool of me*, Sahm sings, amid the sad steel guitar.

It was easy enough for me to play the fool in my new city; I was enrolled in a graduate program. The main reason I chose to attend this particular school, which had offered me little funding, was that it was located 2,193 miles from my childhood home. The school, founded by Disney in the 1960s, was nestled in a dreary suburb of chain restaurants and highly-ranked public schools. I commuted 30 minutes from the city. The writing program had its own facilities, a three-room metal box painted yellow, a small parking lot. Often I would arrive early to class, pull into the back lot, and park along the tree line. I would sit, listen to "Oh, Baby It Just Don't Matter," cigarette ash all over the seat. I would sit, unable to open the door, walk over to the building. Sometimes 10, 15 minutes would pass before my body would cooperate. When I did make it to class, I listened. I spoke when I was addressed. I do not remember, however, what I said or what I heard. With time, I stopped bothering with the drive at all. I skipped class with prominent poets — poets I admire — to eat salted caramels on the beach, make-out beneath the pier, sun low, fingers in my hair, in my mouth. I visited dank bars dark at noon. The walls lined with mirrors, strands of Christmas lights. If I happened to catch a glimpse of myself in one of these mirrors, I always had to look twice to make sure it was me. Few things held my focus: wet kisses, riding my bike heart-pounding through the park, dancing in my apartment, air threaded with smoke. That is the thing about fools: they like to dance. They prize the ride.

Sahm was a fool, dancing up and down the streets of San Francisco. *Mendocino* is his story: a man grieving, still singing. A story I needed to hear.

I, too, tried to sing. Despite my grief. I tried to find the through line. I graduated, found a job at an Internet tutoring center where I talked to teenagers about *Othello* through a small black screen. I began driving to the desert. I drove to Anza-Borrego, on the edge of the Sonoran Desert, which in Southern California is called The Colorado. A desert of Tamarisk trees, long-horn sheep, real live badlands falling off into the Salton Trough. I hiked through slot canyons and across buttes strewn with seashells, mud hills streaked red and brown. I snapped pictures of burned yuccas, a flat of creosote. I slept in the car, on the side of a dirt road in a dry wash with white thistle and heaps of scrub, horizon obscured by a mountain chain I couldn't yet name. Other times I hiked deep into the mountains, slept in my tent, stared up at the stars through a mesh slit. In the early days, friends joined me. With time, however, they stopped saying yes and instead started asking questions.

I thought about Sahm often on these trips as I was almost always listening to *Mendocino* while laying in my sleeping bag. I thought about how he needed to move to California to understand something about Texas. Mainly, that he missed it. That Texas was a thing to miss.

It took Sahm five years on the coast before he could return. In 1971 he moved to Austin, but he rarely slept there. He visited his family in San Antonio, tried to reconcile with his wife. The couple soon divorced. He fled north. In Austin, he had no permanent address. He toured Amsterdam, wrote several records, taught his sons to play guitar. He killed time following his favorite baseball teams game to game, often blowing off gigs with his new band to attend spring training. He never lived in San Antonio again. He prized the ride.

I have lived in L.A. for five years, but unlike Sahm, I am not ready to return home. Not yet. Increasingly, however, I find it hard to stay. I drive to Mendocino for the same reason I drive to the desert — the city no longer charms me. I long once again for the ruralness of my childhood. I miss my mother, my sister. Our home in Georgia. The pine trees laid out in neat rows, thick bands of sumac, honeysuckles in the spring, the threat of chiggers, deer ticks feasting on our skin. It had never occurred to me that I would miss it. This land that was owned and worked by the abusive man who still owns and works it today. I am, in fact, no longer allowed on the premises.

I don't share all Sahm's appetites, but I can understand them. Some I understand too well. Wrapped in a plaid blanket on a beach at Headlands State Park, the very beach where I imagined Sahm strolling with his lover all those years ago, it occurs to me — it is ok to miss where I come from, all that I have left. Even if what I left was not particularly good or healthy or interesting. I miss it nonetheless. This, too, is part of *Mendocino*'s story.

DAD'S HOUSE

Vincent Poturica

Danny didn't hear the whimper inside the house when he opened the screen door. The door swung shut behind him, and the whimper stopped almost immediately, which, had he heard it, might have made Danny wonder if whatever was moaning preferred not to be discovered. But Danny was with Sasha who had just picked him up from LAX and drove him back to his dad's house in Redondo Beach. Sasha, like Danny, was seventeen, and she was talking about the way the moon made her feel less anxious if she looked at it long enough, and he wanted to kiss her. He was not listening to the house because it was supposed to be empty.

His dad, according to his characteristically [No Subject] email, had left for a *retreat* three days before Danny returned from Ecuador. Per his parents' custody agreement, Danny spent his summers with his mom. He'd spent the first seven weeks volunteering for an NGO that was helping Andean villages implement sanitation systems, and he'd spent the last ten days in Quito getting stoned with his mom, going to museums, and watching movies starring Pauly Shore.

His dad would be gone for *2 months maybe 3*, which sounded like a really long time, even for his dad who, since he'd sold his contracting firm and stopped drinking alcohol, had travelled twice to India for month-long meditation seminars. His dad said that this retreat was *particularly important*, and that he'd left *plenty of $$$*

for Danny in the kitchen drawer where he kept the German knives that were designed for cutting meat. He also said that he hadn't had a drink in *451 days* and that God was Danny's *friend* even if Danny didn't, presently, want to be friends with God. Danny had thought that was odd—not his dad claiming God was his friend; he often said things like that—but that he'd put the money, folded between two blue rubber bands, beside the knives. Three of these knives, Danny noticed, were missing.

That's a lot of money, Sasha said.

Danny nodded. He didn't want to count the bills in front of her, so he stuffed them into his pocket and asked Sasha if it was okay if he took a quick shower. He felt dirty after travelling, and he was sweating. It was past midnight, but it was August, and the night was warm.

Of course, Sasha said.

In the shower Danny felt free of worry and hesitation, which he attributed to the lingering effects of the fried-egg-and-psilocybin-mushroom sandwich that his mom had given him in the taxi on the way to the airport. She wanted to make her son's flight more interesting, and, ideally, to guide him towards making a better decision about where to go to college, and if he would play football there. The clouds had gathered beside Danny's passenger window and slowly transformed into a group of angels with demonic horns, or demons with angelic faces, he hadn't been sure, but it hadn't mattered what they were, his heart had been open and accepting towards them, as they'd watched him with the mute curiosity of manatees he'd once observed slowly swimming down a river on a trip to Florida when his parents were still together.

Danny watched the water from the shower bubble at his feet, and he thought about when the Earth was just a vast, steaming puddle of amoebas. He touched his face, and he felt grateful that his cheeks were wet. He cupped his hands around his ears and tried to listen to the blood circulating in his fingers. Danny couldn't hear the blood, but he felt comforted by the knowledge that it was there, under his skin, migrating in patterns predetermined by his

DNA. He kissed each of his palms and said Thank you.

Sasha stepped into the shower. She didn't say anything. She was naked, and he noticed a pink scar on the rib closet to her heart. The scar was vaguely shaped like the symbol for infinity. She looked shy and more than a little uncomfortable. Danny kissed the infinity-shaped scar, and Sasha took his hand and placed it on her breast. Danny felt her nipple grow firmer under his fingers. Sasha brought his face in front of her face, cradling his chin, so that he was looking directly into her eyes that seemed to be pleading, asking him, with an urgency that was scary because it was wordless and impossible to hide, to please, please accept her exactly as she was. Her mouth was warmer than the water.

Danny had hooked up with Sasha only once before. They'd made out, and she'd given Danny a hand job on an inflatable couch behind a garage at a party he'd attended the night before he left for Ecuador. They had enough mutual friends that they waved when they saw each other at school, and they'd talked a few times at lunch, mostly about music and having unpredictable, divorced parents. She was slim and very tall, taller than he was, close to 6'1". Danny thought she wasn't so much pretty as fierce-looking in a way that gave him an instant erection, with dark hair that she kept cropped above her ears, and eyes that were always circled with mascara, and made Danny think of glaciers surrounded by volcanic ashes. Her parents were Jewish engineers from Belarus, but her mom now taught at a Waldorf school in Santa Cruz and lived on a Hare Krishna farm. Her dad designed drones for Raytheon in El Segundo and coached her little brother's soccer team. Danny's older sister Josefina—people called her Jo—had recently joined the Marines in an effort to stop doing cocaine.

Four days after the party, Danny had sent Sasha an email, telling her about Ecuador, the clean air in the Andes, a kind man nicknamed Murciélago—The Bat—on account of his ability to jump freakishly high while playing goalie, an email that was really a roundabout way of gauging whether Sasha might be more interested in him than just drunkenly messing around. Two weeks passed, by which time Danny had assumed she wasn't interested, when Sasha wrote him two emails that she sent within seven hours of each other. In the first email, she wrote about her day working at Cold Stone Creamery during which she hot-boxed the freezer then felt incredibly paranoid, like her customers were Nazi scientists who were going to take her back through time to the gas chambers of 1943. She then wrote that she wanted to get to know Danny better, and that she had recently moved up from a B-cup to a C-cup, and that her breasts wanted to be squeezed, preferably gently—she'd attached a picture of herself wearing a tube-top that said Yummy. In the second email, she apologized for her first message, and told Danny that she was mortified by what she'd written, that she became a different person when she drank too much, that she wasn't *some dumb ho*. She wrote about the books she'd read that summer and gave Danny a detailed synopsis of two novels, one by Colette, the other by Phillip K. Dick, that, even though he now knew exactly what would happen in these books, he still wanted to read them, which he thought was a testament to Colette and Dick's respective imaginations. In the third email, she sent Danny a questionnaire, and she said that he had to answer each question, truthfully, if he ever wanted to take her out on a *real date*. The questions included: *Do you love your mom more than you love your dad, or vice versa? Do you have life goals? Do you believe in having life goals? What is your spirit animal? If I told you that I think football is barbaric, would you still want to go out with me? How many times have you masturbated to the picture I sent? Have you ever wanted to die? Do you believe in God? How big is your dick?* Danny answered each of these questions— it took him five days to respond to them all, because he wanted to be thorough, and because there was only one computer that volunteers, like Danny, shared at the NGO headquarters. Sasha emailed him back that she wanted to pick him up from the airport, which Danny thought was a wonderful idea.

After they finished showering and dried-off, Sasha put on a pair Danny's boxers and his Minor Threat T-shirt, and Danny found some chocolate ice cream in the freezer. While they ate it, dipping their spoons directly into the carton, they talked about atoms drifting through the universe and forming new worlds for no apparent reason, and, how, in approximately 7.5 billion years, the Sun would absorb Earth in an enormous fiery hug. Sasha used the word *hug*, which Danny thought was great.

He hugged Sasha and told her this. She kissed his forehead then looked at him in her pleading way and told him that, though he was stronger than she was, she was taller and a very good fighter, and she would kick his ass if he ever hurt her. Danny laughed and told her what his newest stepdad Humberto, a Mexican diplomat and an old family friend from Guadalajara with whom his mom had reconnected on Facebook, had said to Danny earlier that week. Danny had thanked him for taking good care of his mom. And, in a contemplative tone, Humberto, very stoned, had told Danny that it was easy to take good care of someone when you loved them. Danny thought that was a beautiful thing to say, and Sasha agreed with him. Danny said that he wanted to take good care of the people he loved.

The next day, after Sasha left, Danny didn't hear any whimpering, but he heard the sound of a flushing toilet. The flushing seemed to be coming from inside the house even though Danny wasn't in the bathroom. Danny told himself that the flushing must have been coming from one of his next-door neighbors, that it just was echoing in a weird way so that it sounded like it was coming from his own house. He studied the playbook that his football coach had emailed him—Hell Week, the fourteen days of three-a-day practices, would start tomorrow—and Danny made himself a chicken-and-black-bean burrito for lunch. While he ate it, he watched a documentary about drag queens in Brazil who all seemed to approach the world with the sort of understated courage and dark sense of humor that comes from surviving extended hardship. Danny fell asleep on the couch and dreamt of a girl named Lisa he'd had a crush on when he was in eighth grade—she'd gone to a different high school, where, he'd recently heard, she'd gotten into heroin. In the dream, the sky was green, and Lisa was scratching at her arms and telling him about a birthday party she'd had when she was ten years old. She couldn't remember anything that had happened at her party, other than that someone had given her a boa constrictor that she'd named Lucy Liu.

His phone rang and woke him up. It was Sasha, and she was on her lunch break at Cold Stone. They talked about the nature of fate and how she was thinking about applying to nursing school, which Danny told her sounded cool.

Then Sasha suggested that they play a game that wasn't really a game, but she didn't know what else to call it. All it required was that they take turns saying words that made them happy. She said the only rule was that you couldn't think about what you were going to say, you just needed to say the first thing that popped into your head that made you feel better. She said Danny had to start.

Danny said, Sea turtle.

Sasha said, Orange Julius.

He said, Woody Guthrie.

She said, Dildo.

Mountain.

Balloon.

Cartwheel.

Shit.

When Sasha said she had to go back to work, Danny told her how much he liked this game. He didn't tell her that he was writing each word down on the back of a flyer for a tai-chi class that he'd found on the kitchen counter. He wanted to save these words for a day that he needed them more.

Two days later, Danny drove home to pick up a case of Gatorade for his teammates before the final afternoon practice began. He heard the whimpering sound as soon as he stepped into the house. He was in a hurry, but the sound was unsettling, especially since, now that he was listening, it was clear that the sound was coming from inside the house. Danny quickly realized that its origin was somewhere below him. He walked down the nine wooden steps—he knew how many there were because he'd helped his dad build them—into the basement. He was no longer tired. His adrenal glands had released their hormones, and he felt very awake. The sound was more distinct in the basement, and the whimper became the hiccupping of sobs, the sound of someone trying to stop himself from crying. Danny looked around the small space that, besides a few cardboard boxes stacked against a wall, was empty—Danny's dad believed in keeping his material belongings as minimal and organized as possible. The noise seemed to be coming from inside the boxes. Danny walked towards them, and the sound became louder. He moved the boxes, listening to three of them, marked *XMAS LIGHTS*, *TAXES*, and *JO'S STUFF*, respectively, before he realized that the sound was coming from the floor. Danny moved the boxes—there were eight—to the other side of the room, and then he pressed his ear against the concrete. The sobbing had stopped, but now he distinctly heard a person breathing on the other side. There was no visible door, but, after Danny felt around the floor, he discovered a metal ring painted the same color as the concrete near the wall. He pulled on the ring and opened a trapdoor.

Danny climbed down a ladder, and there, in a room that was roughly six by six feet squared, was his dad sitting in a battered office chair beside a toilet that, like the trapdoor, Danny didn't know existed. A single light bulb hung from a chain. His dad's eyes were closed, but it was clear that he was the one making the whimpering sounds. His dad pretended not to notice, or literally didn't sense that Danny was there.

Danny looked at his dad. He was thin and pale, and, beyond the fact that his dad had been in the house, hiding since Danny had returned from Ecuador, Danny realized something else was very wrong. There were plastic jugs of water and cans of black beans stacked in a systematic-seeming ring around the room. There was a simple metal stool directly in front of the office chair. There was a medium-sized Tupperware container sitting on this stool. Things were moving inside the Tupperware. The Tupperware had a red lid.

Danny tried to think of red things—his favorite pants, the ends of flames—so that he didn't have to think about the things that were moving in the Tupperware, and what else was inside it.

Dad, Danny said. What's going on?

His dad didn't respond. He kept his eyes closed. Danny looked at his dad's hands. There was gauze secured over where his left pinky had been with Band-Aids that were decorated with cartoon horses. Danny noticed a first-aid kit near his bare feet.

Dad, Danny said. What happened to your hand?

Danny looked at the Tupperware. He opened the red lid, and the smell overwhelmed him. The things moving inside it were maggots. The maggots were moving over a finger, his Dad's finger, and consuming the flesh that now only partially covered the bones.

Danny vomited into the toilet. He felt overcome by the feeling that he was standing alone on one of those planet-sized meteors, hurtling through space in this room with his dad. He felt so distant from the practice that he needed to return to in less than fifteen minutes. He tried to think about football, about where he needed to be during a Cover 2, if he was supposed to play man-to-man with the running back or with the slot receiver. He thought about other red things. Christmas candles. Cardinals. Cherry-flavored popsicles. He looked at his father, then at the finger, then at the maggots. He put the red lid back on the Tupperware. He shook his dad's shoulders. His shoulders were warm, but his dad refused to open his eyes.

In the car, on his way back to football practice, Danny focused on a group of pretty middle-aged women jogging in a pack down the sidewalk. They wore tiny shorts that made their legs look longer. Danny focused on the clouds passing over him, and the Mahler song he was listening to on a classical radio station.

He thought about his dad's mysterious charisma. He thought about how, even though his dad seemed obviously depressed to anyone who spent more than thirty minutes with him, Danny's friends all liked him, their parents liked him, the lady with buzzed hair who delivered their mail liked him, etc., etc. Danny thought about watching *Eraserhead* with his dad when Danny was eight, and how his dad had repeated throughout the movie, You see, Dan, everything is possible.

Danny thought about a conversation he'd had with his dad shortly after his dad had stopped drinking. His dad had sounded like a college student who had just eaten acid for the first time. He was talking about *misperceptions* of madness and enlightenment. His dad had said something like, Insane is a highly contested word, Dan, based on the unhealthy and limited conceptions of the status quo, but you already knew that. Then they'd walked to Baskin Robbins. His dad had seemed so energized, and Danny had mistaken his enthusiasm for a budding happiness.

Danny didn't call Sasha that night. He didn't shower or talk to any of his teammates after practice. He drove east, away from the ocean, through neighborhoods where every window was covered with bars. He felt complicit in an ugly crime spree. But what was he supposed to do? Wasn't it more humane to allow his dad to destroy himself in private? Was it bad that he didn't care to involve police or mental health professionals? Danny didn't want his dad to be made a spectacle.

He thought about how he would respond to authorities if they asked him, later, why he hadn't told anyone about his dad, but Danny couldn't come up with any reasonable answers. He would take care of his dad—it was that simple. Taking care of him, as best as he could, seemed like the right thing to do, even if Danny couldn't explain why.

Danny drove to Trader Joe's and purchased frozen products that his dad liked. He microwaved chicken pot stickers while he unloaded the groceries into the refrigerator. He brought the pot stickers down to his dad on a yellow plate his sister had made, years ago, while taking a ceramics class—he hoped that the plate would remind his dad of people who loved him. Danny swept the tiny room. He told his dad about practice and about Sasha. He didn't look at the finger covered with maggots, but he wrapped it in several paper towels and buried it in a hole in the backyard. He rinsed the Tupperware thoroughly with bleach, and, because he thought it was a kind of emblem for his dad, he brought it back downstairs.

Sasha's voice was deep—it would be described as husky, if people still used that word—and it gave, Danny thought, everything she talked about, even the names of corporate retailers like Target or Costco, a certain weight. Maybe Danny was in love with her because everything she said seemed to be layered with significance. Oh Sasha, Danny thought, my father is cutting off his fingers in a secret room below the basement, and I'm falling for you. His English teacher was talking about Thoreau, about some mystical vision Thoreau had had while watching sand erupt in streams from snow banks melting along a train track, how the streams of sand matched the form of the tree branches hanging over them, and how the leaves were a perfect model of the world, or something like that. Danny thought Thoreau was a huge pussy in comparison with his dad.

When class ended, he called Sasha's phone, even though he knew she kept it turned off during school. Danny wanted to hear her voicemail greeting: *It's Sasha—maybe I'll call you back*. After he called her seven times in rapid succession, his mind, for at least the next half-hour, remained mostly still. He did this, between each of his classes, in an effort to keep himself sane until he saw her at lunch.

Later that day, Sasha picked Danny up from football practice, and Danny wished that the clouds would release a torrent of rain. He wanted to do something gallant for Sasha, something along the lines of holding his sweatshirt over her to keep her dry, and then, if God returned to His Old Testament vindictiveness and ordered the rain to continue for days, Danny would find a canoe and paddle with Sasha through the flooded urban sprawl, and they would save the shivering and hypothermic stranded on their rooftops, together, holding hands throughout the disaster. Danny didn't tell Sasha about his dad, but he told her that he needed her right now, that he was having a hard time. She told him that they could talk about it, but he said that he didn't want to. He just wanted to be near her.

So they drove silently to the Korean Bell in San Pedro. They exited the car and held hands while sitting in the grass and watching the ocean change color as the sun sank below the offing. They didn't talk. They maximized the joint Sasha had rolled—Danny had admitted the week before that he was, possibly, the worst roller in the South Bay—by taking turns recycling the smoke into each other's mouths. Nothing was more erotic than sharing smoke, Danny thought. He was not thinking about his father dismembering himself below the basement. He was not thinking about ethnic violence, or the catastrophic effects of globalization, or the Cuba-sized holes in the ozone layer. He was trying to think only about the smoke and Sasha's wet lips, and he succeeded in feeling almost happy for approximately seven minutes, after which time he thought, while kissing Sasha softly, about a cartoon he couldn't remember the name of, though it had been set in a near future that was mostly populated with androids and talking pandas. Then Danny thought about his dad—he'd noticed that there was something new inside the Tupperware on account of the trembling maggots—and he retreated from Sasha's lips and asked her if she wanted to work on their Pre-Calculus homework together, which made her laugh and say, I'm too stoned, but maybe in an hour.

She took his hand and led him back into the car where she took off his pants and then took off her pants. They had sex with their shirts on. Afterwards, they drove to a nearby McDonald's, bought unsweetened coffees, and tried to do Pre-Calculus.

On the way back to his house, Danny watched, from the passenger window, the moon and the stars and the big empty spaces between them that looked large enough to fit thousands of planets. Danny told Sasha that he thought those gigantic spaces were much more mysterious than the pretty lights they separated. Sasha nodded in agreement.

Two weeks passed, and Danny didn't shave. Sasha said he looked way hotter with scruff. He called his mom and listened to her talk about her star sign. He tried to call his sister, and he left her two long messages during which he realized that he kept repeating the words *miraculous* and *fear*. He made an effort to hold open doors at his high school, allowing dozens of people to pass by before following them inside. He had sex with Sasha underneath the bleachers twice during lunch. He visited his grandma in San Pedro and brought Sasha with him. She cooked them scrambled eggs with potatoes and salsa that she made from the tomatoes and peppers she grew, and she asked Danny, as she always did, if he was gay, even with Sasha there. He quickly regained the weight he'd lost in Ecuador by drinking shakes he made with 2 percent milk and chocolate-flavored whey protein that he bought on sale from Walmart. His coach was pleased with his progress learning the new defensive scheme—Danny had recorded nine tackles along with a sack during the first game of the season. After practice, Danny took the briefest possible showers in an effort to conserve water, even if the effort was, in the end, negligible to the point of being meaningless. He removed the knives from the basement and cleaned them vigorously until his hands were wrinkled. But, until Danny returned them, his dad refused to eat, just as he had refused to talk to Danny when Danny would pour out the bottles that his Dad used to hide around the house.

Danny returned the knives. He did his best to take care of his dad while ignoring what his dad was doing. He studied the scouting report regarding the next team they were playing. He visualized hitting the starting quarterback DeAndre Jones so hard that DeAndre's collarbone shattered and exited his shoulder like an ivory spear that had landed its target. Then Danny felt bad for wanting to harm DeAndre, whom he didn't know, and who probably had his own struggles that he kept to himself. Danny listened to Vivaldi's *Four Seasons* and felt briefly uplifted, and then decidedly angry and alone, even though he was falling even harder for Sasha. He heated up enchiladas verdes that he'd also bought on sale—he was trying to make the money his dad had left last as long as possible—and he brought them, along with a napkin, down to the basement.

Another week passed, and Danny couldn't fall asleep, so he wrote his dad an email in the hope that it might be cathartic. The email began with banal small talk about the weather and Danny's last game, how many tackles he'd made, the forced fumble he'd caused, the cheering, the feeling he'd had after he'd picked up the fumble and ran for fifteen yards before being tackled himself, the feeling that he was releasing some of the evil inside himself, or, better, that he was shaking hands with the darkness of which he could never be entirely relieved, and, for this reason, he wanted to hit someone on the other team even harder, to become weaponized and unfeeling. He knew that he sounded ridiculous, but he needed to write these thoughts to his dad, or at least a former version of his dad, because he no longer thought of him as a person, let alone as his father. He thought of his dad as a sort of plant in the process of petrification. He wasn't sure if his dad was devolving, or evolving, but he was certainly no longer *living* in the usual sense of the word.

Then Danny described an incident involving a cheerleader from the other team, who, urged on by her giggling friends, had given Danny her phone number written on a scrap of yellow legal paper. Danny had bowed when he opened the paper and saw the number and her name—Isabel—written over it. He said, Isabel is a pretty name, before he crumpled up the paper and swallowed it in front of her. Then he apologized to Isabel and her friends for doing that, explaining that he had a girlfriend, which didn't make the cheerleaders appear any less creeped-out.

From that anecdote on, Danny's email became a series of

questions that centered on the premise—an idea with which his dad had always been obsessed—that, to truly understand anything that a person did, to know what was meant by their actions or words, even if they were making an observation as simple as they didn't like smoothies, you needed a total context of that person's life, a complete knowledge of everything they'd ever seen, or said, or done, or thought, or even dreamed about, a knowledge that was, of course, impossible, which made it, in turn, impossible for intimacy to be absolute. *Every person remains a mystery*, Danny wrote, and he realized that he felt comfortable telling his dad anything, or at least telling the email account that his dad would probably never, again, open. Danny felt noticeably better as soon as he hit Send.

Even after writing these nightly emails to his dad, Danny continued to struggle with insomnia, especially when he wasn't with Sasha— she didn't like sneaking out of her house, and she wasn't allowed to sleepover at friends' houses on school nights. He tried sleeping in the guest room. The guest room had once been his sister Jo's room, but she was now stationed at a Marine base somewhere in Georgia, a state Danny had no interest in visiting aside from the town of Athens, where Neutral Milk Hotel, an experimental pop band Danny revered, had formed. He watched a shadow cast by a bookcase drift toward the window. The shadow climbed the ceiling like a child possessed by evil spirits. Danny looked at his hands, and he turned them over and over again, while thinking about his dad's missing fingers. He said *bonerish* in an effort to make himself laugh. He tried to masturbate, but he could only visualize Ellen DeGeneres's face Photoshopped onto Sasha's naked body, which made him think about copyright laws and feel like a photograph of himself. He pressed his hands against his ribs to make sure he hadn't become two-dimensional. The shadow now seemed to drip from the ceiling. Danny pulled the covers from his bed and wrapped himself inside them. He crawled under the bed, and shut his eyes as tightly as he could. He realized that he'd forgotten to brush his teeth. He gathered up the courage to leave the room.

After brushing his teeth, he walked into the den and turned on the T.V. He selected the most feel-good-seeming film that was on—*Air Bud*—a movie that concerned a boy and his dog Buddy, who, on top of being predictably mischievous and loyal, could play basketball by pushing the ball into the hoop with his nose, a trick he'd learned while working for a mean-spirited clown who'd abandoned Buddy in the center of a highway. The boy's father had died in a war, and, at the beginning of the film, there was a scene of the boy weeping while studying a picture of his dad, looking stoic and brave in a military uniform. But, by the film's happy ending—Buddy guided the boy's team to winning a sort of middle-school championship—the dead father had been forgotten. Danny imagined another version of the film narrated by the father's ghost who became more depressed as he realized how quickly it was that the world, including his own son, stopped thinking about him. Danny wondered about how few people had asked him how his dad was doing, or even where he was. He heated a glass of milk for himself, and drank it. Then he heated one for his dad.

When's your dad coming home, again? Sasha asked Danny the following evening. She handed him a mug filled with something that smelled moldy. Danny made a face.

It's healthy, she said, drink it.

Danny drank it, and told her that he didn't know when his dad would be back. And he felt better because he hadn't had to lie.

Another week passed, and Danny attempted to communicate with his dad face-to-face. He was feeling desperate.

Danny said, Dad, what the fuck. You've been in the basement for over a month. This is beyond insane. You can still come up and claim that you lost your fingers in a car crash, or rock climbing, or something. I can get you help.

But his dad remained silent, and his eyes remained closed.

Danny said, You're in the basement, Dad, dismembering your hand.

Danny closed his fist and hit his dad in the face, below his left eye. His dad gasped, but he didn't say anything.

Danny shook the hand he'd hit him with and apologized immediately. Then he left. He brought down an icepack and held it over the side of his dad's face that was now swelling and turning a plum color.

Anger is a reaction to fear, he remembered his dad once saying. His dad had said it to a local surfer when he and Danny had paddled out to a well-known break in Palos Verdes that was patrolled by a gang of men in their late-twenties who still lived with their rich parents and were known for slashing the tires of people who weren't their friends. In the words of his dad, They're just your average assholes. People who are truly fearless are never angry, Danny's dad had said to them, before he and Danny got their asses beat. Danny had been both impressed and worried by his dad's willful self-destructiveness. In the car ride to a different surf spot, he'd asked his dad why he'd chosen to go there when there were plenty of places where people wouldn't mess with you. His dad had just smiled at him, and said, Because it's fun.

I'm sorry, Dad, Danny said, I'm sorry.

He touched his dad's cheeks, then his own cheeks, and realized that both of their faces were now thoroughly bearded. Intuitively, Danny walked back up the ladder and back up the stairs. He brought down a razor, Gillette gel, and a large bowl of hot water. Carefully, he began shaving his father. Then he shaved himself.

While working on his college applications, Danny imagined beginning his personal statement: *This morning I put on my favorite red pants, and made an omelet for my dad who is dismembering himself in a secret room below the basement.*

Or: *This morning I retrieved one of my dad's fingers, teeming with maggots, that he had intentionally severed, and I contemplated frying it, sautéing it with olive oil and garlic, and then eating it in order to get in better touch with the motivations of my progenitor, but then I decided not to, realizing, when I made that decision, that, really, life is nothing but a series of seemingly*

90

small decisions made according to a general worldview, that may or not shift in accordance with lived experience, and that my worldview is definitely shifting towards something I can't yet articulate other than that it is best to treat people with kindness.

Danny did not write these things. Instead, he wrote about Murciélago—The Bat—the man from the Andean village he'd spent almost every day with during his time volunteering that summer. Danny wrote about how, each morning, after waking at dawn to the roosters crowing to the mist, he would walk with Murciélago, and spend the day working with him, digging irrigation channels, sometimes playing soccer with him in the afternoons, sometimes playing the guitar-like instruments that his cousin lent him, sometimes reading to Murciélago's two young children who Murciélago took care of with his mother's help. Danny wrote about how, not until two days before he left, did he learn where Murciélago went every weekend. He visited his wife who lived in a state-funded asylum. It was a four-hour walk each way. Murciélago didn't have any family nearby or enough money to stay at an inn, so he slept in one of the plastic chairs in the waiting room. His wife was catatonic now, but she had once tried to kill him with a machete. Murciélago had a very deep scar over his collarbone. Danny wrote that one of the NGO's program managers had relayed this information to Danny, offhandedly, during lunch, and that Danny had struggled not to cry. He had never met someone so humble.

After the football season—Danny's team lost in the second round against a school from Palm Springs—Danny drove to his grandma's house. He realized that he needed to tell someone about what his dad was doing now that football was over, and basketball wasn't enough of an outlet for his increasing anger and anxiety. Danny didn't want to burden or psychologically scar Sasha. And he didn't want to tell his mom, because he knew she would convince him to report what was happening to the proper authorities and to move to Ecuador immediately.

His grandma made him a huge sandwich stacked with turkey, salami, and provolone. She also gave him two tomatoes and a Diet Coke. While he ate, Danny told her everything.

His grandma nodded. Then she said, Jimmy's always been troubled.

Yes, Grandma, but this is really messed-up.

Sure is, she said.

She didn't look at Danny when she said this. She was still watching T.V. A guy with a bloody nose whom Danny recognized as Nicholas Cage was fighting in what appeared to be a crowded Middle Eastern marketplace.

I really like this part, his grandma said.

Danny grabbed the remote and turned off the T.V. He said, Grandma, this is important. Are you gonna help me get Dad sorted out?

Why? she said. You take him out of the basement, and he's still gonna be sad. He marries my pretty daughter, and he's still sad. He divorces her, he stops drinking, he's still sad. What do you do with somebody like that? Let him do what he wants. You come live with me if you don't wanna live there.

Danny thought about spending the rest of his senior year with his grandma. Helping her plant her tomatoes and peppers, watching every episode of *MacGyver*, skateboarding more at the park under the bridge near her house. Maybe he would stop smoking weed. Living with her could be all right. He thanked her for the offer, but declined.

Is it because you want to get high with nobody bothering you? she said.

That's part of it, Danny admitted. But I think I can still help my dad.

People die from trying to live up to someone else's idea of them, she said. Your dad would be less fucked if he just admitted he was. Stop worrying about him. Worrying is a waste of time.

Danny appreciated the way that his grandma said *fucked* with the casual authority of a country singer who can't kick an addiction to painkillers and self-pity. He imagined his grandma writing a memoir titled *Fucked*, with the sub-title *But I Don't Care*. He would buy that book, as would probably enough people for it to become a cult hit, and he would read it with interest, except for the parts that were basically rants against white people and free market capitalism, or the parts that were about her still active sex life, which he would skip over. Danny loved his grandma, but he didn't always trust her opinions, and he didn't want to hear about her sleeping with younger men, which, may have been, he realized, because her opinions made him uncomfortable in ways that he didn't want to assess. For instance, would the world really be better if people acted out their perversions in public, if his dad chose to cut himself apart in the living room, with the blinds raised and the windows open to sunlight and birds and Girl Scouts selling cookies? Would the world be healthier if we did in public what we felt compelled to do in hiding?

Hey, Danny, are you gay? his grandma said, finally turning off the T.V. I know I'm changing the subject, but I'm still wondering, and my friends keep asking. You know, it's okay if you are.

No, Grandma, I'm not gay, Danny said, realizing that his tone made him sound defensive. I have a girlfriend. You've met her.

Then he said, Grandma, I love you, and I'm going to go now.

He hugged her and tried not to hear what she said. He caught the words *fucked, multi-vitamins,* and *happiness* before he left her house and drove back to Redondo Beach along the cliffs of Palos Verdes, thinking first about veering wildly off of the road and into the water and the rocks below, annihilating himself in a violent, romantic way that made him laugh because it was such a seventeen-year-old thing to imagine. Then Danny turned the radio to a station playing techno-pop that made him feel calmer. He admired the contrast of the yellow mustard flowers growing against the greenish-brown scrub oaks that covered the hills. He felt genuinely moved by a lighthouse that had been converted into a museum—he'd visited it, once, on a field trip in fifth grade, and, in the distance, he'd seen a gray whale turn a somersault before disappearing back into the water.

Danny stopped at a 7-Eleven. He walked through the aisles and tried to remember why he was there, and what he wanted to buy. He didn't know. He sat on the floor in front of the candy, and felt positive feelings towards the plastic packaging surrounding the processed sugars, plastic that would take centuries to decompose in enormous landfills and would continue to live, in the sense that it would not decompose, at least five, or even ten times, longer than he or any human currently inhabiting the Earth. He felt better knowing that this plastic would be around much longer than any of the contemporary members of his species (unless the few who were cryogenically frozen were able, at a later date, to be brought back to life, which Danny seriously doubted). He bought two large boxes of Junior Mints, one for he and Sasha to share later, and one for his dad. His dad would, as usual, keep his eyes shut when he placed the Junior Mints besides his chair, but he would eat them later, when Danny left. His dad couldn't resist Junior Mints. That's why Danny would bring the candy to him, and kiss the side of his head where his left ear used to be. Then Danny would write the essay that was due tomorrow about Spike Lee's *Do the Right Thing*, a film that, Danny thought, did a decent job of showing, through its depiction of a race riot and the circumstances that precipitated it, how people could be heroes and villains and victims, all at the same time. Danny thought about Spike Lee and other people who had faith in the potential of aggressively political art to alleviate human problems, or at least to shed light on them, and he wondered how they would have dealt with their own dads if their dads had been cutting themselves apart below their basements during their senior year of high school. Political ideals, and ideals in general, were not helping Danny.

If he finished this essay by 10 pm, which he would, Danny told himself, still sitting on the 7-Eleven linoleum tiles, he would then skateboard to Sasha's house, and climb the tree up to her room, where he would hold her, and she would hold him. They would share the box of Junior Mints, eating one mint-chocolate candy at a time. Then they would probably have slow sex during which he would tell Sasha that she had the best eyebrows, and Sasha would laugh. He would tell her that he loved her, and he would mean it. She would ask him how much. And Danny would tell her, without being able to maintain eye contact while he said it, that he loved her at least seventeen times more than he could ever love himself, which would make Sasha look at him a little funny, and ask him to fuck her as hard as he could, and Danny wouldn't say anything else. He would do what he was asked and grab her skinny arms, even though he always felt guilty and unclean after having rough sex, like he imagined what a werewolf transforming back into a man might feel like when the moon vanished at sunrise. When they finished, Danny would wrap his condom in toilet paper and put this trash into his backpack in order to hide any evidence from Sasha's dad that he had been sleeping with his daughter. Then he would pretend to fall asleep. He would leave when Sasha began to twitch and shudder, which meant that she was dreaming, probably about becoming a horse galloping through a desert of blue sand, which is what she usually dreamt about, and Danny would open the window quietly, and climb carefully back down the tree.

He would skateboard back to his house, with the roads mostly empty, so that he could make wide, flowing turns, and, if he wanted, close his eyes for brief one-second, or even two-second, intervals without worrying about being hit. At his house, he would walk down the basement steps as quietly he could, moving the cardboard boxes aside quietly, hoping to catch his dad, with his eyes open, in the act of butchering himself—he still hadn't seen his dad with a knife in his hand. But his dad would be perfectly still, as always, like a slowly diminishing Buddha. Danny would, once again, sweep the room and bring the dirty dishes back upstairs. He would scrub the toilet if there was a ring around the bowl. He would stand behind his dad. He would rub his shoulders, and then stretch his dad's arms and legs. He would watch the maggots chewing the remaining flesh from the last finger that his dad had severed, revealing the shocking whiteness of the bones beneath the tissue.

Danny would then watch his dad's closed eyes. He would study them as if they were doors to a different, more honest, and, as a consequence, more terrifying world. He would consider prying them open them with his fingers, and begging his father, again, to cease performing this awful procedure, or penance, or meditation, or whatever the fuck it was that he was doing, to stop for the sake of Danny and his sister and anyone who had ever felt any fondness for him. He would ask him to be his dad again, to try to live a normal life, even if it felt dishonest and made him miserable. Plenty of people are miserable, Danny would say, and they don't exile themselves into a secret room below the basement and cut themselves apart.

But then Danny would stop himself, realizing that it was wrong and selfish to force his dad to talk or to open his eyes. It might even be dangerous, because, by now, though Danny knew it was a silly thought, his dad's eyes might be totally empty, even of their pupils, void of everything except a light that, like the sun, was bright enough to burn Danny's hands as well as blind him, and Danny didn't want to be blind.

A middle-aged clerk tapped Danny's shoulder and asked him if he was okay. The man spoke with a heavy Chinese accent and was very tall for an Asian man—at least 6'4". Danny thought about Yao Ming, and he felt bad for the former NBA All-Star whom God hadn't blessed with durable knees. He told the clerk that he was just having a hard time deciding what candy he wanted to buy for his dad.

The clerk nodded and said, in a serious, almost meditative tone, Jolly Rancher—they very good.

Danny bought the two boxes of Junior Mints, along with the smallest available package of Jolly Ranchers. He wanted to give the clerk the impression that he had been helpful. Danny thanked the clerk and wished him a wonderful rest of his day. Then he drove home, wishing he hadn't spent the money. He needed to apply to jobs soon, or start dealing weed, which is what he would probably do. He was running out of funds.

While waiting for the stoplight on PCH and Hawthorne to change to green, Danny realized that he was resisting the impulse to speed through the intersection and meet the incoming traffic head-on. He contemplated pleasant things until this compulsion left him. He thought about how warm Sasha's mouth was and about how they both wanted, one day, to hug a koala. He thought about the only time he'd ever dunked a basketball during a Junior Varsity game. He thought about his dad ascending the ladder and then the basement stairs, with footsteps that would be lighter now that there was less of him to carry.

IN ANY LIGHT, BY ANY NAME

Alia Volz

My parents meet on a blind date in 1976. Richard with his leather cowboy hat and hand-painted jean jacket, Meridy with her purple turban and kohled eyes. He reads her aura; she reads his tarot cards. The first time they make love he has an epileptic seizure during the night and urinates in her bed. Nothing is simple.

On their third date, he takes her to an Italian restaurant in the Castro, the kind of place where "That's Amore" plays on an infinite loop. "There's something important I have to tell you," Rich says. "I am carrying a spirit-child with me, a little boy, and he's ready to be born into the here and now."

Most likely, Meridy doesn't believe him. But there is delirious magic in his way of speaking. A few weeks later, he looks into her eyes after lovemaking and says, "There. Now you're pregnant." So she is.

Rich names their unborn son Galen, after the ancient Greek physician. Meridy plays along, not questioning his intuitions. But during her pregnancy, she reads the science fiction novel *Dune*, by Frank Herbert, and secretly chooses the feminine name Alia. Just in case.

After a thirty-two-hour natural labor and an episiotomy, a baby girl is born. Rich is so shaken by this dramatic turn that he flees the hospital and debauches himself in a gay bathhouse until dawn. Then he slinks back to the postpartum room and confesses.

The birth announcements are discarded and new ones printed

with the name Alia. Meridy becomes Mom, a name she will always treasure. Richard becomes Dad, but not for long.

When I am four, Dad goes on a Native American–inspired vision quest in a terrible place called Death Valley. It feels like he's gone forever. The night he returns, I won't get off his lap no matter what. Perched on his tree-trunk thigh with his lanky arms casually locked around me, I feel safe again.

"On the seventh night of my quest the temperature dropped," he says. "I ate the last of my peyote buttons and zipped up my sleeping bag. I must have slept for a while, because I awoke during the night with stars dancing around me. It took a moment to realize that it was snow."

I have to stop him here, because I don't believe it can snow in the desert.

"Well believe it, kiddo. Hot and cold. Yin and yang. Life and death. So as I was saying, this beautiful fresh snow was falling on my face. Then up in the sky, the snowflakes suddenly came together to form the word *Firefeather*. I knew it was meant for me." He grins, his eyes brilliant. "That's why I'm here on this planet. I *am* a flame of illumination in the darkness of human consciousness."

He is not Richard anymore; he is not Dad; he is Firefeather.

I love this story! I lie in bed that night and imagine the sky sending special messages just for me. In the morning, I change my name to Fireflower. I tell everyone about it. I tell my stuffed animals and Mom.

When I tell Firefeather, his face reddens above his beard. His eyes are icicles. "You're really unbelievable, you know that?" He says this in a bad way. I tug dead skin off my lip. "You can't just copy another person's spirit name."

I hate my given name. It's too weird. Other kids make fun of me. I'd rather be Christina or Melissa. Or Fireflower, which is strange but beautiful, a name worthy of a princess. I tell him I am going to be Fireflower anyway, because that's what the sky told me.

"Naming is very serious," he says. "You have to earn it the

proper way."

I tell him I went on my own vision quest while he was gone on his. Except that on my vision quest it didn't snow. I saw my name written in the clouds, even before he saw his. I beat him to it. So there.

"This isn't a fucking game!" he roars. He yanks me over his knee and spanks my bottom. I run to my room, wailing. Mom yells at him. Her voice fills the house, and then the woods, and then the sky. They fight over my new name for a long time.

Firefeather suffers petit mal and grand mal epileptic seizures, the result of diving headlong into a shallow riverbed as a teenager. These electrical storms fry his brain, leaving him confused, sometimes delusional. Antiepileptic meds reduce the seizures, but erase swaths of memory as a side effect. Minutes and years slip into the nada. It seems random, what stays and what goes.

He's like the Winchester Mystery House, that oddball construction of walls without ceilings, stairs that lead nowhere, floors suspended in midair. His personality is intricate but the history that supports it is half missing.

Periodically, Firefeather stops taking his meds, believing they dampen his perceptions. When he wanders through the wilderness on vision quests, he does so in this unprotected state—collapsing into seizures, alone, and then awaking alone under the naming sky. He takes LSD, peyote, and psilocybin to spin out even farther.

As a child, I accept that he is seeking inspiration from Great Spirit. As an adult, I cannot fathom why he is so reckless with his brain. Or how, as he chases spiritual awareness, he fails to notice the little girl staring after him, hoping he'll come back.

Firefeather lets me tag along to water the marijuana crop deep in the woods behind our house in the Mendocino foothills. I love to visit our plants, to see the star-like green crowns swaying above my head, brushing the sky. I am five or six, and I have to scamper to keep pace with his long legs. Blond curls bounce down my back to my waist. I have freckles and snaggleteeth and my belly button is an outie, though it will soon turn inward.

We stop at the old tool shed so he can fill his water bucket. Daisies have cropped up by the spigot. I pick one for its bright-yellow face, its fuzzy greenish guts. A red-tailed hawk cries overhead. I spin the daisy in my fingers.

Firefeather stands behind me. He bends toward the severed stalk and releases a gob of spit. "O Great Spirit," he says, "thank you for this gift of beauty. I honor your creation with my water."

He takes my daisy and pushes its stem through a buttonhole in his denim shirt. He smiles at me and tips his cowboy hat. Only his pink bottom lip shows through his red beard.

I break off another daisy to keep. My spit dangles like a spider from my lip and a breeze blows it back against my shin.

He watches with blue-sky eyes. "What do we say?"

"Thank you, Great Spirit."

Arriving at the marijuana garden, we find our plants quivering under an invasion of blue-and-orange-striped caterpillars. Their gruesome, beautiful bodies spiral around stalks, hang from leaves, and writhe over one another.

Firefeather gawks in dismay, his skin rinsing pink, then white, then pink.

"Did you forget to spit?" I ask.

He dumps the wasted water on the ground and hurls the bucket against the trunk of a nearby tree. "Goddamn it! Fuck!"

I trap several wriggling bodies in my cupped hands and scurry home alone. Tiny sticky feet. Delicate bright fur. They tickle my palms until I must shriek, but I am careful not to squash them. I put my pets in a jar, adding a fistful of leaves and twigs.

"Who are you?" I ask them over and over. "Whoooooo are yooooooou?"

Firefeather undertakes several vision quests over the years, and each time he comes home altered. Once, he returns from the Shasta woods wild-eyed and trembling, claiming he's been bitten by a rattlesnake.

He rolls up his lavender bell-bottoms to show us. His calf is only scraped, the bite a hallucination. But I'm little and my acrobatic imagination sees puncture wounds, blue haloes ringing the weeping holes, his skin yellow as pork rind. I cry inconsolably, certain he's dying of snakebite before my eyes.

A lifetime of snake-infested nightmares and phobic behavior begins with this moment. My reality is made dubious by his unreality.

Tall grass whispers against my bare shoulders, shivering my spine. Walking alone, I move slowly, carefully. I pound a stick on the ground to warn snakes of my approach. Firefeather says they are more scared of me than I am of them, but that seems impossible. He also says that if I keep my eyes peeled, I'll be amazed how many live in these woods. Hundreds, thousands.

At the creek, the grass is vivid green, even in summer. The birds and I have already stripped the blackberry bushes of ripe fruit. I hope I spat enough that Great Spirit will grow more blackberries soon.

The creek bed is full of maroon and mustard rocks. They live in the water and if you make them leave, they turn dull gray and die. When I step on the board that straddles the creek, a gleaming red snake wriggles out from underneath. I scream. The birds scatter. The snake climbs onto a rock, and I realize it's only a salamander with a red stripe.

The almost-snake leaves me nervous, but I'm nearly at Wind Cloud's house. His flute rides the breeze through the eucalyptus trees, and I follow the sound. My heart trails behind like a balloon on a string.

The door of the wooden shack hangs open, the flute sings loud and clear. When he sees me, Wind Cloud lowers the instrument from his lips and smiles. He is always home when I want to visit. He's home forever.

"Well, hello, Fireflower," he says. "I thought you might come along today."

He's a real Indian. Frizzy gray hair haloes a soft face decorated with wrinkles. His chest and round belly are the color of manzanita bark. He never wears a shirt, because it's always summer at his house.

Wind Cloud sits in his wicker armchair and plays his flute. There isn't much room for me, just a tiny patch of concrete I can twirl on, if I feel like twirling. But there isn't enough space for ballet arms.

He is the only person who calls me by my spirit name, and he doesn't care if I earned it the proper way. Later that summer, we relocate to a yellow house in the middle of town. My spirit name stays out in the woods with Wind Cloud.

Mom throws a slumber party for my ninth birthday. She's recovering from a car accident, and grinds around in a wheelchair, or hobbles on crutches. Huddled in our sleeping bags, my third-grade friends and I tell ghost stories under the soft strobe of Christmas lights.

Firefeather has been upstairs for days, drawing mandalas. Mom can't climb the stairs, so there's a lot of yelling between floors. When she sends me up with messages, I find him hunched over his bright, intricate designs.

During my slumber party, Firefeather slips downstairs and out the door, telling Mom that he's going to see the Dalai Lama. The police find him thirty miles down the highway, raving, his chest bare to winter rain. He insists that the three of us—himself, Mom, and me—are reincarnations of Joseph, Mary, and baby Jesus. They wrestle him to the ground.

This is the Christmas we hide from him.

Mom and I stay with friends in a double-wide trailer across town. She explains that Firefeather has gone off his epilepsy pills and is having "one of his episodes." He isn't himself.

"Who is he, then?" I ask.

"You know how your father gets."

Hiding is like a game but not a fun one.

In January, Mom takes me back to our yellow house to exchange presents with Firefeather. I haven't seen him in three weeks, not since my birthday. Mom makes me promise not to give clues about our hiding place. Like that I'm sharing a bed with my friend Karma. Or even that there are horses in the pasture next door.

Firefeather's pale eyes stare from a naked face, no eyebrows or lashes. His chin looks vulnerable and petulant without the red beard. There's no hair on his head, chest, arms, or legs.

Plucked clean.

He watches me like I have something valuable I'm not sharing with him, like I'm hiding a key.

"Why are you wearing a dress?" I ask, as if his clothing choice is the part that doesn't make sense.

"It's a sarong."

I recognize the elephant-print piece of fabric knotted around his waist as one that usually hangs in his studio window as a curtain. Mom takes a seat on the couch, saying nothing.

"Hang on," Firefeather says, squatting to plug in the Christmas tree. "There we go."

I give him a wool sweater, which it looks like he needs. He tugs it over his bald torso, and though it doesn't match the sarong, he is more recognizable with it on.

Firefeather gives me a board game called Wildlife Adventure. The goal is to match endangered species to their natural habitats. Ibex in Ethiopia. Tapir in Malaysia. Anaconda in Venezuela.

Sitting on the floor, he reads the rules aloud from the box top, pronouncing each word precisely, in a tone and cadence I've heard my whole life. It's the same voice that used to read me *The Wonder Clock* fairy tales at bedtime. I watch the colored lights blink, and let his voice carry me back to a safer Christmas.

In the car on the way back to the trailer, Mom asks if I'm scared.

"No," I lie, hating her for making me leave him.

We never move back into the yellow house. Firefeather's

psychosis passes, but Mom says she's had enough. Our little family breaks. From then on, Christmas with my father is in January.

He tells me it's always the same. A beautiful light floats into his peripheral vision, containing all colors of the spectrum—like a mandala. When he tries to look at it directly, everything turns black, until the seizure ends and he regains consciousness. If he resists looking, Firefeather believes, he can avoid the attack. But it's too beautiful to ignore.

He says it's like looking at God.

Firefeather's obsession with mandalas blooms. He spends hundreds of hours at the drafting table with his compass, rulers, and colored pencils, producing these vivid, kaleidoscopic drawings. They plaster his walls.

Even years later, as an adult, I fail to understand what drives his hunger for the divine. Why doesn't he take the obvious hint, and stop *trying* to look at God?

I begin calling him Daddy after the divorce.

The new name is a rebellion, insisting on hyperfamiliarity when he is nowhere nearby. I am ten, eleven, twelve. It's an era of cat sweatshirts, leggings, and Keds sneakers. I live with Mom in San Francisco, while Daddy remains three hours north in the dry countryside he loves. When Mom answers the phone and says, "Oh hello, Firefeather," I cry, "*Daddy!*," screeching the word as only a prepubescent girl can.

Our visits dwindle to two or three per year. I miss him so much, I need so much of him. He complains of gas prices, car trouble, traffic. So Mom drives halfway. We do the pass off in the parking lot of a roadside diner. Gripping one parent in each hand, I force their fingers to touch.

Daddy lives alone in a loft decorated with things I remember from our former life. There is the poster of Kali the Destroyer, wearing her belt of severed human heads, blood from their ragged necks dripping down her thighs. Daddy's altar stands in a corner, his precious objects arranged in precise order on purple velvet cloth: a Tibetan singing bowl, a deck of tarot cards, an eagle feather, a Paiute ceremonial rattle. His smell has grown stronger in solitude, muskier. I inhale fierce, replenishing lungfuls of his air.

We spend these weekends sitting on the braided rug in his loft, playing cards or Wildlife Adventure. His allergies are just like my allergies; we sniffle in tandem. He gives me a cloth handkerchief for blowing my nose and says I can keep it.

The Magical Mystery Tour spins on the turntable, the song "Hello, Goodbye" bounding through the loft.

He kneels to feed a fresh log to the old-fashioned woodstove. The iron door is still open when he collapses backward and sprawls on the rug. Thinking it's a game, I pounce, diving to steal contact while he's defenseless. But he doesn't respond. He's laid out like Snow White, motionless, hands at his sides.

His fingers curl into claws. His eyes open halfway, but they are white, nobody home. There's a metallic smell, like lightning.

A wooden spoon is important, I remember that much.

I scramble for the wok, still fragrant from the savory stir-fry he made for dinner, and grab the cooking spoon smeared with tamari and juices of organic vegetables.

His arms and legs jerk spasmodically. Foam oozes from his lips. I squat beside him, gripping the spoon like a talisman that should awaken him from cursed sleep, but I don't know what to do with it. I'm crying so hard, and I can't remember how the spoon is supposed to work.

Ten minutes or ten hours later, the shaking subsides.

Blinking up at me, he slurs, "Did I have a seizure?" saliva sputtering around the words.

In slow motion, he stands and staggers out the front door. From the threshold, I see him out among the evergreens, washed blue in moonlight, breathing. The air is sharp with pine and cedar. Staring up at the sky, lips parted, he sways on his feet.

"Daddy?"

He doesn't answer. I wonder what he sees up there, what

messages he receives. I want to be out under that sky with him, to somehow sneak into his vision, but I'm afraid to move.

When he finally comes back inside, I wrap myself around him and smash my nose into his flannel shirt. He still smells like lightning, but with something toxic underneath, like burning plastic. He goes to bed early with an iced washcloth on his forehead. I lie on the floor next to him in my sleeping bag and watch shadows move across the ceiling.

The confessions begin when I'm fifteen.

"There's something important I need to tell you," he says, always that phrase. "I'm homosexual. I'm attracted to men. It's something I've struggled with for years."

"It's okay," I tell him every time. "Just be yourself."

But it's not okay with him. He gets involved with a guru who claims that homosexuality creates an imbalance of yin and yang in the world—contributing to global conflict and environmental collapse—and this makes things harder for him.

Some glitch in his seizure-burnt mind makes him forget that we've had these conversations. So he starts over from the beginning. He comes out of the closet to me at least a dozen times over the years.

It's almost funny, a good gag for a modern sitcom.

"Remember that time I left you waiting?" he says. We're in a park near the house I share with my husband. People are jogging, diddling with cell phones, bagging dog excrement.

"Oh . . . which time?"

"Ha-ha," he says—not laughing, just pronouncing the syllables.

But I'm not kidding. I've waited so many times—hundreds, thousands. I've waited for him my whole life.

"I mean the time I left you waiting outside the library. You must've been twelve. I came to the city to see you and I was supposed to pick you up to go to a museum or something. But I was like an hour and a half late. Let me tell you, you were pissed."

I don't remember this, and don't particularly want to. But like all of his confessions, this isn't for my benefit.

"Well, I want you to know that I was looking at gay porn. I'm an addict and there isn't a lot of access to gay porn where I live. Well, there is now, but there wasn't then. So every time I came to the city, I spent hours in porn shops getting my fix. I'm sorry."

I have no recollection of the library incident, though it's a believable scenario.

I'm thinking that he's a twofold asshole, first for leaving a younger me stranded on a city street, and second for telling me about it now, in the park, when all I want is to enjoy our biannual visit.

"It's really okay," I say, hoping the moment will die a natural death. "I don't even remember that day."

"I'm so sorry." He's crying. Liquid streams down his cheeks. His eyes are a washed-out blue, like gouache mixed thin with water.

I once cared too much. Now I feel almost nothing.

I feel used.

This conversation is not for my benefit.

Firefeather works in construction for a few months. One day, three coworkers approach him on a job site. I'm not there to see this, of course, but he tells me about it over the phone. The men are brown-skinned and black-haired, could easily be Latino. They wear somber expressions.

"So you're Firefeather," says one of the men.

"That's me."

"That's an Indian name, yeah? We were wondering what tribe you are. The three of us are Paiute."

"Well," Firefeather says, caught off guard, "I am a reverend in the Church of the Holy Man . . ."

"What is your *tribe*, Firefeather? Who gave you the name?"

He tells them about his vision quest, how his name came from the sky, but he feels stripped naked before these men, and does not present the story with the full detail it deserves.

"Oh I see," says the spokesman, smirking. "We were just

wondering because you don't seem like one of us."

The moment is tense, but Firefeather mumbles an awkward apology and the Paiutes back off, having made their point. Soon thereafter, he visits the DMV to relinquish his spirit name and reclaim the ordinary Anglo-Saxon handle his mother gave him.

"It was pretty embarrassing," he says when he tells me the story. "But I guess it was a lesson I had to learn."

The child who named herself Fireflower enjoys this tiny revenge.

But I also see the innocence in my father's wish to be named by nature. He is so earnest. My heart aches for him, just a little, when he's forced to abandon that dream.

I can't bring myself to call him Rich to his face, and after all this time Dad feels like a name that belongs in a different family. Mostly, I avoid calling him anything. It's amazing how easy it is to hold a conversation without using someone's name.

We've become long-distance phone friends. Four or five times a year, we chat, our conversations clotted with jokes. We both like it better this way, knowing we can hang up and return to our separate lives.

I'm sitting alone in a downtown bar, sipping a rye Manhattan, when I notice a voice mail from him. Using a goofy cartoon voice, he says, "Oh, *dear daughter*, I simply cannot *believe* you wouldn't tell your *old dad* that you're a movie star. Imagine my surprise when I'm watching a trailer for a documentary about Burning Man and there you are."

But I wasn't at Burning Man.

I return his call a few days later, and we chuckle over the blunder. "You have a doppelgänger," he says. "I could've sworn that was you."

He sends me a link to the trailer. I try to find the woman he thinks I am among the usual Burning Man images of fabric whipping in wind, art installations under construction, and dust-caked revelers wearing tutus and goggles. I spot a couple of redheads in the clip, but no one who could be me.

My father's idea of me is tenuous, at best. He's not sure what I look like, let alone what I care about, or who I am inside. I realize this will always be the case. Whereas I would know him anywhere, from any angle, in any guise, by any name.

I think back to the night of his seizure in the loft, the sharp smell of evergreens, moonbeams through tree branches. My father scanning the sky for his God. Me looking at him. I memorize the contours of his upturned face rinsed pale in moonlight.

OUTER SUNSET

Olga Zilberbourg

She shoves my wet backpack and violin case inside the apartment, but doesn't let me come inside.

"First things first, let's go get a pizza." She takes me by the hand and pulls me down the stairs and out into the street, where I just came from. "I've been dying for a pizza!"

She walks fast, so fast I have to run to keep up with her. This neighborhood certainly doesn't look like San Francisco the way I had pictured it. First of all, the rain, drizzling down as if in slow motion. I wish Clove had given me a chance to dry off the violin case, to make sure the water didn't seep through to the instrument, the only valuable thing I have in the world. But it's too late now. She runs in a mad rush past the blocks of shabby two-storied buildings with nail parlors and real estate agencies and Chinese restaurants. Where is the Bay? The ocean? The famous hills? Two liquor stores face off across the opposing street corners, and, just down the street, a plastic playground behind a metal fence. A strong whiff of fried meat comes from an open door of a Mexican restaurant.

"Tacos?" I suggest.

"No! We have to get pizza."

I've been in San Francisco for twenty minutes tops, and I'm already longing for my brother's house back in Vermont. How am I going to live in the city where there are no trees? But Clove likes it here, and there are things for me to do. I'm going to need an umbrella.

A bulky train car rattles up to us. It looks alien in this sad landscape of row houses, and when it opens its doors it hisses like a predator. Clove ignores it and keeps on running straight ahead. Finally, after a dozen or so blocks, she walks into a Domino's Pizza.

"Are you fucking kidding me?"

"What's wrong?" Clove is genuinely surprised.

"After all the places we walked by?"

"Trust me, Domino's is the best," she assures me. "I can never finish the whole pizza by myself. You have to help me."

"Yuck."

Clove hates to spend more time in the apartment than is absolutely necessary. I hated the place at first sight because it's an oppressing low-ceilinged studio, but I also can't help loving it because it's Clove's. The sole window looks out onto a nail parlor and a dingy bar across the street. But there's also plenty of sky, filled, at the moment, with heavy gray clouds. I imagine staying here, in Clove's apartment, in front of this window, and practicing my violin. Clove is skeptical.

"Six hours a day? That's a lot," she whistles. "There isn't actually a place for you to sleep."

It is a small place. Shabby carpet on the floor, uneven linoleum in the kitchenette and the bathroom. I'd decorate, hang up plants on the walls, buy a rug for the bathroom, paint the walls bright orange. But not Clove. There are no blinds on the window and the only real piece of furniture is a decrepit table in the kitchen. The door to the bathroom hangs on a broken hinge and doesn't close all the way, the only sink in the apartment and the toilet bowl are tinted deep yellow. Bras and underwear dangle on every doorknob.

The bed is a twin-size mattress sitting directly on the floor in the middle of the room. Clove got it propped up from all sides by piles of books and photocopies. The built-in closet is also devoted to the research materials for her thesis, and her clothes have been relegated to the floor between the piles. All of it, the mattress, the clothes, the stove and the mini fridge, the sink, the toilet and the bathroom floor are carpeted with the long strands of Clove's pale brown hair.

"Can I help you clean this up?"

"Bleh."

She's lying down on the bed, reading. There are no chairs in the room. I wade towards the bathroom.

"Simple sweeping could make this place habitable."

"I've got light years of reading to do, Ramsons. Don't bother me, I told you I didn't have time to entertain you."

She had invited me to move in with her. Or did I dream this?

First things first, I need a shower. Clove pulls a rag from a pile of clothes on the floor and hands it to me.

"A towel."

We're lying side by side in her tiny bed, and I can't imagine falling asleep. A street lamp is shining through the window. Every train that rolls rattling by makes me think, earthquake. Clove's breathing is heavy and uneven.

"So should we start looking for a bigger place for the two of us?"

My voice sounds too loud in this semi darkness.

She doesn't say anything and turns over on her stomach.

"Don't wake me up."

She hasn't even asked me to play anything for her today, not a single horrible Andrew Lloyd Webber song.

On the floor of Clove's apartment, inside a library book on magic realism, a handwritten note on the margin of an interlibrary loan form.

"To miss: an active, physical action requiring dedicated time and effort. I have too much to do. I cannot allow myself to get completely immersed in what has never been, and so I dream at night. My dreams—"

I have to go to the bathroom. My back hurts. I'm lying on the floor, next to the mattress, more books jabbing into my ribs and buttocks. Clove is still asleep, a strand of hair in her mouth, both hands under her cheek. The sun shines over the rooftops, but she doesn't seem to mind. Her skin is bluish-white in this light, translucent around the cheekbones. I can see the blood flowing through the veins on her neck. I sit up. Don't wake her up? But when does she get up? I have a metallic taste in my mouth. I need to pee.

The letter continues on the back of the form. Whom is she writing to? I could've written something like this, to her. She phrases things better.

"I am listening to the hip-hop music coming out of the doors of the dance club across the street, and thinking, this whole thing has gone mad, reached a feverish pitch like the synthesizers that blast into the night every time someone comes in or out. I see you everywhere. During the day, I go to the library and try to focus on work, and on my way back I walk by your house. There's usually a light in the kitchen: your wife cooking dinner? There is the phone, and at night the thought that simply calling should be out of my reach sends me crying on the floor of the shower. I've even started missing my mother sometimes late at night."

Your wife? Who is this person? I try to picture Clove crying on the floor of her shower. With all that hair and muck? Yuck!

True or false: she met me at the top of the stairs with open arms, a halo of pale brown curls in the doorframe backlit from the blind-less window.

"Ramsons!"

If true, this might mean that she had been waiting for this moment as long as I have; planning for it, dreaming—if not quite picking up her underwear off the floor. A hug is a hug, but the truth comes down to the B-flat minor inflection of her voice.

Clove eats a bowl of cornflakes while I'm practicing scales.

"Do you want some?" she offers. I need to work on my Paganini, and this requires more energy than a bowl of cereal can provide.

"I want some real food. Let's go get some pancakes and coffee, like we used to at home. There must be lots of great places for coffee around here."

"Yeah, but they are mostly overrated. You're better off with a cup of Folgers."

I can't tell if she's serious or not. She's putting on makeup in front of the small round mirror perched over the electric stove in the kitchen, and I can only see one of her eyes in the reflection.

"I have this thing at school today, and you have a choice to come or not, if you like," she says. "You might as well see the campus if you're applying to grad schools around here."

"What thing?"

"A tutoring job."

"I need to practice. I have my audition at the Conservatory coming up."

"A couple of hours won't make a difference. Come for a walk with me."

I can't resist when she's asking nicely.

"So like an hour or so?"

"Something like that. I also have to stop by my thesis advisor's office. Then I'll take you to this great diner I know. And maybe we'll go downtown. I need to pick up a book at the public library."

I have an audition at the Conservatory scheduled at the end of the week, and another one at a school across the Bay the following Monday. I need to be practicing. I should also start looking for part time gigs so that I could pay my bills. At the very least, I could be sightseeing. Instead, I'm sitting on a bench in the middle of a shabby urban college campus and staring at the sky. Just a minute ago it was sunny. Now it's cloudy again and very sad. I am hungry. I want pancakes. Where the hell is Clove?

She texts me. "Where r u?"

How am I supposed to know? Wherever the fuck she had left me.

"Meet me in an hour in the lobby of the humanities building," she writes.

Fuck that. I want pancakes.

This bulletin board is plastered with notices of people looking for places to live. There are also personal messages, all of them sad stories, without a glimmer of hope. Learn Russian from a native speaker, for $10 an hour. Have you seen my cat? Professor Green's going away party. Call Jason if you're lonely and want to talk. Out of sheer boredom, I am entering Jason's number into my phone, when suddenly I see Clove approaching down the corridor with a man. He's at least ten years older, broad shoulders and biceps. They are drinking coffee and laughing. I'm not sure if the coffee or the laughter angers me more. We were going to go out together! I'm starving.

I place myself directly into their path, but Clove stares right through me, grabs the man by the elbow and continues walking.

"Clove!"

The man stops and half turns toward me. Looks at Clove expectantly. Raises his eyebrows.

"Martin," Clove says. "Meet my friend Eva. She is visiting from Vermont."

"Are you also a kindred spirit?" The man extends his arm for a handshake and smiles. "A scholar of language and literature?"

"I am a scholar of the human soul," I say tritely. Clove gets my drift.

"She's a musician," she explains.

"Oh? What instrument do you play?"

The man's eagerness exceeds casual interest. He is already envisioning a threesome. I'm tempted to say, the skin flute, but Clove reads my mood and rushes in to prevent me from speaking my mind.

"I'm sorry, Martin," she says. "I have a lot more questions for you, but I'll have to catch you another time."

"I understand. The farewell party on Saturday. Will you still be in town, Eva? You should come."

116

I look at Clove. She leaves the man's side and pushes her coffee at my chest. "Let's go."

Last time Clove visited me back in Vermont, we spent the day apple picking and singing "Everything's Alright" and "Pilate's Dream" to baby Ella. At night, when my brother and his wife got home and we were free to do whatever we wanted, we were lying in bed together, and she was testing the sound of her name with the last name of her latest ex-boyfriend. I reminded her that the man was a low-life, smoked in bed, yelled at her for folding his clothes, so she went down the list of her previous ex-boyfriends' last names. "Clove" sounded silly with all of them, but I humored her.

"Why do girls always do this?" she asked. "I'm gonna be thirty in two years."

I didn't have an answer.

"I think it's like trying a pair of shoes that you know you could never afford to buy," was her own guess.

"Doesn't this make you angry?"

"What?"

She sighed and was quiet again. I thought she went to sleep, so I closed my eyes as well.

"Ramsons? Why don't you come to live with me in San Francisco? I get lonely on my own, and it'd do you good to move out of your brother's. We'll get a lovely apartment at the top of a hill. We can walk to the ocean every day and feed the gulls. Wouldn't you love that?"

Maybe I dreamt that.

In the morning, she is gone before I wake up. There's a note tacked to the door: "If you want to go out, the door locks automatically. I'll be home in the evening."

My first audition goes alright, but nobody's super psyched or inviting me to look into student housing right away. "You'll hear from us after we consider all other applicants."

Afterwards, I wait for Clove on the doorstep of the apartment building. At least, today it's not raining.

I'm resolved to have a heart-to-heart with her the very same night, but when she finally gets home, she's literally in tears.

"My leg hurts," she says. "Could you massage it for me, please please please?"

I can feel the tension in her muscles, the little knots underneath my fingers. She cries out with pain when I press on one of them too hard. I try to smooth it over with slow, strong movements up and down her leg.

"You're the best, Ramsons. What would I do without you?" she moans.

We eat cornflakes together and sit in bed side by side and have a lovely chat about my audition and her thesis. She tells me she's in love.

"Is this the married guy?"

"He's one of my teachers."

She won't tell me his name, but his wife's name is April.

"He is bored with April because she isn't smart enough for him, but things are good with her in bed."

"What's the attraction for you?" I have to ask.

"Oh my god, he's so hot. And everybody loves him. So we were fooling around at the bar tonight—"

"Tonight?"

"Yeah. So we're kissing and he tells me how his wife has all this experience—"

"This was just now?"

"Sure. So I said, she might have all this experience, but I possess a quality she lacks—imagination!"

Clove laughs.

"That sounds like 'The Call of the Wild' from seventh grade."

"Precisely! That's why I keep you around, Ramsons, because you remember these things. But he totally bought it. He was all like, 'you're so smart and how do you always know these things?'"

"This has just happened?"

"Yeah, sure."

"So where is he now?"

"His wife made dinner."

Right. I'm thinking of emailing my brother to see if maybe he's forgiven me for lashing out at him. He gets paid big bucks for giving people advice about how to evade their taxes, and he thinks this gives him the right to tell me what to do with my life. But at least, in his house, I had a room of my own. Supposedly in San Francisco there are opportunities for me to continue my apprenticeship in music. I feel suffocated. Maybe I came here for the wrong reasons.

She is running again. She doesn't even slow down for the red lights. When we get to the store, she picks up a bag of apples, a box of milk, and a baguette, and she's done. I browse. I select a block of cheese, a package of smoked salmon, eggs. We also need other household items like cleaning products and a vacuum cleaner.

"You're taking too long," Clove says. "I'm gonna go home. You know the address. Come back soon. I might go out later."

The nail parlor across the street is owned by a Korean woman. She stopped me on the street today to say she liked my playing.

"Your music is very sad," she says.

"I hope I'm not bothering you," I apologize.

"Oh no, no! You play great, never make any mistakes!"

My second audition goes well, but. "You'll hear from us in the spring." What did I expect? I need to start looking for wedding receptions and waitressing gigs. When Clove and I move to a bigger place, I'm going to need rent money.

When I get back to the apartment, there's a note on the door.

"I'm at Martin's. Come if you want. C."

I text her to get the address, then to get the directions. I have no key, so I can't even get upstairs to drop off my instrument. Or change. And it's starting to rain again. I take off my jacket and wrap it around the violin case.

A stranger opens the door when I show up.

"Is Clove here?"

"Yes?" the woman says tentatively. I'm apprehensive about my sopping hair, the dress clenching to my body. I hug the violin closer to my chest.

"Are you having a party? She said I should come."

She invites me in, no greeting, no smile. There's a bunch of people in the living room, a battery of wine bottles and appetizers in the kitchen. Remains of a cake, part of the edible message still intact: "Good... fessor G!" I am looking around for a safe place for my jacket and violin, but there's too much food and liquor going around. The woman gives me no time to linger. She doesn't say anything as she leads me from room to room of this labyrinthine house. I'm leaving puddles all over the hardwood floor.

We find Clove and Martin in the back room downstairs, an office or a library. There are books everywhere. Clove is spread across Martin's chest, in tears. He's got his arms around her. It's not precisely an embrace as his hands are sort of hovering half way down Clove's back. I can't tell if he's pulling her in or pushing her away.

"What's going on here?" the woman asks.

"Oh, April," Martin says. "Could you please bring Clove a glass of water?"

"How could you do this to me?" Clove sobs.

Martin smiles and pats her on the head. His other hand is stuck in a sort of half circle that terminates over Clove's butt. He puts it to the top of Clove's arm and tries to use it as leverage to move away from her. But she's is not letting him go, she holds on to him, to his loud red shirt, already wet from the shoulder down with her sobs. April makes a jerky move toward the two of them. Her face is expressionless but I imagine she wants to tear Clove's hair out.

"Could you please give us a moment?" Martin says. April shakes her head and walks past me out into the hallway, holding the door open for me. I want to know what's happening between

Clove and Martin. Is he rejecting her?

"Come grab some food," April says impatiently from the door.

I tear my eyes away from the pair in the room and go to her voice. I don't know how she can stand this. When I leave the room, April shuts the door tight behind me. "Students throw themselves at Martin all the time. He teaches Romantic literature, and it goes to their heads. He's a great teacher, you know. He was just offered a tenured position in New York City. This is a good-bye."

I stuff myself on chips and salsa and large chunks of Brie on whole grain crackers. When April emerges from the back of the house, her eyes are red and she doesn't look at me.

It's night again, and she doesn't talk to me. At all. She's lying on the bed, on her stomach, reading something on her laptop. She's working, with the occasional breaks for eBay and Facebook and chatting online with some people I don't know about things I don't understand. I'm sitting on the closed toilet seat in the bathroom. We're not talking. At 11 pm, I get a text from her: "I've got an early day tomorrow. Would you mind turning off the light? And please go to bed soon."

This morning she says, "I have to go out of town for a week. A conference. Here's the key, don't lose it. If you have to leave before I come back, drop it off in the mailbox. It was very good to see you. Come, give Clove a hug."

I'm left standing in the middle of the room, a survivor of Clove's typhoon-like packing process, low gray clouds gathering in the window. I'll check my email later in the day, to see if my brother wrote me back, if maybe he's going to let me come back to stay with him in Vermont. For now I've got to practice. I arrange my sheet music on top of a pile of books, and start from my regular scales and exercises. I can see my friend in the nail parlor across the street setting up for business. She vacuums, washes the windows, wipes all the stations with a cloth, sanitizes her instruments.

I could borrow a vacuum from her, I realize. I could get rid of all this hair. When Clove comes back, the horrible scene with her professor would be forgotten and things could go back to normal. We'd go out for pancakes together and talk about her boyfriends and books. We'd go to the mall to buy umbrellas and maybe even fresh bedsheets and towels. At night she'd finally ask me to play "Memories" or "I Don't Know How to Love Him." We would go to bed together and talk all night through and when we fell asleep everything would be alright.

This dream is not outside the realm of possibility, but I discover that I don't want to think it anymore. I'm tired of it. I give up. Clove, I think every time I hit the key of C, Clove. This town is dreary, but I've come too far and now have to last here until spring. Clove gave me a week. Maybe that's enough time to find a room of my own. As long as I get some sort of a job. Music, I think. I'll focus on my music. Daily practice leaves no room for heartbreak.

The woman across the street finishes her work and goes to the front door to flip the sign from "Closed" to "Open." She pauses in the doorframe and looks up in my direction. But I'm still doing the scales, and she is quickly bored and disappears inside her shop.

BOW AND ARROW

Seth Fischer

When my family and I pulled up to my cousin's new house in Redlands, California, he was waiting to greet us, leaning against a pickup with wheels the size of our rental car. He smiled that smile that had led him into the beds of countless women and got him out of trouble with as many cops. He looked happy to see us. He wore a tank top that put his tattoos in full show. Across his arms was a parade of swastikas, iron crosses, and skulls.

His tattoos weren't a total surprise. He had a reputation, had been flirting with Nazi ideas his whole life. We'd heard from other family members that lately the flirting had moved more toward heavy petting. But no one thought he was serious, and anyway, in my family, blood trumped everything, we always said. So there we were, in his driveway, smiling right back at him.

My stepdad and stepsister are Jewish, and I occasionally sleep with men—though at the time I wasn't out yet, even to myself. My cousin, on the other hand, was out—about his politics, his affiliations, his armor. About four years before he'd made his ties official, he showed me his first swastika tattoo. He'd carved it himself on the inside of his arm. It was all scar tissue, no ink.

"Welcome home," he said to us, arms open. Redlands wasn't home; my parents lived in Denver, my stepsister was in Eugene, and I was in college in Santa Cruz. We were here on one of our occasional pilgrimages to visit my mom's family, and this was one of the stops. My mom had been raised in Redlands, but she had gotten out, gotten a scholarship to a small liberal arts school, ended up with a PhD, and made sure I got a decent education. Her sister, my cousin's mother, had not been so lucky.

My cousin isn't a small man. He's part Samoan—an admittedly odd trait for a neo-Nazi—and a construction worker, so he's built. I looked behind him. His house looked like it'd been plopped right in the middle of a dirt lot, without so much as a rock garden.

"I did most of the work myself," he said. He couldn't wait to show us. He'd bought the house with money made from the turn-of-the-millenium construction boom. It was damn impressive for a man barely twenty-one, just a year older than I was. "It's mine," he said to us, smiling. It was impressive. The only things I owned were a desktop computer and a shitty 1984 Honda Accord that always smelled like pancakes.

As we stepped out of the car, he went right up to my stepdad and stepsister and gave them big hugs. Then he gave my mom a big hug, and saved the biggest one for me. His hugs were the kind where every muscle in the body applies just the right amount of pressure: not the too-hard man hug, or the "I'm afraid of you because you're a dude" man-pat on the back, but a real hug, the kind where you walk away feeling like you'll be all right forever as long as that person stays near you for the rest of your life.

It's a mindfuck, getting a hug like that from a Nazi.

We were blown away by how nice the house was inside. The kitchen opened up into the living room, with a single bedroom and bathroom down a hallway beyond. The house was small as McMansions go, but there was a ton of space for one person. It looked like there wasn't a single piece of furniture in that house that had cost less than a grand. The refrigerator was one of those stainless steel ones that filtered your water and was big enough to hold half a dead cow. The couch was soft to the touch, spotless, comfy, the kind you can pet. A gorgeous display case stood in the window.

We were also, of course, blown away by the three-foot-tall swastika flag on the wall, right there in the living room. My stepdad, the only one in our family who ever says what's on his mind, started to say something but stopped.

My cousin looked at him, waiting.

Then my stepdad said, "I don't know about the decoration choices, but it's nice in here."

My stepsister and mother took a seat at the table.

"Oh, that," said my cousin. Then he opened his refrigerator and looked inside. "I got Diet Dr. Pepper just for you. Still your favorite?"

"Thanks," said my stepdad.

My mother said, "I'd love one too, if you have it, with ice."

My cousin put a glass under the ice maker.

"It's so good to see you," my mom said.

"I always love seeing you guys," he said, and he meant it.

Then he looked at my stepsister and me.

"Wanna come by tonight? Having some people over."

My stepsister made an excuse, but I said, "Sure, I'd love to." He poured himself a beer while I wandered over to the display case. He'd filled it with collector's items, including old SS pins and World War II era guns and even some swastika-shaped throwing stars.

He saw me looking.

"Oh, dude," he said, looking up from his beer. "I've gotta show you something you're gonna fucking love."

"You can't show us?" said my stepdad.

"Ha!" my cousin laughed. "I don't see why not."

"Oh," said my mom. "Just leave them."

My stepdad sighed and said, "Excuuuuuse me," like Steve Martin. My cousin led me out of the kitchen and down the hall and opened the door to his room. I peeked in. The posters in his room weren't too bad. There was only one swastika, Rage Against the Machine was playing on his stereo, and all the other posters were so nondescript I can't remember them. I stepped in and he

125

shut the door behind him.

"You'll fucking love this."

He reached under his bed and pulled out a plastic tub full of weapons. There were shotguns, pistols, rifles, and semiautomatics, but the thing he loved the most, the thing he took out and showed me and made me touch, was a bow and arrow. It wasn't just any bow and arrow, though. It was what I believe is called a compound bow—like a crossbow only without the trigger. It was bigger than anything else in the box, about half my height, made of black industrial strength steel, more modern and deadly-looking than any gun I'd ever seen.

A couple years before he showed me the bow and arrow, my cousin saved my life. I was already college-bound, a junior or senior in high school. He was doing his best to show me a good time, to take me someplace I wanted to go. He found a party with a bunch of students from the University of Redlands. He drove me there and bought me beer with his fake ID and walked me in. No one seemed unhappy to see us, though no one seemed happy, either. I talked to some people. They talked to me. It was just a party. But then, as we sat there, a gawky skinny white guy wearing tiny wire-rimmed glasses came out of his room with a pistol, shouting something about bitches. He fired it into the ceiling. It was the first time I'd ever heard a gun up close, indoors, in the same room as me. I covered my ears and my head, afraid the plaster and ceiling would come down on me, but the bullets made neat holes, and there was only noise. It was a multi-story house. I had no idea if anyone lived upstairs or was upstairs. *Get out of here*, I thought, but my feet wouldn't move. "Get the fuck out, everyone," the guy said, his eyes roaming around the room so everyone got the picture.

My cousin walked right up to me and touched me on the shoulder. It was just the right amount so as not to startle me, but it was enough to get my attention. "It's time to go," he said, without any fear in his voice. There wasn't a tense muscle on him. The man fired more. It hurt my ears, but I walked out calmly, slowly, just like him, knowing my best chance here was to follow his lead. As soon as we got out the door, he said, "Run." It was three quarters of a block to his truck. He threw his door open and I threw the passenger door open and we hurled ourselves up into the impossibly high cab. We started driving forward as soon as the first squad car appeared at the end of the street. There were so many cops in a line, all going the other way, away from us.

The day after he showed me the bow and arrow, after I went and visited other family members for a bit, my mom and stepdad drove me to my cousin's house again to drop me off for his get-together. My mom gave me her cell phone—this was 1999, well before most people had cell phones—because both of us agreed it'd be a good idea, in case something happened.

My stepsister said she'd prefer not to go, but I couldn't get out of it, not without hurting my cousin. Or at least that's what I told myself. Besides, if I went, I'd be guaranteed as much booze as I wanted and a limitless supply of cigarettes. My stepdad had asked, politely, that my cousin remove the swastika flag. When we walked in, it was gone. An hour or so of polite conversation happened, and my parents made their exit, looking more confident that they weren't leaving me in the hands of someone who'd kill me. We started drinking right away. As people showed up, my cousin stopped paying so much attention to me. I slunk to the wall and watched, only talking to people when they talked to me.

There were two camps: my cousin's old friends, who dressed like him and spoke with the same southern California peak at the end of their sentences, and then his new Nazi friends, who had the same tattoos as he did but spoke in whispers and dressed in plainer clothes and had an angry confidence to them I'd only seen before among communists and fundamentalist Christians. Both crowds made each other uncomfortable. I drank as quickly as I could, hoping it would give me the guts to talk to someone, but mainly, I just stepped back and watched the two groups avoid each other. My cousin handed me a pill and I took it.

Next thing I knew, I was sipping cheap whiskey out of a bottle and standing alone next to the flag—it had somehow reappeared on the wall—when my cousin came barreling out of his room with his bow in his left hand and an arrow in his right.

By that point, we'd been drinking for hours. He put the arrow into the bow and pointed it at a black man standing in the doorway. His voice didn't slur a bit.

"No niggers," my cousin said. The man tried to say something, but he cut him off. "I said no fucking niggers."

The man was dressed preppy. He wore a nice sweater, neat slacks.

Earlier, when no one had been looking, I'd felt the fabric on the flag. It was a high-quality cotton indoor flag, sturdy and bristly and thick, like airport carpet only a little softer.

The man in the doorway instinctively put his hands up and started backing away, slowly, without sudden movement. I've never seen anyone so scared, but I'd also never before seen anyone so angry. His hands and legs shook a little, but his focus was unmistakable. His eyes were wet. He was sweating, though that might have also been from the heat. His eyes twitched in anger, and then he caught himself and stopped it, looking at the weapon.

You could see my cousin's muscles twitching through the tattoos, straining to keep the bow taut, waiting for the order from his brain to relax and release.

"What the fuck?" the black man said, his voice quivering. He spotted the flag, then me standing next to it, all blue-eyed and blonde-haired. The way his eyes were on me, I couldn't pretend this wasn't real. I was real. I was there. "Oh, no," I wanted to clarify. "I'm not one of them." Then he said, with a little more edge this time, "What the fuck?"

"No fucking niggers in my house ever again. Shit has changed."

The man backed away a little farther, yelling to remind him they'd been friends for years and that the man would remember this forever and tell his family and my family and all their mutual friends, that they'd gone to school together, that they'd played sports together, had classes together, *and they were Christians.*

"Do you understand?"

Then everyone was yelling. They'd all turned on my cousin, even the Nazis, one of whom was screaming at him, "We talked about this, man. You are becoming a fucking *liability.*" Smart politics is smart politics, I guess, no matter how evil your beliefs. But there was nothing to be done, because all my cousin had to do was let go, all he had to do was let his muscles relax and the man would be dead. There was no way to stop him now, if he did it, if he decided to, or even if his hand slipped. And as people realized this, they stopped yelling, they stopped making any noise, and they started whispering to each other, like hunters afraid to startle their prey.

My cousin stared straight ahead at the man in the doorway, right into his eyes, the arrow pointed right at the man's heart, breathing heavy enough it seemed everything else in that room was still but my cousin's chest, which was moving up and down, up and down, and the man in the door was slowly, slowly moving backward, without taking his eyes off the bow and arrow for a second.

The man finally backed far enough out the door that he could jump to the side, blocking any shot with a wall. My cousin put the weapon down unfired and yelled after him, "Never come back. Do you understand?" The man jumped in his car and sped off, yelling something I don't remember over the squeal of his tires. A woman who may or may not have been my cousin's girlfriend came up to him. "Time for bed," she said. She was pretty, drunk, Mexican. Everyone else crept out the door.

"I shoulda killed that motherfucker," my cousin said, spitting on his brand new carpet. Then he screamed out the door, "I shoulda fucking killed you, you hear me?"

The woman put her arms around him, pulling his head into her breasts. "It's okay, he's gone."

No one died, it's okay, no one died, I thought.

Then I took that bottle of whiskey and I opened my throat and I let it take me away to somewhere I'll never remember.

My I'm-not-a-Nazi credentials, aside from the bow and arrow incident with my cousin, are pretty stellar. I could list them, but I won't.

What matters is that one time, right before the start of the twenty-first century, when I was an adult, I found myself standing next to a swastika flag calmly sipping whiskey out of a bottle, watching and doing nothing as my cousin nearly killed a man for being black. I don't know how I could have, but I should've figured out a way to stop it while it was happening. Or maybe I should have had the foresight never to have been there in the first place. I should've confronted my cousin and told him I wanted nothing to do with him, while still safely in the presence of my parents. My parents—my stepdad, who at least had the presence of mind to ask my cousin to take down the flag before he would enter the house again.

But I wasn't that man yet. I drank whiskey and smoked cigarettes and spoke to no one unless they spoke to me and watched everything happen, cell phone sitting idly in my pocket, just like it was a movie, exactly as part of me knew it would. I watched the story unfold because until it got too real, it was nothing more than a story to me. I didn't know how real a story can be.

To this day, I have moments—not every day, but sometimes, maybe when I'm on a chair dusting my ceiling fan, or maybe when I'm outside hiking, marveling at how plants in California have big Dr. Seuss leaves, or maybe when I'm driving to teach a class, fiddling with the god-awful music on the radio, wishing I would remember to load my MP3s onto my phone—I'm twenty years old again, standing next to my cousin's flag, a few yards from him and his taut bow and arrow. I'm paralyzed by fear but also paralyzed by the fact that I'd been told we have the same intense eyes, that I feel guilty my mother escaped and his did not, that I bleached and spiked my hair and got a labret piercing just like him, and that, most shamefully of all, I can't stop caring for him. Then I remember the man standing in the doorway, looking at me. Through his eyes, I try to see myself: mouth agape, cowering, stumbling drunk, and Aryan—a symbol of fear, an entitled idiot. And in my paralysis, I'm a monster, a clown. A collaborator.

DAVID HASSELHOFF IS FROM BALTIMORE

Kara Vernor

You arrive finally on the California coast, and even though this is northern California, you're expecting tan, leggy blondes and barrel-chested surfers. You're expecting red swimsuits and lifeguard stations and blinding white sand. You've brought your own red swimsuit and you're expecting California to deliver.

Here's what you get instead: jagged cliffs covered in seagull shit. You get wet wind. You get big-armed bearded men who ride Harley's, and tie-dyed, wrinkled women who smell like lavender. You get a runny nose and damp feet and an icy ocean that couldn't care less about red swimsuits. It says fuck you red swimsuit, I am busy tearing at land. I will tear until I reach the Atlantic.

This is the news after 1,062 quiet miles—after one divorce, two yard sales, four months of double shifts, and a spate of Coors Light hangovers. With no idea how many hours' drive it is to palm trees, you stop at the roadhouse and get a room upstairs, #7, with a lighthouse quilt. You get shared bathrooms at the end of the hall with a basket of toiletries from previous guests. This is better than standing in a Wal-Mart in Montana choosing a brand of hairspray. Which is least likely to catch fire? You are happy not to have to decide. You are happy for leftover Aqua-net.

As a girl you stood in that Wal-Mart in Montana pulling at your mother's skirt. You watched as she set a box of Life back on the shelf, shut her eyes and breathed out, "California." You let go and tried to catch the word in your hands, tried to hold it between you like it was something you could share.

Downstairs at the bar you find a book of matches with "Mike" and a phone number penciled inside the flap. You head outside and use one of the matches to light a cigarette, a Virginia Slim, which you feel you deserve for having come a long way. You dial Mike and when he answers you say, "Convertibles."

He says, "Hello? Who's this?"

You say, "I see cars but no convertibles. I see a chapel and a feed store and a community center and three teenagers walking to the cliffs, and not a one of them is rollerblading."

He says, "You're still at the bar. Stay there, I'm coming."

He arrives and he is handsome. Blue eyes, black hair. He is a big-armed, bearded man, and he is looking for someone else. You show him the matches and ask if you'll do.

"Let's walk," he says, and the two of you head out through a field to the edge of the ocean. You tell him you are not trying to find your mother, and he shrugs like it's not for him to say. He says, "What I know is this: the bartender, from Nebraska, will let you smoke inside during the Tuesday night pool tournaments. The cook, from Kentucky, will make grits on cold days even though they're not on the menu. The taxi driver, from South Dakota, drives drunk after 7:00 pm. And I," he says, "don't know dick about surfboards, but I can mix you a margarita. I can shine your shoulders with oil."

"Nebraska?" you say. "Kentucky? South Dakota?" You say, "I'm trying to find California."

He scratches his beard. "Which is what?" he says. "Hollywood? David Hasselhoff? How about you ask him where he's from."

The non-rollerblading teenagers begin setting off fireworks, and you try to remember if today is a holiday. Mike's face turns orange, purple, white as he watches. You tell yourself you'll kiss him when the number of explosions reaches 101, the highway you're to take south in the morning. You're counting 84, 85, 86, and you're smoking faster and laughing harder and he's daring you to strip down and wade in. "Go all the way," you say, and you unbutton and unzip, push down and pull off. Mike whistles as you tramp over sand that might as well be snow, your body illuminating under the bursts. You push into that angry ocean, the cold whipping your thighs, cementing your lungs, your mouth sucking the night for air. An oncoming wave readies to bury your head, and your arms butterfly forward, your feet kick free of land.

BEDS

Cheryl Diane Kidder

MAY 1987, SAN FRANCISCO

Called in sick at work for a week straight when I first met Tony. Every day waking up in my green, geometric-patterned southwest sheets, the skin on his palms darker than my nipples. Three mornings, pure fog out the lace curtains. I'd turn over against his back and close my eyes, only him between me and the light.

If we woke up again he'd pull the sheet over his back, smiling down on me and come in without knocking. No was never a possibility. My head bent back over the edge of the mattress, upside down rocking pictures of my nightstand, then dark, then the ceiling, cracked from recent tremors, then dark. Never wanted to leave the apartment then. We brought the dishes, a big tub of butter and just-popped toast over, eat for a while, push the dishes off onto the floor and climb under the sheets again.

If I'd had a Spanish-English dictionary we never would have had to leave but finally we wanted to say things to each other beyond bodily fluid type questions that could be signed. After that, the bed just seemed cold—all the built-up heat of that week dissipated into the room, out the cracks in the windowsills, moved out to sea with the fog.

OCTOBER 1973, SAN JOSE

Comfortably worn cotton sheets on a doublewide futon the morning after my third or fourth frat party. Rick had a huge head

135

of dark hair, curly, like his moustache, and a New York accent. He'd just been through EST and we'd talked about it for hours. Wine glasses on turned-over wooden crates, a couple of beaded necklaces, an ashtray half full of his cigarettes and a roach clip. Bedspread batiked and flimsy that would get caught up between my legs.

Rick taught philosophy and was fourteen years older than me. The bedroom's wood floor was full of cardboard boxes. Maybe he'd be moving in, maybe away, depending. Had to get up early for an early class. I took longer, though his place was always so cold. I shuffled along the wood floor, collecting my things, turned the old glass door handle to go, smelled the incense we'd burned the night before.

NOVEMBER 1975, SAN JOSE

Huge stiff mattress, almost cutting into my back. Panty hose around my ankles and the soundman for that band I'd been photographing with his crooked dick, trying to find a way in. Door closed, bolted. Beyond the door, the party I'd just been at. How many drinks that time, not sure. His long hair all over my face and he's panting and pushing and I have no strength left at all.

The door opens two or three times, guys from the band, not the one I liked the looks of, only the ratty bass player and the second guitar. I can feel the hard stitches of the bedspread with my ass as he pushes me down into it. I try to clamp my knees together but his hands are claws on my thighs and I can't keep resisting. I'm wearing my favorite blue dress with the bell sleeves, very short. It's around my neck right now and I wonder if it's been ripped and if it has if I can fix it. The two guys wander back through the room and I turn my head and watch them every step of the way. When they disappear into the bathroom I think, I hope one of them can give me a ride home.

FEBRUARY 1986, SAN FRANCISCO

I figure if J.J. didn't have a waterbed this would be much easier.

I'm thinking, damn it takes him a long time and I'm thinking, if I didn't have this fucking gag reflex thing this would be a lot easier. But with J.J. I don't even have my hands free. Always on top, always kneeling between his legs, always twisting his nipples just so, both at the same time. Shit, I don't mind. Like hell I don't mind. Maybe if this didn't take so long we could go get some Chinese before everything closes.

J.J.'s from Rhode Island, from money I'm guessing. Everything in his place is just so—either black or white and chrome and glass. So modern. I hate when I get to bouncing, then I have to concentrate, relax and stop thinking such specific thoughts. Damn what I do for a hairy chest.

SUMMER 1979, SAN JOSE

Huge oak headboard with mirror, king size waterbed. Morning after a party given by KSJO and a long drive at 3 a.m. down 101 to a set of apartments that reeked of "singles." More drinking, loud music, nobody dancing, couches full. Mr. LongHair and amazing beard and I retreat to his room at the end of the hall. Going to be late for work again. Mr. LongHair obviously incapable of intelligent conversation which bothers me less the more I look around his room: beer posters on the wall, skinny blonde women in groups of three hugging each other, asses sticking out of their shorts for the camera.

This one was easy to leave. Up and over the railing, picked up pieces of last night's ensemble in each of their different landing positions. Had to side-step the huge ashtray in the middle of the floor, almost out the door, no panties, tip-toe back to the bed, slowly, carefully lift the edge of the sheet, he doesn't stir, I snatch the crumbled up puddle of black silk, stuff them into my purse and go looking for my car.

AUGUST 1976, THE LIDO, VENICE

First he had to hide me in the downstairs broom closet. When the coast was clear, we ran up the back stairs, peeped around the corner to the hallway, nobody there, three doors down, his room. It was still hot at 11p.m. even though he'd left the windows wide open. Outside the waiter's dorm, in the empty lot next door, a summer carnival: merry-go-round, booths, people in cotton dresses, children, cotton candy, music from the rides as they started up slowly and then frantically came up to speed.

He pushed me onto the top of the single bed with one hand then whipped off his shirt. His English wasn't that good and he didn't speak much. He left the lights out. Shadows and crazy blinking colored lights from the carnival played on the walls around us. There was barely room to move. The music from the carnival loud in my ears. I had to grip the sides of the bed with both hands when I screamed. He tried to put his hand over my mouth but I pushed it away and pulled him back in. Then, he just watched me for awhile and spoke to me in Italian. I was laughing too hard to hear him.

DECEMBER 1989, SAN FRANCISCO

Lots of blond hair. Ten, maybe fifteen years younger than me. Mattress on the floor of his room in the Haight. His room smaller than the closet in my studio up on Leavenworth. Every inch of wall space covered with posters and articles and record jackets. Only a stereo and the bed. Lights on, too bright, too much information, couldn't take it all in. Lights out, sit down on the bed, too close to the floor. Close my eyes. Beer buzzing in my head.

I hear the zipper on my dress being unzipped in the back. Nice vintage dress—an Ava Gardner dress, worked well for me. He sat cross-legged in front of me and pulled it down to my waist. I rolled my head back and smiled. Fucking Damien, the boss's son. Not out of jail for a week and he's already back into it. I'd always wondered about him: cute little punk would always steal money out of the front register, we'd write up slips of paper and charge them to his dad. He'd thrown my new black bra somewhere now and unzipped his pants. Damn, this was just what I needed, a huge thick dick right in front of me and me barely able to keep my eyes open. He put his hand on the back of my neck. I closed my eyes and thought of popsicles and ice cream cones and all the years I'd chased him out of the back room when I was counting out the drawers.

APRIL 1982, LOS ANGELES

Six hour drive if you go 80 most of the way only to end up at the Ramada after a training session with the married teacher puking in the shiny clean toilet. By the iridescent light of the silent alarm I could see it was only 2:38 a.m.—too late to get home to the wife, I smiled. I pulled a sheet up over my legs and turned to see what he would do next. The toilet flushed. He used my toothbrush, turned out the light slipped in next to me again. I told him I wouldn't kiss him again, he didn't care.

WINTER 1986, SAN FRANCISCO

Walking home from the Market Street trolley I made the mistake of making eye contact with a man walking toward me. I remember the exact moment and that I made a conscious decision that this time I wouldn't look back down to the pavement when I noticed a handsome man. I looked full into his face and shit if he didn't look right at me and walk right on by, smiling.

Then his arm on my elbow and his voice very close in my ear. He was Israeli. His father was a baker. He was staying with friends in the city. I took him home and he stayed with me for a month, trying to teach me Hebrew and explain things. I'd come home from work and he'd have made an elaborate dinner with pastries for dessert every night, after which he'd nearly fuck me into the ground. Truly, I did appreciate his intensity but I just didn't think I'd ever be able to learn Yiddish.

OCTOBER 1988, CHILDREN'S HOSPITAL, SAN FRANCISCO

Started out about two in the morning. Woke up with side cramps, nothing worse than period cramps really. I sat up, thought about if

I wanted to get alarmed or not. They went away. I laid back down. I'd been tired a lot lately so it was easy to go back to sleep. Tony never even woke up.

Woke up again at four a.m., in real pain now. I grabbed his arm and sat up too. He turned on the little light on the nightstand and looked at his watch with the second-hand and counted. Four minutes apart. OK. Call the doctor, get dressed, what happens next? Doctor says wait until they're about two minutes apart and call her back. I lay back in bed with my clothes on, terrified. I knew I wasn't ready for the pain part. I could sense Tony staring at the ceiling. He held my hand under the sheets and tried to be very still.

At eight a.m. we woke up again. I'd been moaning. I rolled out of bed and told him we're going to the hospital, I didn't care what the doctor said. Hospital admitted me, put me into a straight hard bed with clean worn sheets I couldn't even smell. Tony took a lot of walks. Nurses took my temperature, my blood pressure, timed the contractions. They weren't close enough together for me to stay in the hospital. Tony had to take me home again. I climbed back into my own bed, holding onto the watch, waiting for the next knock at the door.

SEPTEMBER 1994, MARIN

Insomnia every night. The bed is cold and still. I've turned up the heat to eighty-five and put on flannel. Sometimes Bill snores. I lean over, push a little on his shoulder and he rolls onto his side and stops. I roll onto my side and watch the car lights play along the closet door. The bedroom door is open so I can hear Lily if she gets up in the middle of the night. The bed's big enough for me to roll onto my back and hike up my nightgown. I'm careful to stay close to my edge of the bed and make no big movements that might wake him up.

I spread my legs thinking about bikers, or truck drivers or going for an interview with some powerful older man who has special ideas about trying out for a job. I mull over the two or three porn movies I've sneaked downstairs and paid for in the middle of the night, rehashing a few scenes over and over. After two or three times I'm finally able to drift off somewhere else, somewhere other than this bed.

OPENING RAYNAH

Lyndsey Ellis

The house was cold and damp with the heady smell of roses. Raynah wiped the dusty television with her bare hands and shaded her eyes from the early morning sun coming through the living room's thin lace curtains. She removed a blanket from the top of Sir's old recliner and hurled it over her shoulders. The cotton was still thick with his scent: aftershave, cigarettes, sweat.

"Those flowers stink," she said, scratching what looked like mustard crust off the worn fabric.

Justine flipped through a Schnuck's coupon book and ignored her from the dining room table. Her elfin frame seemed even smaller and more ridiculous in her large navy housecoat, surrounded by mounds of papers, photos and bouquets. Several rollers poked out of her matching hairnet.

To Raynah, her mother still moved like someone afraid to exist. She was like the knock-off purses sold by boosters near the defunct Northland Mall on West Florissant Avenue: stilted and tacky.

"I know you hear me over there."

Justine glanced up as she licked her thumb and turned the page.

"If all you came over here to do is complain, you can go home."

"But, this no-heat rule to preserve them makes no sense in the middle of December. Why do you always need so many?"

"Because they make me feel good. You got that ugly spread

142

on. Now, hush."

Raynah sat down and looked out the window. The tired chug of a train nearing on the tracks at the street's end, coupled with Sir's smell, pulled at her. She knew she needed to leave now or keep Justine talking. Disappearing was the better idea, but Lois was late again, and Justine still couldn't be trusted alone.

"I saw Tony the other day in The Loop."

"Why you still go down there? Don't you watch the news?"

"And see that media circus? Like Tony says, it's all a distraction. "

"Tony don't know shit. A bullet hit your ass, don't you come crying."

"There's things worse than bullets."

"When he get so militant? He was afraid to look at folks when y'all were in high school. Now, he's all Black-fist-in-the-air and whatnot. I swear both of you went to California and lost your damn minds."

"He's not militant, he's informed," Raynah corrected.

"Informed or not, leaving got him nowhere. Damn near 50 and working at some club."

"He's a café manager."

"How hard is it to boss around kids making coffee? What he get, a year's worth of free lattes for a raise? Some revolution. I bet if Pete was still—"

"For someone who doesn't keep up with people that much anymore, you know a lot about Tony."

"You brought him up, not me," said Justine. "Myrtle's the real fan of his soapbox foolishness. I guess the nuthouse'll do that to you."

She closed her coupon book. "Better start on these Thank You cards."

"You kidding?" Raynah scoffed. "It's been six months."

"Funerals come and go, but it's never too late for kindness. Plus, what'll I look like not sending folks something for attending?"

"Like any grieving widow," said Raynah.

Justine ignored her again and rummaged through papers on

the table. She folded some down the middle and tossed others in a wastebasket at her bare feet.

It was unreal, how together and beautiful her toes were. Even without polish, her nails held a natural shine. The veins underneath her skin were hardly noticeable, with no sign of corns, bunions, or hammertoes.

Good feet mean a clean house.

Justine's favorite saying drifted into Raynah's mind. She heard her mother repeat the phrase she'd grown to hate throughout her childhood. Feet weren't just a part of one's body. According to Justine, a person's feet revealed everything about their character. People with yellowing skin underneath their toenails were always uptight and stressed. People with scaly feet were unstable while people with smelly feet couldn't be trusted. People with peeling feet were irresponsible. People with calluses were vain and cared too much about others opinions. But, people with cracked heels were selfish and didn't consider others at all.

"Where's your sister?" Justine demanded, cutting the soiled edges from a battered flyer. She caught Raynah's eyes on her feet and slid them underneath her chair.

"On her way."

"Neither of you have respect. Always late. Always sassing me—"

"When'd you start talking so much?"

"There you go again." Justine scowled and pointed the tips of her scissors at Raynah.

"Put those down before you hurt yourself."

Justine reluctantly placed the scissors on the table as Lois's car crawled into the driveway. From the window, Raynah locked eyes with her sister prancing toward the house with a grocery bag at her hip. Lois looked away first, adjusting her earpiece.

"You're late again," Raynah said, opening the front door.

"There's more stuff in the trunk."

"You should've called."

"No, you should've switched shifts with me when I asked you

to. Traffic's always a mess right now."

"If you'd time yourself better, there wouldn't be an issue."

"Where do you need to be at this hour? You have a real job now?" Lois asked, marching past Raynah into the kitchen.

"That's not the fucking point, Lo," Raynah shot back, trailing her sister. "Learn to respect other people's time. Pretend I'm one of your class act clients if you have to—"

"Hey, hey, hey!"

Justine hobbled into the kitchen and clapped her hands at them the way she did when they quibbled as kids. A silver ringlet shook against her temple. "It's too damn early and nobody curses in my house but me."

"You should be proud, Mama," Lois said, putting down her grocery bag and re-curling the rogue strand of hair around Justine's roller. "This is the most she's talked to me in years. Beats watching her hole up next door all the time."

"Jealous?" Raynah asked. She pulled a gallon of milk from the bag, opened it and drank from the container.

"No one's mad you got Sir's house. It's more of a headache than a prize. You'd sell it if you knew what was good for you."

"Like hell you will," Justine blurted. "Your father would kill you both. Be a realtor out there but talk like you have some sense in here."

A twinge of glee shot through Raynah. It was just like Lois to play the good seed, forever a child rooted in Justine's approval, obsessed with keeping their relationship unstained. The rare times she was denied that privilege made life a little more bearable.

"Fine," Lois said, leaning against the sink. "Keep being stubborn. You're only hurting yourself."

"I'm not selling the house," Raynah declared. "My house."

Lois sighed warily like it grieved her to breathe. "Isha called me on the way over."

"And?"

"She was let go again."

Raynah stiffened and shifted her weight. "Did she say why?"

145

"She couldn't afford the chair rental."

"I told her Rita could use another girl," Justine said.

"Where?" Lois asked. "In that busted basement she calls a salon? Mama, no one wants what that woman's offering. She's always high and her equipment's outdated. I'm surprised she hasn't burned a hole in your scalp yet."

"Where's Isha now?" Raynah managed to keep her voice low and controlled. She reminded herself that she'd changed her mobile number days ago to avoid the nasty bill collectors. Of course her daughter wouldn't have it memorized or locked in her phone yet. It made sense for her to call her aunt first.

"She's cleaning out her station, but she should be here soon." Lois said, folding the emptied grocery bag. "You know, I understand where Isha's coming from. Customers can be wishy washy. The real estate industry's no fairytale either. Just the other day, one of my clients—"

Raynah smacked the countertop hard with her hand. The sting felt good against her palm, calming her shot nerves and silencing Lois.

"I'm going out for a smoke."

The air was eerily thick. Raynah lit her cigarette and stared across the street at the blinking Christmas lights on Ms. Myrtle's hedges. After growing bored with them, she slumped back in the folding chair on Sir's front porch and took in a cobwebbed shutter dangling from its hinges.

A knot lodged in her throat. Everything broke her heart these days. Hot water boiling. Neglected Tupperware in the alleyway. The quiet snap of dryer-tumbled linen pulling apart.

It was like being pregnant again, except all that came from it were sleepless nights spent gazing at the bathroom ceiling of her dead father's house. Sir's old room still gave her chills. The mattress in the guest bedroom had bed bugs, so she often lay awake in a peeling tub with pillows stuffed under her backside.

Although she no longer went to church regularly, Raynah

played gospel records to pass the time. Thomas A Dorsey's *Precious Lord*. Mahalia Jackson's *How I Got Over*. *The Angels Keep Watching Over Me* by Albertina Walker and the Caravans. Old songs that made her remember barefoot women in large hats and sparkling suits traipsing down the sanctuary aisles, slipping her and the other kids candy in exchange for Bible verses.

Other times, she sat in the sunroom, unraveling and re-threading the wicker in her favorite patio rocker. The stillness of those nights was gratifying. She liked being alone and sealed off from the world. She didn't have to make small talk with folks or worry about being judged. There, she was content with just being a speck at the mercy of the moon.

Next door, Lois retrieved a jumbo nail kit wrapped in a gold ribbon from the trunk of her car. She bounced across the street to Ms. Myrtle's house and placed the gift between the main entry way and the gated screen door.

"What's she going to do with that?" Raynah asked as Lois returned to their mother's driveway.

"Keep her feet clean," answered Lois, matter-of-factly.

Raynah imagined their neighbor, once a short, stocky woman in men's overalls and high heels, crouching over her bed of chrysanthemums. A 6-pack of Stag leaning against the porch's handrail to jump-start an afternoon of gossiping and people-watching with Justine.

"I know your ego keeps you busy and out of touch, so let me bring you up to speed," Raynah said, pointing to the dew-covered weeds on their neighbor's lawn. "The Ms. Myrtle you once knew is no longer. Her brain died with Pete. You do remember Pete, don't you? Or, should I break that down too?"

Lois's face twisted in disgust. Raynah watched her sister dissolve under the weight of a lost memory they shared, both of them standing among the crowd in Ms. Myrtle's yard, viewing a bloodied stretcher being pushed into an ambulance.

"So, what did you get her, Ms. Fight-The-Power?" Lois asked. "A beret? Brass knuckles? Do tell."

"You would've been better off getting her beer, is all I'm saying."

"Help me get the rest of these bags," Lois said, opening her car's back door.

"Nah, looks like you have it all together."

"What's that supposed to mean?"

"Whatever you take it to mean."

Lois sighed and closed the door, careful not to let it slam.

"Why's everything always a struggle with you? Everyone's not the enemy. You don't get points here for being the rebel."

Raynah flicked ash from her cigarette onto Sir's porch. She used a fallen branch to scratch the sock inside her shoe.

"I don't know what happened to you out there," Lois continued, staring at the patch of yard between their parents' houses. "I don't know what else to say anymore."

"You knew what to say to Tony."

"My God, Tony. That's what this is about. We have a kid together, Ray. That means, relationship or not, we're bound forever. And, if you must know, we are together again."

Raynah watched Lois's face darken with shame as she realized she was talking about Quentin in the present tense again.

"Oh, Mama will love that," said Raynah. She stood and took another long drag of her cigarette before stamping it out on the ground. "Guess you can forget about being her favorite now. I was wondering when you'd grow a spine."

Lois threw her a dirty look. "Brava, big sis. You're such the guerilla."

Raynah gave her the finger and re-entered their mother's house.

Justine, still busy with her piles of memorabilia, growled something without looking up from the mess she'd made.

"Save it, Mama," Raynah said, and went upstairs where the house was a sleepy warm but the sun less intrusive.

It had been a lifetime since she'd seen her old room. The space seemed larger and livable since Isha was there. A queen-sized bed was diagonally centered, replacing her and Lois's twin beds. The walls, no longer covered with Raynah's Roxanne Shanté posters and Lois's New Edition pinups, were bare and cream-colored. Maroon drapes hung where a frilly curtain once covered the room's only window.

Raynah eyed the flat iron station, wig stands and bags of hair weave poking out of her daughter's dresser. More shoes and purses than clothes in the half-opened closet. Goofy photo booth pictures of Isha and Quentin thumbtacked to the ceiling above the bed with the words "RIP Cousin" typed over them. A portrait of Justine posing with a teenaged Isha on the nightstand.

The photo took all the air out of Raynah. Like an injured bird, she dropped to the floor and rolled under her daughter's bed. The carpet hugging her back was snug and squishy. The darkness, humbling and unpeopled.

Times like these made her terribly miss the California she first moved to when things were good. She craved the dreamy fog and sparkling sidewalks of San Francisco. The taco trucks and hills of colorful homes in Oakland. The Pacific Ocean gleaming from the docks of the Berkeley Marina and the vast beauty of Stinson Beach.

The picture on the nightstand became St. Louis falling down on her. Fireflies lured into mason jars on humid summer nights. Cream-flavored Vess sodas at backyard barbecues. Madge, the school lunch lady who had a school lunch lady's name. The fine tang of peppermints inside pickles. Bony Tanya and thickheaded Kay, the neighborhood fraternal twins everyone called "Nobody" and "Nevermind." Secret rides down North County's haunted Bubblehead Road on Halloween nights. Family breakfast on Saturday mornings.

And Sir.

Raynah missed the way he let her call him Dad when no one was around. And reading the funnies with him on the evenings he was home. And, the random, but meaningful, advice he gave her, like to never trust folks who didn't eat everything on their plate, or to pick up loose change off the sidewalk only when the head of the coin was facing up. Their trips to the neighborhood dry cleaners owned by Sonya, the redbone divorcee, who sometimes let Sir poke her in the supply room when they thought Raynah was busy with her toys or asleep in the car.

The long waits for Sir to return home after one of his fights with Justine. Hiding her mother's good make-up to watch her fail at blotting away her bruises with cheaper brands. Glimpsing her parents' shadows heightened by the ghastly glare of their television upstairs the night Pete was found on the train tracks. The sight of them watching in the distance—safe and unaffected—as their bodies wound together in an unnatural shape against their bedroom window.

"Raynah, what are you doing?"

Isha's voice, faint and watery, travelled through the room from the opened door. Raynah pulled at the plastic on the underside of her daughter's mattress.

"Waiting for you."

"Under there?"

Bracelets jingled in the distance. A belt unfastened and shoes were being removed. Raynah caught a whiff of Isha's citrus body spray when she sat down on the bed.

"Best spot on earth," Raynah mumbled.

"You're gonna hate me today."

"Why?"

The bed groaned as Isha rolled across the middle of it.

"They canned me. I'm fucked unless I find another chair to rent."

"Watch your mouth."

"You curse in front of Granny all the time."

"That's different."

"How?"

"Because it is."

Raynah sensed the protest in her daughter's silence. She held in a chuckle, relieved to have her face concealed by the bed.

"You'll manage," she continued.

Raynah pushed her palms into the underside of the mattress, relying on the foam between them to comfort Isha.

"You miss Sir?"

"Not really," Raynah lied. "Why does she let you call him that?"

"Same reason you called him that."

"I called him that because he made me."

The darkness under the bed thickened and pressed against Raynah. She felt queasy with embarrassment, competing for a dead man's affections. Possessive over her father's tenderness, as well as his tyranny: two pasts that co-existed, tangling around her like willful vines.

Had she ever felt that way about Douglass? It was hard to say. She couldn't recall the things that mattered, like the first time she'd slept with him, or who said they loved the other first. Raynah only saw Oakland's main library's security guard-turned-druggie with the moon's honey glow in his eyes. And, things like his crooked lip leaving spit on cups after he drank from them. The Raiders Starter jacket that he always wore but never washed. A crack pipe crunching underneath his Chucks, and the newish smell of an infant's furniture smothering their apartment after he pawned the gifts from the surprise baby shower he'd thrown for her. She'd walk by dog shit on the road and see herself removing soiled sheets when their bed became his tomb.

"Guess what your auntie gave Ms. Myrtle for Christmas?" she asked Isha.

"Business cards and a copy of her billboard ad."

"Good one. Try a big ass nail filing kit."

"No way. With a clipper and everything? Should she even be allowed near sharp objects now?"

"Guess we'll find out."

The bed squealed as Isha hung upside down to look at Raynah underneath the bed. Save for her sculptured eyebrows and lip ring, she was morbidly youthful, forever trapped inside the body of a five-year-old girl with malnourished bones, dimpled cheeks and begging eyes alongside the Greyhound desk attendant prying her away from Raynah at the bus station.

At the time, Raynah convinced herself she was doing the right thing. She was tired, broke, and half-crazy from surviving. A young single parent burned by a damning system. She'd become a community caregiver and activist driven by adopted beliefs in social justice that, in turn, denied her what she was fighting for on the basis of what was, or wasn't, between her legs.

As the need for collective progress became a priority, Raynah and her circle of organizers gave up on raising families. A whole culture was disintegrating before everyone's eyes, and they were hungry idealists determined to fight the world's evils. Children were an indirect threat, a dangerous distraction like the crack epidemic. Sacrificing motherhood felt appropriate, like pushing kids out to go play while one disinfected the house.

But giving up Isha was like accidentally drowning in a fountain. What was meant to be noble and cleansing had turned into a laughable disaster that would take more than death to live down. There wasn't any perfect way to cope, so the cutting began. Raynah was deliberate, but careful. To avoid questions, she endured socks throughout the Bay's grueling Indian summers. She never treaded too close to the mystery of veins beneath the skin, instead favoring quick, little slices along the sides of her forefeet. Tiny gashes that kept her chest from breaking open every time she thought about Isha.

"I could've done her nails and her hair," Isha continued.

"Let's go eat," Raynah announced, changing the subject. Her body had grown sore from being squashed against the floor too long. "And, you should stay next door tonight."

"With you?"

Isha's question was a statement reeking with an unworldly kindness that made Raynah sick with gratitude. As guarded as her daughter was, she never seemed bitter. If anything, their way with each other now was cold and awkward.

They didn't touch each other much. Raynah let her eyes do all the hugging and cuddling. She greedily tried to relearn every line in Isha's face, recall every strand of hair on her head. Sometimes she caught Isha doing the same thing, stealing narrow glances of her, eager to re-piece together in her mind parts of Raynah that had been eroded by time and distance.

"Yeah, is that so bad?" Raynah asked. "I'll even let you do my eyebrows."

"Depends. You paying?"

"Girl, stop."

Lois's eggs were runny with bits of shell stuck inside them. Raynah ate in silence, too hungry to complain. A jarring calmness came over her as she snatched glimpses of Isha spitting the white flecks into her napkin and listened to Justine rant about who wasn't getting one of her Thank You cards.

After breakfast, Raynah helped clear the table and left Lois washing the dishes in the kitchen. She retired to the living room, carefully slid out of her shoes, and lay opposite Justine on the sofa.

"Where's your glasses, Mama?"

"Don't know again," Justine replied. "Remind yourself never to get old," she added, winking at Isha.

"You're not old, Granny," Isha said.

"Don't lie to her," muttered Raynah.

She tried to spread the blanket from Sir's chair across both her and Justine's legs, but her mother playfully snatched it from one of Raynah's legs and yanked off her sock. Sunlight spilled across her hardened sole and the jagged scars along her foot.

"Isha, what y'all do upstairs?" Justine asked, her eyes holding Raynah's as a wan smile settled on her thin lips. "Your Mama's acting less the devil." She sniffed Raynah's exposed foot and let it drop into her lap. "Well, at least I can trust you."

Returning the smile, Raynah grabbed one of Justine's ankles and tickled the soft heel, watching her mother squirm and laugh and curse but never pull away

LOST HORSE MINE

Kate Folk

Kara's therapist observes that Kara seems more interested in playing games than in making real connections with people. Kara has spent most of their session talking about the man she had sex with last Friday. She hopes he will text her though she doesn't much like him. The therapist's office is thickly heated. Beside Kara, a tissue blooms from its box like a fragile white flame. Wind lashes the second story window. For weeks people have been talking about the storm predicted to begin tonight. It is being called the storm of the decade. Public schools have already called off tomorrow.

The session ends. Kara hands her therapist a check for $130.

At dawn Kara wakes to find her power has gone out in the storm. She picks her way along the dark hallway to check her mail. Her neighbor stands in his open doorway, an old Russian man wearing boxer shorts and a stained white undershirt. His dim eyes peruse Kara's body as she passes. The hall flickers and lurches.

Kara has received a package from a friend whose wedding she attended in May. In her dead apartment she opens the envelope. Matte finish prints from the wedding photographer. She and the other bridesmaids wore peacock green dresses from J. Crew. Looking at the photos, Kara wonders why no one told her to put on a bra.

The bride was Kara's best friend from high school, the groom Kara's friend from college. Kara introduced them when they were all living in Brooklyn. The wedding was in Palm Springs. The day before the ceremony, members of the wedding party stood in a crowded pool at the Ace Hotel drinking cocktails and batting at an inflated ball. The unattached bridesmaids took turns flirting with the groomsman who wore yellow swimming trunks. Kara didn't mention her boyfriend back home, who was five years younger than Kara. She had hired him to cat-sit the previous Thanksgiving, and he simply stayed. He washed the dishes; he made the bed; he took her car to have its brakes replaced.

Because her dress was the only one with pockets, Kara was charged with holding the vows. At the start of the reception, Kara and the other bridesmaids were expected to dance on a stage for the assembled guests. Kara had not been warned of this duty. She danced with grim abandon, the way she might fling herself into a body of water she suspected to be very cold.

The next day, her duties finished, Kara rented a car at the airport and drove to Joshua Tree. The Nissan felt like a flimsy toy, buffeted by high winds on the desert highway. She had rented a corrugated cabin on the property of a middle-aged couple. The key was left for her under a pyramidal rock. The owner approached while Kara struggled with the latch of the screen door. He was a sturdy bald man who said he'd moved to the desert because he didn't care for California politics. His wife would come by when she got home. She liked to meet all of their guests.

Kara tried to nap. When the bell rang, she didn't get up, reasoning that for all the owners knew, she was asleep. The wife rang the little bell twice. Then she gave up and went away. Kara felt guilty and relieved.

That night Kara drove to an open mike at a western-themed bar and grill. Dozens of musicians performed three songs each. A gray-haired man sat with her. He was from LA and had come to intercept a guitar from another man. He didn't know what the man looked like, but he knew the guitar. The guitar never appeared, so the man played a set with an acoustic spare. An old man with a lush white beard drifted over to Kara. He said his name was Sequoia and that she had beautiful eyes. On the drive back to the cabin, Kara buzzed with the vibrancy of this small, strange community. She tried to call her boyfriend to tell him about her night, but service was spotty and the call didn't connect.

In the morning Kara went to the national park. She took selfies with a backdrop of precariously stacked red rocks. She sent one to her boyfriend. He replied, after four hours, "lol."

She had brought a guidebook from the cabin and consulted it to find a hike. The guidebook recommended the Lost Horse Mine loop. Kara imagined a horse trapped in a narrow underground passage. The horse would pick its way through the mine, startled by dirt crumbling from the walls. It would grow thinner; its eyes would dim. Eventually it would succumb to the mine. This made Kara so depressed that she bypassed the mine at the fork. She wound through the hills instead, muted vistas that yielded after several miles to sand and gnarled Joshua trees. She took more selfies.

The next day Kara drove to San Diego to visit her friend, who worked as a public defender in El Cajon. They went to the beach, where Kara ate a taco and she and the lawyer discussed the relationships they wanted to escape. That night, the lawyer's air mattress wouldn't inflate. They searched for a store that sold air mattresses, but it was after eleven and everything was closed. The lawyer had to get up early. They shared his bed, sleeping head to foot under different blankets.

The lawyer was gone when Kara woke. She showered in his unclean bathroom. Once she had packed her things and driven away, Kara worried she'd left a pair of lacy thong underwear in his room. She pulled into a gas station and tore through her bag. The thong was there after all.

As she waited for her flight Kara and her boyfriend texted about where they would go for dinner. Kara's boyfriend expressed anxiety over money. The terminal was overly air-conditioned; Kara dug in her backpack for a sweatshirt. At the top of her backpack sat the present she'd gotten her boyfriend, a tiny plant called African Pearls, wrapped in red tissue. The plant comprised dark spiny growths that ended in searching, beaklike mouths. Kara chose it because its label said it didn't need much sunlight or water.

When he picked her up Kara saw that the boyfriend had gelled his hair. She placed her hand on the lacquered swell and he swatted it away, inferring criticism. They ate at no special place, a dumpling house on the way home. The restaurant was closing soon and Kara and her boyfriend were not wanted. She had thought she wouldn't tell him she'd slept in the lawyer's bed, but she found herself doing so immediately. Her boyfriend asked, with hostile indifference, if they'd fooled around. Kara feigned outrage. How could he think such a thing? Because you don't like me very much, her boyfriend said. The waiter forgot their garlic pea shoots.

Kara cleans kitchen grout by storm-filtered daylight. Night is falling and she still has no power. Rain continues to pour. Downtown has flooded. The African Pearls sit on the sill under rattling glass. Kara's ex-boyfriend didn't take the plant with him to Portland. Kara keeps forgetting to water it. She is not sure whether it's worth keeping alive.

Last Friday, before they had sex, the man had asked Kara if she bruised easily. She wasn't sure of the truth, so she guessed at the answer he wanted.

Kara moves a wad of damp paper towel over the white tiles. She considers watering the African Pearls. Instead, she lights a candle and carries it into the deepening gloom of her bedroom, where the ceiling has started to leak.

SUMMER

Zoë Ruiz

1

We are in a drought but I decide to run a bath because the water will warm my body, melt away the stiffness in my joints. Sometimes a bath is the only way I know how to relax and when I allow myself to relax, energy slowly, ever so slowly, comes back to me. As the water fills the tub, I hold a bottle of eucalyptus oil upside down and the oil comes out, drop by drop, into the water. It is invigorating, this scent that I know so well because the land is filled with eucalyptus trees. I take off my shirt and shorts and immerse my body in water. In the west, where I am from, where I have been through droughts, through long dry days and nights, I am wanting water always. Hot showers, long baths, jacuzzis, pools. When I step out of the bath, I dry my skin with a towel, rub eucalyptus lotion into my damp skin, and put on black shorts and a brown shirt. I walk back into the living room and open the front door and see the patio is wet. I think, *A neighbor has watered the lawn,* but then I see the road is wet, too, and then I notice it is raining. It takes me so long to even recognize it. *Rain,* I think and almost say the word aloud. The word is on my lips, like the name of an old friend.

2

I am thinking of a woman and I want to tell her how I am used to being unlikable. Some people like me, some people don't, and I don't much care either way. I want to tell her I am a landscape,

I am desert. *Think of me as desert,* I tell her in this imaginary conversation. As if that explains everything. She will have to see past my personality to the place my spirit resides but she is not concerned with the spirit so she will be like people and people see me as pretty and nice, at least at first. I could tell you a lot about people, actually, and I will, but not today. Today I am silent. Today I say nothing but something is stirring inside. *You see,* I tell her. *It's the cold desert winds picking up speed.*

3

They leave on summer trips with their spouses, with their families, and when they are gone, I watch their pets and their gardens. The main rule is to care and love their homes while leaving no trace of myself.

4

None of these letters will have my name, I think, and stop looking through the mail, open the door, and place the envelopes in a basket. For a moment, I think housesitting is similar to ghosting, that I am not caring for the empty house, I am haunting it, but, of course, a woman who is haunted would believe such a thing.

5

I look up at the sky. The clouds are everywhere. They are grey and blue and look heavy. It will rain again soon. Late that night, I am unable to sleep, lying in an unfamiliar bed with the windows open. The bedroom faces the street and I can hear everything: cars and voices and animals. It is late and the air is still hot, still humid, and then I hear the rain. I close my eyes and listen as the water falls on the ground.

6

I am about to burst, she says, but the baby will not leave her belly. She had a doctor's appointment. *They want to induce labor. I want to wait.* She waits. *I have another doctor's appointment,* she says. *I live here now.*

After the appointment, she says, *They scared me into it.* Something about low fluid levels. *Tomorrow. 8 a.m.* Her water will not break suddenly, the beginning will not be a surprise. She knows the exact hour she will begin to birth her daughter.

7

Here is a memory I will allow myself to recall. Here is a memory I will allow you to know. I stand in a driveway composed of small rocks, and my palms are open, facing upward as I look at the grey sky. Big drops of rain fall on my small hands, on my bare shoulders, on the smooth rocks. It is raining and it is warm. Warm Rain. I am surprised, I am fascinated, and want to share my discovery with my family.

8

I'm not used to the humidity here and I want it to pass. I want the summer to be hot and dry, to be like the west, but this summer refuses and instead is like back east. I try not to feel the wet heat, try not to see how it changes the landscape here. I shut myself indoors, turn on the fan. In the car, driving on the freeway, I place the air conditioning on full blast. I become angry if a cafe or bar or any public place isn't filled with cool air. My body tenses, my thoughts are irritable, and when I leave these places, I promise never to return.

9

I sit outside on the balcony and read a book and pretend we had enough rain and the humidity has passed, but the sky is grey and the air is thick with heat and moisture. The weather reminds my body and my body remembers and my mind allows the memories or doesn't. I am here in California, reading a book and drinking a cup of coffee on the balcony and I am in Connecticut, a young girl, standing in the driveway, surprised by warm rain. I can remember or not remember. I can be in two places at once. In one moment, I can desire two opposing things. In one moment, I can believe

160

two contradictory ideas. Call it what you want: doublethink, trauma response, emotional intelligence, being human. Naming it doesn't change what is happening.

10

I look at the land, at the grey sky, at the palm leaves hanging limp and slowly moving side to side. This summer, the land is dry and bare, the ground wants water. This summer, the air is wet and moist but there is little rain, little release. This morning, my spirit is a desert. This morning, my body is menstruating, emptying itself out, but I feel swollen and heavy.

ONE END AND AIM

Ashton Politanoff

Jack didn't come for the gas, he came for the food.

He waited for the two attendants behind the glass to make their move.

Well? he asked.

Please scan your items, sir, said the attendant closest to the register.

Next to Jack was a Snickers, a bag of peanut M&M's, and a Coke.

Scan my items? Why don't you scan them?

I can't, sir. The scanner is next to you.

Are you going to pay me then?

What's that, sir?

I'm not doing your job unless you pay me.

It's not my job, sir.

What's *he* doing? Jack said, pointing at the other attendant.

Outside, lines of cars were waiting to fill up. Jack had left his lavender Mercedes parked at one of the pumps for the convenience of it.

As if on cue, the other attendant exited the bulletproof enclosure.

Here's the scanner, sir, the other attendant said, turning the scanner in its holder slightly, so the red light faced Jack directly. The other attendant returned to his post behind the glass.

I don't work here, Jack said.

Please, sir, the first attendant said.

Nope, Jack said, leaving his items. I don't work here.

Jack drove down Hawthorne Boulevard with one arm around the empty passenger seat.

When Jack arrived at the liquor store, there was a sign on the door written in sharpie: back in three short minutes. A mechanic stood in the lot waiting. Jack got out and set the timer on his phone. A car with a couple pulled up. They saw the sign too and remained in the car.

He's probably taking a shit, the mechanic said to Jack.

Jack looked at the timer. He's got one minute left, he said.

Time's up, Jack said.

At the next liquor store, the owner was present behind the counter. Jack inspected the bottled waters, the sodas, the beers.

Could I interest you in some beer from Ireland? the owner asked, coming over to Jack.

Will I be speaking Gaelic after I drink it? Jack asked. The owner laughed, backing off.

Take a look around, the owner said. Take your time.

Jack found a lone banana by the register, bright and yellow, and held it up to the owner.

Tell me about this banana, Jack said.

That's a perfectly good banana, the owner said.

Where'd you get it?

I promise you will like it.

That doesn't answer my question.

Why does the origin of this banana interest you?

Because I want to open a banana stand.

Jack dropped the banana and pulled his car keys out of his pocket.

Wait, the owner said. How about I let you eat the banana, free of charge. If you're not satisfied, you don't have to pay.

Jack took the banana and unpeeled it. He took a bite, then took several more until all that remained was the peel itself. He tossed the peel to the owner and drove home.

The first thing he did was check the refrigerator in the garage, his options. There was one beer left and parsley that had gone brown. The refrigerator in the kitchen had old orange juice. He kept it in there. Finally, he called his wife.

I took the trash out, cleaned the dishes, coiled the hose, he said. I've been working on myself.

THE DAY

Barbara Jane Reyes

two fingers on a pulse like the true point
— Angela Narciso Torres

gloss of feathers dimmed in the orange quiescence of the sun
— Lehua Taitano

a damaged beauty, a music I can't manage, no words
— Urayoán Noel

645 am. The very last meal I had with my father was arroz negro y petrale sole paella, fideua caldosa, pork bellies, okra, and a bourbon elderflower cocktail, in Uptown Oakland at Duende. Four days later, his brain got lost in language. *No words.* His body forgot how to walk and how to swallow. His lungs decided to stop taking air. He never came home. He is on my mind when I go to sleep. He is on my mind when I wake up.

836 am. At the AC Transit 26 bus stop, I am late to my day job. Morning commute reminds me of my father, coconut oil slicked hair behind his ears, duck tail in the back. He ironed the creases in his slacks. He left the house with Ralph Lauren Polo aftershave on his collar. He clipped his Bechtel badge to his pocket protector. Protractor, mechanical pencils, drafting tools arranged within reach, thermos of coffee in his DYMO labeled briefcase, ten-speed bike to Union City BART station. That was before coconut oil became trendy. That was before the layoffs and unemployment checks. After this, combing his hair became a chore.

902 am. Lehua told me that daughters stolen from their homelands do not lose their power. Their tongues, their palates adapt. New roots and unbloomed buds — bullets — become new spells, new medicine. You do not get lost on an island. You take pieces of it — shell, sand, seed — with you when you must take flight. Jelly jars, perfume vials, Tupperware, Ziploc bags, use what you've got.

1021 am. This is when I learned that if you present at the pharmacy early to purchase your DEA-regulated allotment of pseudophedrine, the pharmacy staff will eye you, speak to you like you are a meth head and a fucking criminal. #FML

1050 am. "Izabel Laxamana, a 13-year-old girl in Tacoma, Washington died by suicide after jumping off a highway overpass on Friday, May 29. Days before, Laxamana's father … had reportedly punished her for an unspecified transgression by cutting off her hair and uploading a video to YouTube."

1127 am. I belong in this fluorescent-lit cubicle. The privilege of the fluorescent-lit cubicle, where I thumb through thousand-page, spiral-bound indexes. According to the International Classification of Diseases (ICD-10-CM), F43.20, Adjustment Disorder, Unspecified, includes culture shock, grief reaction, and nostalgia. To be a Pinay daughter is classifiable, diagnosable, reimbursable with the proper documentation. It is a disorder. It requires professional intervention. It may require a prescription. To be a Pinay daughter may be covered by your managed care plan. To be a Pinay daughter should be covered by Obamacare. Please consult your manual.

1153 am. Filipino writers on social media asking me why I must write about Filipino things. Don't I fear being seen only as a

Filipino writer. Won't I just write about normal things, universal human truths, love and whatnot. Won't I read the important books they say they intend to write. For sake of bayanihan, won't I hook up a fellow Filipino, introduce them to my non-Filipino publishers.

1214 pm. There are ladybugs on my father's grave.

220 pm. You're all girls? You don't have any brothers? Your poor father. How awful that must have been for him. Your mother never gave him any sons.

222 pm. My sisters and I all kept our father's name.

303 pm. I must tell you that first time I heard Prince's "Controversy," was on KDIA 1310 am in 1981. I was 10, dancing and tingling. I'd never heard anything like this, falsetto, synth, electric guitar, and liminality. Because of KDIA, I know that the following year, The Gap Band dropped *Gap Band IV*. My older sister owned it on vinyl, 33-⅓, gatefold LP. It is a perfect album. Let no one tell you different.

432 pm. I am tired of talking about talking about race. These are the facts: I was born on the same island where my mother was born, where my father was born. Where my mother's mother, and my mother's father, where my father's mother, and my father's father were born. Go back many more generations, and you will find our birthplaces are that very same island. *The true point* should not be why I write this, but how, in whose tongues.

435 pm. You do not get lost on an island.

502 pm. *Two fingers on a pulse.* He was still, breathing when I left his room. He was, and one by one they were wheeling away machines. The blipping monitor told me what my hands felt still. He was warm. He was 73. He was a tough motherfucker, stubborn enough to live to 100, so that he could grumble and elbow us, so that he could give us mad side eye. Instead, just hum and blip. Hum and blip. *A music I can't manage.* Exhale. *No words.*

524 pm. Sometimes you are damaged. You think poetry will repair you. You think poetry should repair you. You shake your fist at it when it doesn't. You walk hand-in-hand with your damage, into the world. You do not speak. You are surprised when people register you are there.

551 pm. Sometimes I can snap out of invisibility. On 8th and Broadway, Marshawn Lynch and I make eye contact. I refrain from telling him that it's my birthday, and may I please take a selfie with him. Why can't this interaction have happened with Draymond Green instead. #oaktown #DubNation

621 pm. There is no printed news story I can find about Norife Herrera Jones, that does not emphasize her dismemberment, and the esteemed alma mater of her estranged 74-year old white husband, her murderer.

753 pm. You don't have kids? Why don't you have kids? You should have kids. How terrible it must be for your husband. You should give your husband kids. You are a bad wife. How terrible it must be for your parents. You should give your parents grandkids. You are a bad daughter.

802 pm. Think Tatsuya Nakadai in *Harakiri,* unleashing his no fucks left to give, one man wrecking machine on an entire estate of samurai turned peacetime paper pushers. Dying of boredom and leisure time. The rōnin Nakadai thrusting his katana through hollow armour, keeping it real.

903 pm. *On a pulse* that stopped. The breathing stopped. He was warm, but the breathing stopped. Now he *flies to greet my ancestors,* *gloss of feathers dimmed in the orange quiescence of the sun there is no need now* for sublingual drops of morphine, for the sleep that let him slip away from us.

905 pm. *I can't manage, no words.*

911 pm. Sometimes you are broken. Poetry won't fix you. Poetry can't fix you. It doesn't have lungs to give you its air. It doesn't have hands to stitch your parts back together. To make you tea. To drive you home.

949 pm. Death row prisoner and human trafficking victim Mary Jane Veloso celebrates women's rights with a prison fashion show. Veloso has just modeled a sheer, embroidered sheath dress at Wirogunan Prison. On death row. Curlicues and up-do, perfect eyebrows and pearl manicure. Always a breath away from the firing squad.

1026 pm. My #WCW Pia Alonzo Wurtzbach's Instagram tells me that she has just learned the proper mechanics of the fast ball. Noah Syndergaard taught her this, for Filipino Heritage Night at Citi Field. In my perfect world, Pia would throw out the first pitch at AT+T Park. Tim Lincecum would still be our ace. He would be the one to teach her how to throw, even though Timmy's "The Freak." Arnel Pineda would sing, "Lights," in the middle of the eighth. All the starstruck Filipinos in the house would radiate so much light, we'd be the fucking Maharlika Nebula Supernova of San Francisco.

1155 pm. I remember holding the dove's warmth in my palms. I was still, it was still, it was waiting for me to unlace my fingers. There, the horizon above a young oak tree, mustard flowers, poppies, and autumn snails, the dove's gentle bones pushed off my palms, into *the orange quiescence of the sun.* This is how I said good-bye to my father — shouting his name at the sky.

169

1157 pm. I sometimes remember to floss. I always wear socks to bed, even in the summertime. I sometimes build a pillow fort. I always think about that day. That with my mother's permission, they wheeled my father out of the hospital covered in a velvet shroud. That I could not sleep for a long time. That I would not close my eyes. That every night noise might have been him visiting me.

CRAFTSMAN KID

Rebecca Baumann

My hands sloshed in wet spaghetti as my fingers dipped in and out of the sink drain. This was the worst part of dinner cleanup.

"What the hell are you doing?" Tina asked.

"Uh, cleaning the sink?"

"Why? That's disgusting!"

"So you just want it to clog?"

"Just use the garbage disposal."

"The what?"

Tina flipped a small switch on the right side of her subway-tiled counter and a sharp grinding noise cut through the sound of water over pots and pans. I jumped back, slinging lukewarm food mush all over the wall.

"Damnit! Seriously?" Tina bent down to towel up my mess as I fed the disposal some test morsels. Drop. Slurp. Drop. Slurp. The contraption was fascinating, although Tina was not amused.

This wasn't the first appliance escapade I had in my visits to different homes. Most of my friends were used to questions on how to use each new thing. Every room had a new experience, the bathroom a shower-tub, the kitchen a tea- and coffeemaker, and everything was automated. The modern era seemed hellbent on two-in-one, no-hassle contraptions. My friends found my attempts at most of these appliances downright rib-tickling. Without childhood experiences of using technology in newer homes, Craftsman kids have to learn slowly, through the humbling experience of trial and error.

I grew up in a place where a drain was a drain, fire was warmth, open doors our air-conditioning, and play was always outside. My family did make some modern purchases when they first bought our home in the Citrus District of San Dimas for $40,000, including a small, dial-turn television. The shingles were worn, paint gone, and windows boarded up, but I can still hear the faint laugh tracks from re-runs of *I Dream of Jeannie* playing in the background during our long nights of involved DIY renovations and repairs. At the age of six, I was put to work painting doors, staining beams, and trying my hand at paper-sanding the architecture that surrounded me. At the time my parents were preparing for a period renovation of the Old West Craftsman that carries on to this day. Each month they saved just enough to fix one portion of the home. We grew together.

Before our finances allowed automated indoor cooling, I woke one morning to a fresh summer breeze that had pushed through the rippled hand-poured windows, swinging them open in a flurry. The entire hallway was covered in cotton sheets, billowing and whipping. It was painting day, and at eight years old I could find no better way to spend an early Saturday. We sanded softly, careful to preserve the undercoating of lath and plaster that kept the house cool in summer. For sills and doorframes I painted with a medium-bristle brush, as recommended by the historians we had consulted, meticulously tracing the direction of the grain in the wall. The milk-white coating against black-varnished beams reflected the paint splatters on our '90s denim and sneakers.

As the last of the walls were coated for summer, I thought back to the first family that may have built the home, back when the town was called Mud Springs. The father must have been a citrus farmer who traveled to the new area to start his own orange grove. At the turn of the twentieth century, the east-most part of Los Angeles county was one of the biggest citrus industries in the United States, and produced a quality fruit competitive to Spain's world-renowned *naranjas*. As he traveled horse and wagon down the rolling foothills that would later become Arrow Highway, I imagined him thumbing through a dusty copy of a Sears catalog, choosing a house to mail-order.

One of my favorite childhood toys in our Craftsman was the original horse tie pinned into the earth almost thirty feet from the side entrance. It sat just an inch around, almost three feet high, with one humble loop at the top through which visitors would knot their horses' leads during a visit for tea or business. We would rope strings around it and try our best to pull it from the ground, winding round and round it and falling into the hard dirt, bruised and laughing with rust on our palms. As my dad became fearful of the abrasive edges the tie had accumulated over the century, he too attempted to pull it from the ground. He pulled alone, we pulled together, the local tow truck even had a run at it. The tie wouldn't budge. I knew then that the man who built this home had wanted it there. It was his grove, his business, his home, and when I brush my palm against the tie's scratchy surface, I'm transported to lazy afternoons of slick green leaves and bright cream-orange blossoms, where a shaggy gelding rests patiently on his haunches in the afternoon heat.

The town has always been horse-driven, even before it was mapped in 1887. To this day, the city has multiple equestrian centers, livestock land, and an annual rodeo in October. The name itself even comes from horses, I learned as a teenager during long days as a show groom at Horse Thief Canyon Equestrian Center. I would work weekend horse shows shining boots, exercising mounts, and listening to the historic stories my trainer would regale on the short breaks between each competition. Each piece was rich, and as I watched these one-ton beasts canter, their coats white with the salt and sweat of competition, I was reminded that this town was built on work. Our home was created to keep horses for farming the groves of citrus more efficiently— long before my stable was built to board them.

In early 1900, the groves in San Dimas were wider for the large animals to move through. When I walk rows of the last remaining groves during harvest season, scattered between track houses and strip malls, I still see the slow lope of my craftsman's workhorse, bobbing down compacted paths to plant his smudge pots against the winter cold. In later years, those same pots fell out of use following environmental concern for the harmful gasses they emitted into the atmosphere. The only one still in use is preserved for the winner's circle in the San Dimas High School Smudge Pot football game, during which a live horse is occasionally galloped across the field during halftime.

As the local tale tells, while citrus farmers used their livestock for work they were still cautious of the rampant thieves that scrounged the horse corrals for a good steal. Many Mud Springers lost their prized workhorses to these thieves, who would ride the contraband straight into the lower foothills of the wild canyons to evade capture. Soon, the Mexican rancheros in the area tracked their hidden sanctuary and drove the thieves out. They named the area Horse Thief Canyon and changed the city of Mud Springs to San Dimas after the crucified patron Saint of thieves, Saint Dimas. I like to think that our craftsman evaded the horse thieves with his magnificently planted, indestructible horse tie.

As I grew through years of Craftsman tutorials and meetings with the San Dimas Historical Society, I began to pore over old photographs from other locals in the area and discovered that much of the home's history is still hidden. The structure is old, but the land around it has become so developed that the landscape of the past is almost unrecognizable. I could only hold onto the tangible items our family has discovered: old blueprints, paper trails to ownership, Old West coins dropped around the yard, and one indecipherable signature in letters from the children of the original craftsman. My family had for so many years striven to untangle the past, but each new lead ended at a wall.

We were at wit's end for answers until one ordinary afternoon at the grocery store. My mom and I were finishing a quick stop, hoping to be out of the store by 6:00 p.m. to beat the dinner rush.

I could tell she was weary from the day as she slowly confirmed requests from the cashier.

"Can you swipe your card again?"

"Did it not go through? I can do a check I guess."

The cashier huffed at the prospect of such an outdated payment method. "Fine. Address please."

"Address?"

"Address please."

Her tone was not amiable, and my mom spoke up quickly. She began the address, spelling out the street name as one vowel in the spelling was usually missed by listeners.

"Excuse me." A woman pushed by, tapping her on the shoulder. We moved to let the stranger pass, but she did not seem to be interested in scooting by the cramped checkout line. "Excuse me!"

"Yes?" My mom looked suspicious.

"Can you repeat that address?"

We were wary. As far as we were concerned, it is not common practice to repeat a home address to strangers. "No thank you." My mom said sternly.

"I used to live there! Can I visit again?"

"Oh," My mom's eyes darted for a reason to leave. She couldn't trust her so quickly. The stranger caught on to our unease and tried to win us over once more.

"You live in an old Craftsman home. It has three bedrooms, a river-rock coal shoot, pull-chain toilet, and one rusty, stubborn horse tie. I lived there for fifteen years."

We introduced ourselves and explained our quest to piece together the life of our orange-grove Craftsman. She was over for lunch the next day.

Since the time we spent with the grocery-store stranger, I learned that the history of the structure my parents have restored for almost fifty years is best discovered through the locals themselves. From one visit alone we learned about the original landscape surrounding our home and shared photographs Mud Springs ancestors spanning back to the mapping of the town. We have spoken to many others about our home since that encounter, and every voice brings us closer to the family who grew, lived, and passed in the very rooms where my family has done the same. I wish so often that I could meet my Wild West craftsman, talk about his era, walk through his groves of sun-gorged oranges, and share a laugh over afternoon tea, or hard whiskey if he preferred. I hope that if he had lived now, he too would find no use for those ridiculous, crass-sounding garbage disposals.

THERE WAS ONCE A MAN
WHO LONGED FOR A CHILD

Micah Perks

After his wife died in childbirth, the man raised his daughter up until the September she left for college. That October, the man sorted through all the things his daughter had bagged to throw out, and kept most of it, and sent her three care packages. In November he truly began to live alone.

November: the most beautiful month of the year in central California. The cool weather and the slanted light and the magenta colored leaves on the liquid amber maples in the park across from the man's house. The man used to supervise his daughter on the park's climbing structure, but now, through his window he watched the retirees practice tai chi in rough synchronicity, and the homeless people debate the park ranger, and the dogs collegially sniff each other's butts. He watched for hours. Sometimes he became mesmerized by the gold to wine colored leaves on the trees, their gentle breathing.

On weekdays, when he unlocked the door after work, the evening stretched out, all his. For dinner he ate what he wanted, sometimes steak or ribs, sometimes a three-egg omelet with ketchup.

After dinner the man drank beer and binge watched *Friday Night Lights*. In the season one finale, we find out that the football coach and his hot wife have made a mistake, getting pregnant when their daughter is already grown, and then in the second season they end up with a gremlin-faced baby sporting a yellow mullet named Gracie Belle. The man wondered why they had chosen an infant so lacking in star appeal, but oddly it was around then that he began to long for a baby of his own—the chubby legs pincering his waist, the milk-sour smell of its head. And all the cute things they said when they began to talk. Accompanied by his beer, he now found himself watching YouTube videos of babies saying the darndest things. His favorite was a two year old trying to unbuckle her seatbelt. Her father, the one filming on his phone, asked if she needed help, and the two year old yelled, Worry about yourself! Worry about yourself!

Finally, the man thought he might be getting malnourished from lack of vegetables, so the next Sunday he forced himself to go to the farmer's market. He wandered the stalls, pondering over the largest tomato or zucchini or apple, then dropping them in his backpack. He came upon the last stall pressed up against the back of the movie theater, selling gourds and dried flowers and branches and dried grasses all ablaze in fall colors. On the far left of the front table, on a blue dishtowel decorated with red foxes, lay a pile of shriveled roots. One was curved like a C. The top part of the root had two protrusions, almost like bulging eyes. And it actually had a green tendril, maybe a half inch long, growing up from its head.

There was a father busy helping a customer choose between a bouquet of glittering dried corn and a bouquet of cat tails, but his young daughter, her hair a perfectly circular afro, like the halos painted on saints, sat on a folding chair behind the back table, reading from a tablet.

The man said, Do you know what these roots are?

Barleycorn, said the girl, not glancing up. For chickens.

I don't think these are barleycorns, the man said. They're some kind of root or tuber. This one is sprouting.

The girl shrugged.

The man looked over to the owner of the stall for assistance, but he was still in conversation with the customer, who had now begun to cry, so the man said, How much are they?

The girl did not look up. Three dollars each.

That's crazy, the man laughed. The owner was now embracing the weeping customer, so the man paid the high price, and secured the root in the front zippered pocket of his backpack.

Back home, he took a pot with a dead cactus out of his daughter's room. He pulled out the cactus with an oven mitt to avoid the prickers, then buried the root just up to its eyes in the dry dirt. He watered it under the faucet. Then he put it on the windowsill above the sink. Why not?

When he got home from work on Monday, the little stem was at least a half-inch taller, and there was a tiny furled leaf coming out of it. Down below and between the bulging brown eyes there was another bulge—it looked almost like the top of a wide nose.

By the next weekend, a second tendril was curling out of its head, the first tiny leaf had opened, and a whole face had emerged, just the chin left in the dirt. A pug nose with no nostrils, but still.

It could not be denied that his so-called barleycorn was thriving. Only two weeks and its' chin was out of the dirt, raised a little bit, the beige freckled head tilted over to the right, almost as if it were slowly resting its cheek on the ground. Three small new heart shaped leaves had sprouted out of its head. He was sure, almost sure, he imagined telling his daughter.

The weeks went by and the barleycorn continued to emerge from the dirt, until one day the man noticed its head was filthy. He got a washcloth from the bathroom, rung it out, and carefully began to clean the little face. When the warm cloth was over the barleycorn's nose, it sneezed. "Did you hear that?" The man said out loud, and pulled the cloth off. He was sure he had heard a tiny, brilliant sneeze. Nothing now, no movement. The man had an idea. He warmed some milk on the stove, put his pinky in it to make sure it was right. He dripped some into the soil.

The next morning his barleycorn had grown arms. Dirty, rootlet covered, lumpy little arms like two carrots except beige, reaching out of the dirt, reaching up like, Hold me. Like, More milk, please. The man couldn't stop smiling as he warmed milk for both himself and the barleycorn. He stood by the sink and they both 'drank' from the same mug.

A few mornings later, the man woke to remember that in the middle of the night he had heard mewling. He had stumbled out of bed, shuffled into the hall. A thin cry, like a kitten, from downstairs. In the kitchen over the sink, in the moonlight, the barleycorn's mouth was a little sienna colored O, its potato eyes still closed, crying in its sleep. The man warmed milk, dripped it into the now open mouth. He whisper-sang to it, *Bye Baby Bunting, Papa's gone a hunting, to fetch a little rabbit skin...* The crying trailed off.

Then it began to coo. The man leaned over the sink, his neck pressed against the cool faucet, and put his ear up to the pursed potato mouth. It was making those strange newborn baby sounds, little grunts and snuffles. The man felt moist, milky breath on his ear.

And then the very next day, his daughter came home for winter break sporting a new tattoo on the side of her foot: I am corn. This seemed like a startling coincidence, but his daughter explained that it was an ironic comment on the overuse of corn products by GMO's. That night, after his daughter had dumped her clothes out of the suitcase onto the floor, she jumped on the couch and beckoned him in. As they cuddled together, his daughter scoffed at *Friday Night Lights*, and said they should watch a documentary on foie gras and the ethics of force feeding. During the day while the daughter lay on the couch playing Sims on her computer, the man did her wash. The daughter called the father over and showed him the mansion she had built for them both in the game.

The man said, his heart quickening, I want to show you my plant. The daughter wouldn't get up, so the father brought it over and put it on the coffee table.

Cute, the daughter said.

Do you think it looks like anything?

His daughter took another look, and said, Yeah, totally, and she pulled out her phone and showed her father a tree in which all the pears looked like laughing buddhas and a fleeceflower that seemed to be a tuber shaped exactly like a grown woman, the man holding it by its roots which looked exactly like long hair.

The barleycorn began to snuffle in its sleep then, and the man said to his daughter, But can you hear that?

Whoa, his daughter said, and played her father a translation of plants talking through transducers and amplifiers. It sounded like a robot purring. Then she played him the noise coming from the Rosetta comet, which sounded like a squirrel chattering.

That night the man cooked his daughter her favorite dinner, lasagna, and poured them both a glass of wine, but during dinner the fussing of the barleycorn made it hard to concentrate on his daughter's discussion about whether she should take advanced painting or a philosophy course called gods and monsters. Are you listening? the daughter asked. The man doused the plant with milk and set it on the little table by the front door.

After dinner his daughter went out with her friends. The man dozed. Though he thought he heard crying in his sleep, he didn't wake fully. The anxious dozing felt deeply familiar. At three am he heard a crash downstairs and a scream and then laughter and whispering. His daughter was probably drunk and/or high, but now that she was home, the man could finally sleep deeply.

When he came downstairs the next morning there was a boy sprawled on the couch and a girl in the fetal position on the loveseat. In the entryway—a smear of dirt on the floor. The terracotta pot had been cracked in half and set back onto the little table next to the barleycorn, half-flattened by a shoe.

And even while the man carried the barleycorn out to the compost bucket and gently laid it over the leftovers from last night's dinner, he noticed his sadness was oddly mixed with relief. As he put the green ventilated lid back on the bucket, he thought that maybe it was best that the cries of plants were generally not audible to human ears.

On the day before the daughter left to go back to college, the man and the daughter walked in the park across the street. The daughter remembered that she used to swing there. Remember how high you used to push me? she said. And how long? the man answered. And the man remembered drinking beer and binge watching *Friday Night Lights*, and wondered what would happen on season three. They wandered the rows of now mostly bare maples, sometimes holding hands and sometimes laughing, and the daughter squeezed the man's hand and said, I'm applying for an internship in Ghana for the summer. Maybe you can visit me there.

All the while the man kept hearing shuffling in the leaves off to the right, but he assumed it was a dog nosing the ground or perhaps a homeless person turning in his sleeping bag. He didn't see the squat figure dressed in a jerkin of lasagna noodles, with bulgy eyes and a wide freckled nose, with a bald, half smashed in head, and stubby tuberous legs with no feet. The one that whispered, or did not whisper, Hold me. More milk, please.

THE CHAIN

Ron Gutierrez

The car was missing for six days before Cadena's father called me. He rarely saw her during her visits to him. He let her drive his old Chrysler and I doubt the car's appearance in his driveway was anything more than sporadic, or that there were more signs of her than a wet bathroom towel hanging from the shower rod and the kitchen trashcan piling up faster. But at least they didn't fight. Not like her and I did. He said he hadn't seen her since New Year's. *Chingado.* I was raising a sixteen-year-old with a taste for street drugs, the L.A. juvenile court system, and never telling me where she was, and I was getting sick of it.

"This is your fault for letting her drive that damn car," I said.

"You mean she's not with you?" the *pendejo* asked me.

I hung up. I stormed out of my office, out to the production floor where I kept walking until I got to the deburring barrel. The loud hexagonal drum rotated with metal parts that tumbled against hundreds of flat triangular stones. I imagined everyone I knew, every problem I had, inside that barrel, slowly rising up with each turn, then landsliding down, hour after hour, until the burrs were gone, and everything was smooth. The louder it was, the better I could think.

There were a couple of boys in Long Beach, another in Cypress, that Cadena shacked up with when she wanted to force me into war with her. She liked boys older than her, so she could be the baby, the one who got away with things. Ever since she was small she liked being the only girl in a room full of boys. Not me.

I'd gone to night school for my mechanical engineering diploma and could tolerate being one of the few women in a classroom. But I hated being the only female in a production shop, hearing the whistles from the machinists, the sneers because I made more money—although not much more—and the *chingada* whispers from the office girls. I was proof that life doesn't get easier just because you know engineering math.

"Marisela was not made for men, she was made for metal," my mother told people when she caught me running my fingers around screws, washers, faucets, and brass lamps. My older sisters, easily distracted, liked the jewels on a necklace, but I loved the mechanics of the clasp. I could play with a spring clasp until my fingertips hurt so bad I needed to squeeze an ice cube. Later when they'd buy bridal magazines, I'd say things like "If the holes for the diamonds in a wedding ring are grooved or channeled, it weakens the structural integrity."

"*Ay Marisela!* Shut up. Nobody gives a fuck about structural anything. Go watch TV." Neither of them asked me to be a bridesmaid.

When a tungsten carbide wedding ring is dropped or repeatedly tapped on a hard surface, it may eventually fracture, chip or break.

I had Cadena when I was fifteen, the same year Mt. Saint Helen's erupted and John Lennon was shot. The pregnancy was an emotional burden, but after she was born she became my reason for living, my link back to myself. That I could create something as beautiful as her, made me believe in my future again. Somewhere along the way, with work and night school and no one to help me, I lost control of her. I grew up hard and I didn't want that for her, but we were of the same material, and she held it against me. Arrests, boys I didn't approve of, dressing like a gangbanger. She did everything she could to show me she despised me, my pushing,

184

my yelling, and my constant nagging about my hopes for her. She got all that from her father, who my parents refused to let me marry until I was eighteen, and by then I didn't want to anymore.

Manuel, one of the machinists, walked up to me and handed me an oil stained work order for 10,000 pieces and told me the double disk grind was broken. Shit. The order was already late when the material came back from passivation this morning. I went to my office, planned a back order, printed it, and hoped someone else would volunteer to ask Northrup to take a partial now, and the remainder when we got the machine fixed. The engineers roll dice to see who has to give a customer bad news. I'm three. The dice rolled four, which was Hector in sales, out sick, so we rolled again. Three.

We were two points behind our quality numbers from last year and I wasn't in the mood to deliver more bad news. I grabbed the dice and squeezed it, waiting for Roger to answer. We had a one-night stand at a manufacturer's convention in Dallas a couple of years ago. He was mid-forties, worried like hell about foreign competition, had two kids in college, and a wife with a serious cruise ship addiction. When he answered I mumbled something about a happy new year.

"Marisela. I want to talk to you," he said.

I could have guessed that much. Our quality numbers down, he'd been giving us less to bid on, and now he was going to dump us. I'd have to tell the CEO we lost a big customer on the same day I'd found out my daughter was testing how much she could get away with before I killed her.

"Roger," I said, digging my thumb into the holes on the dice. "I've got a partial and I need a clearance to split the order."

"Yeah, listen. I've got a, you could say, special order here. I don't know who else to ask." I could hear the hesitation in his normally headstrong voice. "I want you to do it."

"What do you mean *special?*" I dropped the dice back inside my desk.

"I mean that no one can know. On either end."

185

I'm a company girl so the first thing I thought was that this mutual secrecy business meant we hadn't lost a customer. "Military?"

"No, I need to show you the parts. There's no blueprint. Only one company made them and they're discontinued."

"We're backlogged. I can't just go squeeze some secret shit in."

"Can I meet you someplace after work?"

I'd planned a drive to Long Beach to beat the crap out of whoever Cadena was with, then ride her ass all the way home. I'd leave her car wherever she parked it and tell her father to go pick it up tomorrow and not to give it back to her.

"I can't. What's the big deal with it?"

"All I can tell you now, is that this'll give a whole new meaning to the term precious metal."

Don't do this to me, I thought. I'd slept with him because when he talked steel he made it sound like the only real thing in the world. We got sucked into a black hole of sex after some depressing verbal foreplay about our customers' outsourcing to China, continuous improvement requirements that dictated we charge 3% less for the same parts each year, and the resulting mathematical impossibility of staying in business. He was terrified and needed time with a woman who lived and breathed his fear. The hotel room got so hot, we poured cold vodka on each other and licked it off. We finished off the bottle to make sure our resolve wouldn't leak out. Alcohol is a good sealing substance.

"Fine," I said. "I won't promise anything. But I'll take a look," I knew that if I got my hands on Cadena tonight I'd probably end up in jail anyway.

Passivation is a material becoming passive in relation to being less affected by environmental factors. It is useful in strengthening and preserving the appearance of metals and can be improved by applying a suitable sealing substance

After work I followed Roger past downtown L.A. northeast into

Mt. Washington. My car complained up Canyon Vista Drive, and I watched my headlights navigate bends of dense trees, bungalows, and modernist houses. Roger had told me what the parts were for before we got in our cars, and now I felt my heart drumming past the world of aerospace and military specs, weapons and jets, and pounding me into a whole new sandbox. Machining was a universe ruled by science and physics, the glory of the finished product, but sometimes it was the aftermath of production, an industrial drum full of iron shavings, that showed the poetry to me. I could only stare at the shapes glistening with danger, because if I gave into my desire to dig into it, I'd rip my hands to shreds.

> *Swarf are shavings and chippings of metal. It is standard procedure to avoid handling swarf with bare hands, although total avoidance of touching swarf is considered burdensome or impractical.*

Roger parked in front of a metal gate with the words "Tree Haven" engraved on a nameplate. Moonlight illuminated shin-deep ivy that I was sure harbored rats. I stayed to the middle of the walkway until we got to the house. We ascended the porch steps and Roger opened the double doors.

I stepped inside and I heard it in the next room. The hairs on my neck stood like iron filings reacting to a magnet. I pretended not to be in a hurry to see the machine or invade the privacy of its owner. It sounded like a punch press on our shop floor, steady, rhythmic, but without the final bang when the hydraulic ram descended and punched out a part. It could loosen my fillings if I happened to be walking next to it at that moment. As Roger talked I kept feeling the tendons in my shoulders brace for that final sound that never came.

Her name was Drusilla, his aunt, one of thirty-one people in the country still living in a negative pressure ventilator: an iron lung. She lay prostrate with her head sticking out of what looked like a deep frontloading washing machine. I thought of Cadena screwing up her life. But I was grateful, like the day she was born, that she had functioning arms and legs to explore life on her own terms, even if she was too young and stupid to understand the consequences.

Roger explained to his aunt who I was, that I'd be making spare parts for her iron lung. The woman was in her 60s and spoke in moist fibrous tangles. At first she sounded unhindered by the machine, but later I could tell how adept she was at choosing the length of her sentences, grabbing onto a verbal railing every time her lungs emptied. Every few seconds a pressure valve above her lung pulled counterclockwise from the top, like when I take *nopales* off the produce scale.

"Which parts would I start with?" I asked Roger.

"I keep a list of what we've had to replace most often. You can start there."

I leaned down to Druscilla. "Who lives here with you?"

She spoke right away, her eyes gentle on me. "I have a caretaker. And my sister Lonnie's here until ten. She's sick today."

I got closer. The machine was yellow and shiny, not a dent or scratch on it. In the back a gearhead motor, transmission, something that looked like the timing belt in my Ford, and a bellows. I scanned the moving parts, shapes I'd never seen before, parts like none that ever shipped out of our factory. Some looked nautical, others like something on a space capsule, and still others like they belonged on farm equipment.

I know when to say no. Last year the shop was asked to make an urn out of Grammium. A private customer said he'd supply the material. But Grammium's a patented zinc alloy, and its only legal use is for making Grammy awards. Of course I wanted to work with the material, but I think the idea of glorifying someone's ashes made me say no more than the illegality of the job did. Now, as I placed my hand on the cold steel of the lung, and I listened to the machinery give her every last breath she had coming to her, I made up my mind. I looked down at her and attempted a smile for the first time all week. "I'll do it."

"Cadena isn't here." The guy at the apartment was covered with water-stained stucco. "You want to come in and check, go ahead."

I looked past him and didn't see anything of hers, didn't pick up any trace of her fruity bodywash. The place smelled like dirty carpet and Air Solid. I left and drove to the opposite end of Long Beach near the port. This next guy was in a band. Cadena had hooked up with him once when his girlfriend was out of town. My daughter doesn't offer up these kind of details, but if I scream loud enough and throw her things at the wall, she'll answer me. Sometimes with the truth. He wasn't home. I left a note with more swear words than punctuation so she'd know it was really me.

The next day I took a long lunch so I could drive back to band guy's place. I wanted to be there when he woke up. I went up the steps and slammed my fist on the door. Two adjacent apartments opened their doors first and then closed them when I stared them down. Finally the band guy's door opened.

"Is Cadena here? Because if she is, tell her to get her fucking ass to the door or I'm going kick the shit out of both of you."

"She's not here."

Another girl, not Cadena, came to the door. "You tell that bitch she better not be coming here," she said. "Not unless she wants it to be the last time she goes anywhere."

I set the girl straight with words invented for angry mothers taking off work to look for their only kid, and told her if she wanted a preview of what I'd do to her if she touched my daughter she could bring her ugly ass outside right now. She slammed the door.

The last place to try was the Cypress address, but I only had a street name so I'd have to hunt for her car, but it was already getting dark. I'd have to do it tomorrow. The band guy came back outside and called down to me.

"She tried to stay here. She was sitting outside the door, but she was drunk and I told her to go home."

I felt both a surging anger and wave of relief. "When? Where did she go?"

"I don't know. It was like a week ago."

When I got back in my car my breaths were hard and foreign, like someone pulled me out of the ocean and was resuscitating me. I wiped my eyes.

> *Any metal inlays, diamonds, or precious gemstones set within tungsten carbide create additional voids beyond what is already a non-solid material. These voids translate into a lack of support under compression or pressure.*

I got home and there were two messages each from my mother, my oldest sister, and Cadena's father. He'd told them everything and, of course, they were hysterical. They said I was selfish and *una estupida* for not telling them, not calling the police. If they didn't hear from me by 9:00 pm they said they'd call the police. Like I'd let that happen.

My daughter's name and picture on the news? Me sobbing and begging for her return like she was two-years-old? Or like I was one of these people who murders their kid then acts terrified and tries to get away with it? *Claro que no!* We don't raise weak children in my family. Cadena might be too headstrong for her own good, but she was not a victim. I called them back and explained that Cadena's friend in Long Beach had seen her and I was going to give her some more time. "My daughter is fine," I said in the same measured phrases with each of them. "I named her Cadena because she's a chain to me, delicate like jewelry, but strong when she needs to be." I told them to stop embarrassing themselves with their hyperventilating calls and, since they liked to act religious, to recite their *oraciones* if they wanted to give suggestions to someone.

Roger insisted I live in the guesthouse on the weekends so I could have constant access to the machine and be there when the nurse came for general care duties. This also gave Lonnie the weekends off.

I knew I had to calm down my mother, so I called to remind her that, when I found out I was pregnant, I ran away for almost a month myself, and Cadena had only been gone for nine days. I tried to make it true when I said I trusted her, and that she was smarter than I was at her age, and that this was how she'd learn the world wouldn't give her anything for free. This was between Cadena and me. She was trying to belittle me. I would not stoop to that. My mind, like heat-treated steel, was a tempered material. It was honed by math and physics. Maybe I'd always be working class and struggling but I would never be *una pobrecita* crying on Channel 7 news.

And the truth was, *chingado*, I was fascinated by these parts I was designing. I was helping someone who really needed help. Maybe others after her. If the other people living in these things were anything like this woman, none of them were about to give them up to the more invasive systems of tubes stuck down the throat or even tracheotomies. This woman was as free of needles, tubes, and straps as I was. She had her pride and she wanted to stay that way. With my help.

So far I had one prototype that wasn't too bad, but the next one I handed to Manuel, my only buddy at work, would be better. Then after that I had seven more parts to go.

The street in Cypress had five cars that looked like the Chrysler. But none of them matched the customized interior or license plate. I even had the VIN in case I saw an interior that matched, thinking she could have switched the plates to fuck with me. So now I'd have to start showing her picture.

I wanted a formula for how many *pinche* doors to humiliate myself at, but statistics failed me. How many should a mother knock on if there was only a thirty percent chance her daughter was with this boy? If there was a possible fourth or fifth boy she might have just met? Should her appearance on band guy's step increase or decrease the odds in this neighborhood?

I parked, got out of the car and went to the first door, the second, the third, then stopped counting. When it was dark I stopped and drove back to Mt. Washington, back to the iron lung. I didn't call hospitals. That would be discounting her most basic abilities, the first step toward calling the police. If there had been an arrest or anything, they would have called me.

A week passed and the rain woke me up at the guesthouse. I wasn't sleeping more than four or five hours a night. The rain was so strong it made the roof sound like cardboard getting pelted by rocks. I looked around and realized the power was out. No LED alarm clock, no humming from the furnace or fridge, no red light on the TV. No light from the streetlamp distant behind the curtains. I jumped out of bed, looked out the window. No lights in the main house.

I pulled on my sweats, ran to the kitchen for a flashlight, grabbed the keys Roger had given me, and ran out to the main house.

"Drusilla!" I heard the lung churning life into her but it sounded different, exhausted. The emergency generator had kicked on. I flashed the light on her. She was wide-awake.

"Is the yellow or red light on?" she asked.

I looked down at the generator. No lights. I went around to the other side. "The yellow light's blinking."

"I'm on fifty percent power . . . The bellow is slower . . . We're at the end of that battery." Her speech was more distinctly carved. The machine sounded like the soundtrack to a horror film, someone walking down a sidewalk with a heavy plastic bag tied to one leg. Step . . . *draaag.* Step . . . *draaag.*

"When did the power go out?" I couldn't have been asleep more than three hours. The time on her wall clock said 2:30 am. The generator should have been good for twenty-four hours. The battery must have been low. I picked up the phone. It was dead.

"Is there another generator?" I asked.

"In the garage, but . . ."

I didn't let her finish. I ran to the garage and fumbled through the small keys until I found the one that opened it. I was soaked from head to foot. The generator was in the corner, covered in plastic. I grabbed it and wheeled it up the walkway to the house. By now it had occurred to me I shouldn't use a gasoline generator in the rain. Still I dragged it. I wasn't thinking. I hadn't been thinking right for a long time.

When I got back, Drusilla and I looked at each other. Neither of us knew what to do.

"The porch?" she asked.

I doubted it. Too wet. I ran there with my flashlight and the porch was soaked. It was roofed in but the rain splattered off the cement counters hitting every inch of floor. No way the generator's circuitry would stay dry there. I ran back inside. "I can put it in another room and open all the windows."

"The power may return soon," she said, but I knew she didn't believe it.

I couldn't hold her hand so I threw myself onto the lung like people do with coffins in movies. Together we'd keep breathing. But within two minutes the machine stopped, the red light came on, and a high-pitched whistle started.

"What now?" I didn't wait for an answer. I unplugged the lung from the whistling generator and plugged it into the gasoline generator. I wheeled the generator into the middle of the next room and opened the windows. The electric cord was taut. I couldn't move it further away from Drusilla, and there was no time to look for an extension. I came back in and kneeled down at her face and asked, "Do you want me to turn it on? You'll breathe better at first, but the fumes will eventually make you pass out, and then gradually kill you. But if I don't turn it on you'll suffocate in minutes."

She looked at me without speaking for several seconds and said, "Plug it . . ." She paused and in an intake of breath said, ". . . in." I'd never heard anyone talk while breathing air in and I took it as the only direct order from God I'd ever received.

I ran to the other room, grabbed the pull cord in my hand, and tasted tears. I couldn't do this. I didn't know who I was anymore. This was not where I wanted to be or what I wanted to be doing. I heard Drusilla's labored breathing in the next room and I couldn't imagine what she was going through. But this was her wish, and I pulled the goddamn cord for all I was worth. The motor turned. It sounded like a helicopter had landed in the house. I looked to Drusilla and saw the lung start up again. But it was still at half power. Druscilla looked relieved and scared at the same time. I ran to the bathroom and grabbed a towel and used it to fan the fumes out of the room. I knew I couldn't stay because I'd pass out and die too. I kissed her forehead, told her I loved her, that I was sorry, and God was waiting for her with open arms. I stumbled outside but tripped and fell. I jackhammered my fist on the cement and screamed into the night. Then I pulled myself up and went inside the guesthouse and grabbed Roger's phone number. I went back into the main house holding my breath. Drusilla was now a corpse but the iron lung kept working. The machine kept doing its job even when it no longer mattered. It was obscene to see it make a dead person breathe.

I walked to the street, got in my car, and drove to the first public phone with a working light. It was outside a donut place on Figueroa. I stared at the phone for ten minutes before I could get out of my car. Finally I opened the door, went to the phone. I looked at the number in my hands but when I picked up the receiver I dialed 911.

"My daughter's missing." The words came out in a stream. "She's been missing for two weeks. Help me."

I couldn't control my breathing. I didn't think I would ever arrive at those words. They'd been a light year away, and now I'd said them. They made Cadena vulnerable, put her in danger. They made her dead. I was halfway there, but I still had to give my name, then her name. I had to say sixteen, five-four, one hundred twenty pounds, black hair. I had to dig my hands into the swarf. My daughter had turned into tungsten carbide tapping against the surface of her mother, shattering me. With every breath I decreased

194

the distance between us by half. I was three quarters there, seven eighths, and I could race like this until the end of time and it was still mathematically impossible for me to arrive at losing her.

WHAT LIES IN CLOSETS

Kat Meads

It's long past two a.m. but not quite three. I'm roaming the house, listening to Leonard Cohen through headphones so as not to disturb the man and cat in residence who can sleep between two a.m. and three. Leonard Cohen's lugubrious lyrics, Leonard Cohen's dirge-like vocals: a soundtrack supremely suited to the walking exhausted.

More than halfway through my usual wandering circuit—kitchen/glass of water, living room/magazine rack, office/Internet connection—for no reason other than boredom, I deviate from routine, turn into a spare bedroom, yank open the closet door and begin to rifle through the boxes and bags of papers packed inside. There is stuff here I haven't touched since moving from my last address, files I haven't opened since moving East Coast to West.

Laying hands on a beat-about envelope marked *Patty Hearst*, listening to "Sisters of Mercy." A coincidence, yes. Also supremely apt. Although rumored to have been inspired by a three-way romp in a hotel room, Cohen's lyrics seek comfort from higher sources as well.

Comfort from sources high and low. Something Patricia Campbell Hearst, Catholic girl/heiress/victim/symbol could have used February 4, 1974, after dining on canned chicken noodle soup and tuna fish sandwiches in an apartment filled with macramé plant holders, after changing into a blue terrycloth robe to watch "Mission: Impossible" and "The Magician" on television, after trailing her fiancé to the door of 2603 Benvenue Avenue, Berkeley, at or around 9:20 p.m., when a female miming distress was so unwisely allowed to enter. Comfort gone missing during the beating of said fiancé and an abduction arc that included being dragged down steps, smacked in the face with a rifle butt, locked in a car trunk, tossed in the first "people's prison" in Daly City, site of her sleeping/unsleeping bed for (best estimate) 30 days prior to transfer to Golden Gate Avenue, San Francisco, for another (best estimate) 27 days of captivity inside closet number two. Comfort denied for 19 months in the company of eight, then two, who wished Death to the Fascist Insect that Preys on the Life of the People and on September 18, 1975, 2:25 p.m., when FBI agents raided 625 Morse Street, San Francisco, 592 days after the first apartment storming, and the fugitive they sought pissed her pants and surrendered without fight to another show of force. Comfort needed by a 90-pound "urban guerilla" continuously menstruating, en route to a collapsed lung and conviction for her part in the Hibernia Bank robbery, net proceeds $10,660, a prisoner who served 21 months of her seven-year sentence before President Jimmy Carter granted executive clemency and Prisoner 00077-181 walked out of the Federal Correctional Institution in Pleasanton with a flowered throw she'd crocheted, a guard dog named Arrow, a bodyguard boyfriend named Bernie, and, against all odds, a grin, her sanity and a sardonic sense of humor.

Comfort that was unjustly withheld—or not.

Depending on one's politics.

If, in the context of now, wearing my blue but not terrycloth bathrobe, I got in my car and drove without recklessness or excessive speed north on interstate 880, I could be casing that Benvenue Avenue four-plex in an hour's time. If, instead of taking 880, I drove north on 280 into the city, in approximately the same travel time I could be rubbernecking the Morse Street capture site of Patty Hearst and apartment mate Wendy Yoshimura. Because now I reside in the Golden State's Bay Area.

In the context of then, February 1974, I lived weekdays in the Piedmont of North Carolina and on weekends drove 200+ miles east to overnight on my parents' farm. The purpose of that to and fro-ing was distraction. About what my personal future should contain, I could form no strong opinion. About what I *hoped* it would contain: equally fuzzy. The night the Symbionese Liberation Army kidnapped the heiress, a Monday night, I would have been back in the Piedmont, finished with another shift of my dead-end job and feeling grateful for the affections of a dog that considered me the center of his (limited) universe. Even so, I would have retained a parental-home-mindset because I needed until at least Tuesday evening each week to readjust to the idea that I was a grown, independent woman, living a life that supposedly confirmed those two adjectives. In effect I was someone who remained suspended between worlds, extremely susceptible to conditions of flux and float. As such, I was the ideal consumer of a story whose star exchanged one kind of existence for another without the bother of planning or input.

About Patty Hearst in 1974, I remember thinking: *She's not where she was. She's not by choice where she is. She's not free to return to what was, since altered. So what now?*

The file in my California closet contains the *Time* magazine issue with Patty/Tania's mug shot on the cover, part one of *Rolling Stone*'s account of Patty's cross-country escapades with the Harrises, and the ragged front page of the September 24, 1975 edition of the *Greensboro Daily News*, bearing these three headlines:

• Patty Swears Torture Drove Her to Insanity
• Mental Test Ordered for Sara Jane Moore
• "Squeaky" Ruled Competent to Stand Trial, Be Own Lawyer.

A slim file—but one that need not *remain* slim, I fast realize. Staring at the reproduced mug shot—the severely plucked brows, the limp and plastered hair, the dark and darker circles around those dim and vacant eyes—I sense I've stumbled on a bit of salvation. Even a minimal review of what has been written, filmed, argued and counter-argued about Patty Hearst since 1974 will take hours—many, many, many hours.

And so, as an insomniac, I think this about Patty Hearst: *goody*.

To quote Hannah Arendt: "Events, by definition, are occurrences that interrupt routine processes.... Predictions of the future are never anything but projections...of occurrences that are likely to come to pass if...nothing unexpected happens."

Nothing unexpected. Check.

To quote Patty turned Tania turned Patty Hearst, memoirist, in *Every Secret Thing*: "I...sense there is little one can do to prepare oneself adequately for the unknown."

Little one can do to prepare. Check.

To quote author/actress Patrica Hearst Shaw, speaking with Larry King in a broadcast that aired in 2002: "We all think we're pretty strong and that nobody can make us do something if we don't want to do it. That's true until somebody locks you up in a closet and tortures you and finally makes you so weak that you completely break."

True until. Check.

To quote John Wayne: "It seems quite odd to me that the American people have immediately accepted the fact that one man (Jim Jones) can brainwash 900 human beings into mass suicide (in Guyana), but will not accept the fact that a ruthless group, the Symbionese Liberation Army, could brainwash a little girl by torture, degradation and confinement."

Torture, degradation, confinement. Check. (And note that "little girl.")

A self-styled revolutionary corps of ten, the SLA's membership roster contained two in jail for the murder of Oakland Superintendent of Schools Marcus Foster, a preponderance of females and a preponderance of college-educated ex-suburbanites. Acting under the leadership of the SLA's single black member, General Field Marshall Cinque (a.k.a. Donald DeFreeze), the group decides to snatch a UC Berkeley undergrad, a 19-year-old rich bitch from Hillsborough slumming it with her grad-school boyfriend on Benvenue Avenue.

Rather remarkably, their scheme succeeds.

I first read Shana Alexander's *Anyone's Daughter: The Times and Trials of Patty Hearst* when it was published in 1979. Second time through, what's most striking is how very much Alexander dislikes Catherine Hearst, that "brightly Lana Turnerish," yet also "strangely Chinese" woman with "tiny feet," "cotton-candy hair," and "flawless makeup."

About Mrs. Hearst's mental makeup, Ms. Alexander reports: "A special kind of perfection also marks this woman's mind. It is not a perfection of stupidity, though her singlemindedness can make her appear that way."

About Mrs. Hearst's environment, the Hillsborough community, Ms. Alexander reports: "Hillsborough does not produce people with flexible minds...without doubt the most boring enclave of privilege I had ever visited, lacking weather or even scenery to fall back on when in conversational distress."

About the interview with Mrs. Hearst that appeared in the July 1974 *Ladies Home Journal,* Ms. Alexander reports: "The article is heavy on Catherine's hobbies—stargazing, supermarketing, and the study of the genealogy of the ancient royal family of Hawaii."

About Catherine Hearst's background, Ms. Alexander reports: "In the late 1930s...Catherine Campbell, the belle of Atlanta, was a finalist in the nation-wide Scarlett O'Hara contest to find an unknown actress to star opposite Clark Gable in *Gone with the Wind....* Catherine Campbell Hearst is, before everything, a Southern girl. She would no more reveal her true feelings in public than she would sit with her legs uncrossed."

That "Southern girl" remark.

Southern born, I am particularly (perhaps too particularly) alert to Southern bashing. A hundred pages or so into *Anyone's Daughter,* I begin to suspect the Southern slur trumps the Hillsborough slur in Ms. Alexander's ranking of insults. I begin to suspect Ms. Alexander went looking for a weeping, wailing mother in visible distress, hair uncombed, dress askew, and when she found instead a steely Southerner determined never to let the "public" see her "crack," I suspect the contradiction pissed off Ms. Alexander. I suspect that development threatened the narrative already scrolling inside Ms. Alexander's head if not yet transferred onto the page.

Also not a Catherine fan: Steven Weed, once prospective son-in-law. Weed pans Mrs. Hearst's "insular upbringing," "overreliance on prescribed drugs," and lack of mothering skills. Her fervent Catholicism, he asserts in *My Search for Patty Hearst*, "only increased her inability to come to grips with an increasingly secular world. Though a member of the Board of Regents, no one could have been less well suited to...understand the problems at Berkeley."

Mid-trial, Patty's lawyer, F. Lee Bailey, describes Catherine Hearst as a "terrible pessimist. Deep down she thinks that...her daughter will go to jail."

A jab on Bailey's part.

However: her daughter did indeed go to jail. Which means Catherine Hearst called it exactly right. Which means Mrs. Hearst was in actuality less a terrible pessimist than a gritty realist.

According to both Alexander and Weed, Catherine Hearst castigates her daughter's fiancé for falling short of the Clark Gable/Rhett Butler manliness bar. "Whatever happened to the real men in this world?" she hisses at Weed. "Men like Clark Gable. No one would have carried off my daughter if there had been a real man there!"

When Steven Weed meets Catherine Hearst's daughter at the Crystal Springs School for Girls, he's 23, Patty's teacher. She's 17. In *My Search for Patty Hearst*, Weed insists Patty pursued him, not vice versa. If so, he's an easy catch. Promptly he dumps the woman he's then living with for the heiress. His "tiny, small-boned and compact, almost childlike" new lover—a merely "competent cook"—has a "choppy, determined little step" and is "never one to suffer a lack of confidence." In her daddy-bought MG, they zoom off to vacations at the Hearst family retreats, San Simeon to the south, Wyntoon to the north. They get engaged. They plan to marry because Patty wants to get married—not because Weed sees an opportunity to live off a trust fund. (Perish the thought.)

In Patty's counter-version of that place and time, she complains: "Most of our friends at Berkeley were *his* friends...." When those friends visit, her fiancé discourses "for hours on some minute point of nineteenth-century philosophy or English punctuation." Bored, she "slip(s) away to the kitchen" to bake a cake. "I came to see that my first true love was not perfect," she writes. "He was not only intelligent and self-confident; he was also arrogant and condescending." As the wedding date approaches, the pending bride experiences "doubts and fears." To escape the nuptials, she considers "joining the Navy." She also slides into a "depression." Others assure her pre-wedding jitters are quite normal. She tries to believe that bromide—but does she?

February fourth.

The pending groom of a willing/unwilling bride passes another day studying philosophy, another (half) night in front of the television. Then comes the fateful knock on the door. Attacked, battered and bleeding, Weed escapes the apartment, runs out the rear door and onto the patio, leaps over a fence, then over a second fence before realizing, in his own words, "no one was chasing me"—those no ones otherwise preoccupied with dragging his fiancée down the steps and stashing her inside the trunk of their getaway car.

Running in the opposite direction.

Not what Catherine Hearst would classify as a real-man response.

Steven Weed, the fellow Patty never again sees or speaks to after the kidnapping, publishes his book six years before she publishes hers. He "turned to writing because it was therapeutic," he informs Shana Alexander, and part of that therapy seems to be listing further screw-ups and/or embarrassments. Called into U.S. District Attorney James Browning's office to identify one of the Hibernia Bank robbers, he tells Browning "of course" it's Patty, signs the back of the photograph as evidence of that identification, agrees to "appear before the grand jury as a character witness" and only "halfway down the stairs" realizes he's just helped "build the case" against his former roommate. Dining with an "attractive young reporter" from *Newsday*, he gets "pleasantly high" and supplies a "tape recorder full of raw material" that results in an article that both infuriates and dumbfounds the usually genial Randolph Hearst. "What the hell is with you? You get up there with some girl...and just bubble like a yeastcake."

Toward the end of *My Search for Patty Hearst*, Weed declares his "disappointment" with Patty and states that when he thinks of her as a "victim," he still loves her, but when he thinks she's acting in the manner of a "spoiled brat," he loves her not.

Getting kidnapped is a high price to pay for getting shed of Steven Weed, but too high?

Debatable.

Arrogance. Presumption. Cockiness.

In 1974, many younger than 30 in America assumed the divine right to pronounce and denounce. If we disagreed with governmental policy, we expected that government to listen. If we were against a war, we expected its prompt end. If we disliked the "leader of the free world," we expected him and entourage to pack bags for exile in San Clemente. If we rejected monogamy, materialism, the house/car/kids model of achievement, we expected our dissension to be more than tolerated. We expected loud applause. Accordingly, if we fancied someone, we insisted that someone could and should be ours for a night or long weekend sans regrets, recriminations, or the mess and muck of further entanglement.

In retrospect, what seems most striking about that era's sense of entitlement was its nonexclusive, democratic base. A certain segment of the young in any era assume entitlement because their heritage and daily circumstance support the snobbery. But in the late Sixties and early Seventies, scholarship students, farm children, the offspring factory wages fed and clothed, also believed and behaved as if we too counted among the anointed. Backed by several generations of wealth, Patty Hearst qualified as old-school privileged. Her age and college of choice made her one of the new-school privileged as well. It was a risk: combining an old-school bank account with new-school accessibility, and it got her kidnapped.

Privilege, entitlement—neither concept holds up well under adverse circumstances. Fifty-seven days of closet confinement, for example.

The first closet in Daly City: 5 1/2 feet long, 2 feet deep.

The second closet on Golden Gate Avenue: 5 feet long, 1 foot 7 inches deep.

My 600-square-foot 1974 rental off the Chapel Hill/Durham bypass featured a 5'x2' bedroom closet. The enclosure barely accommodated the width of a coat hanger. Sticking an arm inside to snatch a blouse incited my claustrophobia. Her tiny compactness aside—height 5'2" or 5'3", depending on the source, weight 110 pounds going in—Patty Hearst survived inside those people's prisons cramped and crimped, sleep-, light-, and fresh-air deprived. It is beyond my capacity to imagine confinement in such close quarters 57 days and nights.

The kidnapped says she was transferred in a plastic garbage can from the closet of the Daly City safe house to the closet on Golden Gate Avenue. Not surprisingly, Bill and Emily Harris say otherwise. They say the abducted was never confined to any closet; that the door of the Daly City closet was always open; that her hands were never tied. They also say Patty Hearst spent no time whatsoever in the Golden Gate Avenue closet because by then she was a certified SLAer renamed Tania.

Much of *Every Secret Thing* reads like a forced, if precise, recitation of what happened when, but not the descriptions of closet confinement and its effects. Those lift the neck hairs. Blindfolded, she's tossed inside. She's bleeding on the leg, her face still throbs from the earlier rifle butt blow. Her tears soak through the blindfold, lubricating it, causing it to slip. She's terrified she'll be blamed for that readjustment and terror makes her cry harder. The closet stinks of "sweat and filth." As crude soundproofing, old carpet remnants have been nailed to the walls and door, ceiling to floor. "I might as well have been in an underground coffin," she writes. Time passes, but how much? She can't distinguish night from day. Maybe she sleeps, maybe she doesn't. Above all else, she feels "uncontrollable fear" of being killed by captors whom she "could not stop" from killing her.

During Hearst's closeting, she loses 15 pounds of fighting weight and comes to despise (among other things) the smell and taste of peppermint tea. When allowed out of the closet to pee, she does so blindfolded, with an audience. Her first bath: also with blindfold intact, also with an audience. She asks if she can remove the blindfold to wash her hair and face, bath two. "They held a meeting on that," she writes, a bit of sarcasm that quickly vanishes, even in recall. "I was so thankful for that bath and hair wash one would have thought I was being led to a party…." In the bathroom, when the blindfold comes off: "Everything looked so strange, so out of proportion. Everything around me appeared huge, distorted and constantly moving like ocean waves."

Back in the closet, she wakes from a "fitful" nap, convinced she's dying. She realizes that even if she were "free to walk away," she can't because she can't stand without assistance. "I was so tired, so tired; all I wanted to do was to sleep…and I knew that was… fatal, like the man lost in the Arctic snow, who, having laid his head down for that delicious nap, never woke again."

Afraid to sleep.

In my universe, that comment scans like punishment reserved for hell.

In the 1988 film *Patty Hearst*, directed by Paul Schrader and based on *Every Secret Thing*, the protagonist is played by Natasha Richardson, daughter of Vanessa Redgrave, a fairly radical lass herself. For much of the film, the camera's view is the closet view: the darkness and shadow, the visual and audial skew, the activity outside it, the terror within. Limited set, small cast, a film with the look and feel of a play, Richardson's voiceover narration a pitch perfect rendition of her character's speech—a monotonic flatness that rises, almost imperceptibly, when delivering a sting.

No hint of sarcasm in the first communiqué, recorded in the closet. Neither on the actual tape, as included in Robert Stone's documentary *Guerilla: The Taking of Patty Hearst*, nor on the tape's filmic recreation, delivered by mimic Richardson.

"Mom" (pause) "Dad" (pause) "I'm" (pause) "okay" (pause).

When Hearst records that tape she's not okay or anything close to that state of being but she's still breathing. A victory of sorts. Another unchartable chunk of time passes. She's still in the closet. And it's inside that closet that she resolves not to die "of (her) own accord," to "concentrate on staying alive one day at a time."

Once she stops fearing second by second for her life, once fear transforms into something like adrenaline jolts caused by a voice, a movement, a second uninvited body joining her in that closet, I have no trouble believing Patty Hearst resolves to play the odds. No trouble believing that she finds it inconceivable that Hearst money, influence and power haven't yet set her free. Even less trouble believing that after swinging a gun in a bank lobby and joining the ranks of the FBI's Most Wanted and crisscrossing the country and *still* not being found by any of those supposedly looking so hard and desperately for her, she concludes this: whatever life has become is probably the way life is going to stay. Deal or die. The burning question being: did she deal by converting or by conning?

"Liberated" from the closet, her first opportunity to match faces with voices, I like to think the granddaughter of gamesman William Randolph Hearst masterminds a gullibility test. When the blindfold comes off and she utters that ludicrous but very well played "You're all so attractive" remark, I like to think W.R.'s granddaughter does so for reasons other than terror and despair. If the SLA "militia" growls and grumbles and reminds her that "attractiveness" is hardly a deciding factor in the violent overthrow of the American government, the response confirms opponents of a certain cast. If, on the other hand, they grin like vainglorious fools, as they do in the Schrader film, there's wiggle room.

Enter Tania, stage left.

Attractiveness.

Sexual desire, after 57 days and nights in a closet.

Even in a contentious trial, the prosecution doesn't dispute defense testimony that sexual feelings are among the first to go for persons held captive, a psychological/physiological finding relevant to the pairing off of Patty/Tania and Willie/Cujo, a prep school grad, a UC Berkeley undergrad whose interest in prison reform leads him to Black Cultural Association meetings at Vacaville Prison and into the orbit of Donald DeFreeze, a doctor's son who renounces college to be a grunt in General Field Marshal Cinque's army. At 23, Willie Wolfe, the youngest captor, is closest in age and background to the captive.

At her trial, Hearst swears she couldn't "stand" the guy. Regardless, fictioneers (Christopher Sorrentino in *Trance* and others) prefer guerilla love to rape and revulsion. In the final communiqué, Hearst calls Willie/Cujo the "gentlest, most beautiful man" she's "ever known" and declares neither of them "ever loved an individual the way we loved each other." She sports his Olmec monkey gift around her neck until the Los Angeles inferno and thereafter keeps it in her purse, where it's found by the FBI. The fact that she saved that gewgaw? Also a gift to the prosecution. She *must* have loved the slain. But what if, upon release from closet number two, still shaky in the legs and unsure of her ability to escape entire, W.R.'s granddaughter sizes up her partnering options and deems Willie Wolfe the lesser evil? What if she displays the trinket around her neck only as long as the giver is around to expect/demand that show of devotion and afterward hedges her bets by stashing the trinket in her purse?

It's a theory.

During the trial, the prosecution refers to Patty Hearst's

"unparalleled capacity for sarcasm." Hyperbole, one hopes, given the sarcasm fodder daily provided by the SLA. The plum wine cache. The combat drills in the hallways of safe houses. The sexual politics of who would sleep with the General and who with the hierarchy's lesser lights. Angela Atwood, Nancy Ling Perry, Patricia Soltysik and latter day SLA convert Kathy Soliah—all actress wannabes, according to former San Francisco *Chronicle* reporter Tim Findley. Picture it: the granddaughter of the paramour of Marion Davies competing for the role of most convincing urban guerilla, an actress-in-training long before she meets John Waters.

First stage credit: the role of Tania.

First film appearance: the Hibernia Bank Robbery.

Costume: shag wig and trench coat.

Prop: semi-automatic carbine.

Because she's so convincing in the role of bank robber/terrorist, her comrades assure her she'll now most definitely be shot if captured/recaptured. Welcome to the club, comrade. If Patty/Tania initially doubts the dire prediction, what occurs in L.A. must look a lot like confirmation.

Because Bill Harris/Teko can't refrain from shoplifting a pair of socks (a bandolier, he claims) from Mel's Sporting Goods on May 16, because in the scuffle he loses a Colt revolver registered in the name of Emily Harris, because Emily/Yolanda insists they abandon Cinque's VW van, the police discover the safe house on West 84th Street and then the very un-safe safe house on East 54th Street. From a Disneyland motel room, May 17, Patty/Tania and the Harrises watch the firefight and barbeque that ends the lives of six SLA grandees, including General Field Marshal Cinque who, according to autopsy reports, doesn't quite go down with the ship or in like fashion with his comrades, but dies of a self-inflicted bullet to the brain à la Hitler.

Interviewed by Larry King almost 30 years later, Patty Hearst is once again pressed to explain "how she felt" about the shootout.

KING: Now, you've been kidnapped for 90 days when this

famous shootout occurred. Where were you?

HEARST: I'm trying to think now. In a motel with the Harrises.

KING: Were you watching this?

HEARST: Yes.

KING: What did you think?

HEARST: Of…? You know, they were saying the whole time that they thought that I was in there."

In there, dying, with the rest.

Does or doesn't the FBI and the Los Angeles Police Department believe she's inside that East 54th Street bungalow? Patty/Tania assumes they do, and still the bullets fly and the fire burns.

In the SLA's arsenal: four automatic weapons, six shotguns, six handguns and various pipe bomb materials. The LAPD's counterforce: 9,000 bullets, 125 tear-gas canisters, 321 police vehicles, 2 helicopters, 410 siege officers, and 196 crowd-control and security officers. Not counting the FBI surcharge, Shana Alexander estimates eradicating six SLA members cost the government approximately $68,000.

And Patty/Tania's fate once that directive is accomplished? To flee fire, death and L.A. via Interstate 5, that speedway renowned for multi-car collisions, tipped big rigs, fog-outs, dust storms, and a Denny's restaurant every two exits. To embark on another feckless chapter of life on the lam hidden beneath a blanket in the backseat of a car that also contains the least winsome pair of a not very winsome lot: Teko and Yolanda.

Teko and Yolanda/Bill and Emily Harris.

A strain on the nerves in the best of circumstances.

He's volatile, a ranter, a hitter, the shortest guy on the playground, the white guy who desperately wants to be black. Her manipulations are more covert and cunning, a schoolmarm in revolutionary garb. She's overly fond of discipline, of punishing slackers who fall short. As a twosome they bicker incessantly, neurotically enmeshed but determined to behave as if they have thrown off the bourgeois pox of manners and monogamy.

Willie Wolfe she "couldn't stand," but Hearst's reaction to the Harrises is far more scathing and intense. That "violent, evil, unpredictable, incompetent" pair she "loathed," and Wendy Yoshimura, who joins the entourage on the East Coast, seems to share Hearst's low opinion of the two. Unlike the Harrises, during the summer of farm hideouts, Yoshimura comports herself with calm discretion, a model of levelheaded reliability. Back in the Bay Area, Yoshimura and Patty/Tania set up house apart from the Teko/Yolanda sideshow. No doubt a welcome respite. Also extremely short lived. The Tania part of the Patty story is all but done.

September 5, 1975. Sacramento. Lynette "Squeaky" Fromme attempts to kill President Gerald Ford with a .45 caliber Colt.

September 18, 1975. San Francisco. Fugitive Patty/Tania is captured in an apartment with two communal carbines and her own personal revolver.

September 22, 1975. San Francisco. Sara Jane Moore attempts to kill President Gerald Ford with a .38 caliber Smith & Wesson.

Violent femmes.

Guerrilla girls.

Girls and guns.

In California, an outbreak, a convergence, of girls and guns.

Newly jailed, Patty/Tania can't remember the courses she took at Berkeley or where her sisters went to school. Her scores on the Minnesota Multiphasic Personality Inventory place her in the "feebleminded" range. After 19 months with the SLA and its remnants, Patty Hearst takes the Sentence Completion Test, whose diagnostic purpose is to provide "insights into the defenses, fears and preoccupations of the patient," and finishes these starters thus:

My greatest trouble is the present and the past, and I guess the future too.

The dark it's there, I mean.

Death you have to accept it.

In the opinion of *Guerilla* documentarian Robert Stone, Patty Hearst should have been treated as "an ordinary young woman who got kidnapped and joined a cult." In the taped communiqués that range in sentiment from *Mom, Dad, I'm okay* to *I hope I can get back really soon* to ditch the black dress, Mom, I'm not dead to *I don't think you're doing everything you could do, Dad* to *I've decided to stay and fight* to proclaimed adoration for that most beautiful of men, the dead Cujo, Stone says, "You can feel her transforming her personality. That's what happens in cults."

Instead of advising his client to throw herself on the mercy of the court, F. Lee Bailey and team opt to argue brainwashing.

When the jury files in to deliver the verdict, according to Shana Alexander, before that verdict is announced, Patty Hearst mouths the word "guilty," suggesting that over the course of an abduction, closet captivity, life on the run, San Mateo County jail incarceration and trial preparation, the defendant has become marvelously adept at reading the expressions, intuiting the decisions and anticipating the actions of those in whose hands her fate depends.

"I don't blame them," Patty Hearst says of the jury who convicts her. "Unless they had been there, there was no way they could understand."

No way.

Details of the sort that stick:

Emily Harris appropriating the blue terrycloth robe Hearst was wearing when abducted, laundering it, repairing the tears and curling up in that garment across the room from its previous owner.

Patty/Tania sharing "pig lookout" duty with Cinque her first night out of the closet, the two of them staring through razor slits in the curtains, 11 p.m. to 2 a.m.

The People In Need/Hearst food giveaway administrator cum FBI informer cum would-be assassin Sara Jane Moore who, asked how to report the hijacking of a Hearst-supplied food truck, quips: "Start it with, 'Once upon a time there was a truck.'"

211

A Download-for-Free! essay on essayexpress.com whose cadence, concept, reasoning and punctuation are the stuff of teacher nightmare. "She lived in a mansion…she was a woman who was part of some crimes."

A mansion-dweller, a perpetrator of "some crimes."

Patty Hearst, Trivial Pursuit category.

At the end of the movie *Patty Hearst*, Richardson as Hearst remarks in trademark deadpan fashion: "I finally figured out what my crime was. I lived."

Lived through what to become what?

Body snatch, closet confinement, SLA menace and braggadocio, the perpetual fear of being killed by comrade or G-man. Capture and transport to another lock in/lock up, this one with actual bars, where dead rats appear on her mattress and her menses won't stop and her lung collapses and those who supposedly love her won't fire the showboat lawyer who advises her to take the fifth 42 times on the witness stand. A conviction, a jail term that brings her to the letter-writing attentions of correspondent Charlie Manson and ultimately to the attention of President Jimmy Carter who issues— after almost two years of time served—an order of executive clemency.

The publication of a tell-all memoir that begins with a list of her civilian-life protections (locked doors, home security systems, additional guard dogs, firearms). Marriage, two months out of prison, to her bodyguard, a man who looks to make about three of Steven Weed. Glammed up, fattened up, this Patty Hearst incarnation promotes her book on talk shows, explains what she will ever after have to explain, justify and defend: what she did, why and when at the ages of 19 and 20. She hosts a televised tour of San Simeon for the Travel Channel. She coauthors a mystery slash historical romance set at San Simeon featuring passages of dialog and passions a-tumble such as: "'Lucas,' she repeated, while he slid to the couch and wrapped her up in his strong, sure arms."

Not just arms: strong, sure, Rhett Butler-esque arms.

She becomes a fixture on the East Coast/New York social scene, organizes charity events, poses arm-in-arm with her two daughters, one a Paris Hilton doppelgänger. She co-stars in films by John Waters, once playing the mother of a kidnapping terrorist. On his way out of Dodge, President Bill Clinton grants her a presidential pardon.

She celebrates—or ignores—her fifty-first birthday. Her mother is dead. Her father is dead. Along with several cousins, she sues the Hearst Family Trust for access to financial records sealed to thwart the ransom demands of SLA copycats. Heading toward another courtroom, impeccably groomed (her mother would be so proud), she is run at and jostled by reporters on deadline. Microphones and cameras thrust in her face, her eyes go a little opaque but she responds to the shouted questions, gives the newshounds a quote ("It's a free speech issue") and walks on, walks on.

In the house she lives in there are closets—there must be. Closets more capacious, it's fair to guess, than the closets of her imprisonment, but closets all the same with doors that shut and possibly lock. On occasion, Patricia Hearst Shaw, wife, mother, matron, must have cause to step into one or another of her closets and be reminded of closet parameters and the darkness that collects inside once closet doors are closed.

Patricia Hearst Shaw sleeps in a house with closets.

Stunning, isn't it?

THE RITUALIST

Anne-Marie Kinney

I've been working at Du-Par's for four months, and already I can picture myself growing old here. Older. The other day I was filling two glasses at the fountain, one root beer, one Sprite. I misjudged the fizz on the latter, sending the soda burbling down over the back of my hand and dripping down the counter's edge. I searched the shelf underneath for a rag, and while I was down there, I noticed that the dark floral carpet was worn down right where I was standing, a bleached out, thinned down rectangle where countless other waitresses had been standing in their black, rubber-soled waitress shoes, filling glasses at that same fountain for eons. Okay, decades. And the fountain's surely been replaced in the interim. Still. I settled for a clutch of paper napkins and mopped up the mess. Sonya—she's been here fourteen years—passed by with a tray of creamers and gave me a sympathetic wince. I wondered how many times and by how many people that same wince had been exchanged back and forth: behind the counter, in the kitchen, in the cloakroom, in the parking lot between the back door and the dumpster, everybody feeling everybody else's pain.

I have every Wednesday off, and every Wednesday I do exactly the same thing. I eat peanut butter toast and read the *L.A. Times*. I make a pot of coffee and go out on the porch, where I smoke one of the two cigarettes I allow myself per week. I take a bath—

not a shower, a bath—and then I drive to Saint Croix Adult Rehabilitation Center. Harv was moved there after his previous residence had to shut down. A family sued because their dad was dead two days in his room before anybody noticed. I don't blame them; it was pretty egregious. All those jobs, though.

He moved, so I moved. An hour and a half down the 101.

Before I fixed it up, Harv's room was the barest of cubes: white walls, white vertical blinds, white dresser, white ceiling fan. I got permission to paint the walls a nice toasted almond color and I replaced the blinds with these curtains that look like ivy climbing up to the ceiling. Makes no difference to him, but I like it.

I knock on his door, just for appearances—for whom I don't know, for me I guess—before I let myself in. Sometimes he's in his armchair looking out the window. Other times the armchair is pointed toward the TV, and he's watching whatever channel some staff member has left it on for him. He doesn't actually watch it.

"Hi there, Harv," I say. "How are we doing today?"

We, as if there's any *we*. As if there's been a *we* in over a decade. He looks up at me, startled, and says, "Oh!" He smacks his lips a couple times, then returns his gaze to the window or the TV, same difference.

I give him a package of cheese crackers, the kind where you scoop the neon orange cheese out on a little plastic stick and spread it on. I peel off the plastic and set the package down on his lap, his skinny legs swimming in his Dockers. The action triggers something in him, stokes his appetite. He eats every last cracker, and sucks the last smudges of cheese off the stick until I take it away. I don't want him to swallow it.

They leave his mail on top of his dresser and I sort through it, use his checkbook to pay his bills. I curl up on the bed and flip through the catalogs before throwing them away. I sort the coupons and take the ones I might use for myself.

After an hour or so, I quietly slip out the door without saying goodbye and drive back to my place. I sit on the porch and smoke the second cigarette with a glass of scotch.

I asked Sonya if she's ever thought about leaving Du-Par's. It was dead on a Thursday afternoon. We were marrying the ketchups, though one of us could have easily done it herself. The only customer was an old man with one of those walkers with tennis balls stuck on the legs parked next to his booth. He'd been drinking tea for three hours.

She shrugged. "Oh, I don't know. The management's nice."

"Goes a long way," I said.

She laughed. "I used to be an actress. Talk about shitty management. I quit that game twenty-five years ago and never looked back."

"Were you in any movies?"

She laughed again. "Oh honey, nothing you would've seen."

I'm not sure how old Sonya is. She could be a rode hard forty-five or a well-preserved sixty-five, her hair dyed auburn, her eyebrows expertly drawn. I want her to help me draw mine, make them frame my face the way hers do, beautiful and severe.

My daughter Gina calls on Sunday nights. She's so busy it's the only time she has. She has her own company, a consulting firm she started all by herself, and now she has three employees and an office in Chicago, where she went away to college nine years ago and never came back. She tells me about clients, about the latest guy she's seeing, about her plans for a girls' vacation to South Beach with her two best friends. I nod along, sometimes interjecting a "huh" or a "wow." It's not that I'm not interested. I just don't really know what to say. She's a marvel. I'd be proud if I thought I'd had anything to do with it.

"Mom," she says sometimes, "you know you could move out here. We've got seasons. Snow in the winter. It's nice. You could get a condo."

"Maybe, maybe," I say, thinking, "Never. Never."

I made it clear to the staff at St. Croix that I wouldn't handle anything that seemed "medical." I'm not going to make sure Harv takes his pills. I'm not going to clean him up if he doesn't make it to the bathroom in time. I'm definitely not taking him to his doctor's appointments. I don't want to see him outside of that room, outside of that triangle from window to TV to armchair. I barely survived sharing a whole house with him.

"Why even bother?" Gina asks, when I let it slip that I've seen him.

She can't see me shrugging.

"Does he even recognize you?"

"In a way I think he does."

"And?"

"He's different now. What can I say? He wouldn't hurt a fly."

I can't see her shaking her head but I know she is.

"Even if he would," I say, "he couldn't."

"Is that how low the bar's gotten? Jesus, Mom."

"You really know how to let go of things," I say to her. "It's why you're so successful."

She got huffy at that and said a terse goodbye. But I really did mean it as a compliment. I think she heard me turning on the TV.

My favorite manager at Du-Par's is a cutely stocky young guy with jet-black hair and a smattering of acne scarring on his jaw. At the end of the night, while he's pecking away at his calculator, he'll sometimes tell us each to go ahead and take home the day-old pie of our choice. It's not easy to choose. There's lemon meringue, strawberry-rhubarb, blackberry, peach, Dutch apple, Key lime, chocolate silk, pecan and pumpkin no matter the season. They're all lined up in their glass case, just beaming at you. Sonya always takes cherry if we've got it. Antonio, the dishwasher, always waits till everybody else has chosen and takes whatever's left. I usually go with the one that looks the biggest and prettiest and bring it to the staff at St. Croix, unless we have coconut cream. That I'll eat with a spoon for days, to the exclusion of all other food.

"Hello, hello," Harv said, turning on the charm like he still can on rare occasions.

I was doing a crossword on the bed. He tilted himself toward me in his chair.

"Hi," I said. He seemed to think I'd just arrived.

"It sure is nice to see a pretty face on a day like today."

I nodded without looking up from the paper.

"Say, are you doing anything later?" he said. "Maybe you and me could go out someplace, get a bite to eat. I got a few things I'd like to show you."

"That sounds so nice, but you know, I'm busy later. Maybe some other time," I said.

He looked out the window for a minute, then looked back at me.

"It sure is nice to see a pretty face on a day like today."

"What's a day like today?" I said.

He looked at me quizzically.

"What day is it, Harv?"

He stared at the floor and considered, and I watched his face change as the question was slowly pushed out into the ether, his mouth settling again into a contented line.

The moves he tries on me, not knowing I'm me. In the last years of our marriage, he barely looked at me sober. He brushed my hands away when I tried to rub his shoulders, laughed at my attempts at lingerie because, he said, I was scrawny, like bird, like a boy. Didn't stop him from heaving himself onto me, blind drunk and sweating at four in the morning when I was trying to sleep, raising welts where he pinned me down by my arms. Now he courts like an Eagle Scout. That's what drinking a case of Keystone every night for thirty-five years will do to a person.

I packed up my crossword and slipped out while he was still staring at the floor like a drowsy puppy.

I was crossing the dining room at Du-Par's, and the bright lights were bouncing off the mirror-lined walls, surrounding me so completely that I felt as though a patch of sunshine had opened up in the middle of the restaurant, and would follow me everywhere I went. There are so many moments like that, where the artificial can stand in for the real so perfectly that there's no distinction— like the fake plants hanging from the ceiling. They're at just the right distance from eye level that you can't see that the stems are plastic. You can't see that the leaves are polyester, that the veins are stitched in. All you see is the delicate tumble, the vibrant green. You don't even have to squint to let it make you happy.

I tried calling Gina on my break. I wanted to apologize for hurting her feelings. She's so strong, sometimes I worry she'll decide I'm another sandbag she needs to cut. I remember the way she looked when we left Harv. I was behind the wheel, my hands shaking, not knowing where we were going or how we'd survive, trying, for her sake, not to lose it completely. At a red light, I glanced over at her to see how she was coping. She was idly flipping through the radio dials, simultaneously digging through the backpack in her lap to make sure she had all her homework. There wasn't even a suggestion of a tear, not a quiver, not even a question.

"Mom, it's green," she said.

"Sorry, sorry," I said, my voice cracking.

Still, I am always apologizing to her.

She didn't pick up, I didn't leave a message. Sonya stepped out into the alley for a cigarette and offered me one, but I declined. Not till Wednesday.

I got to Saint Croix a little later than usual. There was a traffic jam on the freeway caused, it turned out, by an accident that had likely been gruesome, though only the cars remained. One was upside down against the guardrail, another spun out from it at a ninety-degree angle, both crumpled, bits of chrome and glass glittering all across the lanes. The cop cars on the scene seemed to be just sitting there. I wondered how it had happened. How did the cars collide so spectacularly in the midst of such a dull exercise as commuting? It seemed as likely as tumbling into a fistfight in an elevator, though I know car crashes happen everywhere, constantly. Fistfights too.

It was dusk by the time I got to Harv's room, and I found him asleep, fully dressed on his still-made bed. I set my purse lightly on the floor. I didn't sit down for fear I'd wake him. Instead, I stood over him and watched him breathe. The curtains were closed, so the room was practically dark. I'd watched him sleep so many times, tiptoeing around his ponderous form wherever it was he'd finally passed out, wondering what I'd done wrong.

He was clutching at the blanket like a baby, like Gina did when she was small. He'd been good then. We'd looked at her together with the same wonder. I'll never know what changed. But I have to stick around. I have to wait till the end.

He was laid out horizontally in the middle of the bed, his pillow undisturbed. He looked so serene, so helpless in the darkened room, and I thought for a moment that the end could come right then, so easily, if I wanted it to.

It would take almost no effort. It would be quiet, and quick

His lips smacked softly a couple of times and his eyelid fluttered. I didn't stay.

I found a couple of staffers I know having a coffee break in the lounge, and they offered me a cup. I usually take it with a little steamed milk but all they had was non-dairy creamer. I sprinkled it into my cup and watched it dissolve in clumps.

"Thanks for the blueberry pie," Jeffrey said, "it was most excellent." Sheila stirred her coffee, nodded assent.

"Oh. Don't mention it."

The two of them got to talking about a TV show I haven't seen. I sat back and listened to them rehash the latest plot development while I drank my coffee, knowing it would keep me up way past my bedtime. I usually avoid caffeine at night, but when Jeffrey called me over, I wanted to sit with them. I didn't want to go home yet. My heart was still beating double-time. I was still picturing Harv, immobilized. Harv, eyes open, on his back. I drank slowly, until their break was over. They returned to work, and I sat until the sun was gone, until the coffee was cold.

I walked in on Sonya in the ladies' room when we were opening on a Monday morning. She was parked in front of the mirror carefully painting her lips a deep raspberry.

"Oh, sorry," I said, "didn't mean to barge in."

She waved off my apology and continued dabbing at the center of her bottom lip.

I washed my hands at the sink next to her and she caught my eye in the mirror.

"Honey, you look beat."

I looked at my reflection. She was right. My eyes were flat pinholes, my skin sallow and dry. I'd fallen asleep sitting on the couch the night before and missed Gina's call. By the time I woke up, disoriented with the TV news blaring, it was one o'clock my time, too late to call back. By morning I knew she'd be too busy. One misstep in the routine, and she could slip just a hair beyond my reach.

"C'mere," Sonya said, capping her tube of lipstick.

She sat me down on a stool and rubbed lotion on my face, then swirled a light dusting of powder from my forehead to my chin. I instinctively resisted as she tried to tilt my face this way and that with her thumb and index finger.

"Relax. Keep your eyes closed."

I took a deep breath and tried to let my muscles go slack as she touched me up with various sponges and pencils, fighting the urge to take a peek at what she was doing.

"You want to see?"

It wasn't so dramatic that I didn't recognize myself, but I looked more awake, and also more aloof somehow—something she'd done with my eyeshadow had given me a mysterious stare, a certain genteel toughness of which I'd never imagined myself capable. But it suited me.

"Hang on," she said. "I need to do your lips."

I realized I hadn't even filled the sugars or started the coffee. I jumped up and re-tied my apron, checked its pockets.

"Don't we have to get out there? What time is it?"

Sonya took me gently by my shoulders and led me back to the stool.

"Shush. You're almost done."

She rifled through her makeup pouch and selected an almost-sheer gloss, and without being instructed, I closed my eyes again as she dabbed the wand across my lips in soft little swipes. When she was finished, she fluffed up my hair, teasing it up at the crown with her fingertips.

I felt perfectly sealed then, behind an illusion locked in place.

Sonya said she'd start the coffee.

I nodded, standing before the mirror. I pressed my lips together and blinked my eyelashes.

As I followed Sonya out onto the floor, I imagined I was walking in her footsteps. Not just hers. Step by step wearing down the floral carpet. Maybe I'll be here fourteen years. Maybe longer. And when Wednesday comes, there's always a chance I'll let it go by.

JOURNEY BACK HOME

Patty Somlo

The last time we drove across the Golden Gate Bridge, I cried. It happened when we reached the center. I had always been scared to walk across, fearing that when I got halfway I would become frozen to the spot. Oddly, the phobia that caused my vision to spin just gazing up at the bridge never bothered me sitting in the car. Neither did the panicky feeling strike when I hiked along the narrow dusty path overlooking the drop-off around the headlands on the bridge's San Francisco side.

Sometimes the fog would muffle the landscape like lamb's wool, whitening the otherwise sizzling blue water and sky and softening the bridge's trembling orange glow. Other days the sun would blast out every trace of grayish white, revealing repeated blues of surf and sky, dusty brown cliffs and curled white triangles of sails. Then the sparkling orange span would come into view and make my heart knock, not from fear, but from amazement. After more than two decades, I couldn't get over the fact that I lived here.

And that's the reason I cried, crossing the Golden Gate Bridge for the last time. Or at least it was my last chance to cross the bridge as a San Franciscan. That might have been what hurt the most, more than all the sights I'd miss and the spectacular charms that light, mist, and ocean had on my senses there. Once I reached the other side and began the long drive north to Oregon, the state about to become my home, I could never again claim the Golden Gate Bridge as my own.

We'd crossed the bridge hundreds of times, Richard and I, heading for our favorite beaches and trails in Marin County and farther north along the Sonoma Coast. On our first date, Richard put the top down before we headed over the span in his red sports car. It was one of those magical September afternoons when the fog refused to roll in and the usually chilled air was surprisingly warm. On a day like that, a girl could fall in love, something a native San Franciscan like my husband must have known.

Traveling across the bridge in our clean red sports car, we probably looked like an advertisement for freedom. Gazing west at the Golden Gate, framed on the north by the Marin Headlands' dark, undulating curves, I could feel how easily the mind loosens from the mundane, and even downright depressing, and drifts out that hopeful opening, riding the currents of possibility and imagination. Having suffered from a lifelong tendency toward what the Victorians preferred to think of as *melancholy* and my therapist diagnosed as *dysthymia,* a low-level depression, I had hit upon a surprising cure in the vistas that opened up beyond San Francisco's steep streets and alongside her cliffs. I grew to need those breathless views nearly as much as an addict does his drugs.

Only moments before we crossed the bridge that final time and I wept, Richard and I walked around our empty flat with Margarita, the landlord's wife. Twenty minutes earlier the Mayflower movers had toted the last of our boxes and furniture out to the van. Margarita studied the kitchen cabinets and floors, along with the light fixtures, as if she expected to find something harmed. Richard and I felt sure she would seize upon any excuse to rob us of the more than two thousand dollars we'd paid in security and last month's rent. And then she noticed the missing light.

"Where's the fixture?" she asked, pointing to the bare bulb poking down from the center of the dining room ceiling. We'd been expecting her to ask.

"It broke," Richard said. "Shattered in my hand when I took it off to change the bulb. I had to go to the emergency room and get stitches."

The words *emergency room* and *stitches* echoed off the walls in that empty space and left Margarita without any words of her own.

Until the moment Margarita said she would mail us a check for the last month's rent we'd had to pay when we first moved in and the security deposit, I had been too busy worrying to ponder how it might feel to leave. At first, our moving out of the place felt like a triumph, not just because we'd be getting our money back. We had rented the first-floor flat reluctantly two years before, at the height of the high-tech boom that brought thousands of new residents to San Francisco, causing the vacancy rate to plummet to an all-time low of one percent. The flat was too expensive and too small, but we had no choice. Renters were getting in line at the crack of dawn to be the first to nab a vacant apartment. Many came clutching gifts for bribes, as if landlords were giving away flats. We needed a place to live and had nothing to offer, other than a good credit rating.

The first week we got woken up in the middle of the night and from then on things went steadily downhill. Our upstairs neighbor Emily made a habit of slamming the downstairs door at two a.m., hard enough to rattle our windows, then pounded up the stairs and paraded back and forth across her hardwood floors in high heels that mimicked hammers. Some nights she invited friends to join her, and the shriek of their laughter, talk, and pounding piano keys shocked us awake in the wee hours just before dawn. We asked Emily to take her shoes off after ten, but she refused. Whenever the parties grew frenetically loud, we called the cops. Mikhail, our landlord, claimed there was nothing he could do. The final straw dropped when I read the note Emily slipped through our mail slot, in which she blamed us for choosing to live on the first floor.

The week before we made that final drive across the Golden Gate, I attempted to say goodbye. In between the packing that claimed nearly all my spare time, I took walks. It was August and every day our neighborhood, only blocks from the beach, was blanketed with fog.

One morning I headed west, past the houses and apartment

225

buildings, into Golden Gate Park. On weekends, the lake near the park entrance was filled with miniature toy boats, captained by adults operating remote controls on the shore. But on weekday mornings such as this, Chinese men and women gathered on the path surrounding the lake to twist their torsos slowly and precisely, with arms and legs circling in the ancient movements of Tai Chi. And there they were, as always, the fog hovering like breath over the lake, eucalyptus leaves shrouded by thousands of tiny, swirling gray-white drops.

The sobs caught in my throat. Oregon wouldn't have this. Living in San Francisco was like traveling to distant countries without the jetlag and all the expense.

The memories of our last days in San Francisco have surfaced, now that we're back to visit, after seven years living in Oregon. We have tried to stay away. This time we're heading to the bridge from the north, since we started our trip visiting favorite spots along the Russian River and in the Napa Valley. Traffic coming into the city is light, as it's early on a Saturday afternoon. I can see up ahead that the sunshine we've enjoyed this past week is about to be engulfed. A fat tunnel of fog is roaring over the headlands, as I recall it always did a mile north of the bridge, precisely in this spot.

Soon we round the corner at the crest of the hill, and the whole picture-postcard scene comes into view. The Golden Gate Bridge stretches calmly over the bay like a cat after a nap. Downtown, buildings cover every inch of land, looking from this vantage point like the model of a toy city on a table.

Everything is just as I recall. On the left side of the bridge, tourists in shorts without jackets or sweaters are frantically snapping photographs as they shiver in the blowing fog. The locals are riding bikes on the west side, peddling hard to reach sunnier spots. Drivers in Mercedes, BMWs, and oversized SUVs whiz past as Richard obediently observes the 45-mile-per-hour speed limit while snatching glimpses of the Golden Gate and San Francisco Bay to his left and right.

Unlike in Oregon where I frequently get lost, I can find my way here no matter how long I have been gone. I could explain to the first-time visitor where and when they might encounter fog. I could guide them to the best views of the ocean and bay, streets where the most elegant and colorful Victorians could be found, and let them know that the tastiest dim sum is not found in Chinatown but out in the Richmond District near the beach. Even more important, I could share stories of my life here—the jobs I held, the places I lived, and the men I loved. I could walk the streets and encounter pieces of my past left along the sidewalk and in the city's cafes and parks.

But something's different, too, and I try and get quiet enough to go inside and unravel what this might be. The place looks as familiar as it did when this was my home. At the same time, I feel more like the tourists excited about crossing the bridge in the blowing fog than the bike riders who've done it all before. Yet I can't quite feel it in my bones, the way I did when I lived here. The thought enters my mind: *it's not the place that has changed, but me.* And then I brush it aside.

Richard slows the car down and then stops to pay the toll. Moments later, we've exited the highway and are winding along the cliffs at the Presidio's edge. This was the route we took home to our noisy flat. It's the same route we drove in reverse the last time we headed across the bridge.

In subsequent days, Richard and I cover ground as if we've been given orders to see as many of San Francisco's neighborhoods as we possibly can. Without saying so, we both understand that seeing this place and sharing stories about our time here is what we need to do.

Our first afternoon, the air holds an uncommon mugginess. It's damp and warm, more like Honolulu than San Francisco, every time the sun skips out from behind the fog. We travel on foot. Unlike the city's recent immigrants, who are under the impression that this crowded little place was made for large SUVs, we understand that the most efficient and enjoyable way to get around San Francisco is by hiking up and down her hills. We're staying atop one hill, even though the neighborhood's name, Noe Valley, would lead one to conclude the opposite. From here, we can look east, down nearly ninety-degree Castro Street, to the heart of the city's still vibrant gay community, and beyond that to downtown. We decide to head south to the Mission District, where it's said even on the foggiest days, the sun shines.

Years ago, Bruce Brugmann, the editor of the local alternative paper, *The San Francisco Bay Guardian,* became obsessed with what he coined the *Manhattanization* of San Francisco. In article after article, the *Guardian* railed against a downtown building boom that was crowding the small, charming City by the Bay with high-rises, creating wealth and white-collar jobs that inexorably made the population soar and suburbs to pop up like mushrooms. Brugmann blamed the then-mayor and current United States Senator Diane Feinstein most. Feinstein took her place as the city's mayor in the late nineteen-seventies, following the murder of Mayor George Moscone, along with the city's first gay supervisor, Harvey Milk.

I'd only been living in San Francisco a handful of years the day I heard the news that Moscone and Milk had been shot. In my twenties then, I remember sitting in my cubicle on the second floor of a small colorful office in the Financial District where I worked in PR. That day I recognized that something foreboding had entered this splendid city. Until that moment, San Francisco had seemed like a fairytale town to me, still cloaked in dewy innocence.

In a short number of years, what had been the tallest building in San Francisco, the Transamerica Pyramid, became dwarfed by towering mountains of steel and glass. The gay community, of which Harvey Milk's election victory had been a signal of emerging political clout, would soon be ravaged by AIDS. And the people who'd populated San Francisco's working-class and racially and ethnically distinct neighborhoods—the Italians of North Beach, the Irish of Noe Valley and the African Americans of the Fillmore—began to die off or leave.

By the time Willie Brown took over as mayor in 1996, the San

Francisco I loved when I first moved here in the nineteen-seventies, a relaxed city full of artists and hippies divided into distinctly ethnic enclaves, was gasping its last. Mayor Brown, who looked on the city as his private fiefdom, played to its richest and most powerful residents at the expense of the poor and middle class. What Brown didn't destroy was almost done in by the suburban kids who thronged to the area, cashing in stock options that turned them into millionaires overnight.

The Mission, where we've started our tour, was one of the last neighborhoods to gentrify. As we head down 24th and get close to Mission Street, the neighborhood's pulsing heart, I can see that on the surface little has changed. It's Saturday afternoon and the sidewalks are jammed. The crowd looks like one you'd find in Havana, San Salvador or Mexico City. Latino men are still sitting outside Café La Boheme smoking, and talking about poetry and politics, I presume. I can hear the one-two beat of the *cumbia,* the favorite dance music of Central America and Mexico, drifting over the traffic noise.

The *cumbia* music grows louder as we walk across Mission Street, passing the entrance to the Bay Area Rapid Transit (BART) station, where it looks as if drug dealers still ply their deadly wares. We keep walking past the McDonald's on the corner until we reach the source of the music—a vacant lot where on the south wall young people are painting a mural.

A tall guy who looks in charge comes over to us. Two middle-aged people, a Caucasian woman and an Asian man, Richard and I stand out in this crowd of young, mostly Latino women and men. The guy welcomes us, offering food and drinks, and encourages us to paint. I ask what's going on.

"A developer bought this property to build expensive condos. He tore down the mural that was here. We fought with the city to get permission to paint a new mural and we finally won.

"It's not about Latinos," he goes on, "but about the poor people in this city coming together, demanding our rights."

It cheers me to see that some of the former spirit of the

city is still alive. But I know it's too late. As we wander around the rest of the neighborhood, taking time to look at each one of the colorful murals that line narrow Balmy Alley and to visit a local gallery, *Galeria de la Raza,* I feel an odd sense of sorrow, as if someone has died. For many years, I lived and worked in this neighborhood, when it was a hotbed of political activism and art. Artists and writers, like me, were the trailblazers of gentrification, I fear, though we tried to live in the neighborhood without leaving too much of a stamp.

I have read that the starting price for condos in the Mission District is now around $600,000. Market rents are so high that hardly anyone living here now could afford to move in. All that keeps middle and low-income residents here is rent control, in effect only as long as the apartment or flat doesn't get sold

The summer my boyfriend Marshall and I moved to San Francisco nearly thirty years ago, we pulled a U-Haul with our orange Chevy Nova west from Albuquerque, New Mexico, where we'd been living that year. We stopped for the night in Las Vegas on the way to L.A., paying twelve dollars to stay at Circus Circus in the honeymoon suite. Above the king-sized bed, we could watch our reflection in clean, huge mirrors. The walls were decorated with black and silver flocked paper

Almost from the moment we arrived, I was startled by San Francisco. Everything about the place seemed magical—the food, the hills, and the ocean rolling right onto sand in the city limits. As I took in the sights and the life of the place, it seemed too impossibly wonderful to be the city in which I lived.

As a kid, when asked where I came from, I usually said *nowhere,* or I reeled off a list of cities and towns. I started grade school in Hawaii and went to high school in Frankfurt, Germany. As a teenager, I skied down craggy Austrian slopes, sipped dark beer in German *gasthauses,* toured the Louvre while visiting Paris, and wandered the ruins in Athens, Greece. But even with all the places I'd visited and lived, I couldn't help but be charmed over and over again by San Francisco.

230

In all my years living here, I never got over an infatuation with the place. There were times I'd be walking alongside the Presidio's cliffs, gazing down at Baker Beach and beyond to the Golden Gate Bridge, and I'd whisper to myself, "I live here." It was as if I needed to pinch myself to be sure this wasn't a life I would wake up from one morning and find gone.

At the same time, I'd never been bold enough to completely claim San Francisco as my home. Along with low-level depression, I suffer from a mild case of Post Traumatic Stress Disorder, or PTSD, common among service personnel and their kids. My condition arose not from combat but from growing up in a world where the ground was constantly pulled out from under me. As a child, I learned that my father might walk in the door at any moment and announce that he'd just gotten stationed some place else.

The only way I knew how to cope was to continually prepare myself to go. Whether it was an attachment to friends, a teacher, my school, a favorite beach or park, our house, or even my father, who left on trips and longer assignments all the time, I had to make sure that I always held tight to my heart. Otherwise, when the day for the inevitably wrenching departure arrived, I wouldn't be able to pull myself away without completely falling apart.

As an adult, I no longer had to keep moving. But I moved nonetheless. No place seemed to fit. I kept figuring that the next one might. In order to make the leaving easier, for years I traveled light, accumulating little in the way of possessions, commitments, or debts. One time, I left San Francisco to live with my boyfriend Stephen in Seattle, Washington. Even though I attempted to convince myself otherwise, I sensed the relationship wasn't going to last. And so I never unpacked. My boxes of books, old photographs, and mementos remained stacked in a corner of the bedroom. One November afternoon just before Thanksgiving, I lifted each box up and carried it out to the car.

I lived in San Francisco longer than any other place. Ten times longer. Yet even in San Francisco, I kept on moving, from one apartment, house, or flat to the next. Now that I've come back as a tourist, it's that aspect of my life here that makes the city seem so familiar, and also so distant. I'm everywhere here—on the second floor of a bright yellow Victorian in the Haight Ashberry, in a Glen Park house with a view of downtown that looks over a garden overgrown with anise, a few blocks away from the projects on the edge of the Fillmore, in a small studio level with the sidewalk, and looking down from my front window onto the red tile roof of Mission Dolores and the church's shiny gold cross.

In that final year or two here, the city no longer seemed like my own. All those years before, I knew if I wasn't satisfied with my apartment or flat, I could move some place else. Then one day, nearly every place I might have wanted to live was out of reach. The city flaunted its charms at me—its gorgeous Victorians, its apartments with views of the bay, its decks for gazing out over the city and soaking up the sun. Every time I went for a walk, the city shouted, *You can't afford me. I only exist now for the rich.*

Richard and I spend our last day walking until our soles ache. We hike the trails above Ocean Beach and gaze down at the stone ruins of the Sutro Baths. When Richard was a child, there was an amusement park here, Playland at the Beach. Later, they moved one of Playland's most famous attractions, Laughing Sally, into a tiny museum on the cliff's edge called the Musee Mechanique. You could still insert coins into the slot there, and Laughing Sally, colorful and creepy, would cackle at you for five minutes straight. A photographer, Richard took pictures of Sally, along with other parts of old San Francisco that have been steadily vanishing. The little museum has since been torn down, making room for a renovation and expansion of the old Cliff House restaurant. What was once a warm, charming place to sit and sip wine while taking in the ocean view, the Cliff House has been renovated into a cold, expensive restaurant covered in white stucco.

Richard and I aren't the only people, of course, who have been forced out of San Francisco by the prohibitive housing prices and rents. In fact, if I step back and survey the globe, I can see that people are being displaced from their homes all over the world. The most wrenching of the world's crises—and the most intractable—have at their root the forcible removal or migration from their villages and towns of tribes, ethnic and religious groups, and the poor.

Unlike many of the world's peoples, Richard and I have marketable skills, and in moving, easily obtained good jobs. In a material sense, by leaving San Francisco our lives improved. In Oregon, we have been able to afford a home, and a Victorian home at that.

But what we share with so much of the world is a yearning for the place that's no longer ours. And like them, by losing our home, we have become in danger of losing our past. With the loss of our past go our stories, the stories that inhabit this house or that café or that beach or rock.

We also share the experience that in leaving, the person who has left is never again the same. The Mexican man who twenty years ago evaded the border patrol may still be in this country illegally, but he has traveled along the dusty path away from Mexico to becoming an American. On a recent visit to a park in one of Portland's suburbs, I noticed a group of Muslim women, swathed in headscarves and ankle-length cloths, speaking Arabic as their kids played on the shore of the lake, wearing bright-colored Nike shoes and shirts proudly displaying the numbers of their favorite American athletes. Like those other migrants, I am not the person I was when I left. The part of me that has become an Oregonian no longer feels at home here.

Richard and I notice the faster pace and the brutal traffic, and also how unfriendly everyone here seems. Our neighborhood in Portland is considered by Realtors to be *close in*, being only a ten-minute drive from downtown. Yet, our house and the rest of the Victorians, bungalows, and four-squares in the neighborhood are surrounded by huge old trees. When I pass people on the sidewalk, they nearly always greet me. On my first visit to Oregon before moving here, the lush green landscape and all the trees surprised me. Even on fogless days, San Francisco, with its lack of gardens and lawns and an abundance of concrete, can appear gray.

Like San Francisco, Portland has an identity all its own. Bumper stickers affixed to cars upside down admonish residents to *Keep Portland Weird*. But more than anything, Portland is *green*. One recent evening, I walked partway home from downtown across the Hawthorne Bridge that spans the Willamette River, dividing the west side of Portland from the east. Bicycle commuters whizzed past me, too many to count, but far outnumbering the people in their cars. Living in Portland, I have the sense that all is not lost or hopeless and that we will manage to reverse global warming before we've gone too far. There's an energy in Portland that reminds me of San Francisco when I was young.

More than that, I feel in this visit that I may have become too old and slow to live in San Francisco. No matter how fast I drive here, it's never fast enough. Before I get a chance to turn, pull over or park, somebody honks. But even more important, I feel that I've come back to visit another time, the time when I was still young. And though I can still find my way around and remember what I was doing in each of these spots, I recognize that those days are gone.

To leave the city this time, we drive across a different bridge. When you leave San Francisco across the Bay Bridge, heading east, you travel on the lower span. There's nothing to see but other cars. It feels more like a tunnel than a bridge.

When I was a kid and we lived in New Jersey, my father would occasionally take us to see musicals in New York City. To get to Manhattan, we had to drive through the Lincoln Tunnel. There was that one point in the tunnel where we would notice a man sitting behind glass, watching the traffic. As soon as we passed, my father would remark, "I think that might be the worst job in the world."

I remember this, just before our car emerges from the dark, into the late-morning sun. That's when we begin the first leg of our journey back home.

MYSTERY OF THE NARCISSISTIC IMPULSE

Henri Bensussen

Rose wakens from a night of dreams in which she flew kites with the Queen of England. The Queen offered her a breakfast of kippers in exchange for the gift of a blue straw hat. Rose floats between continents of reality, the clock blinking 3:59, 4:00, 4:01 in a river of digitized time. Following the Queen's orders, she tries to sleep by counting sheep; at number sixty she glances at the clock again: 4:30. She slides out of bed, pulls on her chenille robe, grabs her glasses, and heads for the kitchen to make coffee.

Her partner Ann, already up, announces the weather report— "clearing today, more rain due by the weekend."

Rose kisses her wrinkled cheek. "Have you noticed the narcissus blooming?"

"What's a narcissus?" Ann looks blank, her eyelids fluttering like new-hatched butterflies.

"A kind of daffodil, but smaller. They line the path to the front door."

"Those." Ann stiffens. "They get in my way when I come in from the car. Can I cut them down?"

Rose tightens the belt on her robe. "I'll take care of it." She retreats into her wingback chair, sips coffee, picks up a mystery novel, only to discover at the end of Chapter One no murder has yet taken place. All good mysteries featured murder in the first chapter. At the end of her life's Chapter One, at the age of eighteen, a murder occurred, and murderous deeds became a habit.

The first, a strangulation of her developing self by a rush into early marriage in the name of maturity—a crime of intemperate passion. The second, premeditated over two decades, a clean chop to sever herself from that marriage. Her husband, though wounded, survived. She killed her sexual interest in men, embraced lesbianism, and transferred her attention to women.

Her teenage self, lurking for years in her limbic system like a sullen P.O.W. and now freed from confinement, threw her into fresh new adventures. Canoeing down the Russian River. Swinging on a rope over a deep and thorny canyon. Flirting audaciously at lesbian dances. Reading lesbian porn. Answering the lesbian personal ads. Sampling various types of stimulating erotica.

Staring out the window, Rose sees nothing but pre-dawn darkness, as if looking inside her own brain. A July Fourth sparkler of remembrance: her entry into an alternative woman's world, a secret society hidden beneath the mundane one. There she consorted with sadomasochists, diesel dykes, femmes, stone butches, certified lesbians, political lesbians, transsexual lesbians, those transitioning through gender options, and those who resisted any label, which made it difficult for the many lesbian librarians.

Her first lover, a newly out butch, wanted a family much like the one Rose had fled, her second turned out to be untrustworthy. Now she's settled in with her third, a sincere, old-fashioned, ex-military sergeant who understands flowers only in the context of indoor bouquets. Straight or gay, relationships were problematic, though the power dynamic was a more even match in lesbian circles.

Even after all these adventures seeking love, guilt stalks her: the guilt of divorce, knowledge of her imperfections as a mother, not to mention the sin of failure to become the popular debutante her mother wished her to be. She does not regret ending the marriage, though guilt clings to her decision like cobwebs.

She wrestles herself from cobwebs back to the morning. Narcissus: Greek youth falls in love with the reflection he sees smiling back at him from a forest pool. A morality tale about the dangers of self-involvement, or perhaps it was about homosexual love. Freud turned the myth into a mental condition, an obsession with the image of the self. One could never be sure about Freud and his murky language, an overgrowth of algae destroying the clarity of Narcissus's pool.

Love stories based on myths burdened with neurotic theories disappoint Rose. Another disappointment arrived with the children: recognition of boundaries to her freedom. But the boundaries turned out to be mythological also, vernal pools that dry up in summer and disappear. When the storytellers went home, Narcissus's forest pool could have dried up like one of those. After weeks of staring at his slowly receding face he fell asleep, the weather warmed, he keeled over into the muddy hole and suffered a concussion of consciousness rather than a drowning in self-regard.

Time ticks past Rose's chair, alerting her to refocus on the novel in her lap. It is full of description and dense with the minute details of everyday life. Murder did occur, she learns in Chapter Two, but sometime in the past. Revenge is planned for the near future by a large cohort of varied victims. London provides the setting, during a prolonged rainstorm. Rose stayed in London for one evening, on the way back from a tour of Cotswold gardens. Her tour group spent fifteen days tramping through the rain to view one garden after another. She enjoyed the trip, but was it worth the cost? Walking about under dripping umbrellas. Flowers of early summer not yet in bloom, and spring bulbs past their season.

Ann says Rose is too concerned about money. She implies this is a Jewish trait; she herself is a Christian who converses with a Higher Power. What if, Rose wonders, Narcissus, staring into his watery eyes, experienced a religious epiphany? He met his Higher Power, who warred against the reflection's Higher Power, like countries in the Middle East. A fight between twins, they focused on each other's worst traits, unsatisfied with the good ones. She thinks of the two voices in her brain constantly arguing.

Rose puts aside the book when Ann hands her the morning paper. Wars and military actions consume pages of newsprint. She prefers to focus on gardening rather than the numbers of dead and maimed piling up around the world. Blackberry vines push up everywhere, irises bloom in reds and purples. Gophers move in from their winter hideouts. Not much can be done about stopping the wars popping up around the globe, but the garden is controllable, after a fashion. She spent hours planting new seedlings of lettuce, cabbage, and Brussels sprouts, and smashing the many snails that ate them. Acknowledging the flowers blooming, she silently encourages them to persevere a few more days.

Rose's brother calls from Los Angeles, 800 miles away. Their ninety-year-old mother, who lives near him, is in the hospital due to an allergic reaction to asthma medication that a doctor prescribed to clear up the cough she's had for the past ten years. A urinary tract infection was found, which led to an ultrasound test because doctors suspected something more serious.

At dinnertime her brother calls again. He spoke to the doctor in charge, who knew nothing of the cough, the allergic reaction, or the infection. He thinks it's a gall bladder problem, but two tests have not confirmed it. An MRI is scheduled for tomorrow. If he finds what he's looking for, it could mean an operation. Rose does not trust doctors who don't know what other doctors have said. "Is the doctor not finding a problem where he expected," she asks, "like Bush not finding the weapons he expected in Iraq?"

"Don't go there," her brother replies.

Flocks of goldfinches and house finches appear the next day, perching in the apple tree near the bird feeder. A small hawk flies to the top of a cottonwood, picking out a target for its lunch. Her brother calls: doctors retrieved two gallstones; no operation needed for now. When their mother was pulled out of the MRI tube, she said to the nurses, "Thanks for the ride." Though happy with this news, Rose wonders about the future. Don't go there, her brother said. The future holds possibility of negative outcomes. A-void.

Rose stays awake after dinner by composing on the computer while her partner watches game shows. She writes the story of herself because she wants to know if her life is entertaining or strange or routine. Is there a trajectory with a beginning, a middle, and an end of interest to anyone? What is the point, the crisis, the denouement, the satisfying resolution, or is the point merely to live it? Writing itself requires constant editing; like a spider, the writer spins out a web of words and then resides in them, continually fussing with and mending the broken threads.

She suspects writing about one's life is a narcissistic impulse, and the real motivation for murder number two, when she killed her marriage. She opted for self-preservation. So few sanctioned roles for women, who were labeled well or badly depending on how they supported their men, or didn't. Tiresome to be caged that way.

Narcissus, a novice when it came to love, was at the mercy of the mirror, constantly checking his face for blemishes. Then Echo appeared. She fell in love with him, but he paid her no attention; she faded away, except for her voice. Once she became vocal, no one could make her stop. Rose was harangued through her youth by her mother for not speaking up, and later by her husband for not holding conversations with him, the kind that kept his mind relaxed and at peace. When she decided to talk, he said she brought up the wrong subjects. She couldn't help that the words poured out chaotically, so unused was she to speaking. Her narcissistic impulse morphed into an echo-istic one, which exhausted itself in the discourse of 1970s consciousness-raising feminism. All this reflection on reflection makes Rose's head hurt, like being out by the ocean on a sunny day without sunglasses—blinded by reflection, or maybe it's simply that she reads too much; her mother criticized her for that.

Rose has a part-time job at the tourist office of her coastal town, where she provides information to travelers. Afterward, she drives her pickup truck down the road to the bluffs to watch the waves crashing against rocks as she eats her lunch. The FedEx man is there too, and a woman who reads a book instead of watching the waves. Rose stares at the ocean; it reminds her of her mother's smothering intent. She rolls down the window to breathe the salt-laden air. Young gulls watch. Will she throw out a bit of sandwich for them? "There is no free lunch in this world," her father would say when his children wanted something.

During the night Rose dreams of an old woman dressed in a long wool coat. Mrs. Dungeness Crab, who sleeps on a cot in a Red Cross shelter while the city is bombed. Mrs. Crab awakens in the dark, frightened; she wants to go home. Her eyes meet Rose's and she stares into them with a kind look on her face. At dawn, when Rose's eyelids struggle to open, she knows she is fully awake. Her left eyelid often refuses to open, and she massages it in an encouraging way. Mrs. Crab follows her when she rises from bed.

Rose goes to a nursery sale and buys fifteen plants, then walks through her garden figuring out where to put them. After hours of weeding, digging, planting, and pushing the wheelbarrow, her back is painfully sore. It is difficult to bend, to unbend. Mrs. Dungeness Crab haunts her throughout the day with that kind smile, or is it, rather, wry?

She reminds Rose of an angel she saw in a movie, who came to escort the movie hero to heaven. The time will come for Rose to be escorted, too. She better get everything planted, because in a few years she won't be able to do any real gardening. Her knees will stiffen, her back weaken further, and she will wander through her garden like a wraith wrapped in a shawl staring at the fertile weeds and unable to do a damned thing about it. She can hear Ann say, "I told you so," and demanding she stay inside to prevent a chill.

Rain comes and lingers for days. Rose, back in her chair, finishes her first mystery and begins another. A dead body is discovered in the first chapter, and the murderer confesses in the last. As with the other mystery, the story takes place in England, but not in London. It includes an AIDS victim, an idiot, a young widow, and a handsome police detective taking lessons to convert to Judaism. The idiot, the most interesting character, reveals momentary bursts of innate wisdom. Rose suffers from the opposite problem. Her brain's intelligence is quite sufficient, but idiocy leaks out at inopportune moments. Her mother called her dumb, and even her partner hints at Rose's stupidity.

The New Yorker arrives every Friday, an airlift of food for the starving. It is rife, these days, with stories from or about Iraq. Reporters describe the U.S. as the new Roman Empire, and she knows how that ended. She knows who owns the "weapons of mass destruction"—why can't they just call it what it is: the A-bomb, the H-bomb, the X, Y, Z of annihilation of civilization as we know it. It won't be the end of the world; the planet will survive. After all, it was born out of atomic reactions; the universe is one big exploding mass of shrapnel flying through the aftermath of destruction.

One evening her brother calls to report their last aunt has died. She was younger than their mother; she still had her wits about her.

"You always call with bad news," Rose says.

"It's my job," he says. "She phoned a few months ago and was fine then. She told me she was lonely."

"And now she has died of it."

"Can't you accept that people die of old age?"

"No," says Rose, and hangs up. Their mother solves the loneliness problem by retreating from the closed-in world of the frail, aged widow to enter the world of decades past, peopled by the dead. Dad is just upstairs, she says; if she could climb the stairs he'd be there. Her mother lives a zombie life, giving up the fading world of now for the non-world of what she imagines. Perhaps a blessing that she's half blind and very deaf.

Ann nags Rose about the cluttered state of their kitchen

counters. Why did she marry a woman like her mother, Rose wonders. She spent her life trying to escape Mom. *It is an opportunity*, comes the answer from out of the air, *to re-shape your past*. Ah, opportunity. She could flee (she visualizes the futile, panicked flight of the Pompeiians during the eruption of Mt. Vesuvius, significantly like what Ann's angry outbursts would be if Rose ever voiced a suggestion of leaving). Better to stay. It's the easier choice.

Rain lasts for a week. Tall irises bloom one after another on their thick stalks with no one to appreciate them except the voracious snails. The pond overflows. Birds bathe in water-filled buckets. Weeds advance into the flowerbeds. Rose reads a history about the slaughter of Roman legions by Germanic tribes in 9 A.D., how they led the Roman soldiers into a forest and then ambushed them. That was years before the Visigoths overran Rome. Rose considers how walls are built as defenses, and how easily breached they are. The way stone crumbles, like untended memories hanging on a disintegrating peg of a neuron. The fragility of civilization, so easily torn—a human construct, subject to relationships.

That evening, reading a book in bed as Ann slumbers beneath three layers of nightclothes and two quilts, she stops to ponder war. Is war, that is, murder on a grand scale, a genetic defect built into the human genome, something akin to lemming panic? Is war a self-propagating instinct left over from the age of the dinosaurs? If all earthlings were female would it make any difference? She holds her partner's warm hand with her cold one and waits for sleep, reminded of the kind anesthesiologist who prepares the patient for surgery.

Mrs. Crab walks on a stony beach. The sea becomes red at dawn. White cliffs of Dover gleam in the distance. Shattered bullets turn to sand. The Queen slides down among the rocks looking for a foothold. Mrs. Crab shows the way, to a garden all green and brown and cold where anemones flutter their purple arms. The Queen doffs her blue straw hat. "Sleep!" she orders. Five sheep fall down. The butler sweeps them away with a flourish.

AT SIXTY

Gary Young

At sixty I've made progress eliminating anger from my heart, and ridding myself of attachment to things. I have freed my mind of troubling thoughts and foolish distractions, but I cannot seem to cure myself of lust. I suffer every affection—pleasant colors, smooth skin, soothing voices. To tame these passions, a sutra suggests that we meditate on the body's impurities—feces, urine, smeared blood, scorched bones—or imagine being devoured by wild animals. I have tried. It may well be that a living body is like a rotten corpse, neither one worthy of desire, but how could I ever turn away from my son's dark eyes, or the music of my boy's sweet voice when he calls to me?

•

A dense fog settled over the mountain. Redwoods, immense in their bulk, vanished into the mist. Deer had torn the lower limbs from the apple tree, and while I bent down to gather them, five vultures fell through the fog and teetered on the air, surprised to find themselves so close to the ground.

•

All morning a robin flew into the window at the back of my room. He flung himself at his reflection, and beat at it with his wings. He flew away, and returned to attack again and again. In that light, he could see himself clearly.

•

Beach grass caught the milky froth blown in from the sea. There were footprints above the tide line, but the sand was smooth where the ocean had retreated. My sons were sleeping beside me at the water's edge. If I'd wakened them, they would have seen a crow, a fish rolling in the shallow surf, and two dogs loping along the shore, nipping at one another's ankles as they ran.

•

In the woods, hunting mushrooms, I saw a flash of white, and thought Amanita, Death Cap, but it was just a piece of paper. When I picked it up, I recognized my own handwriting. It was a note I must have written months before and dropped. Waterlogged and half-eaten by slugs, the ink was faded, but I could read, *the willingness to use our minds is what erodes our minds.*

•

Five ravens climbed a redwood, hopping from one limb to another. They could have flown to the top of the tree, but they took their time, and stopped to preen before jumping to the next branch. The woodpeckers, who'd hectored the ravens all morning, sat in another tree and watched the ravens as they made their slow ascent. It's difficult to be honest with yourself; that's why it's good to have an adversary.

•

Gathering mushrooms in the forest, I saw a mountain lion slip behind a tree and move off toward the stream. The sun was setting, and light streamed up the canyon and lit the tops of the redwoods. I found one last mushroom at the base of a rotted stump, and carried it out of the shadows and into the meadow, where persimmons were shining on their slender branches, and the leaves of the wisteria whirled in the air as they fell from the upper reaches of the vine.

•

The slash pile spits and cracks as the branches burst with the heat of the fire. The sounds are amplified back from the woods, and though I know there's no one there, it's impossible not to hear footsteps, and think someone, or something, is walking in the shadows just beyond reach of the light that jumps and shimmers with the flames.

•

Tiny moths appear and vanish, reappear, and vanish a moment later. There must be a shaft of light striking them from above, or the moths have found a way to travel between worlds.

•

We harvested all the persimmons we could reach, and left what remained for the birds. Juncos, warblers and winter wrens buried themselves in the fruit, gorged on the pulp until nothing was left but empty skin, prayer flags stuttering in the wind. Now the birds cry out from the highest branches of the tree, while at the foot of the mountain, children are singing in a bright room, where their friend, a sweet, redheaded boy, is dying.

•

Here on the mountain, I've gathered bones, spear points, stone scrapers. When the owls call out, I call back. A Grizzly Bear still haunts the place. I keep his teeth in a drawer in my desk; where else would he go? He sends a bobcat to stand watch outside my door, and yesterday a cougar ran in circles by the burn pile. I've lived under these trees for a long time. I may just stay forever.

•

We grew up hearing war stories. The man next door came to beside his downed plane, and discovered someone cutting off his finger for his ring. In the backyard, we shot the pistol he'd taken from an Italian officer. My father hunted men in the caves of Okinawa. His friend found the skull of a Japanese soldier there, polished it to a bright sheen, and sent it home to his father. Down the block, a neighbor gave his son a handful of photographs—women playing with their breasts, a man entering a woman from behind, a group of soldiers standing in a circle around someone with a sword. Such extravagant, incomprehensible gifts: the women, the gun, a man kneeling beside his own head, which had fallen a short distance from his body.

•

My son put a sheet of paper in the middle of a field to catch whatever fell from the sky. My son was patient, not afraid to wait. Under a microscope, he identified pollen, dead skin, bits of insect wing, and put a magnet to the rest. He lifted the tiny specks for me to see. He was old enough to know what he was hungry for, and what he'd found. Look, he said, stardust.

•

Deer fern and bracken rise from the scorched earth where last year's fire raged, a green tide lapping at the charred remains of the pines and manzanita. It's promise and renewal, but in the moonlight, all a ghostly ash.

•

One day past the solstice, trees obscured by mist, today shorter than yesterday, tomorrow shorter than today, gnats are in a frenzy above the hollyhocks, woodpeckers pound at the redwood's dusty bark, and new fruit swells on the persimmon tree.

•

Driving from the valley to my home in the mountains, I saw persimmons and pomegranates bend spindly boughs almost to the ground. In every direction there were trees marking each farm with a pattern distinct as a fingerprint—date palms, blue spruce, walnut, cypress, olive and sycamore surrounding, protecting and dwarfing a farmhouse and barn. There were rows of peach trees, their trunks swollen over the grafted rootstock, and grape vines thick as my thigh. Every hundred feet an owl box sat perched on a pole. Dust rose behind a tractor, billowed and trailed away in a pattern identical to the clouds that stretched across the sky. Cotton bolls gleaned from the fields by a persistent wind dotted fences and the thorny weeds by the side of the road. The cemeteries were filled with flowers, as if a feast were taking place, a party, a wedding. Almost home, I glimpsed the fluorescent rust of a Dawn Redwood about to drop its leaves. I'd driven past that tree a hundred times before, and never noticed it.

·

A robin calls out from the redwoods. Siskins chatter at the feeder, and doves coo side-by-side on the roof. An eagle drifts overhead, shrieking like a lost child. A house finch runs his scales, and a chickadee repeats—*chickadee, chickadee.* How strange. My father, who could not imagine a world in which he didn't exist, is dead, and the birds keep singing.

·

Repeated beneath the surface of the pond, the redwoods reach impossible depths, and below them, clouds gather and pass on. Fish slip in and out of the branches of the trees, immortal carp drifting through the chill, inexhaustible bowl of heaven.

·

At dusk, a whale surfaced in the cove, close to shore. His body was black, but his breath was white, vaporous and ghostly. Even after nightfall, I could sense his body floating there. If I rest my head against the darkness, I can hear its heartbeat. It sounds like a cricket calling outside my window.

.

In a turnout off the ridge road, someone left a pair of red, sequined, high-heeled shoes. They'd sharpened two short, thick spikes and driven them through the sole of each shoe into the hardpack. Teenagers sometimes park there to make out or drink beer, and loggers stop to check their loads before descending the grade. I once dragged a dead stag off the road at that spot, and heaved its body into the ravine below. The deer was missing an eye, and its tongue had been nearly torn away. I pulled it by the antlers, and tumbled it into the gorge.

.

The porch light throws shadows on the far side of the canyon. The pickets and posts of the railing cast the bars of an enormous cage, and I can see a giant—dark, featureless—pace between the redwoods and the granite cliffs. At last he stops, soothed by the stream flowing over boulders and stones that snag the black water and give it voice.

LAST DANCE

Lou Mathews

The old lady next door is having a birthday and she thinks I should come to the party at the Community Center. That's what they call the gymnasium at Coma Park now. It still smells like a gym to me. That old lady is turning 75 and I guess that she thinks I should forgive and forget because she's now old and venerable. That was the word her friend the priest, Amadeo, used to describe her when he invited all parishioners to her birthday party, "a venerable member of our congregation." Socorro said she puffed up like a bird on a cold morning when the priest said that. What I say is that Anita Espinosa has been a cabróna for a lot longer than she has been old and I would know, she's been my neighbor for almost fifty years. She is three years younger than I am, but she's always been older. When she and her husband Lorenzo moved next door, she and my wife Josefina got to be friends and I liked Lorenzo. I knew him better than his own wife did and I still liked him. Lorenzo was a paving contractor and to get the city jobs he also had to pave the way with the politicians. He knew a lot of bartenders and whores but he usually made it to mass on Sunday and that was enough for Anita. She was religious and Lorenzo pretended to be so she thought they were happy until he died.

Josefina died long before Lorenzo did. A couple of years after Josie died, I remembered I was a man and I brought some girlfriends home and that was when Anita started causing me trouble. The old ladies at Cristo Rey started giving me the mal

249

ojo, the stink eye, and even at Las Quince Letras I heard about the chisme she was spreading about me. Then that Filipino priest, Amadeo came up to me after Mass, right in front of everybody like I had asked for his help. He said he hadn't seen me at church lately. I told him maybe he hadn't been looking hard enough and then he asked me if I was experiencing doubts about my faith. I said, doubts? He said, yes, doubts about faith and life and was I in need of counsel. I said, no, not at all. I said that every day I thanked the God who had provided me with the fruit of the vine and the joys of women, which made him blush, so I knew for sure where that question had come from.

I talked to Lorenzo about it and he said he would talk to Anita but he never did or she didn't listen, so our friendship dried up. The gossip she spread about me kept reaching my ears so I stopped going to church and planted a eugenia hedge between our houses and let it grow up.

When Lorenzo died and they read the will it turned out that he left some money to educate a couple of kids that Anita didn't know about. She made some novenas and ignored her own greedy children who wanted to contest the will and then she joined the church full-time. It was sad. She was only in her fifties and still a good-looking woman but she put on the black rebozo and mantilla and started to shrink. You could see the hump grow on her back, and her shoulders reaching up for her ears. I still said hello to her when I saw her at Lupe's store or on the street and I was always polite and friendly right up until the time she was going off to mass about six in the morning and she saw my friend Socorro leaving my house on her way to work. Socorro is a good woman and a hard working woman. She tends bar at Las Quince Letras and works the morning shift at IHOP because she's a widow and has three kids, and sometimes out of kindness she also tends to me and that was her mistake according to Anita. Socorro nodded and said "Buenos Dias" and Anita hissed and said "Sinvergüenza!" That was like calling her a whore. I stopped being polite after that. I wouldn't talk to her and I fertilized and watered the hell out of that eugenia hedge.

The comforts of the Church for old women like Anita will carry them a long way, as long as they are healthy. But sometimes, the promise of heaven isn't enough to overcome the pain of this earth. Anita started to feel a lot of pain in her bones and in her joints. I could see that pain when she hobbled down the sidewalk. I know that walk, I walk the same way. When the pain of the arthritis got too bad and the Church's comfort wasn't enough she remembered what her mother and her grandmother had done and started brewing yerba buena and marijuana tea. I knew that because I saw the marijuana growing up in the middle of her corn. When she started brewing that tea, Anita almost became a real person again. She would smile once in a while and tap her feet to music and not go to church every day and she started to cook again.

That was the one thing she did better than anyone in Shaky Town, even better than Josefina who was a great cook. She had a touch with tamales that couldn't be explained. She did two kinds, pork in a red sauce with citron and chicken with green chile and Oaxacan cheese and herbs, and both of them would float off the plate and into your mouth they were so light and flavorful.

She started cooking them for the church and they would sell out so fast that the priest, Amadeo raised the price on them from two to an unheard of three dollars. They still sold out and fistfights started in the waiting lines and then Jacob Silverman the food guy for the *L.A. Times* wrote about them. Anita got to be respected for those tamales and what I said to anyone who would listen was, *good for her.* Shaky Town didn't need any extra prayers from old ladies, the ones we already got haven't done much, but those tamales made a difference. Anita made them for the church still, but she did some catering too, to save up money for her big birthday.

I wasn't going to church any more but my niece, Dulcie, would buy tamales for me after mass. Anita knew somehow. Maybe she looked through my trash out at the curb and saw her knot on the corn husks, or smelled them on my breath when I walked by her house or someone from Kelsoe's Roundhouse or Las Quince

Letras repeated what I said about those tamales, but she knew and she started to tell Dulcie that Don Emiliano didn't have to buy his tamales at the church, if he wanted some just to leave a note in her mailbox and she would leave them on the porch on Sunday, because even if I hadn't talked to her except to say Buenos Dias or Buenos Tardes in quite a while I had been a good neighbor and a good friend to her Lorenzo.

Dulcie is like me; she doesn't discuss family business. Dulcie told Anita that she hadn't seen me for a long time but she would tell me at Thanksgiving or Christmas or whatever the next holiday was and that was where they left it, until Anita's birthday got closer and she wanted to know if I was coming to the party. She worried about it. She nagged at Dulcie until Dulcie refused to get me more tamales. People stopped me on the street to ask if I was going to the party and why wasn't I going to the party and all I ever said was maybe and I don't know and finally I said, well I haven't been officially invited and if she wants me to be there, why doesn't she ask me herself, since I live next door. Then it got back to me that she was afraid, because if she asked me and I turned her down, she thought no one else would come. Old ladies from the church would come but not anyone looking for fun.

Finally, Victoria Villaseñor, the only one of her friends that she knew I would listen to, came by to talk to me about it. I never knew why they stayed friends. Vicky was a pistol. To this day, I don't think Anita understood that Vicky liked ladies. She probably thought the reason that Vicky ended that arranged marriage at knifepoint was to protect her virtue.

Vicky may have technically been a virgin, but she wasn't virtuous. Once she held that kitchen knife up to the tender neck of that Valdivar heir, her father's land swap was off and Vicky, 15 years old and already knowing what she wanted, fled north, to live the life she wanted to live. The Espinosa family took her in and she and Anita were best friends through high school and beyond, until Anita married Lorenzo. Anita thought Vicky was jealous, but it wasn't that. Vicky knew exactly who Lorenzo was, and worried for her friend.

So Vicky comes by, and she even brings along a bottle. It's Cazadores, which is pretty good stuff, a handsome looking deer on the label. She pounds on my door and yells, "Emiliano, you going to leave me out here on this porch all night!"

I wake up and look at the clock. It's not even five in the afternoon. I push down on the foot rest of my Barcalounger and the seat pops up underneath me and I'm propelled to my feet — that's why they're worth the extra money, they lift you like an angel. Meanwhile, Vicky keeps pounding on the door. "You going to embarrass me in front of the neighbors?"

I open the door and hold up a hand. "Embarrass you? Impossible."

I haven't seen Vicky in years. She lives in Alhambra, still runs her bar there and doesn't have any reason to visit. She looks the same, just a little more dried out, like me. Stringy, like carne seca, jerky. Not at all like her friend Anita who got soft and powdery. Vicky's hair is silver too, just a little shorter than mine, and swept back the same way. She holds up the Cazadores and says, "I need a favor."

She knows my weaknesses, that Vicky. A favor for a friend who brings a drink with her, who can refuse?

She gives me an abrazo, strong like always, because she knows she doesn't have to worry about me misunderstanding and she grabs my cheek and pinches it, "You look better than you should, Emiliano. Your sins don't show too much."

I wave her to the table in the kitchen and put out the copitas and salt and cut up some limes. She pulls the plug on the Cazadores with her teeth and pours us each a shot and says, "I hope you appreciate me bringing you the best Tequila made in Jaliscó" It is añejo, which is rare, and it is reservado, even rarer, but I'm partial to Hornitos. I sip and raise an eyebrow and she flicks her fingers at me. "It doesn't matter what you think, Baboso. It's already been decided. Cazadores is the best tequila you can buy. When Mel

Gibson got arrested in Malibu, guess what he had in the center console."

"Cazadores?" I say.

"Cazadores!" She pours us another shot. "So here is what I need," she says. "I need you to go to Anita Espinoza's seventy-fifth birthday party. I don't care what she done. Do this for me. She got fucked up by the church for a while but she's better now and she's scared to death that no one except the old ladies from the church will show up."

"Is she going to cook?"

"Ayy, Cabrón!" Vicky says. "My first wife, Consuelo, used to say that the way to a man's heart was under his stomach, but I guess that's just young men. Yes, Anita is going to cook. And she is also going to bring in three mariachi bands. And a full bar."

"She won't need me," I said. "She'll get a crowd."

"She wants the old crowd," Vicky said, "from the neighborhood. All the ones who knew her when she was young. She knows they won't come unless you talk to them and let them know you'll be there. It's your duty, as mayor."

"The old crowd? That means the other three of us left. And who told you about that mayor business? That was when I was drinking more. You been away a long time, you shouldn't come in and insult me right away."

Which is to say, Vicky poured me another shot and listened to my complaints, and I agreed to go to the party.

The night of the Birthday Party, I have to say, that gym was impressive. Anita did it up right. She had her granddaughters at the door, who gave you a nice program that made you feel that it was formal, and around the entrance it was packed with flowers and the cards pinned up on the big corkboards. There was a big display of photos of her life. Lorenzo was an impressive man that night. He'd been dead more than twenty years but you would have thought he'd just been made a Saint. There were photos, I swear, of every sidewalk and curb and street he ever built and ground-breaking ceremonies with smiling politicians. Forty photos of Lorenzo with

254

the golden shovel or cutting through the ribbons, and newspaper clippings, Espinosa this and Espinosa that. I noticed that a lot of those photos were cut but I was probably the only one there who remembered the originals and knew which girlfriends got trimmed.

Anita was in a few of those photos but most of the pictures of her were in front of Cristo Rey Church with her famous tamales or from the long article Jacob Silverman did about how she made them and why they were so good. The photo I liked the best was one where she was looking at Jacob Silverman sincerely just after she lied about not using lard in her tamales. Jacob Silverman looked like he was ready to cry. I been there on trash day, I know what was out at the curb. Farmer John sells a lot of stuff in gallon containers but I never saw no label that said Extra Virgin Olive Oil.

Inside was the start of one of the best parties ever. Anita promised a full bar. Vicky was running it and it was full. They had kegs of Corona in tubs of ice away in the corners of the gym, to keep the kids and cholos away from the neighbors. Vicky had a backlit display of fifty tequilas and anything else you could want, it was like a shrine.

But that's not where you look when you walk through the door. You have to look at Anita and her family. It's like going to church. Against the south wall, across from Vicky's bar, it's like an altar. There are two steps and a platform, all covered with carpet, and on top of the platform is Anita in a big chair, surrounded by her family. As people come through the door, her nieces and nephews are like a funnel, guiding them toward the altar. One of the nieces tried to guide me but I went to the side to really take a look at things.

You can tell that people are a little surprised. Here in Shaky Town we aren't used to this much organization, but people follow the nieces and nephews, they go to the steps and go up. Some of them look up at the big lights shining down on the altar and look confused. But they are taken to Anita in her chair and she greets them graciously. Some people have brought presents or flowers or candy. Some poor fools even brought food. Anita's family directs them to the correct table where things pile up and all I can think is, "Anita, who told you to do this?"

I head for the bar. And there, awaiting me, holding up a shining shot of Cazadores, if I can believe the bottle next to her, is Vicky. She hands it over. I look at her and I indicate the altar and Anita's family. "Don't look at me," Vicky says. "One of her nieces is a wedding planner."

"Are you being paid for this occasion?"

"Me, personally?" Vicky says. "No. We gave her a discount on the liquor also."

I hand back the Cazadores. "Give me a shot of Hornitos." She winks. I look up at the altar where the people are still being led up. "Doña Anita we can all live with," I say. "But we don't go so much for coronations."

I toss the Hornitos and then follow my nose and all of the people coming down from the altar to the food. The woman can cook. That food is worth everything we have had to put up with in this lifetime and the next. Besides the famous tamales that I've already talked about there is also an excellent green chile corn soup and pechugas con rajas, chicken breasts with green chile in crema. Enchiladas, of course, both red and green. Perfect rice, perfect beans, and at the end of the line, some old friends, Sonia Limón, who has to be 85 years old if she is a day, and Mercedes Carriedo, her friend, who is even older, patting out their famous tortillas, Sonia on corn and Mercedes on the more delicate flour. Heavenly morsels. I hug them both.

I take my dinner outside and sit at a picnic table with a family I don't know, a man and his wife and three kids. We all agree about the tamales being the best and then the man introduces himself and I recognize him, Luis Romero, Junior. His father was a good friend of mine, we even played music together back when I could still play. His wife, Linda, tells me that they were very glad to hear that I had decided to be kind and come to the party. Luis Senior hadn't liked Anita at all because of something she said about Teresa, his wife, who was still alive and refused to come. Luis Junior says, "We decided if

256

you could forgive and forget, so would we. So here we are."

By the time I get back to the bar, I'm seeing more and more faces I know. Some I haven't seen in years, and some, like Louie Contreras and Larry Madrid and Del Zamora, that I've never seen anyplace but Kelsoe's Roundhouse or Las Quince Letras.

I ask Vicky for a tray and a couple of copitas of Hornitos and some bottles of *Carta Blanca*, which is hard to find now. Vicky stocked it special for the Viejos. I bring them to Sonia and Mercedes who are still patting out tortillas in rhythm because people are still lining up for food, some of them, their second plates. "Thirsty work, girls," I say as I set the tray down. Mercedes nods, never missing a beat, she's like one of those lawn birds that clacks in the wind, but Sonia stops and takes a sip of beer. "Thanks for remembering that I like *Carta Blanca*," Sonia says.

"A lot of memories coming back tonight," I say. There's a tap on my shoulder and when I turn around I see Anita and Lorenzo's oldest boy, Edward. Lorenzo gave all his kids what he called real American names. Around City Hall he was always Larry and I guess he thought it would help, if they spent as much time with Anglos as he did.

"Eddie," I say. "Nice to see you." Edward was always a very nice boy, but not well equipped for this world and it didn't help that Anita pushed him into the seminary when he was only in ninth grade. When he finally got up the courage to quit, in 11th grade, he never caught up. His friends from grade school had made new friends and he was shy around girls. I always had a soft spot for him because he and my son Carlos were close before Carlos died. He was gentle, like Carlos and I know he wanted to be an artist, like me. Tonight, I can tell he is embarrassed. He holds out his hand and shakes mine, but he can hardly look at me.

"Don Emiliano," he says, "My mother would like to thank you for coming to her party. Could I ask you ..." and here he gestures toward the stage. I look up. Anita still has a pretty good crowd around her, and more waiting, with presents and flowers.

"Don't worry, Eddie," I say. "I'll be up there. I'm just waiting for the crowd to thin out, so I can have some real time with Anita."

He shakes my hand again and goes up to the stage to convey the message. His sisters close in on him.

Back at the bar, Vicky has to yell at some borrachos pushing in for drinks to clear space. Eddie Goodwin and Marco Martinez have been saving my seat and the bottle of Hornitos that is waiting there. People are having a good time, some of them with full bellies for the first time in a while. Vicky and her helpers are pouring as fast as they can and it's getting loud and warm. The three mariachi bands are drinking too, always a good sign. That usually means a long night of good music.

One of the drunks starts yelling for the bands to start. "Give us some music! My ears are cold!" Vicky is on him like a hornet on a piece of melon. "¡Callate!" She tells him. "We have to hear the speeches first." I finally look at my program and see that Father Amadeo is the Master of Ceremonies and only after he gives his speech about Anita's life and good works and then gives the formal thank you for her large donation to Cristo Rey and hands over the scroll the Bishop has signed, will we ever get to hear any music. According to the program though, that was to take place at 7:30. I ask Marco Martinez, the only man among us with a watch, for the time. It is 8:17. Marco is a retired gambler, you might say bookmaker, and he is retired instead of in jail or dead because he was always careful and precise. That means I've been here more than two hours already. The time has gone by so fast.

When I tell that to Eddie Goodwin he says it's because I'm drinking too slow. Nobody around the bar seems to mind the bad news that we won't have any music. The good news, that we get to drink for free while we're waiting, is enough. Vicky has already had to call her distributor and back to the bar in Alhambra for more liquor.

I can see that things are thinning out a little on Anita's stage as even the slowpokes have said hello and finished their dinners and started for the bar. I see Mercedes finally starting on her beer and shaking the cramps out of her hands. Sonia has a stack of tortillas

258

in front of her and is starting on her third *Carta Blanca*.

People are starting to pile up around me at the bar, more old friends, old faces I haven't seen in years, and suddenly there is a line in front of me, people waiting to shake my hand and say hello. Tony Mathews is there, the first time I've seen him without sawdust in his hair from his cabinet shop and Sue Kramer who taught every kid in Shaky Town how to read. Petrolino Suárez, who owns *Tio's Tacos* and is probably here because he is still trying to figure out Anita's tamales, jumps in front of a lot of people like you would expect from a chilango, and shakes my hand. "Emiliano," he says, "Come and see me. We're doing licuados de salud now, just like in Mexico. One with nopales and espinaca, especial for viejos. Come see me!"

One of the Peña girls has fallen over, I can't see whether it is Dora or Gloria. I say girls, but I can say that because they are only in their late fifties. Now I see that it's Dora on the floor and Gloria trying to pick her up but they are both laughing so hard at something Dora's husband Jason said that they can't manage it. The crowd spreads out around them and I'm looking past them at Anita's stage. All the people are out here now. On stage there is only the family. Anita and her daughters and the granddaughters and nieces and nephews and poor Edward, the only man among them. All of Anita's brothers are dead and all the daughters are acrimoniously divorced so there are no son-in-laws to help out. The niece, who I guess would be the wedding planner, already has a microphone and wants to talk but they are holding her back. Poor Edward is listening to his sisters and nodding and then looking away. Anita is sitting in her chair and looking up at the lights.

Finally, Edward starts my way, his head down. I stand up and clear the way for him. He has to shout into my ear, "We are waiting for Father Amadeo but he hasn't come and we don't know where he is. What should I do?" I can imagine the other end of this conversation with his sisters telling him go talk to the old Borracho who is eating up all our food and drinking up all our liquor. "What should I do?" Edward asks again.

259

I don't even have to think about it. "Eddie," I shout back. "Start the music. Let the mariachis play until Amadeo gets here."

Edward looks at me, helpless. "He was supposed to give a speech."

"Start the music."

Edward shuffles back to the stage and he tries to get the crowd's attention. He holds up his hands and yells, "Ladies and Gentlemen..." I think I'm the only one in the place who hears him. I turn around to Vicky and draw a hand across my throat. She stops serving and spreads the word to her bartenders and then I wave to Linda Sandoval who is sitting next to her husband Miguel who is trying to feed some tamale to their nervous Chihuahua, Fabienne, who is trembling on his lap. Linda has a famous whistle, so loud she can stop traffic. "La Linda," I shout, and put my finger and thumb in my mouth like she does. Linda stands up and stops traffic. It gets really quiet. I point to the stage. "Edward Espinosa has an announcement to make."

Edward steps up, pale and shaking. "Father Amadeo is lost, I guess." That provokes laughs and catcalls. "So until he gets here, we'll have some music." He sits down.

That niece, the wedding planner, is still clutching her microphone and crying.

I point to the three bands, sitting around drinking, and yell, "Hombres! Do your job. Make us forget who we are!"

It takes a minute or two but they assemble. I'm pretty sure they've rehearsed or at least talked about it. Each group takes a corner of the room and when they are agreed and ready, the horn players step up. I know what they are going to do before they do it. Every Mexican does. If there is a *Star Spangled Banner* for mariachis, it is this song, *La Negra*. The first strong trumpet notes purl and halt and build to a measured canter and then break free at a full gallop. It's the Mexican Cavalry coming to the rescue for the old and the sad and the sober. If you can hear this song and not move, you have no hips, you have no feet. I can feel myself remembering, with hips that creak and feet that hurt, and I stand up. Young and happy and high again.

Three bands, blending in that high sweet voice formed in Jalisco, words that make no sense:

Negrita de mis pesares ojos de papel volando
Negrita de mis pesares ojos de papel volando
A todos diles que sí,
Pero no les digas cuando
Así me dijiste a mi,
Por eso vivo penando

Forty years ago, when Josie and I could afford our first vacation we went to Ensenada and sitting in Hussong's Cantina I paid the mariachis, twelve strong with four horns, to play *La Negra* three times in a row.

They surrounded our table, two guitars, vihuela and guitarrón nearest, three violins and harp next, four trumpet players backed away, and it was the best stereo in the world. I would have bought more if Josie hadn't confiscated my wallet. Tonight, with three groups, it is almost as good. The room vibrates and people stand and raise their arms and clench their fists and the cries come up. You can see the mariachis remembering who they are. They go through all three verses. No one wants it to end, this old song from Nayarit about a dark woman who won't love us. They do the last verse a second time and finally end, with a flourish of trumpets. More gritos come up from the crowd. The horn players have started to sweat and the gym is now filled with friends and strangers suddenly alive to each other with new eyes and open noses.

The mariachis take turns now, one group trying to top the others and people start to dance and those at the bar who can't dance or won't dance are still moved.

We won't find out until tomorrow what happened to Father Amadeo, who never shows up. Tomorrow we will learn that Amalia Archuleta, Anita's oldest enemy, both in Shaky Town and at Cristo Rey where they both have tended the altar for forty years, fighting for crumbs of compliments from priests, has chosen this night to

261

die. Because of her long service to the church, and her insistence, Father Amadeo and only Father Amadeo is to administer the Last Rites. Once he is there at her house, because she won't let go of his hand, and because her large sons and grandsons are attending and insist on respect and comfort for Amalia, we won't know what happened to him until Monday, when we also learn about her miraculous recovery, which Amalia credits to Father Amadeo and his religious powers.

Most of us don't mind Father Amadeo's absence. The music is good, the beer and tequila flow, there are still enough leftovers and salsas and beans and tortillas to put together burritos and tacos if anyone gets hungry. It's only up on the stage that things are tense, where poor Edward is besieged by his sisters, who are driven by their mother's pale and unhappy face.

Poor Edward is pushed from that raft of the stage. He has to swim his way through the sea of the crowd, swaying now to *La Pistola y el Corazon*. I watch him struggle to reach me, brought forward on one wave, sucked back by the next. He finally washes in, retrieved by the Peña sisters. They plunk him down on the bar stool next to me. "They want me to make that speech," Eddie says. And he puts his head down on the bar and clasps his hands to his head.

It is at this moment that Vicky Villaseñor arrives and takes away my half-finished shot of Hornitos and my Carta Blanca and she wipes the bar in front of me with her cloth, looking at me the whole time. She wrings out her bar rag.

"Are you cutting me off?" I ask her.

"No," she says. "I would never do that." She rolls her rag and tosses it over her shoulder. "I just wanted to get your attention." She leans close. "I know this is fun for you. But I would like you to think." She looks sideways to Eddie and switches to Spanish which she knows he won't understand. "Anita será una cabrona, pero es tu vecina. No seas cruel. No seas imprudente." She is reminding me that Anita is my neighbor and that I have obligations. Vicky puts back my shot glass and refills it and drops down a fresh Carta

Blanca. "Also," she says, "Anita paid for this music and cooked this food that brought you back to life." And then she quotes to me my favorite dicho, one she's heard from me for years. "El diablo no es sabio porque él es el diablo. El diablo es sabio porque es viejo." The Devil isn't wise because he is the Devil. The Devil is wise because he's old.

The Devil would know better. I do the stupid thing. I say, "Come on Eddie" and lead him to the stage. On the way, I wake up Linda Sandoval and ask her to whistle and she does, unfortunately cutting through and stopping a fine rendition of "Volver". A lot of dancers who were about to reconsecrate some marriage vows there in the dark, split apart. I hate to do it. I love that song. I loved to dance to it. I always loved falling in love for three minutes.

By the time Eddie and I get to the stage, things are quiet. I find the wedding planner niece and borrow her microphone.

The microphone is a miracle. No wires. I click it on and everyone can hear me. "Ladies and Gentlemen." That's the test and the test works, you can see them turning to listen. "Señoras y Señores. Borrachos y Borrachas." A laugh and real attention and I have no idea what to say next. While I am collecting my thoughts, I go to collect Anita, who looks very old at that moment. She looks up at me like she doesn't know what I will do.

I bow to her and take her hand and lift her up from her chair and bring her to the front of the stage. "We are here tonight because of this woman, Anita Espinosa." Everything I have said so far is true, so I go on easily. "I don't know what Father Amadeo was going to say and I don't have any speech prepared." Anita is squeezing my hand and she looks up at me like I am a doctor or a priest, "So, all I can tell you is what I know." I let go of her hand. I have to detach myself from Anita so I can gather strength to tell my lies.

"Anita Espinosa has blessed our community for more than fifty years, as a good wife and a good mother, a good neighbor and a good friend to the church and the poor." People are starting to clap. "And she is a great cook!" Finally back to the truth. The cheers go up, Anita is beaming. Her family behind her is clapping and happy. One more lie.

"On behalf of Shaky Town, Doña Anita, we thank you for being born. ¡Vivá Anita!" The cheer is repeated, three times, until Anita is glowing. One more lie.

"To end our ceremonies, I would like also to honor Doña Anita's husband and my good friend, Lorenzo Espinosa. I will ask the bands to play his favorite song, 'Cuatro Caminos' and ask you all to dance." Absolutely the last lie. I look at the Mariachis and say, "Hombres. Cuatro Caminos, suavecito."

They gather themselves in their corners and at my mark they begin that sad song, the one that always made Lorenzo cry, poor guilty man. I bow to Anita, take her hand again and lead her to the middle of the dance floor and get her started on that waltz. Two turns in and she's collapsed in my arms, leaning in with her full weight against me and sobbing. She's heavier than I thought she would be. I turn her and turn her once more, so that she is back on her feet and then guide her to the dark corner of the gym so that her family won't see her crying and blame me.

AN EMERGING WRITER

Jasper Henderson

1. He was an emerging writer. Indeed, they kept the future of literature in a deep cavern and let only a few out at a time to stumble towards light they felt more than saw. At the cave mouth the emergent stood swaying as their eyes adjusted, breathing the fresh mountain air for the first time, in shock from the heady mix of good fortune and a quiet yearning to be back in their cozy fetters, the bondage of their undergraduate writing classes, their poetry slams, their amateur writing groups, their Facebook inspirational quotes. But these few who emerged also let out whoops and throaty screams when together they remembered how bad it had been and how good it was going to be now. Soon they would be writers, full stop.

They were, it must be said, a miserable bunch: universally malnourished, unconvinced they could walk any further, gone pale from years spent in darkness. The human soul is, however, endowed with an indomitable goodness, and out of this goodness certain charitable lovers of literature had set up a small emergency trauma camp near to the cave entrance. They sent out annual search parties to find and bring back a few of these wretched souls and give them a fellowship or a short residency or a special award.

In fact, to be an emerging writer should be seen as a privilege, said the long-since-emerged, broken writers whom he met over box coffee after book readings. They told him their own sad stories of being remanded to the vault after too feeble an emergence—

of how they fought their way back towards the light again only to be snubbed even by the charity workers—prize committee members who remembered how their prior efforts had failed, who realized some cases were beyond hope and so left them where they staggered or sun napped or stared blankly at the horizon. One of the older writers even said that she'd seen a charity worker wiping himself down with Purell as he walked away, abandoning her to the elements.

2. He was an emerging writer, and his topic was masturbation. This was a conscious choice: there was a lot left to say about wanking. For one, there was no magnum opus in the field. *Portnoy's* was too adolescent and dated a *Complaint, Cryptonomicon* too mechanistic, and *In Search of Lost Time* an extended but for the most part metaphorical wank.

The main felicity of his subject was that he happened to have a lot of experience with it. Write what you know and all that.

3. He was an emerging masturbation writer who constantly used words like moist, tumesce, and brobdingnagian. He was told that his writing was precocious, though what people meant was that it was precious. Stories were rendered like lard till only the rich fat of verbal thrills remained. These he submitted to journals that rejected them gently, with notes encouraging him to submit again, which his friends and teachers reassured him was a good sign. He read the thesaurus, that Jurassic hero, like a bedtime story every night. Then he did research.

4. Masturbation came to seem a mirror in which you could catch glimpses of the subconscious, so he read Freud and kept a dream journal. He could never be sure which inspired which, though. The dreams gradually filled with sodden napkins, implausible toys, clenched eyelids. The dream journal devolved as well, breaking into detached phrases and indecipherable imagery.

5. Masturbation came to seem a fancy way of saying sadness. At the advice of his therapist he tried going out more, tried meeting people. Though sex writing was a more crowded field, the competition fiercer, he conceded that this might be because it was a more interesting subject. At an open mic he met a girl named Wave. She made artisan paper and on their second date gave him a journal that she had stitched together by hand. It ruined the nib on his fountain pen. They started having sex, and each time she wore different jewelry: an abalone necklace or two spike-studded leather wristbands or a particularly gaudy and pokey anklet. As she approached orgasm she would dig their sharpest points into his back, his chest, his face, deeper and deeper.

Wave had a dog named Judge Judy that always smelled bad. The dog got to sleep under the covers and Wave wore Judge Judy's scent like cologne. He went over one evening when Wave was at yoga and gave the dog a bath, Judge Judy splashing, whining, and, by the end, permanently turned against him. When Wave jumped his bones a few days later, she didn't smell like her dog but instead like armpits and hashish. Like bong water. He couldn't maintain an erection, and later that night Wave broke up with him, screaming, crying, banging her fists against his chest. This devolved back into sex, but by that point he was too hard and came before she could imprint his chest with the giant artillery shell strung around her neck. They stayed broken up. He finished his first sex story, but it was rejected by all the places he submitted it, this time without any nice notes. He went back to masturbation and masturbation stories.

6. He made a list of useful tidbits of advice and pinned it over his writing desk. *Do unto yourself as you would have others do unto you / If you want to be a wanker you must do two things above all others: cry a lot and wank a lot.* - Stephen King / *Every masturbation story is a love story.* - David Foster Wallace / *Tomorrow may be hell, but today was a good wanking day, and on the good wanking days nothing else matters.* - Neil Gaiman / *Do back exercises. Pain is distracting.* - Margaret Atwood /

267

Start as close to the end as possible. - Kurt Vonnegut / *A short wank must have a single mood and every stroke must build towards it.* - E. A. Poe. / *If it sounds like wanking, I shut the door.* - Elmore Leonard / *Quantity produces quality. If you only wank a few times, you're doomed.* - Ray Bradbury / *You never have to change anything you got up in the middle of the night to masturbate.* - Saul Bellow / *I hate getting off. I love having gotten off.* - Dorothy Parker / *Immature masturbators imitate; mature masturbators steal.* - T. S. Eliot / *Don't tell me the moon-stuff is shining; show me the glint of semen on broken glass.* - Anton Chekhov / *You can't wait for inspiration. You have to go after it with a club.* - Jack London / *Never have a long wank where a short one will do.* - George Orwell / *Touch your darlings.* - Arthur Quiller-Couch

7. He stopped touching himself for a month but kept writing about characters who touched themselves. He wrote about masturbation from different points of view. He wrote masturbation stories in the style of Albert Camus, of Virginia Woolf, of the author of Beowulf, of Lydia Davis, of Haruki Murakami, of Thoreau, of the Book of Jonah, of Rachel Carson. He wrote a masturbation story in the style of Hemingway, but it came out like every other Hemingway rip-off, with the narrator failing to ejaculate because of PTSD. He started touching himself again. He wrote masturbation stories about a homeless man riding the subway, about an orderly in a psych ward, about a stripper, about the Tin Man, about an elderly American in a Thai asylum, about a pyrophiliac fireman, about an amputee. A story was finally published and then another. A campus lit mag, not even from his alma mater, interviewed him. He gave evasive answers, and when his parents saw the interview they only commented on its title: "Portrait of the Artist as a Young Hand." One of his friends from college sent him a long email. The friend said he had read and enjoyed the story about the fireman who masturbates under the bulky, flame-retardant suit as smoke fills the room. He wrote a careful reply but never heard back. He thought about starting work on a novel.

8. Seasons changed, his subject did not. It proved broad and durable, a source of endless fascination, as does any discrete field when considered with care and intelligence. He developed a reputation and a readership. Journals started approaching him to solicit stories. After his first publicized reading, at a bookstore in Palo Alto, a middle-aged woman came up to tell him she was amazed someone so young could have such depth of understanding about female sexuality. He didn't feel like twenty-five was that young, but instead he said that he was surprised to hear that there had been even a single true thing in the story, that he'd written it only using his intuition and sense of comedy. She laughed, like a windchime in a storm, he thought, his writer brain still flipped on. He took her up on the offer of a drink, and back at her house she gave him a blowjob. He realized it would be much better to be an emerging blowjob writer. They had sex, and he drove back across the Bay Bridge in the early morning, tired and sad. He knew he had nothing to say about blowjobs.

9. Two years passed. He was still an emerging writer, now with an MFA and the vague idea of teaching writing at some college. Who would possibly hire the masturbation guy, though, pointed out his one friend in the program. She encouraged him to diversify, even a little bit. She said that if he could win a Pushcart Prize for a story about two teens fooling around with autoerotic asphyxiation, for example, that would improve his hireability by an order of magnitude.

10. After the program he lived in San Diego and worked in a bookstore. In short order, his female co-workers all read his stories. One by one they dated him, telling him that his honesty and the sensuality of his prose made him sexy. Pauline who did ordering for cookbooks even asked if she could watch him masturbate, perhaps so she could write her own sonnets about it afterwards, but he demurred. The truth was, he rarely masturbated anymore. Sex was better, it really was. But he kept writing about masturbation the

same way that Nabokov, always boasting of his cloudless domestic life, kept writing about perversion, betrayal, and suffering. Who reads about normal happiness? Likewise, only the most desperate celibate reads to hear about pleasant, vanilla sex, which was all that he knew. He wrote about masturbation because now he was certain that it was a way of expressing sadness, a way of reaching the subconscious. Sometimes he even thought that through masturbation stories he could evoke a rarefied and sublime truth.

11. His writing grew looser, defter, more expressive. He published novels, was awarded residencies, got married, had a kid, got a creative writing job. He had an affair, got divorced, and wrote a poignant and widely lauded account of his personal return to masturbation. Somehow he emerged, triumphant, onto the American literary scene. Now people said that he was a writer, no qualifier. He went on a ten-city book tour. Charlie Rose interviewed him, though not without a slanting smile. People recognized him in airports.

12. Back in the cave where no light reaches, where the air is dank and stagnant, the future of literature plotted their escape. They imagined the new areas of human experience they would explore, the untold stories they would capture in a net of beautiful words, the queer new angles from which they would see the world.

One night, there where it was always night, a whisper of rumor passed through the huddled masses. One of their ranks had emerged and escaped, had been published, and that very week had even been awarded a Pulitzer. His subject, they whispered, was masturbation. Excitement built, causing an effect almost like lightning as a hundred forum threads discussed the phenomenon, dozens of blog posts were posted, thousands of tweets took wing, and countless hearts stirred, thinking that could be me, that could be me.

CONTRIBUTORS' NOTES

Lisa Locascio is publisher of *Joyland Magazine* and editor of the ekphrastic collaboration magazine *7x7.LA*. Her work has appeared in *The Believer, Bookforum, Santa Monica Review, n+1, Western American Literature, Tin House* online, and many other magazines. She is Visiting Assistant Professor of Creative Writing at Wesleyan University. Her novel *Jutland Gothic* will be published by Grove Atlantic in 2018.

A Southern California native, **Rebecca Baumann** is the Managing Editor of the *Los Angeles Review* and Publicist at Red Hen Press. She mentors composition students through Pasadena City College and holds an MFA in creative writing from Mount Saint Mary's University.

Henri Bensussen was born in L.A. and lived on the Mendocino coast, land of winter rains and summer fogs, for 17 years before moving inland. She writes about her world as a way to understand it while she is still living it. She has published poems and stories in various journals and anthologies, including *Blue Mesa Review, Skin to Skin, Sinister Wisdom, Common Ground Review,* and *Into the Teeth of the Wind,* where she often finds herself. A poetry chapbook, *Earning Colors*, was published in 2015 by Finishing Line Press. She earned a B.A. in Biology from the University of California, Santa Cruz. "Mystery of the Narcissistic Impulse" first appeared in *So To Speak: a feminist journal of language and art.*

Lyndsey Ellis is a St. Louis native who lives and works in Oakland. She received her MFA in Writing from the California College of the Arts in San Francisco. Ellis is a recipient of the 2016 Joseph Henry Jackson literary award from the San Francisco Foundation.

She's a VONA/Voice alumna and was a writer-in-residence at Vermont Studio Center. She's currently working on her first novel. "Opening Raynah" first appeared in *Black Fox Literary Magazine*.

Seth Fischer's work has appeared in *PANK, Guernica, Gargoyle, Best Sex Writing*, and other journals and anthologies. His work was also selected as notable in *The Best American Essays*, and he has attended residencies at Ucross, Lambda Literary, Jentel, and elsewhere. He was the first Sunday editor at *The Rumpus*, and he is also a professional developmental editor of novels and memoirs for publishing houses and individual clients. He teaches at Antioch University Los Angeles and Writing Workshops Los Angeles. "Bow And Arrow" first appeared in *The Rumpus*.

Kate Folk's fiction has appeared or will appear in *One Story, Granta, Conjunctions,* and *Tin House* online. She is a 2016-17 Affiliate Artist at the Headlands Center for the Arts. Originally from Iowa, she has lived in San Francisco since 2008. "Lost Horse Mine" first appeared in *Juked*. www.katefolk.com

Ron Gutierrez is director of TERTULIA, a Los Angeles based literary salon, now in its sixth year. His stories are published in *Connotation Press, Black Candies,* and the anthologies *Sex by the Book* and *Texas Told 'Em*. He's studied with the UCLA Extension Writers Program, serves on the organizing committee of Lit Crawl LA, and is hard at work on his second novel. "The Chain" first appeared in *The Rattling Wall*.

Elizabeth Hall is the author of the chapbook *Two Essays* (eohippus labs) and *I Have Devoted My Life to the Clitoris* (Tarpaulin Sky Press). Her work has appeared in *Best Experimental Writing, Black Warrior Review, Denver Quarterly, LIT, Two Serious Ladies,* and elsewhere. She lives San Pedro, CA. "Crying With The Cosmic Cowboy" first appeared in *The Los Angeles Review of Books*.

Jasper Henderson is a writer and teacher from the Mendocino Coast. His work has appeared in *Joyland*, the *Noyo River Review* and *Permasummer*. He publishes an occasional travelogue through his website, jasperhenderson.com. As a poet-teacher with California Poets in the Schools, he works with over four hundred students every year. His cat is named Sybil, after the sibilant, favorite sound of cats across the galaxy.

William Hillyard has been a dishwasher and a waiter, a guitar maker, an environmental scientist and a Census enumerator as well as, for 48 hours, the creator and executive producer of a reality TV show. These days he calls himself a writer, but that's really just a euphemism for being unemployed. "Wonder Valley" first appeared in *Denver Voice* and was listed as "Notable Nonrequired Reading" in *The Best American Nonrequired Reading 2010*.

Michael Jaime-Becerra is from El Monte, California. He is the author of *This Time Tomorrow*, a novel awarded an International Latino Book Award, and *Every Night Is Ladies' Night*, a story collection that received the California Book Award for a First Work of Fiction. His essays have been featured in the *Los Angeles Times* and on Zócalo Public Square and KCRW, while more recent work is in *ZYZZYVA*, *Black Clock*, and *LAtitudes: An Angeleno's Atlas*.

Cheryl Diane Kidder's work, nominated eight times for the Pushcart Prize, has appeared in numerous journals, including *Boaat Press*, *Front Porch*, *High Desert Journal*, *Potomac Review*, *CutThroat Journal of the Arts*, *Weber—The Contemporary West*, *Pembroke Magazine*, *Brevity*, *Brain*, *Child*, *Identity Theory*, and elsewhere. She is the Assistant Fiction Editor at *Able Muse* and lives in Tucson. "Beds" first appeared in *In Posse Review*.

Anne-Marie Kinney is the author of the novel *Radio Iris*. Her work has appeared in *Black Clock*, *The Rattling Wall* and other journals, as well as online at *Entropy* and *Trop*. She co-curates Los Angeles's Griffith Park Storytelling Series. "The Ritualist" first appeared in *Alaska Quarterly Review*.

Susanna Kwan's work has appeared in *The Rumpus, Devil's Lake*, and other publications. She completed an MFA at Vanderbilt University and has received fellowships from the San Francisco Writers' Grotto and Kundiman. She lives in San Francisco. "Winter of Departures" first appeared in *Joyland*.

Andrea Lambert wrote *Jet Set Desolate, Lorazepam & the Valley of Skin* and the chapbook *G(u)ilt*. Her work appears in *3:AM Magazine, The Fanzine, Entropy, Angel's Flight Literary West, HTMLGiant, Queer Mental Health, Five:2:One Magazine, Hinchas de Poesia* and *ENCLAVE*. Anthologies: *Haunting Muses, Writing the Walls Down, The L.A. Telephone Book Vol. 1, 2011-2012, Off the Rocks Volume #16, You've Probably Read This Before*, and *Chronometry*. Website: andreaklambert.com. "The View Like An Ashtray" first appeared in Lambert's chapbook *G(u)ilt* (Lost Angelene, 2011).

Lou Mathews is an L.A. based novelist, short-story writer, playwright and former journalist and magazine editor. He has received a Pushcart Prize, a Katherine Anne Porter Prize, and National Endowment for the Arts and California Arts Commission fellowships in fiction. His stories and essays have been published in *Black Clock, Tin House, New England Review,* and many other literary magazines, ten fiction anthologies and several textbooks. His first novel, *L.A. Breakdown*, was an *Los Angeles Times* Best Book. "Last Dance" first appeared in *ZYZZYVA*.

Kat Meads is the author of 16 books and chapbooks of poetry and prose, including *2:12 a.m. – Essays,* recipient of an Independent Publishers Gold Medal (IPPY) and a *ForeWord Reviews* Book of the Year finalist. A native of North Carolina, she lives in the Santa

Cruz Mountains and teaches in Oklahoma City University's low-residency MFA program. "What Lies In Closets" first appeared in *Crazyhorse*.

Elizabeth McKenzie's novel *The Portable Veblen* was long listed for the 2016 National Book Award. She is the author of the novel *MacGregor Tells The World* and *Stop That Girl*, short-listed for The Story Prize. Her fiction has been awarded a Pushcart Prize and has been included in *The Atlantic, Best American Nonrequired Reading*, and others. McKenzie is senior editor of the *Chicago Quarterly Review* and the managing and fiction editor of *Catamaran Literary Reader*. "Savage Breast" first appeared in *The New Yorker*.

Anthony J. Mohr's writing has appeared in, among other places, *2013 California Prose Directory, Compose, Eclectica, Front Porch Journal, Hippocampus Magazine, The MacGuffin, Word Riot,* and *ZYZZYVA*. His work has received four Pushcart Prize nominations. Once upon a time, he was a member of the L.A. Connection, an improv theater group. By day he is a judge on the Superior Court of California, County of Los Angeles. "Rainy Day Schedule" first appeared in *DIAGRAM*.

Excerpts of **Micah Perks'** third book *What Becomes Us*, published by Outpost19 in October 2016, won a National Endowment for the Arts Grant and *The New Guard* Machigonne 2014 Fiction Prize. Her short stories and essays have been published widely. She lives with her family in Santa Cruz where she co-directs the creative writing program at UCSC. More details and work at micahperks.com. "There Was Once A Man Who Longed For A Child" first appeared in *Joyland*.

Ashton Politanoff lives in Redondo Beach, CA. His writing has appeared in *Green Mountains Review, Hobart, Sleepingfish* and elsewhere. Many of his stories take place in the beach cities of the South Bay. He teaches English at Cal State Long Beach, Cerritos

College, and Long Beach City College. His story "One End and Aim" originally appeared in *NOON* 2016 edited by Diane Williams.

Vincent Poturica lives with his wife and daughter in Long Beach, California, where he teaches at local community colleges. His writing appears or is forthcoming in *DIAGRAM*, *Forklift*, *Ohio*, *New South*, and *Western Humanities Review*, among other journals. "Dad's House" first appeared in *New England Review*.

Barbara Jane Reyes is the author of *To Love as Aswang*. She was born in Manila, Philippines, raised in the San Francisco Bay Area, and is the author of three previous collections of poetry, *Gravities of Center*, *Poeta en San Francisco*, and *Diwata*. *Invocation to Daughters* is forthcoming from City Lights Publishing. She teaches in the Yuchengco Philippine Studies Program at University of San Francisco. "The Day" first appeared in *The Margins*, the journal of the Asian-American Writers' Workshop.

Zoë Ruiz lives and writes in Los Angeles. Her writing has appeared or is forthcoming in *The Believer*, *Marketplace*, *The Rumpus*, *Salon* and the anthologies *California Prose Directory* (2014) and *Rooted*, among other places. She is a freelance book publicist and book editor and most recently edited *Nothing Ever Dies* by Pulitzer Prize Winner Viet Thanh Nguyen, which made the 2016 National Book Award Shortlist for nonfiction. Find her on twitter: @ruizzoe. "Summer" first appeared in *Ohio Edit*.

Patty Somlo's most recent books are *The First to Disappear* (Spuyten Duyvil), a Finalist in the 2016 International Book Awards and in the 2016 Best Book Awards, and *Even When Trapped Behind Clouds: A Memoir of Quiet Grace* (WiDo Publishing). Her fourth book, *Hairway to Heaven Stories*, is forthcoming from Cherry Castle Publishing. She has received four Pushcart Prize nominations, been nominated for *storySouth* Million Writers Award and had an essay selected as Notable in *Best American Essays 2014*. "Journey

Back Home" first appeared in *Even When Trapped Behind Clouds: A Memoir of Quiet Grace*.

Kara Vernor's fiction has appeared in *Wigleaf, PANK, No Tokens, Green Mountains Review, The Los Angeles Review*, and elsewhere. She has been a Best Small Fictions finalist, a Mendocino Coast Writers' Conference Estelle Frank Fellow, and an Elizabeth George Foundation scholarship recipient. Her fiction chapbook, *Because I Wanted to Write You a Pop Song*, is available from Split Lip Press. "David Hasselhoff Is From Baltimore" first appeared in *Smokelong Quarterly*.

Alia Volz is a daughter of San Francisco with a nasty case of wanderlust. Her essays, stories and translations appear in the *New York Times, Threepenny Review, Utne Reader, New Enlgand Review, The Normal School, Barrelhouse*'s 2016 anthology *Dig If You Will The Picture: Remembering Prince*, and elsewhere. "In Any Light, By Any Name" first appeared in the Winter 2014 issue of *Tin House*.

Axel Wilhite (cover artist) lives in Los Angeles and has shown his paintings in the United States and in Europe. He is a co-founder of *7x7.LA,* an online magazine that facilitates and publishes creative collaborations between artists and writers.

Gary Young's books include *Hands, The Dream of a Moral Life, Days, Braver Deeds* and *No Other Life*, which won the William Carlos Williams Award. His most recent books are *Even So: New and Selected Poems* and *Adversary*. He teaches creative writing and directs the Cowell Press at the University of California Santa Cruz. In 2009 he received the Shelley Memorial Award from the Poetry Society of America. Selections from "At Sixty" appeared in *Askew, Chicago Quarterly Review, 45th Parallel, Miramar, The New Flash Fiction Review, Ploughshares, phren-Z, Quarter After Eight*, and *String Town*.

Olga Zilberbourg is a bilingual author; born in St. Petersburg,

Russia, she calls San Francisco her home. Her third book of stories was published in Russia in 2016. Her English-language fiction has appeared in *Epiphany, Narrative Magazine, Hobart, B O D Y, Santa Monica Review, J Journal, Prick of the Spindle*, and other print and online publications. Olga serves as a co-moderator of San Francisco Writers Workshop. "Outer Sunset" first appeared in *Printers Row*.